The Iron Realm

Book One of the Iron Soul Series

J.M. Briggs

Published by J.M. Briggs
www.authorjmbriggs.com

Printed in the United State of America
Third Printing 2017
ISBN 978-0-9967826-2-3

Dedicated to Mom, Dad and James who I have the privilege of loving, liking and respecting. Thank you for all your support in this adventure and putting up with my long tirades about this book.

1

Growing Magic

Magic. The word alone conjures images, sounds, and ideas from the mind. The belief in magic and the practice of harnessing its strange energy has been present in humanity since the very beginning. There is a reason for this. A reason why, even in an age of science, magic and the unknown that it encompasses is always present at the fringe of human thought. And there are a few in this world who know that reason. And there is a place that was about to become a new haven for it.

Ravenslake, Oregon is a small city tucked away on Oregon's Highway 20 with a land grant university that justified its existence. The University of Ravenslake provided the majority of jobs to the town and its student population made up the bulk of the residents. While a pleasant town with an attractive main street, decent small mall and two small movie theaters, it wasn't what one called vibrant. In the summer the city was a ghost town that survived on some tourism, students that stayed in the area and the teachers who spent their summers enjoying activities on the lake that gave the town its name or in the nearby forest.

Main street retailers switched out their stock come August as the tourists departed and the students returned to the collection of brick buildings that dominated the center of town. The large box store on the end of town was putting all its back to school supplies at the front of the store with cheap furniture and appliances for the college students just to the right of the pens and binders. The faculty of the university were returning from their summers to prepare for the students and the administration hall clock was receiving its annual maintenance.

Bookend Coffee was a favorite of the students of the University of Ravenslake and the employees were scrubbing the shop in anticipation of the start of the school year. The coffee shop had the distinction of being right at the edge of campus and having a large loft over the café area where students could sit and read. Years ago the owner had started a shelf of free books on the understanding that others would bring a book to replace it. At Bookend this concept had grown until six shelves of old and worn paperback books lined the three walls of the loft sitting area. Today the loft was completely empty save for one woman sitting at a small table and glaring at the empty chair across from her.

A few of the students that had already returned to town had climbed the stairs to the loft with their coffees and pastries only to turn around and rush back downstairs at the sight of the woman. She was beautiful with long dark hair plaited over one shoulder and with an air of experience despite appearing to be barely middle aged. It was known that she was at least fifty, but her hair remained dark brown and her face largely remained wrinkle free outside the frown lines between her green eyes. Her hands raised her cup of coffee to her lips and she sipped slowly as she kept eying the chair across from her. In front of her was an open three-ring binder holding a printed academic paper on Hildegard of Bingen with bright red notes all across it. A red pen sat at the top of the binder just waiting for her to find the next mistake.

Footfalls on the stairs made her look sharply over at the stairway up to the loft, but she quickly returned her attention back to her paper. Setting down her coffee, she picked up the pen and made another notation before turning the page. The newcomer reached the loft and strode towards her table without hesitation.

"You're late," she informed the newcomer as she looked up at him after capping her pen very deliberately.

He was older than her with soft white curls that had a ghost of auburn color in places and a short neatly trimmed beard. His brown eyes warmed at the sight of her and he looked her over quickly, checking for any sign of injury and irritation.

"Oh stop mothering Merlin," the woman huffed with a roll of her eyes. "I'm quite alright." Her voice carried a slight accent to it that might have been British or maybe even French, but was too faded for certainty. "It is quite rude not to call and inform me that you will be late."

"My apologizes Morgana," he replied with a sheepish, but wide smile as he plopped down into the chair across from her. Setting his coffee down, he twisted to unshoulder his satchel and sling it across the back of the chair. Then he raised his coffee to her in a silent toast before taking a long drink from it. "Lovely," he announced a moment later as he set it on the table. "But it is nice to know you care."

"Don't fish for compliments Merlin, it's unbecoming for a man of your age," Morgana informed him sternly. "But you have news for me, Merlin. I would hear it."

The man continued to smile and continued as if he had not heard her. "But really my dear Morgana le Fey, you must call me Ambrose." His brown eyes locked with her green ones. "You only call me by my old name when you are irritated with me. My name doesn't blend in this time as smoothly as yours."

"And Ambrose is such a common given name," Morgana remarked with a raised eyebrow. Smirking when another student backed down the stairs of the loft instead of coming up, she took a sip of her coffee and turned her attention back to him. "Ambrose," she huffed, "You missed the first of your department meetings and sent only coded messages. People were asking me where you were. You'd better have a good reason."

"Indeed," the older man replied as his smile fell away. "I'm afraid that the news is not good." When Morgana opened her mouth to ask, Ambrose held up a hand and shook his head. "Please Morgana," he asked softly. "Give me a moment."

Morgana paused and nodded, her stern expression softening. Silence descended around them, weighing on the pair like a thick fog. Looking over at him, Morgana studied Merlin with concern. He was wearing his standard clothing of jeans teamed with a dress shirt and tweed jacket with an elegant silver triskele pin on his left lapel. Nothing had visibly changed, but for the first time in a long time Morgana could see him as he had been so long ago, in a long simple robe with a bronze triskele talisman hanging from his neck and wielding a great twisted wooden staff in his hand.

Then their eyes met and Morgana felt a rush of magic, the greatest force in her life that had been so still and silent for many years.

Suddenly she could smell the woods, feel the morning mist on her face and feel the wind in her long loose hair. The sound of birds chirping as a small animal moved through the underbrush overwhelmed her. Magic weighed down upon her, pulling her further into another place and another time.

Then it was gone. Morgana took a shaky breath and found Merlin standing next to her chair with a hand on her shoulder. Turning, she met his wide eyes.

"I'm sorry," he told her. "That was-"

"It's alright," Morgana told him quickly, trying to recover from her own discomfort. She brushed a loose strand of hair behind her ear and gestured for him to retake his seat. Her fingers fiddled with the silver triskele pendant that hung around her own neck. "We've both felt…. it growing stronger. Just tell me what you found."

Merlin retook his seat and nodded. He took a breath before he spoke, "The gates are failing. I checked all of the Old Places and it is the same all across the isles. They won't hold much longer."

"The gates are iron," Morgana protested weakly. "The Sídhe… they can't just-"

"It's been almost three thousand years and even enchanted iron may rust." Merlin interrupted gently. "We always knew that the gates might not be a permanent solution. When iron was common it worked, but you have to look hard in the modern world to find iron. Everything is steel and plastic now."

"So they are returning?" Morgana questioned, dropping her eyes to her hand. It was shaking. She quickly pulled it off the table and clutched her hands together in her lap. "When they find me… when they find us both…"

"We still have some time," Merlin reminded her, his voice soft. "Do not despair, Morgana," he commanded her. "And the signs say that the soul will return to us soon."

"Merlin…" Morgana looked up at him and shook her head. "The Old Ones are waking up. It is not just the Sídhe we must contend with. The eldest of the old spirits are stirring. While you were in England I checked on some of their resting places and it is the same. There is movement and I can feel their power rising." Morgana gestured around with her hand. "This new age calls to them. I don't know why, but soon they will be waking."

Merlin's eyes widened and he paled slightly. They both fell silent and Merlin stared into his cup of coffee, seeking answers in the swirl of coffee and cream. "Then we face both the ancient forces. It is no wonder that magic is growing stronger," he remarked. "It would seem that the war is to resume."

"How can you say that so calmly?" Morgana hissed. "We barely survived the Sídhe on the Isles and you can't have forgotten when they broke through into the Norse lands. We were lucky not be at war with those Old Ones at the time. To face both at the same time-"

"You and I have both faced Old Ones with success in the past," Merlin reminded her, raising his hand. "Perhaps it is a sign that the soul is ready, that the time has come."

Morgana opened her mouth to speak but failed to make a sound. "You are such an optimist," she whispered as she slumped back in her chair. "We've been hoping for the end of this for three thousand years with nothing to show and yet you still say that every time the soul is reborn. We don't even know for certain that there is an ending to all of this."

"I have to believe in that," Merlin told her. "Everything else I once believed has been stripped away by the ages."

Morgana studied him carefully across the table, detecting something more in his thoughts. He fiddled with his hands and kept his eyes on his cup.

"What else do you know?" Morgana sighed. "What more could there possibly be?"

"I have also detected the presence of reincarnations of Gwenyvar and Luegáed," he admitted without looking up.

Morgana's body tensed and she clenched her teeth as all traces of sorrow vanished into a rage. "That's it then," Morgana growled as she glared at Merlin. "We might as well kill the Soul once we identify it and try with the next reincarnation. With the rising levels of magic we could-"

"Morgana," Merlin scolded as he looked up at her sharply. "How can you even suggest-"

"It always goes the same way when they are near," Morgana hissed in low voice. "And you know it. They always betray him and cause a downfall at the critical moment. If he dies quickly then we can at least get him back in another nineteen to twenty years if we use our magic. That might still give us enough time-"

Merlin's gray eyes were cold as they studied her, but she refused to squirm under the gaze. Morgana lifted her chin and met his eyes squarely. "Sometimes," Merlin told her slowly, "I forget how…. pragmatic you were raised to be." He shook his head sadly as the chill faded from his eyes to be replaced with weariness. "Your 'foster mother' did you no favors."

"Merlin," Morgana uttered in a quiet voice. "It is always the same. They are cursed to repeat those events when together. Gwenyvar and Luegáed, Guinevere and Lancelot, whatever you want to call them will betray him when it will hurt him the most and cause the most damage. There is a reason why when the humans began to tell the King Arthur story they wound those tales together. That betrayal is buried so deep and runs so true that they still knew it even after hundreds of years. Need I remind you of-"

"It could be different this time," Merlin interrupted. "We have to believe that things can get better."

"You are too optimistic old man," Morgana scoffed, but her shoulders sagged in defeat. "But have it your way if you wish. The Soul has been through this song and dance before and this time will be no different."

"Ah Morgana, even the Soul is not an island. Like all humans it is affected by the world it lives in. He is shaped by his time and place in the world." Merlin smiled and nodded to himself, "And the right person can change everything."

Morgana raised one of her dark eyebrows as she considered the man across from her. "You've been reading too many of your own myths, Ambrose," she declared. "Of course I suppose being a literature teacher doesn't help."

"Oh, and as someone who is three thousand years old you can tell me just how accurate the history books are," Merlin teased with a smile. "My dear Morgana, you teach another form of literature, whether you like it or not. At least my version is honest about what is fiction."

"There are days that I hate you," Morgana informed Merlin with a soft sigh. "I will give it a year."

"Give what a year?" Merlin asked her with a tilt of his head.

"The new form of the Soul," she said calmly. "It has a year to show some promise despite Gwenyvar and Luegáed's presence, if not then I will exercise my pragmatism."

"You know I will not agree to that."

"I know, but I don't need you to," Morgana replied. "We both also know that if things go badly that you will not stop me," she told him as she met his eyes with a cold glint of determination.

Merlin swallowed but said nothing more on the subject. Giving him a moment, Morgana returned her attention to the paper in front of her after collecting her red pen. After watching her for a moment, Merlin reached into his bag and pulled out a worn hardcover book. He flipped the book open to the midpoint but watched Morgana scowl at the paper in front of her for another moment.

"Graduate student?" Merlin finally asked.

"Yes," Morgana told him as she made another red note without looking up. "He doesn't hold much promise either."

2

Welcome to Hatfield

Excitement filled the air of the Hatfield freshman dorm corridors even as the smell of sweat and the heat of too many bodies made it difficult to breathe. One tall blonde girl maneuvered her way through the corridor, with a duffle bag in one hand and a backpack over one shoulder, leaving the man and the woman following her far behind as she strode to one of the doorways that lined the hallway. The number 321 was marked on the door in shining letters. Grinning with excitement, the girl pulled a single metal key from the pocket of her jeans and unlocked the door.

Her smile fell only the tiniest bit as she stepped inside and examined her new dorm room. It was smaller than television shows and movies made it seem like it should be. But it was filled with sunlight from the large window directly opposite her that looked out over the lawn between the university's dorm buildings. Only the fact that her roommate already had a magenta bedspread with white floral designs and matching pillows and boxes stacked by the door prevented the room from being identical on both sides.

Desks stood on either side of the room next to the window and flush against the twin beds that were each against their own wall. Closer to the door were chests of drawers with flat tops and mirrors hanging above them to make them suitable vanities. Stepping further into the room, the girl saw that small closets were built into the wall closest to the door creating a narrow entry space. The right side of the room was empty of boxes and any sign of her roommate as though the invisible line had already been drawn right down the middle of the space. She tossed her duffle bag on the bed and shrugged out of the backpack, before placing it gently in the desk chair on her side of the room. The noise outside in the hallway fell away for a moment as the young woman took in a long breath. This was finally it.

"Oh hey, you must be Alexandra," a masculine voice suddenly said from the doorway, breaking the moment. She spun to face the new arrival.

A tall handsome young man with short blonde stood just inside the door with a stack of boxes in his arms. He stepped further into the room and gently set the boxes on the bed of her roommate before straightening up. Stepping closer, he held out his hand and smiled at her.

"I'm Arthur Pendred," he introduced. "I'm helping Jenny move in. It's nice to meet you, Alexandra."

"Alex," she squeaked as she accepted his hand and met his blue eyes.

There was a rush of warmth over her as she inhaled the scent of smoke and heard the crackling of charcoal. Then there was a metallic ringing that echoed twice before it all vanished.

Alex blinked and took a breath as she tried to orient herself. She was in her new dorm room and Arthur was looking at her expectantly.

"Uh I prefer Alex," she managed, giving Arthur a shaky smile. "Alexandra is a bit stuffy."

"Nice to meet you, Alex," Arthur replied, releasing her hand. "I've only got a few more boxes to get for Jenny and then I'd be glad to give you a hand with your things."

"Great!" Alex cheered a bit too loudly before lowering the volume of her voice. "Uh, thank you, that's really nice of you."

She shoved aside the brief flash of... something as a reaction to the excitement or maybe a scent on Arthur's clothing. Maybe he'd been camping in that shirt or something recently. Alex was about to inquire about the nature of Arthur's relationship with Jenny when a suitcase was shoved through the door and a man stumbled in. He was just over six feet tall with a receding hairline of brown hair and behind his glasses, he had gray eyes like Alex's. He set down another suitcase and sighed in relief as he stepped fully into the room, fanning himself.

"Uh this is my dad, Michael Adams," Alex told Arthur, gesturing to her father.

Realizing that there was company in the room, Michael Adams finished catching his breath and looked curiously at Arthur. The young man just smiled and stepped forward, extending his hand once more.

"Nice to meet you, sir," Arthur greeted pleasantly. "I'm Arthur Pendred, I'm your daughter's roommate's boyfriend."

Alex's shoulders sagged slightly at Arthur's statement, but she smiled and pulled one of the suitcases further into the room. Her movement was just in time as her mother darted into the room to avoid the bustle of the crowd, loaded down with shopping bags. Moving quickly, Arthur stepped out of her way so that she could deposit the bags on Alex's side of the room. Turning to her daughter, Alex's mother brushed a strand of graying blonde hair from her face.

"This place is insane," she remarked to Alex before looking around the room. "Oh dear, where did we lose your brother?"

"Here," a higher male voice called as a young man dashed into the room. He glanced at Arthur and then at his sister, but shrugged off his presence. Instead, he set the plastic bin he'd been carrying down and pushed it to the side with his foot. "How much longer do I have to do this?"

"That was only the first load Ed," his father said, ruffling his son's brown hair.

Edward pulled away from his father and straightened his hair the best he could before giving his sister a look while his parents exchanged amused glances behind his back. "Why do I have to help?" Ed asked his mother, pretending he wasn't a pouting fourteen year old. "First we had to help Matt move in and now I have to help Alex move in, but they won't be around to help me move into my college dorm room."

"Yeah well deal with it kid," Alex told him as she picked up the plastic bin that Ed had brought up and moved it over to the desk. "Just one of the joys of being the youngest."

Arthur chuckled and gave a small wave to Alex as he moved towards the door. "Looks like you've got help, so I'd better go get the last of Jenny's stuff."

"Right," Alex said quickly. "Nice to meet you, Arthur."

"Just remember to lock the door if no one stays up here," Arthur reminded her before he vanished out the open door into the throng of moving people and boxes.

"Who was that?" Alex's mother asked with a smile. "Your roommate's brother?"

"Liz," Michael scolded, "That was her roommate's boyfriend."

"Oh," Elizabeth sighed. "Too bad." She winked at Alex and gestured to the boxes. "Why don't you start unpacking and we'll get the rest of the boxes. That way you can leave the door open for us and Arthur."

"Thanks," Alex told her mom with a grin as she pulled off the lid of the top box in the waiting stack.

"Ah, that means I have to carry more," Edward protested.

"Come on," Michael told him. "Parking is only supposed to be for fifteen minutes."

Elizabeth started to follow her husband and youngest son out of the room, but turned back to Alex. "Don't forget to start making a list of things you need," she reminded Alex. "We'll go shopping this afternoon for anything you think of."

"Right mom," Alex agreed without looking up as she pulled out the first stack of textbooks.

Moving over to the desk, Alex slid the books onto the shelves above the desk. She didn't bother with ordering them by class just now and instead shoved them up as quickly as possible. Her Jane Austen books and other favorites were given more respect and placed much more gently on the lower shelf. A small plastic box of school supplies was shoved into the top drawer of the desk before Alex turned her attention to setting up her laptop.

She'd just gotten some music started and turned the volume up enough to hear over the people in the hallway when Arthur returned with another three boxes stacked in his arms. Despite barely being able to see over them, he maneuvered into the room with ease and set them down on Jenny's side of the room. Alex opened her mouth to ask him what music he liked when a beautiful young woman about her age walked into the room with a suitcase and canvas shopping bag.

While Alex was tall and had a slim athletic build with blonde hair that she'd inherited from her mother, this girl was of average height and curvy with Hispanic coloration and an elegant face. Her long dark brown hair was wavy and Alex felt a twitch of jealousy on her face that even made her cleft chin seem feminine and pretty. Nearly jumping forward, the girl dropped her bag on the bed and left the rolling suitcase standing near the doorway to approach Alex.

"Hi Alex," she greeted cheerfully. "It is so nice to finally meet you! I'm Jenny."

"It's nice to meet you too," Alex told Jenny with a smile of her own. "Texting can only do so much."

"Well at least we were able to iron out a couple of things in advance that way," Jenny replied with a shrug before glancing Alex over. "I admit I was hoping for someone I could swap clothing with, but maybe we can still share shoes. What's your size?"

"Eight and a half," Alex replied, slightly startled at the sudden conversation change.

"That's perfect, so am I," Jenny told her before glancing down at the blue high top canvas shoes that Alex was wearing. "Those are cute."

Looking over Jenny's head, Alex spotted Arthur leaning against the closet door and watching with an amused smile. He must have seen Alex's look of concern because he laughed and announced, "Don't worry she's only like this when she's really excited and has had too much coffee."

"Arthur," Jenny hissed, flushing slightly at the cheeks and tugging at her bottom of her shirt. She looked up at Alex, giggling at the three-inch difference between them. "Sorry about that," she apologized a moment later. "Guess I probably should have skipped the second espresso."

"Probably," Arthur agreed as he came up and slipped an arm around Jenny's waist and rested his chin on her head. "Anyway, what else can I help with?"

"That's it for me," Jenny told him as she looked at the stack of boxes that were now awaiting her. "I just need to get organized."

"Then I can help Alex's family unload," Arthur offered as he looked back at Alex.

"Thanks," Alex told him as she glanced between them. "Uh, are you a student here?"

Arthur laughed and ran a hand through his blonde hair with a chuckle. "Yeah I am, sorry I probably should have said that earlier. I'm a freshman here too and majoring in political science."

"Arthur's a member of the football team," Jenny proudly told Alex. "He's already been here for a month."

"That's great," Alex replied automatically as she turned back to her boxes and began to unpack the rest of her supplies. "And your major was communications right Jenny?" Alex asked, thinking back to the texts she and Jenny had exchanged since they'd been assigned together.

"That's right," Jenny answered as she began unpacking her own things. "I can't believe how small this closet is."

Alex chuckled as she opened a suitcase and began to unload her supply of jeans and t-shirts into the dresser. Her family returned a few minutes later with more boxes, greeted Jenny quickly and left to retrieve the last load with Arthur's help and a promise to talk with Jenny more when they returned.

"I never asked, why did you pick Ravenslake?" Alex asked Jenny as she finished emptying one suitcase and shoved it under her bed.

"Arthur was offered a full ride scholarship here and second string on the varsity team," Jenny answered with a cheerful tone. "I came to see it with him and … I don't know what it was, but it just clicked with me. Surprised me since I figured I'd go to Berkley or somewhere closer to San Francisco and Daddy. Plus Arthur loved it too, despite offers from bigger schools."

Turning, Alex found Jenny gently hanging up her clothes with a soft smile on her face. Jenny looked over at Alex and shrugged. "This place just feels right I guess. My dad told me that finding a place to be happy was really important for college since I'd never learn anything if I was miserable," Jenny laughed softly. "And I had been figuring I'd be trying to convince Arthur to pick the same school as me, not supporting this one so much."

"It is pretty far from San Francisco," Alex agreed.

"Farther than it is from…." Jenny hesitated as she tried to remember, "Seattle?"

"Close," Alex replied with a shrug. "Spokane. My older brother Matt is at the University of Minnesota so compared to him I stayed in our backyard. He's already back at school, but you'll have the pleasure of meeting my younger brother Ed as soon as they get back."

Alex stepped back and looked at her side of the room. A couple of empty boxes were stacked by the door now with two half-unpacked ones shoved under the desk until she could get to the pile of small items inside. It was already taking shape, but she'd feel better once she was could make up the bed.

"You made arrangements for the fridge and microwave, right?" Jenny asked her suddenly. "Here between our desks would be a good place for it. And it gives us some prep space."

"Sounds good," Alex agreed, putting a makeup bag on the top of the dresser. "So how long have you and Arthur been together?" Alex asked. "I mean that you are living separately."

"We've been together for three years," Jenny informed her. "Ever since the start of sophomore year, but the coach here insists on the players living in singles the first semester so they can train. So good news you'll probably only have to put up with me for the first semester."

"Too bad," Alex said as her eyes went to the pile of shoes that Jenny was loading into a door organizer on the outside of the closet door. "I could have gotten used to borrowing some of those shoes." Jenny held up a bright yellow pair of strappy heels that made Alex's feet hurt just looking at them. "Maybe not that pair," Alex amended quickly.

The next two hours were a blur as the last of Alex's things were brought up and her father and brother left to collect the mini-fridge and microwave they'd arranged to rent for the year. Arthur had vanished to football practice and Jenny was humming softly while she unpacked on her side of the room. Working alongside her mother, Alex unpacked everything for her desk, her clothing and the stuffed beagle she'd debated leaving at home. Her mother smiled as they finished making up the bed with the dark purple bedding they'd bought last week and placed the stuffed beagle on one of the pillows.

"There, now Galahad can look after things," her mother announced.

Alex glanced over at Jenny's side of the room with a soft blush, but her roommate just grinned at the stuffed animal before reaching into a box and pulling out a worn teddy bear. A moment later the bear was sitting on its own pillow.

"That's Zoe," Jenny told Alex with a smile. "I've had her since I was six."

"I've had Galahad since… forever," Alex volunteered.

"Two and a half," her mother filled in before picking up a small spiral notebook that they'd been writing things down in. "I didn't think Galahad would survive this long." She didn't give Alex time to respond before looking over at Jenny, "We'll be heading to the store as soon as the boys get back. Would you like a ride?"

"No thanks Mrs. Adams," Jenny said quickly. "I'm good and if I think of something I'll get it after the initial rush."

Alex's mom nodded but still had a thoughtful look. "Then how about you join us for dinner? That is unless your parents are town…"

"That would be nice," Jenny replied politely. "Dad couldn't leave home due to an appeal of one of his cases and Arthur is tied up so much lately with football."

"Excellent," her mother declared, "Then you'll join us tonight."

There was a heavy thud as Alex's father steered the cart holding the mini-fridge into the side of the doorway. Everyone jumped and looked over at Michael as he tried to adjust the angle of the cart enough to get through the doorway. After a moment of struggle, Michael rolled the cart into the room, followed by Edward carrying a microwave.

"Now where do you girls want this?" He paused and looked around the room. "Well, that's much better." He grinned at Alex, "I think you'll be very happy here honey."

"Yeah," Alex agreed with a smile and glance at Jenny. "I think you're right."

3

Myrddin

834 B.C.E. Snowdonia Wales

A young man, no more than fifteen, stared transfixed at the rise and fall of the flames before him. The fire burned in a small dug-out pit surrounded by bare earth. A soft breeze blew past him, but barely affected the flames as the woven branch fence a few feet to his left blocked most of the wind. He pressed down the bellows in his right hand, pushing more air into the fire before repeating the process with the bellows in his left hand. In front of him, the two bellows joined into a single tube leading right up to the fire and with each depression of either bellow, the flame jumped.

His knees were beginning to ache from kneeling so long on the ground, but he did not shift his position, too afraid of losing the rhythm he'd established. His auburn hair seemed on fire itself in the glow and his brown eyes were alight with awe, anticipation, nervousness and a touch of fear. Heat rolled off the small fire as it consumed the charcoal, and the young man thought he could see the glowing crucible even through the flames. He wanted to wipe the sweat from his brow, but he couldn't risk losing the heat; not when it was so close. His tunic felt sticky against his skin in the front while he felt a chill at his back, but he kept the steady pace of the bellows: up and down.

There was movement to his right and he risked a quick glance to see another young man, a little older than himself, carefully bringing a stump of wood near the fire. The older boy vanished and returned carrying a pair of carved stones closely bound together. These stones were carefully placed against the wood, exposing a small opening at the top.

"It's almost ready Myrddin," the boy told him as he studied the fire.

"I know," Myrddin replied, fixing his eyes back on the flames and ignoring the sting of the smoke.

"Don't worry," the older boy told him. "It will be fine."

"I don't wish to do this once again, Candon," Myrddin informed him softly. "The last casting-"

"It happens," Candon stated before leaning towards the fire. "Almost there, it should be perfect."

Myrddin didn't reply as the tension doubled. This was where he'd made the mistake the last time. He didn't want to do so again.

"Is it ready?" a deeper older voice questioned behind Myrddin. He knew it was a rhetorical question, asked only for his benefit.

"Yes," Myrddin answered, grateful that he didn't have to face his uncle as the knot of nerves returned to his stomach.

"Candon, take over the bellows," the man ordered.

Candon knelt next to him and in a practiced movement took the right bellows from Myrddin's hand as he raised it and finished the movement of pushing it down. Myrddin shifted to the left allowing Candon to take over. Climbing to his feet, Myrddin was thankful when his sore knees did not buckle underneath him.

"Ready?" the man questioned, giving Myrddin a serious look.

"Yes Uncle Dewydd," Myrddin answered with a quick nod.

His uncle said nothing more, but reached for a pair of heavy tongs and handed them to Myrddin. Dewydd moved over to the stone casting mold that was waiting and gave Myrddin an expectant look. Carefully, Myrddin reached into the flames with the tongs and touched the crucible. He took a breath and tightened the grip of the tongs on the glowing container. Then, moving slowly, he pulled the crucible from the fire. Blowing on it, Myrddin tried to dislodge the charcoal that remained on the lid before he walked over to his waiting uncle and the mold.

No one said anything as Dewydd used a second set of tongs to brush the last of the charcoal from the lid before lifting it off. Inside the crucible was glowing hot bronze, made of the perfect mixture of tin from the southern peninsula and copper from nearby mountains. It was liquid fire and Myrddin's heart jumped at the sight of it.

"Myrddin," a soft strange voice called, startling him. "Myrddin," the voice repeated. It was warm and gentle but sounded somehow distorted.

Giving his head a tiny shake, Myrddin focused on bringing the crucible directly above the stone mold and carefully poured. It was the perfect temperature, and it flowed smoothly out of the crucible and into the opening of the mold. Myrddin would have sighed in relief had he not been so tense. The last time a scrap of charcoal had ruined it all and they'd had to melt it down, but this time he would get it right.

The mold filled, leaving only a glowing orange spark of the liquid fire visible at the top of the hole. Checking quickly that his uncle and cousin had control of the mold, Myrddin moved the still glowing hot crucible away from them. With no small degree of reverence, Myrddin set the crucible to the side. Finally taking a breath, he tasted the smoke in the air and the metallic tang of the bronze. He gave himself only a heartbeat before he returned to the stone mold where his uncle was eying the golden top with a stern gaze.

"The pouring looked good," Candon offered him breaking the silence.

"The truth will be in the sword," his uncle reminded them gruffly, but then he looked at Myrddin with a small smile. Placing his hand on the young man's shoulder, Dewydd added, "But you did everything right."

They settled into silence all staring at the stone which held something precious to Myrddin. Some time later, his uncle prodded the glowing top gently, but the metal did not shift. Candon and Myrddin needed no instruction and carefully pulled the stump of wood away so they could lay the mold on the ground. Myrddin unbound the heavy rope that tied the two stones together. He looked up at his uncle and received a quick nod.

"Myrddin," the voice called once again. It sounded far away and echoed. Forgetting the mold for a moment, he looked over towards the fence just to reassure himself that there was no one there.

"Myrddin," Candon urged, "Open it."

Nodding, Myrddin picked up the top stone and lifted it away. He set it to the side without much thought as his eyes locked onto the cooling sword that he'd freed from the stone. The very top of it was still orange with a rapidly dimming glow while the rest of the metal that had been locked in the cold stone was giving off only the barest heat. It needed polishing and some shaping of the edges, but there it was.

Dewydd handed Myrddin the second set of tongs which he took eagerly. Using the tongs, Myrddin finished freeing the sword from the stone as the last of the heat faded and with a smooth movement walked over to a large tub of water. Hissing filled the yard as the warm metal met the water and cooled. Myrddin waited until the sound had stopped and pulled the sword from the water. Holding it up before his uncle he waited with baited breath.

His uncle smiled and nodded, clapping Myrddin on the shoulder affectionately. "There you are, boy," he said. "Your first sword. You've come a long way from ax heads and arrow tips."

Myrddin was impatient as they cleaned the furnace and the workspace, placing wood over the small furnace pit in the ground. They moved efficiently in long practiced movements, but Myrddin's mind was on the sword and the metal working stones waiting at his own home. It would take some time, he knew, to smooth out the bronze completely, to carve a handle and rivet it into place and his hands were already itching to start.

Myrddin had long lost track of how many bronze socket axe heads he'd help to make over the years, but a sword…. that was new and he would be keeping it. This piece wouldn't be traded away but would be his. Swallowing when they'd finished, Myrddin touched his hand to the cooled bronze and smiled. The metal was rough to the touch from the stone mold, but it was free of any impurities that might have weakened it. He glanced up to see an amused look on his uncle's face and an understanding one on his cousin's. Blushing slightly, he bid them both a good night.

Myrddin turned to the low roundhouse that belonged to his uncle and started towards the front of the yard. The conical thatch roof sloped down, almost touching the ground and hiding the woven wood and daub wall. He followed the curve of the house, passing the entry porch and stepping onto the wide and worn path in front of the house. The sun was close to setting, hanging just above the mountains that rose over his village. Myrddin's eyes scanned the collection of thatch and daub round houses as people began to prepare for nightfall. One of his uncle's neighbors saw the sword in his hand and gave him a smile. Nodding in return, Myrddin turned right and headed up the low hill for his own home.

This roundhouse stood apart from the others just enough to ensure that they had more space. Myrddin wasn't certain how much larger it was than the others, but the point of the rooftop was higher and the interior seemed more massive. Of course, some houses in the village were barely seven feet in diameter while he'd always hesitated to measure out his mother's domain. The path wound up the hill along the woven wood fence that kept his mother's pigs pinned. A large brown dog was lying at the entrance of the roundhouse and raised its head as Myrddin approached. He took a moment and patted the animal's head before he pulled back the pelt that provided the house with privacy.

"Mother," Myrddin greeted as he stepped inside.

The roundhouse was a single large circular space and the first thing Myrddin saw when he stepped inside was a set of shelves directly opposite the door. His mother's precious possessions were displayed there including a jet necklace from the western coast, several bronze and gold pins for her cloaks and jars of perfumes that she only ever opened on the most special occasions. There was a fire in the square stone hearth between the doorway and the shelves where his mother usually sat on one of the low wooden seats. There were two beds, one against the right wall and one against the left wall, each piled with blankets and pelts. His mother's loom was near her bed to the right along with a collection of pots and baskets holding her supplies.

"My son," his mother replied from her seated position before a low table.

Myrddin said nothing else and retreated towards his bed in silence. His mother returned her attention to the work spread out on the small table. There were two candles burning in carved stone holders, each one with the triskele carved into them and the small bronze dish in the center held some kind of ground herbs. Myrddin watched as his mother chanted soft words under her breath and added some ground minerals to the herbal mixture. As much as he wished to begin work on the sword, he knew that his mother would not accept the noise. Instead, he tended to the hearth fire and quietly began to work on a reed basket that he'd begun the previous day.

"Myrddin," the female voice called once again. "Myrddin, come to me."

He shivered and picked up a blanket, wrapping it around his shoulders. A sick feeling was churning in his gut at the sound of the voice. He was the son of a priestess, the grandson of a priest, and had always been… different. Once he'd heard his mother speaking of hearing the ancestors, but this voice just didn't seem like that of an ancestor.

"Myrddin," another female voice, this one familiar and stern. "Myrddin!"

He jumped and spun towards his mother, swallowing and wondering how long she had been standing there trying to speak with him. Instead of being seated at the table she was right next to him with a questioning look on her face.

"I am sorry Mother," he told her quickly.

She looked at him and it was all Myrddin could do to hold the gaze. Then she blinked and giving a soft sigh, lowered herself onto the ground next to him and the hearth.

"What did you hear this time?" she asked without looking at him.

"A woman," Myrddin told her softly. "But… it didn't sound right."

"How so?"

"I'm not sure," he tried, "She sounded far away and there was something strange about the voice. I've never… heard anything quite like it before."

His mother's back straightened and she took a long slow breath. Turning, her eyes went to the sword that Myrddin had left on his bed.

"Was it," Myrddin swallowed, "One of my father's-"

"No," she answered sharply, her eyes jumping back to him. "No," she repeated in a softer tone. His mother raised her hand and touched his cheek. "It was not a Sídhe, Myrddin," she told him. "But there are other things that speak to mortals in such a way." Her hand dropped back to her lap. "Tomorrow go up the mountain lake to work on your sword."

"The lake is a third of the way up the mountain," he protested. "Mother it is nearing winter, it could snow."

"Go up the mountain," his mother commanded. "Take the sword, go to the lake and work on it there."

Myrddin wanted to ask more questions, but his mother took the basket from his lap and began to determinedly weave the basket. He struggled to find his voice and then the wrong question came forth.

"Is this about my father?"

"No…" his mother sighed, "Not completely." She looked down at the basket in her hands, her brown eyes moist. "Myrddin, in all my travels across the islands of our ancestors I have never heard of another child being born of a Sídhe and a human. Your birth… was special and it attracted attention." Turning her brown eyes on his son, she pleaded, "Please my son, just go to the lake and maybe you will get the answers that I never could."

4

The First Day

Michaels Cafeteria was loud at 8:30 in the morning with crashing dishes, clattering tableware, heels on the tiled floor and students who had already had too much caffeine. The large space had sunlight streaming in through the windows that lined three sides of the dining area. Tables in a variety of sizes filled the space with small walkways weaving between the chaos of chairs and tables. One side of the room was lined with booths under each of the large windows.

Alex tapped her foot to what little she could hear of the music that was playing as she waited for her omelet. She looked over her shoulder to decide what else other than a loaded with peppers omelet sounded good. The final side of Michaels Cafeteria was dominated by a long serving bar piled with fruit, yogurt and cereal options. In a semi-circle around the bar were small counters with signs that made it look like a full food court. Most were closed at the moment, but the one in front of Alex was taking hot breakfast orders.

She held a plate in each hand, one holding a few pieces of bacon and hash browns while the other held some scrambled eggs. The counter next to the hot order station had bread and bagels along with a toasting machine and opposite across the way was the drink station where Jenny had gone to check the selection.

"Orange juice, apple juice, chocolate milk, fat-free milk, 2% milk and of course a huge dispenser of coffee," Jenny reported as she walked back over and took the plate with the scrambled eggs from Alex. "Yogurt selection looks pretty good too."

"I'm not a yogurt person," Alex replied giving a small shudder. "But the watermelon is calling my name."

"Here you are girls," a male voice called to them. "One ham, onion, red pepper and cheese omelet." Alex stepped forward and let the cafeteria worker slide the omelet onto her plate. "Your hotcake will be up in a just a second," he added to Jenny.

Alex sidestepped over to the bread and bagels, setting her plate on the counter so she could put a piece of bread into the toaster. She snagged a piece of bacon off her plate and took a bite while watching the industrial toaster cycle the bread through. Jenny joined her a moment later, grabbing a bagel and some cream cheese.

"Any sign of Arthur?" Jenny asked as they walk to the long food bar.

"Nope," Alex told her, quickly glancing around the room.

"Oh," Jenny chirped, "There he is! In the far right corner."

Alex squinted towards the corner, but couldn't make out anything more than two male shapes seated at the table at the distance. She snatched up some pineapple and watermelon on a small plate before walking to the drink station as Jenny kept glancing to where she thought she'd seen Arthur.

"Eyes on the road," Alex told Jenny as the girl nearly rammed a boy getting some milk. Jenny flushed but nodded before setting her tray on the counter so she could get some coffee and milk. Chuckling at her roommate's action, Alex poured herself a glass of orange juice.

"Now where did you see him?" Alex questioned.

"This way," Jenny commanded as she began to weave her way through the other students and towards the back.

It was indeed Arthur seated at the back table, dressed in a University of Ravenslake t-shirt that was already starting to look well worn. He stood up and pulled out the chair next to him for Jenny, kissing her cheek before she sat down.

"Morning honey," Arthur greeted before turning his smile towards Alex. "Morning Alex, I hope you both slept well."

"Pretty good," Alex replied with a shrug as she set her tray down and the table and sat down next to a boy she didn't know.

"Good," Arthur responded with a quick nod. "Alex this is Lance Taylor, he's a wide receiver on the football team with me."

Lance was a strongly built African American man who was at least three inches taller than Arthur. Like Arthur, he was wearing a university t-shirt, but his was under an open flannel shirt. Both of the football players had trays stacked with food and several glasses of juice.

"Nice to meet you," Alex told him with a smile. "Alex Adams."

"And Lance you remember my girlfriend Jenny Sanchez."

"Yeah I do," Lance told Arthur before looking at Jenny. "Nice to see you again."

"Right," Jenny blurted out. "I remember you now, last Friday Arthur introduced you." Jenny shook her head and gave Lance an apologetic smile. "Sorry, I have a really bad memory for names and faces."

"Don't worry about it," Lance assured her. "You're a communications major right Jenny?"

"Yes," Jenny replied with a nod as she poured some syrup on her hotcake. "Alex is an English major," she informed Lance with a nod towards Alex. "And of course Arthur is political science. How about you?"

"Geology," Lance informed them with a smile. "I'm an outdoors person."

"Oh, where are you from?" Alex asked after swallowing a bite of her omelet.

"Portland," Lance answered before digging into a sausage link.

"So, ready for your first class?" Arthur asked, glancing between Alex and Jenny.

"We actually have the same first class," Jenny informed him with a smile. "It's one of those general education classes."

"Reason and Critical Thinking," Alex filled in. "9:30 with …" she trailed off and pulled her folded up schedule from her pocket. "Professor Williams in the Hamilton Building."

Beside her, Alex was aware of Lance also pulling out a sheet of paper. He chuckled and asked, "Mind if I walk with you? That's my first class too."

"And now I'm depressed," Arthur huffed. "My first class is Principles of Chemistry."

"You could always switch to join us," Jenny suggested eagerly.

"I'd have to redo my schedule," Arthur told her gently. "I was lucky to get into International Politics this semester and wouldn't be able to get into another science class for the Gen Ed requirements."

"Okay," Jenny sighed. "At least we've got Personal and Exploratory writing together this afternoon." She leaned over and kissed her boyfriend quickly before frowning, "You taste like apple juice."

"I like apple juice," he replied. "You're just weird."

Shaking his head, Lance chuckled and sipped at his coffee, giving Alex a small smile.

The Hamilton Building was an old brick building on the east side of campus that mostly housed the offices of the History, Philosophy and Political Science departments. The classrooms were all small whitewashed squares with only a few windows and lacked a decent Wi-Fi signal and sufficient outlets. In fact, there were outlets only at the front of the room and in the very back, neither of which was the ideal seating location. Lance, Alex, and Jenny had arrived in time to find places all together in the respectable middle of the room, not too close and not too far from their lecturer.

Professor Williams was one of the older members of the faculty and yet could still cheerfully skip through his classroom and hear even the slightest whisper. Naturally, their first hour of class was consumed with the presentation of the syllabus and Alex's first introduction to the notion that college professors didn't care if she showed up. They had ten minutes at the end which consisted of Professor William challenging them to consider the difference between logical thinking and critical reasoning along with assigning the first chapter of the textbook. When Alex stumbled out into the sunlight, she tucked her tablet under her arm and breathed in the fresh air with relief.

"What do you think?" Jenny asked her, turning her face up towards the sun.

"Not bad," Alex replied with a shrug. "But I have no idea what the difference is between logic and critical reasoning."

"I think logic is more scientifically based," Jenny offered. "You know, absolute truth while I think critical reasoning may be more human nature and behavior based."

Alex turned to look at her roommate with a new hint of respect in her eyes. Jenny smirked in response and winked at Alex.

"I'm with Alex," Lance admitted, "I wouldn't have thought they were different except that the class is called reason and critical reasoning."

"Well I'll see you both later," Jenny said to them with a glance at her phone. "I've got to run if I want to get a water before my next class."

"See you later," Alex called with a wave to the departing Jenny who gave them a quick wave over her shoulder.

"Bye Alex," Lance told her with a nod before he jogged off to call after another boy who was leaving the building.

Sighing softly, Alex adjusted her messenger bag and slipped her tablet into it. She pulled out her sunglasses and slipped them on before stepping further away from the building. Her eyes scanned the moving crowds of students as she started walking towards the administration building, searching for anyone she recognized from her dorm. The buildings became less crowded quickly and Alex found herself walking up a long sidewalk towards a large classic university building complete with a massive clock tower. There was a large open park in front of the administration hall with lots of leafing trees and students were lounging all about.

Having nothing better to do, Alex moved off the main path and sat down in the grass. She shrugged off her messenger bag and set it down next to her. Pulling out her map, Alex put her finger on the administration hall and let her eyes trace the route back to her dorm room. According to the map, the large modern building constructed from pale brick and steel to her right was the Fine Arts building. The one to her left was Miller Hall and she didn't know what classes took place there. Turning, she looked at a smaller building beyond Miller Hall on the left that was the Health Center.

Leaning back on the grass, Alex stared up at the blue sky and listened to the low hum of the people moving around her and other students on the lawn talking amongst themselves. She felt a twinge of regret at not going to University of Washington or Washington State with her high school friends. Compared to Spokane, Ravenslake was so small and had so little to do. Alex swallowed the lump in her throat and closed her eyes. She was just a little homesick, she assured herself quickly. Her parents and brother had left the day before and she didn't have any real friends on campus yet. But she had Jenny, who seemed friendly and wanting to make friends just like she did, and Arthur and maybe Lance. That made Alex feel a bit better, and maybe she'd meet a few more people in her next class.

Alex sat up and checked the time on her phone, wondering if she should get something to eat before her next class. She didn't feel very hungry, but packed her map back into her bag and stood up. Following the long sidewalk south, Alex headed for the University Commons where her RA had assured her a full food court could be found.

One turkey sandwich and stop off at her dorm room later, Alex was sitting down in the fifth row of her 12:30 Survey of Calculus class in the Meier Building. This room was much more modern with permanent large seats arranged like stadium rows. Each chair had a small fold out desk attached to the right side that swung up and into place. At the front of the room, a middle-aged African American woman who Alex assumed was Professor Bailey was writing on the whiteboard.

Waving to a girl she recognized from her floor, Alex took a quick drink from her water bottle and turned to watch the remaining students file in. Everyone looked about the right age to be freshman, but there were three nontraditional students in the mix as well. Alex was about to turn back to the front when a young man with short dark brown hair entered the room. There was nothing remarkable about him, he was cute and dressed casually, but as he walked down the aisle his eyes met Alex's.

Suddenly she was enveloped in the thick scent of old books. Pages turned around her and low voices sounded like there were off a great distance. Then the smell of garlic washed over her before Alex snapped back to reality.

Taking a quick breath, Alex stared at the young man who was gaping at her with a stunned expression on his face.

"Aiden," a voice called out. "Come on man!"

The young man, Aiden, turned towards the voice instinctively and started towards it. He had taken a few steps when he looked over his shoulder at Alex with a confused expression. Lowering her eyes, Alex focused on her tablet. She kept taking slow and long breaths, trying to sort out what was happening. First, there had been that weirdness with Arthur and now with this guy. Risking a look up, she found him sitting with another boy two rows ahead of her. He looked up at her over his shoulder making Alex look down quickly. She was relieved when Professor Bailey announced the beginning of class and started to go over the syllabus. Alex barely heard a word of it and rushed from the room as soon as the professor dismissed them.

When she made it back to her dorm room, Alex was relieved to find Jenny absent. Tossing her bag onto the bed, Alex sat down on the edge and rubbed her eyes. After a moment of consideration, Alex set an alarm on her phone and walked over to her laptop on her desk. She tapped her fingers impatiently as the machine booted up and accessed the internet. Then she hesitated. Alex stared at the search engine screen for may have been minutes before typing in 'seeing and hearing things'.

There was so much. Search results ranged from visual and auditory hallucinations tied to late life blindness, schizophrenia and post-traumatic stress to spiritual awakenings. Alex found none of them particularly comforting. She went through the other symptoms of suggested mental disorders but didn't think that anything else applied. The alarm on her phone went off, startling Alex out of her research.

"Okay, Alex," she told herself. "It's probably just the stress of college and being homesick. Don't panic yet."

Moving automatically, Alex grabbed her things for her next class and started walking back towards the Meier Building. She moved through the crowd of students with little difficulty until she reached the stairs and had to blend into the natural flow of movement. The classroom was at the far end of the hall and Alex slipped inside with a sense of relief. Once again she second guessed her decision to attend class, but she wasn't ready to go to the Health Center and announce that she'd had two hallucinations.

The classroom was far more similar to high school than the others had been with free standing chair and desk combinations in rows throughout the midsized room. There were three windows on the far side that looked over at the next building giving the room a closed off feel that didn't help Alex's nerves at all. There were only a few people in the room and the professor's tweed-clad back was turned to the door as he wrote points of the syllabus on the white board. Hoping to be seen by her new professor, but avoid any more unpleasant contacts, Alex's eyes went to the back row.

Another girl was already seated at the back with a notebook open in front of her, nibbling at her thumbnail. She had long red hair styled with a crown braid and was wearing rolled up jeans which revealed a tattoo on her ankle. It looked familiar to Alex, with a J, T and maybe two R's, but she couldn't place the symbol. Alex moved to take a seat and smiled as the girl turned to look up at her. Alex's eyes met the girl's blue eyes and she felt the world fall away again in a surge of panic.

Her hands were moist and touching rich thick clay as she inhaled the dusty earthen scent. Dry particles in the air irritated the skin of her face and arms. There was dried clay on her arms even as the moist clay caught under her fingernails and caked her hands.

A desk crashed to the ground as Alex backed into it, breaking eye contact with the girl. Unable to regain her balance, Alex stumbled over the leg of the desk to the ground, hearing a few people cry out. Her eyes rose to the girl in the back row who was now standing and staring at her with a look of shock.

"Are you alright?" an older warm voice questioned her before someone knelt beside her.

"I'm fine," Alex replied automatically, turning to look at whoever had come over. She wished she hadn't as her eyes locked with a pair of warm brown ones.

The smell of an old forest overwhelmed her as the classroom fell away from her sense. Birds were singing around her from amongst bright green leaves that rattled softly in the wind. Her feet were sinking into moist earth and a cool mist settled on her face and arms.

"Young lady," a distant voice called. "Are you alright?"

"Uh," Alex muttered before swallowing. "I'm not sure."

A pair of hands helped Alex to her feet and she blinked a few times before risking another look at the person helping her. He was a bit taller than her and clearly her professor, wearing a tweed jacket with jeans. Her eyes were drawn to the strange silver pin on his left lapel that looked Celtic.

"Take a seat," the man advised as he guided Alex to a desk. "I was afraid that would happen," he added in a more cheerful voice. "They pack these small rooms so tightly. We'll all have to careful."

"I'm fine now," Alex assured him as she sat down and focused on pulling out her things for class.

The professor remained beside her for another moment and Alex thought she heard a gasp from the back of the room but wasn't certain. Surely one small sound couldn't carry over the noise the other students were making. Alex looked up cautiously at the professor standing beside her. He was looking down at her with a pleased and gentle expression.

Leaning forward, he whispered, "It's alright. There is nothing wrong with you. This will pass."

Before Alex could form any kind of reply or think of a question, he called the class to order and introduced himself as Professor Ambrose Yates. He took a moment to do a quick survey of the students in the class for their majors before he launched into explaining the syllabus for Literature of Western Civilization. Alex wanted nothing more than to vanish into the background, especially given her less than flattering introduction, but Professor Yates went around the room and had each student introduce themselves including their major, hometowns, and reason for taking the class. For most it was pretty standard; the class was a mixture of freshman and sophomores who were either taking the class to fulfill a general education requirement or were English majors getting started.

The girl in the back whose eyes Alex could feel throughout most of the lesson was apparently named Nicole "Nicki" Russell and was an anthropology major. If Nicole's gaze wasn't bad enough, Alex noticed Professor Yates glancing her way multiple times during the hour. She wanted to brush it off as concern for her fall, but couldn't shake the dread that was knotting in her stomach.

When class ended and the professor assigned them to start reading Shakespeare's A Midsummer Night's Dream Acts 1 and 2, Alex was halfway packed. She rushed towards the door but saw Nicole slip out ahead of her. Alex felt trapped as she stepped out and found Nicole waiting a little down the hall from her. The classroom's location at the end of the hall and away from the stairs meant that Alex was stuck. Despite her intentions to the contrary, Alex locked eyes with Nicole and was relieved when nothing happened. She saw Nicole relax a little as well and stubbornly moved forward.

"Alex," Nicole called to her, reaching out to grab her arm.

Alex tried to shrug her off, but the girl had a remarkably strong grip. "What?" Alex snapped, turning to face Nicole with a glare.

Her tone surprised Nicole who looked uncertain for a moment before her facial muscles tightened. "What did you see?" Nicole questioned her.

Starring at Nicole, Alex could think of nothing to say. "What are you talking about?" she asked in a small voice.

Nicole's gaze softened a little and she eased her grip but did not let Alex go. "I smelled a thunderstorm and fresh cut grass," Nicole informed her. "There was a field and lightning. What did you see?"

"Nothing," Alex responded, pulling her arm away. "I don't know what you're talking about."

"Liar," Nicole said under her breath as Alex started to walk away. Despite the people around them, Alex heard the word and flinched.

Jenny was in their room when Alex made it back. Her roommate looked up from her desk where she was painting her nails and watching some television show that Alex didn't recognize. Smiling widely at Alex, Jenny gave a little wave before blowing on her nails.

"How were your classes?" Jenny asked cheerfully. "Mine were awesome! I think this semester is going to go really well."

The sick feeling in Alex's stomach intensified at the words and she was lost for a moment. Forcing a smile, Alex dropped her things on her bed before turning to her dresser. "They went fine," Alex forced. "I'm just a bit twitchy from all the excitement," she told Jenny as she pulled out some running clothes. "I'm heading out for a jog."

"Oh," Jenny responded with a curious glance over Alex. Her expression softened and she turned fully in her chair to face Alex. "I'm sure tomorrow will go better."

Alex looked over at Jenny with surprise and then gave her a small real smile. "Yeah," she agreed. "I hope you're right."

"Enjoy your run," Jenny told her before turning back to her computer screen. "And give Galahad a hug."

It was the best advice Alex had heard all day so she picked up the small plush dog and gave him a tight squeeze before changing. She grabbed her phone, keys and put the map of campus in her pocket, just in case. Alex glanced over at Jenny one more time before she left the room and headed down the stairs.

The University of Ravenslake campus was on the southwestern side of Ravens Lake and the South Santiam River marked the northern edge of half the campus. The dormitories were located near the river, giving some of the rooms a nice view of the water and winding trails that ran along the bank. A small path out the back of Hatfield Hall led straight to the trails. Alex waved to some other students who were arriving home and started walking down the path towards the water. She stopped once she was down the hill and near the water to stretch, wondering briefly why the town name was one word while the lake was two words. A few students were out on the trail and Alex could see a bike coming towards her in the distance. Taking a deep breath, Alex tried to put the strange happenings of the day out of her mind and began to run.

The campus buildings faded from her consciousness as Alex focused on her breathing and the sight of the lake ahead of her. The trail followed the river to the mouth of the lake and then turned southeast to follow the shore. Alex left the last of the campus buildings behind as the trail curved between the lake and the university's arboretum.

Waving to fellow students, Alex let her eyes trace the far shore of the lake where there were only a few stray cabins and docks. Up ahead the trail vanished into a small parking lot at the side of a busy city street. Beyond that, Alex could see the homes, shops and office buildings of the older section of town. The trail restarted at the other side of the parking lot and Alex guessed it followed the lakeside through the rest of town.

She slowed down and came to a halt before the parking lot and the start of North Riverside Drive. Using a bench, Alex stretched out her muscles while she debated going further or turning around. The ringing of her phone interrupted the debate and she pulled it out with a practiced motion to answer it.

"Hello sweetheart," her mother greeted warmly. "I know you just finished your classes, but I wanted to see how they went."

Alex swallowed. She wanted to say that she was seeing and hearing things. That other kids on campus were seeing them too and she had no idea what was happening. She wanted to ask her mother if she could come home and join Kayla and Hannah at the University of Washington in the spring.

"Rough huh," her mother said on the other end, interpreting her silence. "It's going to be a transition," her mother reassured her gently. "The first week and finals week will be the hardest."

"I'm not sure this was a good idea," Alex choked out.

"You loved the school when we visited," she reminded Alex. "You're just nervous because you don't know anyone yet and are a little homesick. It will pass. Your brother had a similar experience when he started college, remember him calling home every night for the first week."

"Yeah," Alex managed to reply.

"And now I'm lucky if he calls once a month," her mother grumbled before adding, "Give it time sweetheart."

"I think I may be sick," Alex blurted out.

"It's probably just nerves," her mother said, switching into pediatrician mode. "But keep an eye on your symptoms and keep a list. If you're not feeling better by the end of the week go to the Campus Health Center," her mother ordered. "And remember to take your vitamins and drink lots of fluids."

"Yes Mom," Alex answered dutifully. "I'm just…I don't know."

"Give it time sweetheart," her mother urged. Alex heard a beeping in the background. "I'm afraid I'm being paged," her mother informed her gently. "One of the other doctors is ill so I'm on a long shift at the clinic today."

"Bye Mom," Alex said softly. "Tell Dad I love him."

"I will," her mother promised. "I'll talk to you soon."

The call ended and Alex sighed. Collapsing back on the bench, Alex stared out over the lake. She looked down at her phone and pulled up the notepad feature. With a frown and a huff, she typed in:

Symptoms: visual, auditory and olfactory hallucinations started the first day of school.

5

The Second Day

The alarm clock blasted out a cheerful pop song from its spot at the edge of Alex's desk. Groaning, she reached up and turned it off, snatching her mp3 player from the dock. Alex brushed a strand of loose blonde hair out of her face and looked over at Jenny's side of the room. Jenny was already up and putting on mascara in front of her vanity.

"I think we should get a plant," Jenny announced as she spotted Alex moving in the mirror.

"A plant?" Alex repeated still not fully awake.

"Yeah," Jenny told her, turning to face Alex. "Something alive and green." She gestured to their room which still lacked personal touches beyond the photos they'd both put up. "We should get a rug for the middle too."

"Uh okay," Alex agreed, rubbing her eyes. She looked over at the clock with a frown. It was eight o'clock, but she didn't remember setting it.

"Are you feeling better?" Jenny asked her as she sat down on her bed. "I came back at six to see if you wanted dinner and you were already asleep. I turned your alarm on when I got back from dinner to be on the safe side."

Tossing back her comforter, Alex glanced down. Sure enough, she was still in her running pants and shirt. She'd come back to her dorm and laid down under the covers with Galahad to calm down, but that was the last thing she remembered. Jenny was watching her with a concerned expression, but put on a smile when Alex looked back at her.

"Tell you what, how about you get dressed real quick and join me for breakfast," Jenny suggested. Seeing Alex's hesitation, she quickly added, "Arthur has morning football training so it'll just be us. You really should eat something since you skipped dinner."

Nodding, Alex climbed out of her bed and grabbed her toiletry kit and slippers. Jenny gave her an encouraging smile before she started packing a bag for her first class of the day. Alex slipped out into the hallway where other students were moving around and talking. She strode down the hall to the communal bathroom, waving to a few of the other girls on their floor. Steam was billowing out of the large shower area to the right of the main door and the tiled walls amplified the chatter of the line of girls who were using the long counter of sinks and mirrors. Thankfully, a sink was free at the far end and Alex set her bag on the counter before looking at herself in the mirror.

There were no bags under her eyes and she looked fine except for her messy hair. Considering her reflection for a moment, Alex thought about how long she'd slept. Maybe everything she'd seen and heard yesterday was because she was overtired and stressed. Letting out a long breath, Alex smiled slowly at her reflection.

"New day," she told herself before pulling out her toothbrush.

After brushing her teeth, washing her face and taming her hair, Alex felt much better about the world. Jenny was double checking her schedule for the day when she returned and waited patiently while Alex pulled on some clothes.

"Sorry if I worried you," Alex apologized while brushing her hair back into a ponytail. "I'm not sure what happened."

"Stress," Jenny told her, standing from her desk chair. "If Arthur wasn't here I don't think I'd be coping very well." Jenny shrugged as she collected her key and student card. "And I called my Dad last night just to hear his voice."

"What about your mom?" Alex asked before she thought better of it.

"My mom died when I was ten," Jenny answered wistfully, "Cancer."

"I'm sorry," Alex replied quickly.

"It's okay," Jenny assured her with a smile that didn't quite reach her eyes. "We're still getting to know each other, it's a process."

Alex remained quiet until they sat down at a two seat table against the left wall of Michaels Cafeteria. There were students moving and talking all around them in a rush of noise which was strangely comforting.

"So I never asked your parents what they do," Jenny told her as she cut apart her omelet.

"My dad is a journalist and mom is a pediatrician," Alex explained and recalled something Jenny had mentioned a few days ago. "Your dad is a lawyer right?"

"That's right," Jenny replied with a proud smile. "He became a senior partner two years ago."

"That's nice," Alex acknowledged. "That means he's one of the bosses of his firm right?"

Jenny chuckled, "Close enough."

"What's your class this morning?" Alex asked to move the subject away from parents.

"I've got History of Media and Society and then we've got History of Civilization this afternoon," Jenny reminded her. "You've got science right?"

"My general physics class is this morning," Alex replied after taking a sip of her juice. "My physics lab is only on Thursdays."

They ate in silence for a few minutes, but then Alex noticed Jenny looking over her shoulder with an odd look.

"What?" Alex questioned.

"Two people across the room keep looking over at us," Jenny told her.

"Cute boys?" Alex asked with a teasing smile before turning to look over her shoulder.

She froze as she spotted Nicole and Aiden, two of her hallucination triggers, sitting together at a table and looking at her.

"Do you know them?" Jenny asked with a nod towards them.

"I have a class with each of them," Alex admitted as she turned back to Jenny, determined to ignore them. "I wouldn't say I know them."

Jenny looked at her, clearly waiting for more, but Alex dug into her eggs and ham even though her appetite had vanished. After a moment, her roommate looked over at the pair once again with a warning look before turning her attention to her yogurt and blueberries. They split up soon after so Jenny could make it to her class and Alex could get back to the dorm for a shower. As Alex waved and started to walk away, Jenny caught her hand.

"Why don't you meet Arthur and me for lunch today," Jenny suggested, "Eleven fifteen at the Commons Food Court."

"You sure?" Alex asked. "You haven't been able to spend much time with him." Studying Jenny's expression, Alex added, "I'm alright Jenny, seriously. I'll see you later."

"If you change your mind it shouldn't be hard to find us," Jenny added tentatively before she took a step away from Alex. "Have a good morning."

"You too," Alex replied, giving Jenny a smile and turning to walk across the lawn to their dorm.

After a shower, Alex felt a bit better even if she was a bit rushed in getting to her morning class. The Natural Sciences Building was a large three story looming brick building near the west edge of campus with a modern steel and brick addition on its north end. The main entrance had cases of awards and an old fashioned, but beautiful metal astronomy display of the solar system in a large dome. There were two sets of staircases leading up, and someone had been kind enough to post paper signs by each one to guide the new students. Following the signs, Alex made her way into the new side of the building and located room 203.

It was a chemistry classroom with large black topped tables that each had a set of drawers built into the side and gas nozzles in the middle. There were two chairs at each table and a few students were already sitting, spread out through the room's six rows of three tables. Once again, Alex glanced around to see if she knew anyone but tensed as she spotted Aiden sitting in the back of the room. He looked up at her and gave her a small smile before gesturing to the chair next to him. Alex set her things down on the front row table closest to the door and sat down, turning her back on him. As she was unpacking her things, someone walked behind her and pulled out the second chair next to her and sat down. She didn't even have to look to know who it was.

"Go away," she grumbled, not looking at him.

"How about we start with hi nice to meet you, I'm Aiden Bosco," he suggested in an entirely too calm voice. "Ignoring it isn't going to change what happened."

"Nothing happened," Alex growled stubbornly.

"That was convincing," Aiden chuckled. "Look it's weird, but it only seems to happen the first time."

"Go away," Alex repeated as she glanced up hopefully at the clock.

"Look," Aiden said in a much more gentle voice. "It freaked me out the first time, it happened with my best friend two weeks ago. I got back from a road trip with my family and went to see Nicki and suddenly I'm seeing her grandmother's clay studio. She told me that she saw something with you yesterday, the same thing that I saw: a big field and a thunderstorm in the distance with lightning."

"If I tell you my name will you go away?" Alex asked tensely.

Aiden chuckled and leaned forward in an attempt to see Alex's face, but she refused to look at him. "I already know that you're Alex Adams; Nicki was in class with you when you did introductions," he reminded her.

Alex opened her mouth to reply when her attention was caught by another student walking into the room. He had a slight built and was a little taller than Alex, but shorter than Aiden. He had sharp cheekbones that made Alex jealous, a few freckles and bright green eyes. But around his right leg, all the way up to his waist was a metal leg brace and he was half leaning on a wooden cane with a carved head. Alex swallowed and watched as he took two steps into the room, knowing she shouldn't stare. Then the young man turned and looked at her, his green eyes meeting her gray eyes. Alex would have screamed in frustration if she could have when it happened again.

There was a sense of warmth as the scent of freshly baked bread and cookies surrounded her. The sound of jazz music was coming somewhere in the distance. She was looking up at dried flower bouquets tied with red ribbon hanging from a beam on the ceiling.

Alex snapped back to reality to find the young man leaning against her desk and taking a few slow breaths. Dropping her eyes, Alex put her hands on her lap as she tried to stop them from shaking. Aiden put a hand on her shoulder and said something to the young man who moved away a moment later. Alex heard him sit down at the desk directly behind them.

"That was Brandon Fisher," Aiden told Alex once she stopped glaring at her tablet. "I met him yesterday in my technical writing class."

"Shut up," Alex hissed, but Aiden ignored her.

"Fresh bread and cookies, jazz music and dried flowers," he supplied. "That was my vision, Nicki hasn't met him yet."

"I told you-" Alex started to say, but the professor tapped a wooden ruler against his desk at the front of the room. He was an older man with a no-nonsense feel about him, dressed in a three-piece suit.

"Enough chatter," the professor announced. "Welcome to General Physics 1; I am Professor Whittaker. I'm going to assume that those of you taking this class in order to fulfill your general science requirement have signed up for a lab as well. If you haven't, then I urge you to see if you can still register."

Ignoring Aiden, Alex focused completely on Professor's Whittaker's introduction to the class. She'd been introduced to physics in high school with Newton's Three Laws of Motion and the spectrum of light, but Whittaker quickly made it clear that they were going much further than that. He announced that by the end of the semester they would have a basic understanding of the physical laws, their applications, heat, electricity, magnetism and light. She noted down her assignment as the class wound down and ignored Aiden as she packed up. As soon as Professor Whittaker dismissed them, Alex bolted for the door and let herself get swept up in the wave of students leaving classrooms.

Alex returned to her dorm room to drop off her textbooks and found a note on her desk from Jenny once again inviting her for lunch. She glanced over at the clock and nibbled at her lip. It was 11 o'clock so she had time to meet up with her…. Alex paused, Jenny was trying to be her friend and Arthur was her boyfriend. They were nice to be making an effort, especially Jenny who was probably wondering what disorder she had. Decision made, Alex made sure she had her student card and grabbed her things for History of Civilization which started after lunch.

The University Student Union Building was the newest buildings on campus and had replaced an old brick classroom building. On her first tour of the campus, the building had clearly been the pride and joy of the school as it served as the main hub of student activity and housed most student services. It was a tall building that mixed brickwork, metal, and lot of windows together over four floors. The shaded lawn across from the main doors was filled with students eating sandwiches or out of to-go containers as they lounged on the grass.

Walking inside, Alex looked around the long food court seating area that dominated the first floor of the commons building. The space was two stories high above Alex's head with a curved ceiling that was a decorative mix of wood, metal, and round lights. A walkway circled the food court with a large curved staircase linking the first floor and the second floor. To her right was the entrance to the administration offices, financial aid and the enrollment office through one imposing set of double doors. To the left was the food court with a collection of counters that each had their own type of food and menus.

Yesterday Alex had just grabbed a sandwich from a large display of prepared foods, but today she decided to try something new. Moving past the checkout stations, Alex scanned the various counter shops for any sign of Jenny or Arthur. Her eyes landed on a familiar purple top and head of long black wavy hair in front of the custom sub shop. Grabbing a tray, Alex walked towards Jenny to confirm it was her roommate.

"Hi," Alex greeted as she came up beside Jenny.

Her roommate beamed at her as she turned, but her expression grew concerned as she studied Alex. "Rough morning?"

"Not the best," Alex admitted. "Where are you two?"

"We don't have a spot yet," Jenny informed her as she checked her phone.

"Alright," Alex told her, "I'll find you." She stepped away from Jenny and headed for the counter that smelled of burgers and fries.

"Hey Alex," Arthur greeted, surprising Alex and making her jump. "Sorry," he apologized.

"Oh hey Arthur," Alex answered with a soft blush. "Sorry, I didn't notice you."

"Can't blame you," Arthur told her a wide smile. "That smell is rather distracting isn't it."

One of the chefs came over to take their orders before shooing them to a waiting area off to the side. Alex grabbed a bottle of water from a cooler and leaned against a metal pillar in the center of the food court with her tray to wait for her food.

"So how are classes?" Arthur asked. "Haven't seen you since yesterday morning."

"Classes are fine," Alex answered honestly. The classes themselves were fine; it was her fellow students she was worried about.

"I'm sensing a but," Arthur informed her with his smile falling away. "Everything alright?"

"Just some weird classmates," Alex told him quickly, "I'm sure it'll pass. I've just been sort of stressed." Alex shrugged, "I've never been away from my parents without a coach and team around me before."

"I didn't know you played sports."

"I don't anymore," Alex answered, "Well I'm going to sign up for intermural, but I wasn't…. I mean I wasn't exactly the sports star."

"Which sports?"

"I did a lot of cross-country, soccer, and track in high school," Alex replied.

"Then you should like the intramurals here," Arthur told her. "But I hope you'll make time to attend the local games."

"Course," Alex said quickly, trying not to blush again as Jenny walked over to them with a sub sandwich and iced tea on her tray.

She glanced at their empty trays and smirked. "I suppose I'll go and get us a table."

"Thanks, Jenny," Arthur told her, beaming at her. He leaned forward and kissed her quickly before Jenny walked over to the checkout station.

"What about you?" Alex asked, "Your classes I mean."

"They're good," Arthur answered with a shrug. "I was able to get into one of the more advanced Poli Sci classes this semester in addition to 101. Plus I'm getting my math and English requirements out of the way."

"I think every freshman is," Alex remarked.

Thankfully their numbers came up and they collected their burgers and fries. There was a line at the checkout as more and more students filed in to get lunch, but they quickly spotted Jenny near the far wall once they were through. Joining her, Alex felt like she could finally relax and threw herself into listening to Jenny's excited description of her classes and Arthur's stories from practice.

At 12:15 Alex had to drag Jenny away from Arthur so they wouldn't be late to their first History of Civilization class. It was back to the Meier building, but in one of the recently upgraded classrooms on the first floor. It was a large lecture room with long white tables on either side forming a long aisle down the center. Each of the tables had outlets between every two chairs. A large rolling computer station stood at the front of the room, hooked to the projection system which was shining the first slide of a presentation on the large white screen.

A beautiful, but stern looking woman with long dark braided hair and wearing a tailored black waistcoat stood at the front of the room. There was a something instantly intimidating about her that made Jenny and Alex fall silent. Jenny touched Alex's hand and pointed to a table safely in the middle of the room at the end of one of the long desks. Students filed in, talking as they did, but quickly fell silent. Glancing up cautiously at her newest professor, Alex saw the woman's lips curve into a smirk, but the professor kept her eyes on the computer screen.

"Hi Alex," a familiar female voice said to her right.

Alex looked up in alarm to see Nicole walking past with Aiden who gave her a quick wave. They settled on the other side of the room, one row ahead of them which made Alex feel only a little better.

"Wait," Jenny spoke in a low voice, "Aren't those the pair from this morning?"

"Yeah," Alex whispered back. "I'm got a few classes with them. They're a bit …" Alex trailed off. If they were crazy then didn't that make her crazy? She'd have to look up shared hallucinations and see if there was such a thing. "They're strange," Alex settled on. "But harmless," she added quickly on impulse.

"Okay," Jenny replied slowly, "But if you need Arthur to beat them up or scare them off let me know."

"Attention," a sharp feminine voice with a slight accent called from the front of the room. Alex looked up sharply to see their professor stepping away from the computer. "It is now 12:30 and we will begin. I am Professor Cornwall, and I drew the short straw in the history department to teach one of the freshman classes as one of my colleagues is on sabbatical. You will find me a highly knowledgeable professor and fair to those who put in an honest effort, but a harpy to those who think they can sail through my class. Therefore I will remind you that all students are allowed a certain number of withdrawals with no penalties to their records."

Alex could almost hear a collective swallow of fear around the room. Professor Cornwall was silent and let her eyes track across the fresh crop of students. Her eyes stopped on Nicole and then on Aiden before sweeping towards Alex's side of the room. Gripping the edge of the desk, Alex was about to look away when the Professor's eyes met hers, slamming her eyes shut.

She could smell water and salt with the wind blowing her hair back from her face. Opening her eyes, she gazed down at a wide flooded valley with small islands linked by wooden causeways far below her. She stood atop a high hill that rose sharply from the earth. It was surrounded on three sides by water and in the distance across the water, she could see forested rolling hills. Strange haunting music began to echo up from the lake valley below.

Green eyes moved away from Alex and she tightened her grip on the edge of her desk as she fought the urge to run. Professor Cornwall finished her stare down of the class and then turned her attention to the slideshow.

"Now class, today we will go through the syllabus and my expectations for this course. You'll find a full copy not only of this presentation but also the print syllabus on the course website."

Forcing herself to focus, Alex pulled up the course website on her tablet and followed along as Professor Cornwall went through a rapid explanation of class dates and subjects. Professor Cornwall did not slow down the whole class. In quick succession, they were given the date of the final exam, covered the requirements of two group projects, went over Professor Cornwall's attendance policy and were introduced to the discussion point system. By the end of the hour and fifteen-minute class, Alex was feeling tired and overwhelmed.

"You are dismissed," Professor Cornwall told them. "I look forward to seeing who remains on Thursday."

"I am torn between fear and awe," Jenny whispered to Alex as they packed up.

"Yeah," Alex agreed with a small smile. "She's pretty intense."

Swinging her bag over her shoulder, Alex stood up and looked back at the front of the classroom to find Professor Cornwall looking towards her with a strange expression. Alex swallowed nervously, but the professor kept watching. Frowning, Alex realized that the professor wasn't looking at her at all, but was instead watching Jenny. She looked across the room to find Nicole and Aiden packing up and speaking quietly. Sensing her gaze, Aiden looked over at her as he pulled on his backpack. Next to him, Nicole offered her a small shrug.

"Alex," Jenny called. "Earth to Alex."

Looking back at her roommate, Alex blinked and quickly smiled. "Sorry," she apologized quickly.

"We're done for the day," Jenny announced. "How about we walk over to Main Street. I heard that there is a great coffee place right at the edge of campus and I'm dying to explore more of town."

"Uh, sure," Alex agreed with a quick nod as they walked out the door. "That's a nice idea."

"Plus we can meet more people," Jenny added. "Tide us over until the weekend parties start at least."

Alex fought the urge to look over her shoulder at Professor Cornwall as Jenny linked their arms and guided their way out of the building. To her surprise, Aiden and Nicole walked past her without a word. Aiden simply gave her a little wave over his shoulder on their way out.

6

Lady of the Lake

834 B.C.E. Snowdonia Wales

High above his village, Myrddin could see the dusting of snow on the mountains while the highest peaks vanished into the gray clouds. He sighed softly and tightened his cloak around himself before lifting his bag over his shoulder. The dull shape of his sword bumped his back and the weight of the metal working stones at the bottom of the bag felt comforting. At his side hung a small pouch with some food and a dagger strapped to his belt. His right hand gripped a strong wooden walking staff that had small signs carved into it for protection. One of his neighbors looked over at him curiously before giving a quick bow which warned Myrddin of his mother's approach behind him.

"Do you have everything?" his mother asked in a gentle tone that surprised him.

Myrddin turned to his mother and studied her face, finding a trace of fear in her normally calm and collected features. His mother reached for him, placing one hand on his shoulder and the other touching his cheek. They remained that way for some time, his mother memorizing his face.

"Take care, my son," she whispered before leaning forward and kissing his forehead gently.

"I will be back," Myrddin said seeking to reassure her, but it sounded like a question to his ears.

"I don't know," his mother murmured. "I hope so, but you were born for a reason. That much was revealed to me. Remember that you are the son of Awena, priestess of the western mountains and that I am proud of you."

He swallowed thickly and before he could change his mind, he stepped forward and embraced his mother. Her arms came up and around him, holding Myrddin as she had not for many years.

"Go," she ordered as she released him. "Go on Myrddin."

Myrddin nodded and took a few hesitant steps backward before he turned to follow the path away from his roundhouse. Determined not to look back Myrddin focused on the path that wove between the numerous roundhouses. Everyone was already starting their days with many men and their children walking towards the mountains with packs and mining tools. One young boy carried his bone pick over his shoulder and Myrddin could tell that his stone hammer was tucked into the bag slung over his shoulder as he followed his father towards the copper mines. Myrddin fell into step with them and allowed their morning chatter to distract him.

"Myrddin," the strange female voice called to him, still sounding so far away.

The morning mist had barely lifted when Myrddin reached the split in the path. One well-worn path continued on, twisting its way around the mountain while another faint trail headed up the slope towards the peak. He looked up at the rocky mountainside that offered no shelter and the tilted rocks that were broken apart all over the ground. Thick dying grass covered the area as the chill of autumn hung over Myrddin and he knew it would only get colder as he ascended. He tightened his grip on his bag, stepped off the worn path and began to climb the mountain.

He did his best not to ponder on what being awaited him up the mountain as he worked to keep his footing on the uneven terrain. The ground was cold and unforgiving, but Myrddin was thankful that the snow remained only at the highest point of the mountain. Despite his nervousness, his feet knew the way to go and how to climb. Many times he had joined his mother in gathering plants from the highest points of the mountain and she had shown him the largest of the mountain lakes which was his destination.

A standing stone loomed before him, marking his progress up the hill and Myrddin gratefully stopped to drink from his water skin. Turning around, he looked down the mountain and smiled softly as he saw his village. He was too far to see anyone moving, but the field boundaries made of mounded earth were clear and there was still enough green in the grass that the thatched roofs of the roundhouses were distinct. After catching his breath, Myrddin touched the standing stone gently and moved on.

He was nearly out of breath when he reached the precipice of the mountainside, but forced himself to take a few more steps. Myrddin gazed over the long deep blue lake before him which was nestled in the carved grooves of the mountain. Harsh cliffs and steep rocky slopes surrounded the long irregular lake as small creeks and waterfalls fed into it from the upper reaches of the mountain. Mist still clung to the steep peaks just above the lake enclosing the small valley with a chilly veil.

The water rippled softly in the wind, but everything felt still as if waiting for something. Myrddin hesitated to breathe, hesitated to move closer to the water; a feeling he had never had at the lake before. He had skipped stones here as a child, but now this place felt strange and wrapped in a shroud of something beyond his reckoning. Then, slowly, he descended down the side of the valley, watching his footing carefully. His staff made a gentle clinking sound against the rocks that echoed across the water with each step he took. Finally, he stepped onto the narrow rocky beach at the edge of the water where he paused to look over the long stretch of water.

Gently lowering his pack to the ground, Myrddin drew a small bronze dagger from his belt. He gently ran a finger over the smooth polished bronze blade before inspecting the carved wooden handle riveted to the metal. Looking out over the lake, Myrddin released a small sigh before bringing the dagger back over his head. Then with one smooth movement, he launched the dagger over the water and watched as it hit the water and vanished. The ripples spread out and he held his breath, waiting.

Myrddin noticed the ripples becoming stronger rather than weakening. Water began to churn in a circle, the height of the small wave growing higher and higher with every moment. Gasping, Myrddin stepped back, nearly tripping over his bag as small streams of water burst forth from the water towards the sky. The shimmering strands of water wove themselves together above the surface of the lake. Then a figure stepped through the veil of water, the flowing drops cloaking it without making a sound and Myrddin found himself looking into deep green eyes.

Everything around him faded into a thick mist that clung to his skin with an icy touch. The air was thin and he could not breathe. Voices in the distance were singing a strange song that he could not understand but filled him with loneliness and despair. Moving forward, his footfalls echoed and he looked down to see a floor of polished black stone with ripples of white and silver. A deep voice shouted a strange word and he was pushed forward by an unseen force. The word was repeated and he was pushed forward once again even as he braced himself against it. Light burst forth before him as a strange doorway of stone and glowing metal with glowing marks of it appeared just in front of him. A wall of strange rippling light filled the doorway and Myrddin was filled with fear. The strange voice shouted the word one more time and Myrddin was forced into the wall of light.

"Myrddin," a voice called out to him.

He gasped for air and fell to his knees as the world resettled around him. Pebbles slipped through his fingers as Myrddin grasped at the rocky terrain beneath him.

"Myrddin," the voice repeated, but he was loath to look up at the being that had appeared from the lake. "Fear not," she urged him. "You will not have to experience that again for some time."

Slowly, Myrddin raised his head to look back at the strange being. She looked human at first glance with long black hair flowing over her shoulders and small several small braids scattered throughout. Softly glowing water droplets created a circlet on her head that illuminated her face in the low light of the overcast day. Her features were elegant and graceful in form, but strange blue and black flowing lines circled around her eyes. The woman's skin made him think of polished bronze, a rich tone much darker than his own skin and shimmering even in the low light. She was unnatural, not of this world, but his mother had promised she was no Sídhe.

Myrddin realized that she was smiling at him and dropped his eyes from his face only to see that she was not standing on the water as he had first thought. Instead, the water was rising around her creating the silvery white gown that she wore and flowing down behind her back to form the blue cape at her back. Stumbling to his feet, Myrddin swallowed, unsure of himself.

"That, Myrddin, was the Connection," the strange being told him. "It occurs when two beings of magical power come together for the first time. We both see a moment or an impression of the other."

"Who- what are you?" Myrddin asked, trying to remain calm and wishing desperately that his mother had better prepared him. "Are you an ancestor?"

"No," she answered calmly, sounded amused by the question. "I am not Sídhe nor have I ever been a Child of the Iron Realm. I am of another realm. What you saw when we formed our Connection was the moment of my banishment to your realm."

She held out her hand and a shape burst from the lake, flying into her hand. Holding up the bronze dagger that he had cast into the water, she remarked, "You forgot to put it beyond the realm of humans." Then she took the dagger's blade with her other hand. "That is very important Myrddin, the item must transcend the realm of use and the living to give strength to the ancestors," she reminded him. The woman bent the bronze blade with a smooth motion that twisted the metal out of shape. "That's better isn't it."

Myrddin watched as the woman knelt onto the surface of the water and reverently placed the dagger on its surface. It vanished into the depths once again the moment she released it and Myrddin swallowed.

"I thought Mother was sending me-" Myrddin started.

"I know," the being replied, "I am not offended, Merlin."

The name startled him as she had called him by his true name only moments before, but he brushed it aside.

"Was it you who called me?" he questioned, trying to stand tall and not fidget.

"It was," the woman answered. "It was time that we met, you are old enough now Merlin. I am Cyrridven, although your mother called me the Lady of the Lake. It was good of you to bring an offering to your ancestors." Cyrridven frowned slightly, a faraway look in her eyes. "Your ancestors will need the aid and strength of the living in the coming days. The Iron Realm will need the strength of her children."

Her words sounded like a promise of things to come and sent a chill through Myrddin's body. Through sheer will, he forced the response down and focused on the present.

"Why did you call me?" he asked in as even a tone as he could manage.

"You know what you are, do you not Merlin?" she asked in return. "You are aware that your father was not a human, but a member of the Sídhe who slip into this world to steal and torment."

"I know," Myrddin confessed his voice tight and his fist clenching. "All of my clan knows it; only my mother's position protected me as a newborn."

Water rippled as Cyrridven moved closer to the shore, a gentle expression on her face. Myrddin didn't dare move closer to the water and Cyrridven stopped a few feet from him with the edges of her watery gown lapping at the shore.

"You are the only child ever born to both the Iron Realm and Sídhean, you were born singular and special in this and all realms Merlin," she assured him in a soft tone.

"My name is Myrddin," he snapped at her, before promptly shrinking back with fear.

"Myrddin is the name your mother gave you," Cyrridven agreed without any sign of anger. "But Merlin is the name the world bestows on you."

"How can the world give a name?" he questioned in a doubtful voice.

Cyrridven laughed her voice musical like his aunt's flute blended with running water. She paused in her laughter and smiled brightly at Myrddin.

"Oh, child," she told him, "There is so much that you must learn. Did your mother tell you nothing of me?"

"No," he informed her with a shake of his head. "She said that I might gain the answers she could not."

"And you shall," Cyrridven agreed. "Your mother met me once, sixteen years ago when she discovered she was with child from a Sídhe raider. She wandered these mountains calling for the voices of the ancestors for guidance. When she came to the water I appeared and passed on a message that you would be a beautiful and strong lad who had a great purpose ahead of him. Your mother is a great priestess of the Iron Realm, but she is no mage. You, Merlin, shall be."

"Why?" he asked her, "I've been training to be a priest and I've learned to cast bronze. Why do I need to learn… this?"

"Great danger is coming," Cyrridven informed him, her face tightening. "A new Sídhe leader has risen and she is not content to merely torment humans or steal children. The Iron Realm is the central world in the great Tree of Reality and she wants to rule it. Scáthbás wants to take the whole of existence for the Sídhe." Cyrridven's lips curved into a small victorious smile, "But the realm's magic is gathering a defense of its own," her eyes locked on Myrddin's, "And you have a central part to play."

He wanted to run home, he wanted nothing to do with this strange being and her words of danger. The Otherworlds were not to be toyed with and the ancestors were to be honored for the protection they provided the living. Terror gripped him that the thought that the current lull in hostiles by the Sídhe against his people ending. Myrddin swallowed and looked back at Cyrridven before taking a few steps back from the lake. She said nothing and did nothing to stop him as he grabbed his bag and staff. Myrddin scrambled up the side of the valley and jumped towards the path that would lead him home, never turning around to see if Cyrridven was still watching him.

7

The Third Day

The problem, Alex was finding, with spending your first two days at college suffering strange flashes isolated to a small group of people that you kept running into was that it made a person start their third day of classes with a very paranoid view of the world. Wednesday started with Jenny's alarm clock going off a few minutes before her own with an overly sugary pop song. After making themselves presentable, Jenny and Alex met Arthur and Lance at the Michaels Dining Hall. To Jenny's amusement, the boys were late and they found themselves waiting by the doorway while Alex kept her eyes open for any sign of Aiden, Nicole, Brandon or worse Professor Yates or Professor Cornwall.

Breakfast was a calm affair with everyone reporting on their Tuesday classes or in Alex's case giving a highly edited report. Jenny was loving her Journalism and Media class, Arthur had found his political science 101 boring, but had met some of his fellow political science majors and while Lance had nothing good to say about his pre-calculus algebra class he had nothing but good things to say about his geology teacher Professor Bates.

Alex's nervousness only grew as she listened to the others discuss their positive experiences. Aiden had said that the weird visions had only happened the first time between people so maybe it wouldn't happen again. She paused at her own thoughts, when had she started calling them visions instead of hallucinations. Then again as far as she knew hallucinations weren't usually shared and she couldn't understand why the different visions for each person. Alex snapped out of her thoughts when Jenny poked her arm and called her name.

"You with us Alex?" Arthur asked with an amused smile as she could have sworn that his eyes twinkled.

"I'm sorry," she apologized quickly with a glance at all three of them before her eyes settled on Jenny. "I don't know where my head was."

"I was saying that maybe after our last classes we should go the recreation center and see what fall activities they have," Jenny repeated with a raised eyebrow.

"Sounds good," Alex agreed quickly with a smile before looking at the boys. "Can you join us?"

"No," Arthur replied with an apologetic look towards Jenny, "Football practice. We've got a game in Arkansas this Saturday."

"Arkansas," Alex repeated with wide eyes. "They don't give you much time to adjust to college before sending you out."

"That's why the football players were all here weeks before the rest of the students," Lance told her with a chuckle. "It's the price of glory." Lance slapped a hand on Arthur's shoulder. "And Arthur here might even be starting quarterback."

"Seriously!" Jenny gasped at her boyfriend who had ducked his head. "You didn't tell me that!"

"It's because Will has a bad cold," Arthur rushed to say. "The doctor is worried he might even have pneumonia."

"It's still a big deal," Jenny told him, leaning around the round table to kiss him quickly. "The coach clearly sees how talented you are."

"She's right," Lance agreed with an easy going smile. "I almost wasn't going at all and it is unlikely that I'll actually play."

Smiling, Alex watched the pair for a moment as Jenny beamed at the embarrassed Arthur before turning her attention back to her cereal. They settled into a comfortable silence as everyone focused on their food. Alex jumped when Lance's phone started playing a guitar riff. Quickly, Lance turned off the sound and held up the phone for them to see.

"We'd better get moving ladies," he told them with a smile.

"Yeah," Arthur sighed. "Principles of Chemistry awaits."

They gathered up their trays and quickly moved over to the trash washing area in a flow of students who all had 9:30 classes. Once they were outside Lance and Alex waited as Jenny and Arthur kissed again.

"See you for lunch," Arthur promised Jenny before looking over at Alex and Lance, "You'll join us right?"

"Sure," Lance replied, pleased with the invitation. "I haven't tried the Commons yet." He looked at Alex and asked, "Any good?"

"Better than the dining hall," Alex promised before sighing. "Pity my meal plan is mostly Michaels meals."

"Everyone's plan is mostly Michaels meals," Jenny huffed before stepped away from Arthur. She gave him a little wave and led the way southeast towards Hamilton.

Reason and Critical Thinking was spent with Professor Williams questioning the class on the first two chapters of the books and their thoughts on the differential between logic and critical reasoning. Apparently, Jenny had been pretty close in her thought process on the first day. Professor Williams sat on the edge of the first-row desk and summarized the difference as critical thinking was how humans actually thought while logic was how we rationally thought we should think using the Socratic method versus Aristotle's logical reasoning approach as an example. By the end of class, Alex had a long document of notes and a pleased smile on her face due to things making sense.

After a quick goodbye, Jenny and Lance left her standing outside the Hamilton Building and rushed off to their next classes. Alex wandered back to Hatfield Hall to retrieve her statistics book while debating whether or not she should go to class, remembering that Aiden was in it with her. Finally, she settled on arriving right before the bell so she could ensure she sat far from him. Professor Bailey was watching the clock carefully as Alex walked in.

Aiden saw her come into the room and nodded to her as their professor started to call the class to attention. Nothing happened when their eyes met and Alex relaxed into her chair. Sadly, Professor Bailey proved to be a rather dull professor who never strayed from her flat monotone voice. Worse was now that they were off the syllabus discussion, the Professor spent the whole class writing information on the board which made the monotone hard to hear, but it was still not enough to ruin Alex's good mood. At the end of class, Alex packed up her things and looked over at Aiden once again. Their eyes met and she grinned when nothing happened. He raised an eyebrow at Alex and chuckled before turning his back on her to walk out the door. Right before he vanished into the throng of students, he gave Alex a small wave over his right shoulder.

Lunch in the commons was noisy with all the students around them clamoring for their food and Arthur speaking much more loudly than normal at their small table. He recounted a story from his and Jenny's high school days in San Francisco much to Jenny's embarrassment while Alex tried to hide her grin behind her hand. Jenny only half-heartened threatened Arthur while watching Alex's mood out of the corner of her eye. Lance smiled even as he kept his head down and hid his chuckle. Alex promised to meet Jenny back at their dorm once their classes were over before Jenny and Arthur headed off to Personal and Exploratory Writing hand in hand.

Literature of Western Civilization had a good start as Nicole only looked up at her as she walked into the classroom. Again nothing happened when their eyes met and Nicole gave only a small nod to acknowledge her before going back to braiding a small wisp of her hair. Alex slipped into a desk near the wall, grateful to avoid falling over a desk today. Professor Yates entered the classroom, wearing a different tweed jacket, but with the same pin and carrying a leather briefcase in his right hand. He was humming softly with an occasional whistle as he walked up to the front of the room.

"Welcome back class," he greeted them all with a wide smile as he set down his briefcase on the front table. "I'm glad to see you all back here today. I'm certain that you all read the first two acts of *A Midnight Summer's Dream*, but we will discuss it today anyway."

Strained chuckles filled the room as students tried to look interested in the lesson plan. Pulling a marker from his briefcase, Professor Yates turned to the whiteboard and wrote: Act I and the names of the first characters introduced.

"Let's begin," he told them as he turned back to the class. "What is established in the first act with the couples that Shakespeare presents?"

They worked through Act I and Alex got the distinct impression that Professor Yates found it all a bit dull. In the span of only fifteen minutes, he ran through the plot of the first act with the ruler of Athens about to marry the Queen of the Amazons whom he had conquered and the dispute over the marriage of the woman Hermia who wanted to marry Lysander and not Demetrius. Meanwhile, a group of craftsmen was preparing to perform a play for the ruler's wedding creating a play within a play.

Act I established that two men were in love with Hermia, but another woman Helena loved Demetrius who used to love her. To escape Hermia and Lysander plan to run away together, but Helena goes to tell Demetrius so she can see him. Yes, the symmetry of love was out of balance and yes Theseus and Hippolyta symbolized order Professor Yates agreed before erasing everything he'd written on the white board. Picking up the marker again he wrote one word on the board: Fae.

"Act II is the introduction of the magical elements of the play and the best-known characters," Professor Yates announced as he spun back to the class. "Most people don't remember the humans, but they vividly remember the supernatural creatures. We're going to start by looking at the roots of Shakespeare's magical characters of Robin Goodfellow, Oberon and Titania as they relate to the mythology of the British Isles."

The sudden change in the professor's energy and the shift in the lesson made the students glance at each other in surprise. Professor Yates noticed the confused glances and chuckled.

"This is a bit unusual," he conceded. "But literature is the art and power of the written word and many works of literature capture not only the moment they are written but aspects of a world that have been lost. One of the key themes of *A Midnight Summer's Dream* is the relationship between reality and fantasy, a theme that Shakespeare takes directly from older mythology. Now despite the rise of Christianity, many of these stories and legends survived, which is one of the reasons that this play was able to speak to the masses. The people in the audience knew what these beings were."

Professor Yates paused and wrote the names Oberon, Titania and Robin Goodfellow on the board with a flourish. "A Midnight Summer's Dream was written well before the Victorian alteration of the Fae into the tiny winged magical creatures that you grew up with. Shakespeare's audience was familiar with a very different kind of Fae. The origins of Shakespeare's Oberon, Robin Goodfellow and Titania are very old. These are stories that survived from the time before the Romans all the way through the rise of Christianity."

Professor Yates pulled a stack of papers from his briefcase and held them up. "Your homework assignment for Friday is not only to read Acts 3 and 4 but also to complete this worksheet about the Fae. You will find a selection of information and links on the course website, read them and use the information to complete the worksheet. This should be an easy assignment, but spares you a long lecture on the mythological roots of these characters."

Professor handed stacks of worksheets to a blond boy whose name Alex couldn't recall and a girl named Susan at the front the room. Both stood and dutifully passed out the sheets of paper. The professor remained silent at the front of the room, but erased the names of the Fae and instead replaced it with a single word: Changeling. When Alex received her sheet she looked it over quickly. There were only three questions.

Professor Yates cleared his throat at the front of the room and whistled sharply to regain the class's attention. "The Fae are prevalent throughout the entire play so we'll have plenty of time to consider them, but for now let's look at the origin point of the dispute between the Fae King Oberon and the Queen Titania."

He pointed at the word Changeling on the board. "The Changeling is the point of dispute and never speaks in the entire play. In some adaptations, there isn't even a visual appearance of the Changeling. This is a human child that has been taken from its family and replaced with a supernatural being which is also referred to as a Changeling. The folklore of Changelings is most often bleak, dark, and horrific, with the Fae taking children for their own personal gain. A great deal of mythology has the Fae treating these stolen children as property with some darker and much more violent examples," Professor Yates informed them with a dark look passing through his eyes.

"It is also important to note that on the human side of the equation, human families were encouraged to mistreat and seek to trick the Fae Changeling to get their real child back. Some myths had children being put into fireplaces and ovens to drive out the Changeling. Those thought to be Changelings were often horribly abused and even murdered. Even in the 19th-century people were still killed in the British Isles on the suspicion of being a Changeling. That's how strongly these stories influenced people even after Christianity replaced the older religions."

Professor Yates smirked at the stunned expressions in the room before he continued, "So, does knowing the mythological roots of the child who is at the heart of the dispute which sets off the strange series of event change anything? Is there significance in what elements of the old stories Shakespeare chooses to use versus those he doesn't? In doing so, is he telling the audience something beyond the common interpretation?"

Alex stared at the professor with a look of surprise and curiosity. Smiling, Professor Yates held up his copy of *A Midsummer Night's Dream*. "Let's turn our attention to the text of Act II shall we," he pointed to a student in the second row whose name Alex thought might be Tyler. "Please start us off."

The bell rang soon after they'd covered the major parts of the text and Yates dismissed them with a shout, "Remember to do your worksheets on the Fae and to consider how Shakespeare's first audience may have seen his interpretation. Read Acts III and IV for Friday.'

Packing up her things, Alex considered the Professor's question of the changes that Shakespeare had made. She'd read A Midsummer Night's Dream and watched one of the films in her high school. Did the mythology matter? Was it possible that audiences who knew the roots of the fae and Changeling stories would see something else in the story than people who grew up with modern fairy tales? Swinging her bag onto her shoulder, Alex tensed as she noticed Nicole waiting by the doorway. Alex grit her teeth and walked through the doorway, feeling more than a little irritated and uncomfortable as Nicole fell into step beside her.

"Interesting wasn't it," Nicole observed calmly with a smile. "Too bad we can't look at more mythology in this class, that's what I love most."

"So you're taking this class to fulfill your general requirements?" Alex questioned politely as they moved down the hallway towards the stairs.

"Sort of," Nicole answered with a shrug. "I'm Anthropology remember. The stories we tell are very important. Plus I enjoyed English class in high school."

The stairs were crowded making it impossible for Alex to get away from Nicki until they reached the bottom. Alex rushed out the door, but Nicole didn't seem at all bothered by the pace she was setting and stepped out into the sunlight just after her.

"Alex," Nicole called before Alex stormed away. "Why are you resisting so much?"

Turning back to Nicole, Alex crossed her arms and scowled at the redhead. "What? Resisting what? If you've got an explanation for hallucinations that doesn't end with I'm crazy then I'll listen."

Alex saw Nicole's expression sadden before she shook her head and stepped away from her. "Aiden was right about you, wasn't he?" Nicole asked her sadly. "That's really disappointing." Then Nicole turned and walked away from Alex, leaving her standing in front of the Meier building with a strange tightness in her chest.

"Alex!" a voice shouted from behind her. She spun to see Jenny leaning against one of the trees on the lawn surrounding the building. Her roommate beamed at her and gestured her over.

"Hi Jenny," Alex greeted with the best smile she could muster.

"I figured I'd meet you halfway," Jenny told her as she straightened up. "It's faster to go to the Rec Center from here than the dorms."

Jenny linked her arm with Alex's and started heading south towards the huge two-story red brick building that housed the school's exercise programs and rock climbing wall. Alex only half-heard Jenny talking to her about her classes and a party she'd been invited to on Saturday to watch the football game as she fought the strange urge to look for Nicole over her shoulder.

Doing her best to stay cheerful and keep up with Jenny, Alex enjoyed a tour of the student recreation center and left with descriptions of wellness classes that would be starting up Monday along with a list of intermural sports. Jenny was humming softly with a contented smile as they walked back to the dorms. Alex kept looking down at the list of intermural sports, her eyes automatically going to soccer. She didn't have a team to sign up with, but the university free agent program would assign her to a team and let her meet some new people.

"Cheer up," Jenny said sweetly from her side. "I bet you'll meet a lot of great people in intermural."

"The trip to the rec center was for my benefit," Alex realized with a start.

"Yeah," Jenny confessed gently as they reached the doors of Hatfield Hall. "You've seemed kind of lost. I know that everyone deals with starting college in their own way, but I'd like to see you enjoying it more."

Feeling humbled, Alex swiped her card key and pulled open the door for Jenny. Her roommate beamed at her and breezed inside with Alex following.

"I've got homework today," Jenny informed her as they entered the stairway. "How about you?"

"A bit," Alex told her as she followed Jenny up the stairs. "Reading for each of my classes, some statistics problems that are due Friday and reading and a worksheet from Literature class."

"Okay," Jenny replied with a nod as they reached the third floor. "New plan do homework until dinner and then meet up with Arthur and Lance at Michaels after they finish practice. They're leaving Thursday for Arkansas."

"Are you sure you wouldn't rather see Arthur alone?" Alex questioned carefully as they walked to their door.

"He's bonded with Lance," Jenny answered as she pulled out her key. "Honestly I've never seen him click with someone as quickly as he has with Lance. They're talking about going on a weekend backpack trip and camping as soon as they can. Arthur has never been interested in the outdoors like that." Her roommate chuckled softly, "It's kind of adorable in a weird way and I like Lance. It's nice to see Arthur so happy."

Alex wondered if she detected a note of jealousy in Jenny's voice, but wasn't sure. Instead, both sat down at their respective desk and started their homework. Alex began with the math problems and signed into the university math homework system which she found a nice alternative to constantly erasing her work on paper. When she finished that, Alex turned her attention to A Midsummer Night's Dream and read the next two acts quickly to refresh her memory.

A human named Bottom was given the head of a donkey while in the forest by Robin before Titania is enchanted to fall in love with Bottom as a trick to punish her by Oberon. As she reread the scene Professor Yates words came back to her about the Fae. She'd always considered it just a trick, but there did seem to be something more malicious behind it. Oberon didn't care if Titania was in love with another if that love humiliated her. Closing the book, Alex dug into her bag and pulled out the worksheet that Professor Yates had assigned. She set it next to her and logged onto the course website. The Fae information links were listed under the A Midsummer Night's Dream materials and Alex clicked the first one to an Irish mythology site.

Looking at question one she frowned: What is the Irish Gaelic name for the Fae and what does it say about them?

Turning her attention to the site, Alex had only to read the first line. Apparently, the old Irish Gaelic name for the Fae was the Sídhe which meant 'people of the mounds'. Alex wrote this down on her worksheet along with it meant that they lived underground, but she also added that mythology said that after the Sídhe were defeated they withdrew into another world. It was more science fiction than she was expecting, but interesting and a major change from the fairy in the forest stories she'd grow up hearing.

Question two read: What is the moral alignment of the Fae?

Alex scrolled through the site slowly as she read about the different stories and attributes of the Fae in mythology. Apparently they were very much like Oberon in the play: largely amoral without much regard for how their actions affected humans. It certainly explained his treatment of Titania, but also his almost kind interest in the human lovers. Alex paused as she wrote in the answer that the Fae were amoral and largely concerned only with what benefited them or entertained them. Had Oberon actually been helping the lovers or just using them as entertainment while he punished Titania? Shaking her head, Alex turned her attention back to her worksheet.

Question three read: What are the Unseelie and Seelie courts and where did their mythology come from?

She finished reading the site's history of the Irish Sídhe, but there was nothing on the courts. They sounded familiar from a book she'd read years ago. Alex's first thought was that they were the good and evil courts, but she frowned remembering the answer to the previous question. Going back in her browser Alex found another link that looked promising and clicked it. This one covered the classifications of the Fae.

Leaning forward, Alex read the document quickly and glanced at the images of the medieval and later artwork. According to the author of the short document on mythology evolution, the Seelie Court and Unseelie Court actually entered fae mythology much later, potentially not until the medieval ages. This separation was probably inspired by the Vikings with their separation of elves into Light and Dark categories since the two magical beings were so similar, but this separation occurred hundreds of years after the Fae entered human mythology.

Grinning, Alex closed her web browser and slipped the worksheet into her things for Literature class. She picked up her reason and logic textbook to read the next assigned chapter, swinging her chair around and lifting her feet onto the desk.

"I'm starving!" Jenny chirped as she stood up from her desk and stretched. Her roommate's phone beeped with a text message and Jenny scooped it up with a smile. "It's the boys," she announced. "They want to know if we're ready to join them for dinner."

"Yeah," Alex replied with a shrug as she lowered her feet. She put a scrap of paper in the textbook and tossed it onto her bed. "I'm good to take a break."

"Great," Jenny said as she texted them back. "There, the boys are waiting for us." Closing her phone, Jenny snatched up her keys and student card. "I'm almost done, how about you?"

"Nearly," Alex replied as she picked up her own key card. "Maybe a run after dinner will help me think."

"Whatever works," Jenny answered with a shrug as they headed out the dorm room door. Alex reached and turned the lock behind them, letting the door close and latch on their way out.

8

The Fourth Day

Thursday dawned with a different song playing on the alarm clock and a sigh from Alex as she reached up to turn it off. Strange music and voices still lingered in her mind for a moment from her dreams before fading away as she pulled back her comforter. Jenny was already up and moving around her side of the room with her heeled shoes clicking on the tiles of the floor.

"You're right," Alex groaned as she forced herself to sit up in her bed. "We need a rug or something."

"Maybe today after classes we should run out," Jenny suggested as she went to her dresser to check her reflection.

"I've got my physics lab today," Alex reminded Jenny as she climbed out of bed and cringed when her feet touched the cold floor. "I'm not sure when I'll be done; the class is usually until 5:30," Alex finished as she hurried into a pair of slippers.

"That's not a problem. If you get done around five then you can join me for dinner with the guys. They're leaving early in the morning and have a practice tonight starting at 6:30 until late." Jenny shrugged and added, "If you can't join us then we'll just go shopping when they're at practice."

"That's fine," Alex agreed as she gathered up some clothing and her shower kit. "Are we meeting them for breakfast?"

"That's the plan," Jenny answered. "I've got some homework to wrap up while you're in the shower and then we can head over."

"Then I'll wish them luck this morning," Alex remarked. "You'll leave the door unlocked?"

"I'll be here," Jenny promised her as she sat down at her desk and Alex grabbed her shower kit.

Breakfast was amusing as Lance and Arthur both had homework with them at the table that they were rushing to get turned in before the team left for Arkansas. Jenny seemed used to Arthur's half responses as he tried to work, eat and pay some attention to the conversation. Lance, on the other hand, didn't even try to be social as he talked quietly to himself as he did some algebra problems.

Since Jenny and Arthur had 8:30 classes, they headed out first and left their empty trays for Alex and Lance to take care of. After sitting with a silent Lance for ten minutes, Alex gathered up the trays and returned them to the washing station. She bid Lance a goodbye and he pulled himself out of his homework enough to give her a sheepish apologetic smile. Returning to her dorm room, Alex collected her physics materials and checked the subject for the day on the syllabus.

To kill time, Alex checked her email and looked back over the Fae worksheet to make sure that her answers made sense and weren't just jumbles of facts. For a moment she could almost grasp the dream that had ended with her alarm clock; it had involved the Fae somehow, but Alex couldn't pin down the memory. The ringing of her phone alarm made Alex jump and she set the worksheet aside. She gathered up her things for the day and double-checked that the door was locked on her way out.

Professor Whittaker had a long collection of notes and equations waiting on the board when Alex walked into her general physics class. Aiden was sitting in the back of the room today and was tapping his fingers as he read a book open in front him. He didn't look up and Alex quickly slid into the same seat near the door she'd taken on Tuesday. Pulling out her textbook, Alex skimmed through the first chapter that she'd only glanced at on Tuesday night. She barely noticed when someone sat down next to her with a strange metallic sound.

"Hi," a male voice greeted.

Alex looked up and flinched slightly when she met the green eyes of the young man Aiden had referred to as Brandon. The young man didn't react to her unfriendly response. "I'm Brandon Fisher, most people just call me Bran," he supplied as he held out a hand to her. "Sorry, but I find sitting at the front more comfortable for my leg," he informed her with a gesture towards his leg brace before he offered his hand again.

"Alex Adams," she answered with a hint of hesitation, taking his hand carefully and shaking it. "No problem." She glanced over Aiden with suspicion only to have Bran chuckle beside her.

"Don't worry, Aiden didn't put me up to this," Bran assured her.

"You two know each other?" Alex questioned carefully.

"We had our weird flash when we were in technical class together and ran into each other at Book Nook," Bran told her before noticing Alex's confused expression. "It's his family's bookstore on Main Street, he's usually there."

"Oh," Alex said, turning her attention to the front of the classroom. "Look I'd rather not talk about… the flashes," she added in a whisper.

"Fine," Bran replied as he pulled out his own textbook. "Physics only then."

"Good," Alex responded as Professor Whitaker turned to the class and dusted off the chalk dust from his hands.

"Great," Bran finished softly, leaning forward on the edge of the table to adjust his leg. The brace clicked softly against the metal stool and Bran leaned his cane against the wall to their right, relaxing into position as the lecture began.

General Physics passed without too much pain and Alex learned that Bran was actually majoring in physics which softened the blow when Professor Whitaker used their current positions to assign partners for in class work. When class was dismissed and the homework assigned, Alex packed her things up quickly as Aiden approached them. To her surprise, he walked around the front of their table and started talking about the homework with Bran, completely ignoring her. Swinging her bag over her shoulder, Alex said a quick bye to Bran and headed out to meet her friends for lunch.

Everything was nice and normal all throughout lunch despite Lance and Arthur still doing homework. Jenny called over one of her classmates, a girl named Aisha to their table and introduced her to Alex. While the boys sat eating their burgers and fries over their homework, Alex learned that journalism was much more complex than she'd thought.

It was with no small level of trepidation that Alex followed Jenny into the History of Civilization classroom. Professor Cornwall was more than a little intimidating on her own and the vision didn't increase Alex's comfort around the woman. Glancing around, Alex quickly located Nicole and Aiden sitting in the same seats they had on Tuesday and talking quietly to each other. Nicole's long red hair was styled in a series of braids wrapped around each other that made Jenny stare as they took their seats. A moment later Professor Cornwall glided up the aisle to the front of the room, silence falling in her wake.

"Good afternoon," Professor Cornwall greeted them, waiting a moment for the class to return the greeting. After a moment of hesitation, they all rushed to do so.

Professor Cornwall set an elegant leather satchel on the computer cart at the front of the room and pulled out her materials while the class waited. Then Professor Cornwall looked around the room, noting every student with a quick look over. As the professor's eyes moved over her, Alex found herself sitting up a little straighter and trying to look ready to learn.

"Let's begin," Professor Cornwall said a moment later. "As I informed you last week we are going to start with the earliest civilizations and examine the core components of Stone Age technology and society."

The Professor strode over the wall and flipped a switch, turning off every other light in the room. A moment later the projection system turned on and an image of a human hand outlined on a stone wall with a burst of color shown onto the screen. Without missing a beat, Professor Cornwall launched into lecture mode.

An hour and twenty minutes later, Alex and Jenny stumbled into their dorm room and collapsed on their respective beds.

"That woman is something else," Jenny groaned as she rubbed her head. "Maybe I should have dropped the class when she warned us. How is that an entry level course?"

"Yeah, but at the risk of having to take a worse semester down the road to get enough credits to graduate on time," Alex mumbled into her pillow as she curled up against it.

"Don't you have another class?" Jenny asked as she kicked off her shoes.

"Not until 3:30," she answered as she toed out of her sneakers and listened to them thud to the floor with satisfaction. "I can have a quick nap."

"I'm not waking you up," Jenny warned as she curled into her own comforter. "My brain hurts."

Groaning, Alex reached over to the bag she'd dropped on the foot of the bed and wrestled out her mobile phone. She set an alarm for 3 in the afternoon and placed it up on the desk.

"Happy?" Alex asked Jenny, as she snuggled down.

"Just so long as you don't wake me up when you go, yeah," Jenny replied and Alex could hear the smile on her face.

Sleep came quickly but was not peaceful as a nightmare crept into Alex's mind. She was standing alone in total darkness, one hand braced on a smooth rocky wall to her right. Music floated to her from somewhere in the darkness, a haunting melody that she had heard before. Reaching out, Alex found another rock wall to her left and carefully mapped the tunnel that surrounded her. Strange voices spoke, their words echoing along the rocky wall, but Alex realized they were coming closer. She opened her mouth to yell for help, but an icy feeling in her chest stopped the sound from escaping her throat.

Then her phone beeped loudly, startling her from the nightmare. Sitting up slowly, Alex took in a deep breath and grabbed her phone to turn off the alarm. She pulled herself out of bed, brushed her hair and gathered her things as quietly as she could manage.

Alex found her way to a larger classroom in the Natural Science Building with square black-topped lab tables spread throughout. Judging from the cabinets of beakers, cylinders, flasks that dominated one side of the room and the fume hood in the corner it was usually a chemistry lab. A short balding man with a thick beard stood at the front chalkboard, writing on it from a sheet of paper in his hand.

"Tables are labeled," he announced as Alex came closer. "Just sit where I put your name."

Sighing, Alex found her name right at the top of the list on the board. With a surname like Adams, she was naturally at table one. Alex located the table which was marked with a propped up piece of paper. Another girl with dark hair and glasses was already sitting there. Alex slid into a seat across from the girl and smiled when the girl looked up at her.

"Hi," she greeted. "I'm Alex Adams."

"Helen Baker," the girl replied with a slight shrug before she turned her attention to the phone in her hands.

Alex unpacked the assigned workbook and her tablet and waited in silence as the rest of the class trickled in and found their seats. A boy with red hair sat down and smiled at Alex and Helen before taking out a notebook full of doodles. He introduced himself as Rob Anderson before he pulled out a green ballpoint pen and resumed doodling.

"Hey," a familiar voice said as someone sat down next to her.

Eyes widening, Alex looked over at Aiden who was sitting next to her and pulling out his tablet.
"What are you doing?" she asked in a low voice.

"Check the board," Aiden told her, gesturing towards the front of the room where Aiden Bosco was listed under Robert Anderson and Helen Baker.

"You've got to be kidding me," Alex growled as she glared at the board.

"Funny how we keep running into each other," Aiden observed with a chuckle. "Let's play nice and pass physics lab, Alex."

"Did you do this on purpose?" Alex demanded with a cautious glance towards the board.

"Yes I hacked into the school system just to take this lab with you," Aiden replied with an eye roll. "You're a bit paranoid aren't you," he teased.

"Alright," Alex huffed. "Fine, we're in a lab group together. I can be civilized if you can."

"Have I not been civilized at some point?" Aiden asked with a slight tilt of his head. "Not my fault we're in so many classes together. You've got two with Nicki after all and I don't see you accusing her."

"Well your girlfriend has backed off," Alex remarked as she turned her attention to her tablet.

"Nicki is not my girlfriend," Aiden told her with a smile. "Her interests run parallel to mine, not perpendicular."

Professor Hammon called the class to order and started handing out the syllabus as well as the first in class assignment. Alex barely restrained her 'oh' when she realized exactly what Aiden meant and he chuckled softly. He quickly turned his attention away from Alex to focus on Professor Hammon as the syllabus and class schedule were outlined. To Alex's relief, the Professor ended the class early after handing out a worksheet on the echo and sound wave experiment they were to come to class prepared for the next week.

"Now take a few minutes and get the contact information from the rest of your group," Professor Hammon told them all. "The catch of me releasing you early today is that you should meet at least once before next Thursday to have your process planned out. We will spend only half an hour covering the material and you will need almost the entire remaining hour and twenty minutes to complete your work. You are free to go."

Bringing up a new text document, Alex quickly entered her group's names and phone numbers. At Aiden's suggestion, she added emails too since they would probably need to share documents at some point. She was sending the information to them when Rob leaned over to speak with Aiden.

"Hey man, haven't seen you in while. How'd the family road trip go?"

Alex ignored their conversation as she packed her things. Rob departed a moment later with a quick goodbye to everyone and Helena followed a moment later. Aiden, on the other hand, seemed to be packing up slowly, waiting for Alex.

Sighing, Alex looked over at the departing Rob and then over at Aiden. "Friend of yours?" She asked, trying to make casual conversation that in no way related to the hallucinations.

"Local kid like me," Aiden replied with a shrug. "And he's a good customer at the bookstore my family runs." He gave Alex a cautious look and added, "That's where the books in the vision you got from me came from and the garlic I can guess came from my dad's cooking. He's Italian and proud of it."

"I thought we agreed not to talk about that," Alex said sternly as she stood up and pulled her bag over her shoulder.

"No, we agreed to be civil," Aiden replied. "Very different."

Marching out of the classroom, Alex picked up her speed when she noticed Aiden following her and nearly tripped on the stairs leading outside. The sunshine blinded her and Alex fumbled for her sunglasses as she slowly moved towards a patch of shade. Behind her, the door opened and she heard more students come out, but Aiden's footsteps nearly echoed to her ears.

"Alex," Aiden called out as he jogged towards her, "Look just one thing then I'll leave you alone."

She hesitated, but turned towards him, the shadow of the building falling over them as they stood off the main path. Aiden had his hands raised in a calming gesture, but lowered them and slid them into the pockets of his utility jacket.

"What?" Alex asked him sharply, drawing herself up to her full height and nearly glaring at him.

Aiden didn't seem affected and calmly asked, "Have you ever believed in magic?"

It wasn't the question Alex expected, but she answered quickly. "No, I don't believe in magic." She turned on her heel and started to walk away from him.

"I didn't ask if you do believe in magic," Aiden called after her. Alex stopped and he walked up behind her. "I asked if you ever believed in magic?" he reminded her as he stopped two feet behind her.

Turning slowly to him, Alex searched Aiden's face for any clues to what he was thinking. He had a soft smile while he watched her and his brown eyes seemed oddly bright.

"Have you ever believed in magic?" Aiden asked softly. "Ever in your life?"

The air around them felt heavy and thick as something rose within Alex, the strange pulse of unknown sensation she'd had the second before each hallucination occurred. Sounds of her classmates and traffic faded into the background as she stared at Aiden and tried to form a response.

"Of course," she admitted softly, a whisper that hung between them. "Don't we all when we're young?"

"I like to think so," Aiden said kindly before his eyes grew sad. "So why are you fighting this so much?"

"Fighting what?" Alex asked, her tone taking on an edge of panic. "You think this is magic? I've never read a story where magic caused hallucinations and nothing else!"

"Maybe we're still only at the beginning of the story," Aiden suggested gently. "Don't you want to know more about this? See where this goes?"

"You're talking about magic!" Alex hissed at him. "Yes I believed in magic when I was a kid, but I grew up, did my time in high school and I'm trying to get ready for the real world!" Alex's shoulders slumped and she took in a deep breath before adding, "Magic isn't something that happens in the real world, even if we'd like it to."

"Except that maybe it does," Aiden pressed as he took a step closer. "Come on Alex, you believed once. Try to believe again, just for a few days."

"And then what happens when we have to accept that it wasn't magic, that magic isn't real?" Alex asked him, "What do we do then when that hurts?" Her eyes burned with unshed tears that she refused to let fall, her throat already tight from the unexpected words.

"What do you do when you give up something too important to lose in the name of being 'grown up'?" Aiden replied sadly before he turned away from Alex, giving her a small wave over his shoulder as he walked away.

Tightening her grip on her bag, Alex swallowed in an attempt to control her chaotic emotions. Her feet felt heavy, but she forced herself to start moving towards her dorm. Everything seemed fuzzy and her mind couldn't quite connect her thoughts together. Her question to Aiden kept replaying in her mind and his words answered it in a terrible re-enacting. She just felt drained and weak.

"Alex!" a voice shouted behind her, cutting through the haze. She slowed her pace and relaxed as she recognized Arthur's voice. Turning, she stopped walking and watched as he jogged up to her.

Arthur's blond hair was windswept and he was dressed in his jeans and a faded old t-shirt that Alex couldn't read. He paused when he got closer to her and his wide smile faded into a concerned look.

"Alex," he called gently, "Are you alright?" He placed a hand on her shoulder and examined her face.

"Yeah," Alex assured him quickly, desperately trying to keep her voice steady despite the flutter in her stomach. Her hand quivered, but she quickly tightened it to hide the movement. "I'm good."

Arthur's blue eyes took on an edge of suspicion as he looked around the area and spotted Aiden looking over at them from across the lawn. Aiden quickly turned and resumed walking away just before Arthur looked back to Alex.

"Do I need to beat someone up?" he asked her seriously, his eyes nearly sparking.

"No," Alex nearly shouted with a short giggle. "No you don't," she amended, tension draining from her shoulders. Taking a deep breath, Alex silently rejoiced as the knot in the chest eased.

Considering her carefully, Arthur gave a brief nod and stepped up next to Alex. He extended his arm to her with a widening smile. "Then shall we make our way back to the dorm?"

Alex accepted Arthur's arm with a genuine smile and laughed softly as they started walking. Neither spoke for a few minutes until Arthur broke the silence as they moved past the Administration Building.

"Do you want to talk about it?" he asked softly, but still looking ahead.

"Talk about what?" Alex questioned, her voice sounding much calmer than she felt.

"What is bothering you, seriously Alex you looked like you might cry."

"I…" Alex swallowed, almost painfully. "I don't know."

Arthur let it drop for a little longer until they were walking past Upham Hall with Hatfield Hall only a short distance away. "You know I consider you a friend which means that you can always come to me if something is bothering you."

"Thank you," Alex replied, honestly grateful for the statement.

"Or if you need a football player to frighten someone," he added with a grin.

Laughing softly, Alex looked towards Hatfield Hall and dropped her arm from Arthur's. "That's sweet of you," she told him, not meeting his eyes.

"Friends look out for each other," Arthur replied with a small shrug, but the words rang with conviction and authority.

"Yeah…" they were by the main door of Hatfield Hall. Alex moved towards the doorway to go and get Jenny for dinner. "Do you believe in magic?" Alex asked in a rush before blushing at even asking him that question.

"What?" Arthur questioned with a surprised look. "Do I believe in magic?"

"Yeah," Alex replied, shifting uncomfortably.

"Maybe," Arthur answered slowly a moment later. "I don't not believe in magic and there's a lot we don't understand about the universe." He gave her a bright smile, "And I absolutely believed in magic when I was a kid. So yeah, I think I might."

Alex smiled slowly and pulled out her card key. "Uh Jenny wanted to have an early dinner with you guys before you had to leave, I'll go and get her," she told him nervously as she reached for the door.

"I'll be waiting," Arthur promised as he pulled out his phone and started to text Lance. "It'll be nice to spend some time with friends before the travel and practice chaos of my first college game," he added without looking up from his phone.

The door's lock clicked open and Alex pulled the door ajar. She stopped in the doorway and turned back towards Arthur, only to find him watching her with a knowing smile.

"Thanks," she said softly with a tiny smile. He grinned and nodded, causing her smile to widen as she walked inside Hatfield Hall.

9

The Sídhe Ride

834 B.C.E. Snowdonia Wales

The atmosphere of Myrddin's roundhouse was tense as he ran the polishing stone down the length of the bronze sword with care and tried to ignore his mother's accusing gaze. Never before in his life had he defied her. The Priestess Awena was well known for her knowledge of the mystical world and her abilities as a healer. His grandfather had been a noted priest who had taught his eldest child the mysteries of the Earth well.

It had been that reputation that protected Myrddin when he was born from a Sídhe father, but he felt no fear of her wrath. Instead, when he looked at her he saw the gray hairs in her long auburn braid, the wrinkles on her proud face and the slowness in her steps. Her anger bothered him; he was still her son and she his mother, but it did not worry him. Despite the tension between them, the sounds of him polishing the blade and her working at her loom were in time with each other, a rhythm born of the deep connection they shared whether they wished it or not.

"You should return to the lake," Awena told him for the tenth time that night. "Winter will be upon us soon and trekking so far up the mountain will be too dangerous."

"I repeat to you mother: I have no reason or need to return."

"Does it not bother you that you ran?" his mother challenged, it was the fifth time she responded in that way to his remark.

"No," he answered shortly, gripping the wooden hilt of the blade tighter.

"It should," his mother returned as she looked back to her loom. "I did not raise a coward."

"Should I trust her?" Myrddin questioned. "There have been plenty of priests through the Isles who did not approve of you bringing me into this world. You did that on Cyrridven's advice."

His mother's movements stopped suddenly and there was a sharp intake of breath that made Myrddin look towards his mother with alarm. Still sitting by her loom, her hands were shaking softly in her lap as she stared at her son as if she had never seen him before.

"She told you her name?" Awena breathed. "A being such as that gave you her name?"

Swallowing, Myrddin looked back to his sword quickly and kept his eyes low. His mother's side of the roundhouse remained still and silent. Outside the roundhouse, the wind was picking up and Myrddin could hear the villagers moving about as dusk approached. Part of him wished to find some excuse to go outside for even a few moments to escape the heavy silence in his home, but it felt vital that he show his mother no weakness.

The silence continued as his mother moved away from her loom and began grinding herbs. Myrddin glanced towards the doorway quickly as a chill rushed through him, but the doorway was secured with a hide covering. Focusing on his sword, Myrddin tried to ignore another shiver which passed quickly. But then there was another and then another much sooner after. Unable to shake the cold feeling despite sitting next to the hearth, Myrddin put aside the bronze sword and stood up to grab his cloak.

"Myrddin?"

"Just a chill," he informed his mother quickly.

"It's quite warm," Awena disagreed, standing gracefully from her seat. Her earlier irritation and shock fell away as concern crept into her eyes. "Are you feeling ill?"

"No," Myrddin assured her as he clasped the cloak securely around him. "I'm fine mother."

Despite his assurance, Awena crossed the room to him and inspected him. Myrddin was unable to contain a shiver as another spike of cold rushed through his body.

"Then why are you shivering?" Awena questioned, her eyes narrowing.

"I don't know," Myrddin confessed. "Truly mother I don't know."

For a moment he thought that his mother might leave it there, but then a sudden scream from outside made them both turn towards the doorway. Another scream echoed through the village quickly followed by more. Myrddin glanced at his mother before lunging forward to grab his sword. It wasn't as sharp as he wanted, but it gleamed in the firelight and fit snuggly into his hand. Awena rushed to the doorway and pulled back the pelt as more screams filled the night.

A fiery glow rose up from thatch roofs of the village as flames roared and villagers ran screaming. Myrddin's eyes adjusted quickly to the flickering darkness and he heard his mother gasp in horror as three strange horses with tall pale riders dashed through the village. One of the rider's pale horses reared before the flames, exposing its shimmering fur which glowed like a rainbow in the moonlight. Its rider tossed a lit branch onto a nearby thatch roof, increasing the reddish glow. The rider was taller than any man in the village with pale luminescent skin that had a fierce glow in the firelight. His long white hair glowed in the light of the flame with two long twisting horns rising from his forehead.

"Sídhe," his mother breathed fearfully.

Myrddin couldn't look away from the Rider. The screaming faded and the cold chill settled in his limbs, leaving him numb and staring dumbly as his village burned. Behind him, his mother was shouting to the other villagers and chanting words he'd never heard before. People began running toward their roundhouse and the Sídhe moved to intervene.

Bronze flashed in the fire as an axe was thrown at the Rider. It impacted into the creature's chest, knocking him back on his steed, but then the Síd merely reached up and wrenched the axe head from its chest. Another man swung a sword at the horse, but the unearthly beast showed no pain.

"Myrddin!" his mother screamed in his ear, shaking his shoulder. "Child I need you!"

Her plea reached him through the chill and Myrddin turned to look at her, gasping for air. His mother was standing straight and tall behind him, her left hand raised with blood dripping from a cut across her palm and a dagger clutched in her right hand.

"Mother!?" He gasped, moving quickly to her side. "What are you doing?"

"The Sídhe cannot withstand the blood of our realm," she told him, her eyes looking past him at a rider. "Quickly, fetch me a bowl."

He wanted to argue with her, to demand an explanation, but years of obedience won out and he rushed back into the roundhouse. Scooping up a small bowl, Myrddin scrambled back to his mother's side. Blood was pooling in her hand and she was carefully dripping it on the ground in a circle and a look of intense concentration.

"My father taught me this," she told him softly as he returned to her side. "Never thought I'd dare to use it, I don't have his powers. Call the others towards us," his mother told him. "The closer they are the better."

Confused, but determined, Myrddin strode forward and shouted for the villagers to come towards his mother. More screams filled the night as one of the villagers tried to run towards him only to be knocked to the ground by a Síd Rider, and the infant she was carrying ripped from her arms. The Rider's horse reared, bringing its hoofs down on the woman's back with a sickening crunch. Myrddin shouted once again to the others, fighting back panic. In the firelight, he could see his uncle Dewydd swinging his bronze sword at a rider to no effect as Candon scrambled towards him. More screams and more shouting filled the village as the smoke thickened around them.

"Myrddin!" Awena called desperately.

Spinning, Myrddin's throat tightened as he found his mother on her knees inside a circle of her own blood, her left wrist sliced open and bleeding into the bowl in front of her.

"Mother!" He gasped, moving towards her.

"Step over the line, be careful!" His mother snapped before raising her right hand towards him. It was shaking badly and her face was terribly pale.

Myrddin obeyed and carefully stepped over the bloody line in the earth to join his mother in the circle. Taking her offered hand, he knelt in front of her, his eyes falling to the bowl that was filling with her blood despite his efforts not to look.

"I need your power," Awena gasped softly. "I did not inherit my father's magic."

Gasping, Myrddin nearly collapsed when a tugging pulled the air from his lungs and towards his mother. Their joined hands began to glow softly, his very skin giving off a faint light that instantly drew his eyes. Around him he heard the villagers rushing past them, hiding beyond his mother's circle, but his eyes remained locked on his hand against his mother's as the glow intensified. Breathing became more difficult as his energy drained away, flowing from him to his mother and leaving him weaker every moment. Collapsing forward, he caught himself on his free hand, gripping the cold earth beneath his fingers with fear and desperation.

Hoofbeats echoed off the mountains, the horses snorted and the villagers screamed as the Riders rushed up the hill towards Myrddin. He ripped his eyes away from his hand, looking towards the Riders who were almost upon them. Awena tipped the bowl of blood, spilling the thick red liquid to the ground. She gasped out a few more words, her voice strained and weak, but her last word resounded through the air like a shout.

Lightning flashed, the glow exploded into a blinding light and the earth around them shook as the thunder rolled. The circle of blood began to glow red around Myrddin and his mother before spreading outward like flowing glowing water, illuminating the earth all around them as it extended ever outward. The cry of a Rider made Myrddin look back at them in alarm as they reached the top of the hill. The first horse reared as its hoof touched the blood and Myrddin gasped as the horse's leg began to turn into vapor. Eyes widening, the Rider leapt from the horse but was unable to avoid the spreading magic. His foot touched the glowing liquid and he screamed as his own body dissolved.

The second Rider tried to move his horseback but was quickly encircled by the magic Myrddin's mother had conjured. Villagers cheered as the horse began to be turned into vapor and the Rider screamed as the rivers of glowing liquid surged up towards him as he sank to the earth when his horse melted away into mist. The last Rider glared at the villagers, still clutching the screaming infant in its arms. Setting his eyes on Myrddin, he maneuvered his horse back.

"You think this is a victory?" he asked the villagers, his voice echoing in the suddenly still night. The voice had a beautiful music quality that frightened Myrddin even as he felt lulled. "Your tricks, your blood and your realm will not hold us back forever." He looked down at the infant and then smiled wickedly. "I shall gift this one to Queen Scáthbás. Remember the mother's death as you have nightmares of this child's fate."

The Rider spurred his horse back just in time to avoid the rivers of brightly glowing blood that were flowing down the hill towards the village, never running dry. Everything was still, the horse's hooves echoing as the Rider fled and the villagers all watched too frightened to breathe. When the hoof beats faded some cheered while others began to cry.

"Awena!" A pained voice cried and Myrddin turned to see his uncle carefully stepping into the circle.

His mother was collapsed on the ground, completely still with her hand still gripped in Myrddin's, but the once bright glow faded rapidly. Dewydd knelt beside her and gently pried her hand from Myrddin's before picking her up in his arms.

"Sister?" he called softly. "Awena."

Swallowing, Myrddin studied his mother, his heart gripped with fear. Her face was white, her wrist and hand covered with her own blood and her breathing so shallow that he could barely detect it.

"Mother," he called, crawling towards her. "Mother, please?"

Awena took a short, painful breath while she opened her eyes. Desperate brown eyes met dimming brown eyes, but his mother smiled softly.

"My son," she whispered. "So much power, they will not be able to return for years to this village."

"Sister," Dewydd repeated gently. "What can I do?"

"Nothing brother," she replied in a warm weak tone. "There is no return from this."

"But mother, you're a healer," Myrddin argued. "A priestess of the land."

"And now I go to join the ancestors," she told him softly. "Myrddin, I love you and I …" her voice cracked and was too low for him to hear the rest even as her lips moved.

Awena stilled in her brother's arms, her son's warm hand against her cooling cheek.

"She joins the ancestors," Dewydd informed Myrddin and the assembled village before turning his eyes on his nephew. "You are now the priest of the western mountains."

Myrddin stared at his still mother, unable to speak, but he slowly raised his fingers to close her eyes. The Priestess was gone; the link between the living and the ancestors had been shattered. He wanted so much to scream, to cry and mourn as a child for his mother, but already the weight was pressing on his shoulders. All around him, his village waited for him to speak. He was their priest now. He was their link and they needed him. Releasing a small breath, Myrddin softly whispered a goodbye to his mother and his childhood before rising to his feet.

"Put out the fires, save what can be saved and then gather our dead," he finally managed. "We'll return them to the earth once the living are tended to."

Dewydd nodded solemnly at Myrddin before he lifted his sister into his arms and carried her into the roundhouse. The villagers remained for a moment to watch Dewydd until he vanished into the building before they started down the hill to the rest of the village. Taking a long breath, Myrddin looked down at the blood circle that his mother had made and his eyes were drawn towards the bronze sword he had dropped when his mother reached for him.

Hand shaking, Myrddin reached down and picked it up, gripping the hilt tightly. He looked over at the roundhouse for only a moment before he turned his attention towards the smoldering village. Then his eyes were drawn upwards, towards the high slopes of the mountain where one waited who could answer his questions. But that would have to wait.

In three days' time, those who had survived were protected from the elements with new roundhouses. The night before Myrddin had sent his mother to the ancestors on a grand funeral pyre that burned all through the night. The few charred bone fragments that had been gathered in the morning were wrapped in her favorite shawl for transport to the stone circle at midwinter where the funeral ritual would be completed for her. It was a small comfort to Myrddin to know that his mother's strength had become a part of the world around him. She was a part of the realm now, watching them, guiding them and giving power to the earth to protect them. But as he collected his staff and supplies for traveling up the mountain, Myrddin acknowledged that he would have preferred she was next to him.

A mist hung over the lake and the mountains were cloaked with low clouds as Myrddin began to climb down the valley towards the water. His staff clacked against the stones with every determined step and his cloak rippled around him in the breeze. Stopping at the water's edge, Myrddin glared out over the water and tightened his grip on his staff.

"Cyrridven!" He shouted out across the water. "Show yourself Cyrridven!"

Before him the water rippled and swirled as it had only days ago, rising from the surface of the lake to take on a human form. Today, however, Myrddin was not in awe and watched as Cyrridven materialized from the water with indifference.

"Hello Merlin," she greeted gently with a soft sad smile. "I know what drove you to return. I am sorry, Merlin," Cyrridven told him softly, moving closer to the shore. "Awena was a great daughter of the Iron Realm. She will join the ancestors and give her strength to the world."

Myrddin bowed his head slightly at her words, knowing that she spoke the truth. Even in his rage, he was unable to disrespect such an important truth. Cyrridven's compassion washed over him like a gentle wave, easing his anger and bringing his grief forth like a spring.

"Is this my fault?" he asked her in a quaking voice. "When I refused to listen and fled, did I cause this?"

"No," Cyrridven promised him. "Even had you stayed that day and come every day hence, I would not have been able to teach you enough to change what occurred."

"How did you know?" Myrddin asked, looking at the rocks on the shore. "How did you know that the Sídhe attacked my village? That my mother was dead?"

"I embraced this realm long ago and became connected with it. I felt the Sídhe ride," Cyrridven explained gently, "I felt the Blood of Earth turn them back with the help of powerful magic and knew that it could only have been you and Awena." Cyrridven shook her head, her hair floating gently in the air. "And I know the cost that Awena would have been called on to pay. The ritual that she used is powerful and needed more power than she could call upon without offering the realm her life in exchange."

"Why?" Myrddin asked weakly, unsure of which why he wanted answered first.

"I told you that the new Queen of the Sídhe Scáthbás seeks power beyond merely the occasional torment of the Children of Earth. Her people have a vast empire across many realms, but it is not enough for her. She seeks to solidify her power by gaining mastery of this realm and begins by bringing human slaves and children back from Earth."

Her words were frightening. Everyone knew of the Sídhe and their tricks to trap adults or their theft of children who became their slaves in another darker world. Myrddin's thoughts turned to the child that the Sídhe rider had taken and he fought back a shudder.

"What is the Blood of Earth?"

"The Blood of Earth is the blood in the veins of the living children of this world. Within the blood of humanity is something that is poison to the Sídhe. By combining her blood with your magic you mother was able to create a barrier around your village that saved your people and will last for some time."

"Something in the blood?" Myrddin repeated, "But I have both Sídhe blood and human blood, so how is that I live?"

"You live because the world decided for you to live," Cyrridven informed him with a smile. "You have a purpose, dear Merlin. You are a Child of the Iron Realm and were gifted with magic, but you also carry certain powers from the Sídhe. Merlin, you were born to protect this world."

"But I couldn't even protect my village, my mother had to die!" He argued, his anger flaring hot in his chest.

"Then I will teach you, Merlin," Cyrridven assured him. "I will teach you everything I have learned about the magic of your world and the Otherworlds. I promise you that when the time comes, you will be prepared."

Myrddin tightened his grip on his staff and nodded sternly. "Very well Cyrridven, let us begin."

Cyrridven smiled and raised her hands in before her, summoning up water from the lake's surface. Flowing around her body and into her hands, the water formed a cauldron. Cyrridven breathed on the flowing water which turned slowly to ice before Myrddin's eyes, solidifying into a shimmering cauldron that she held gracefully in her hands. A surge of water rose from the lake, forming a pedestal for Cyrridven as she gently lowered the cauldron and allowed it to rest on the spout of water.

"Then let us begin with a potion, Merlin," she told him with a smile. "Gather what I require before the next full moon and in a year and day, you shall gain inspired knowledge from the Iron Realm itself and full access to all the magic you were born with. This was the task given to me when I entered your world and vowed to aid the Children of the Iron Realm by the magic of this world."

Looking at the ice cauldron, Myrddin dismissed all questions in his mind and looked back at Cyrridven's face. Nodding, he leaned forward on his staff. "As I said Cyrridven, let us begin."

10

Soccer and Swords

Voices echoed off the high domed ceiling above the bleachers and basketball floor in the gym as students moved through rows and rows of tables, each proclaiming a club name or school activity in a variety of bright colors. Alex walked alongside Jenny through the throng of students who were examining the various stations.

"I can't believe the boys are gone again," Jenny huffed as she glanced over at a table for the fashion club. "That's two weekends in a row."

"Only half their games are home games," Alex reminded her calmly for the third time that afternoon. "Homecoming is next week and they have home games the rest of September and all of October."

"And then the pressure goes up for spots in the college bowls," Jenny remarked. "Is it too much that I want to see my boyfriend?"

"No," Alex quickly replied. "But it won't last forever. Come on find a club or something to take your mind off things," Alex suggested with a gesture to a nearby booth.

"I'm not sure," Jenny sighed, "Nothing is really speaking to me. The Spirit Squad doesn't have tryouts until spring."

"Maybe you should try a dance club or something, or join an intermural sport," Alex tried, "I just got my assignment to Corvus for women's soccer. My first practice is tomorrow, should be fun."

"No thanks," Jenny told her before stopping and looking over at Alex. "I'm sorry Alex, I don't mean to be such a downer," she apologized.

"You just miss Arthur," Alex said with a nod. "It's okay, I don't take it personally."

"Thank you," Jenny replied with a small smile. "So Corvus? Weird name."

"I looked it up, apparently it is the Latin word for raven," Alex informed Jenny with a small chuckle. "I think the team captain is a science major."

"So you've got soccer," Jenny observed. "What else are you looking for?"

Alex grinned as they turned a corner and pointed up ahead where a few mats were laid down and two students were fencing in their white jackets and masks.

"Fencing?" Jenny asked, "Really, fencing?"

"I've always wanted to try it," Alex defended quickly. "According to the club website, they allow you three sessions with free equipment rental to try it out." Taking Jenny's hand, she tugged her forward towards the demonstration.

"Well," Jenny shrugged as they watched a match, "I suppose it will keep you out of trouble."

"Yes," Alex laughed, "Because I'm such a troublemaker."

"We've only been rooming together for two weeks," Jenny teased, "Too early to tell."

By the late afternoon when the fair began to wrap up and students packed up their booths. Alex was grinning as Jenny slipped a flyer for ballroom dancing club into the back pocket of her jeans. Jenny slipped her arm into the crook of Alex's as they stepped outside into the sunshine.

When Alex woke up on Sunday, she shook off the familiar nightmare of the dark tunnel and the strange voices, more easily than she usually could. Instead, she was nearly shaking with excitement and energy. On her morning run, Alex enjoyed the scent of freshly mowed lawns and the shining sun in a clear blue sky. Jenny was not so eager about the day when Alex returned her and banished her 'overly cheery' self from their dorm room while she got some more sleep. After a shower and a quick trip to Michaels Hall for breakfast, Alex changed into suitable practice clothes as Jenny rolled out of bed and started getting ready for church.

There weren't many people around campus this early on a Sunday morning, but Alex saw a few joggers out as she walked towards the practice fields. She played with the team information sheet in her hand and wondered how many of the girls on the team already knew each other. Maybe a lot of them were locals who had been to high school together, maybe- Alex shoved the thought away, there was no point stressing about things just yet, but nervous butterflies were rapidly taking the place of her happy excitement.

The school's practice fields were on the southwest end of campus near the stadium and old gym. When Alex arrived there were already several teams out on the four practice soccer fields and she searched around until she spotted the group in the purple jerseys in field four. A large group of girls was stretching and putting on the light purple jerseys as she jogged up and put her bag with the others and changed into her cleats. She recognized three other girls from her classes and gave them a quick wave as she started stretching.

"Alright, team Corvus!" A cheerful female voice called out and Alex looked up sharply in alarm.

Nicole Russell walked out onto the field with a clipboard and huge smile. Their eyes met and Nicole's mouth opened and closed silently before the wide smile returned. "Most of us know each other from high school, but we've got a few girls who were assigned to the team by the recreation center so let's start with introductions and favored positions. Also, tell us how much experience you have.'

Standing up with the others, Alex shifted nervously as Nicole introduced herself as Nicki and the team captain. Every girl introduced herself, some rambling more than others, and indeed many of the girls had played on the local high school soccer team. When it was Alex's turn, she met Nicki's eyes and introduced herself and informed them that she had played midfield all four years of high school getting an even wider smile from Nicole.

At Nicole's command, the team split into scrimmage groups against the goalies, but Alex's arm was caught by Nicole before she could get very far. She turned to look at the redhead girl who had an amused expression on her face.

"Of course you'd be one of the random girls assigned to my team," she observed. "I should have guessed that A. Adams was you, but I convinced myself that there were probably plenty of Adamses in the university."

"Sorry to disappoint," Alex remarked, crossing her arms. "What excuse should we give to put me on another team?"

"Another team?" Nicole repeated before saying, "Alex don't be like that. I'm sure we can handle being on an intermural soccer team together."

"Can we?" Alex questioned, raising an eyebrow.

"Look," Nicki said, taking a step towards her. "I know Aiden can be like a dog with a bone when he's curious, but from what I understand you two haven't spoken outside of class for over a week." Nicole offered her a small smile, "I'm really a nice person once you get to know me."

Alex bit her lip slightly as she considered the redhead in front of her. Before she changed her mind, she agreed, "Alright, I suppose we can't just avoid each other forever, Nicole."

"That's the spirit," Nicki told her. "And please, it's Nicki."

"Adams! Russell!" another voice shouted and they turned to see the other players waiting for them. "We practicing today or what?"

"Coming," Nicki shouted back before nodding towards the field. "Come on, my first day as captain. I've got to make a good impression," Nicki told her with a wide and almost evil smile.

At the end of practice, Alex understood the evil smile. She hadn't thought she was out of shape from the summer, but Nicki had given her and two other midfielders a series of brutal drills after a three-mile run. Nicki herself was a forward but spent most of the three-hour practice calling out positions for the other players to take against the midfielders. When Nicki ended practice they all eagerly went to shower with an agreement on next practice and individual copies of their game schedules for the month of October.

Nicki jogged after Alex as she left the old gym shower room and called, "Hey Alex wait up!" Against her better judgment, Alex stopped and waited for the shorter girl to come up beside her. "Nice practice today," Nicki complimented her. "I'd say you should play on the school team, but I'd honestly prefer for you to stay with us."

"Thanks," Alex replied with a shrug before she gripped the handles of her bag. "I had fun," she admitted quickly.

Nicki grinned and nodded, but then turned serious. "Nothing else has happened to you right?"

Tension flooded her body; she didn't have to ask what Nicki was asking about. "No," Alex said, nearly hissing the word. "Nothing weird has happened."

"That's probably good," Nicki replied thoughtfully. "I've been having nightmares lately, where I'm in this horrible dark tunnel, there's this strange music and then I feel…" Nicki shook her head and looked back at Alex who was desperately trying to keep her face neutral. The description of Nicki's nightmare matched hers too closely to be a coincidence. "Sorry to bring it up. What I really wanted to talk about is fencing club."

"Fencing club?" Alex repeated dumbly before she caught onto the conversation, "What about it?"

"I saw you take a form yesterday," Nicki told her. "I just thought it was fair to warn you that Aiden is in fencing club. Professor Bosco, his father, is the primary advisor of the club and the fencing instructor."

"Oh," Alex sighed, "I see."

"I just figured I should warn you," Nicki told her. "But I'm in fencing too, the first meeting is tonight and we could partner."

Alex gave Nicki a nervous look, "Uh I'm not… I don't swing that way."

Nicki snorted, trying to control a laugh, but failing to control her smile. "Don't worry, you're not my type," Nicki managed between soft giggles. "I was just giving you an option with a buffer from Aiden."

"I'll just skip it," Alex told her with a frown.

"You shouldn't do that," Nicki protested with a shake of her head. "Aiden can be a pain in the ass, but he's not a bad guy. He'll back off, but in the meantime, you can't let him influence what you do for fun."

Giving the other girl a searching look, Alex considered the words and then asked, "Why do you care so much?"

"I get it," Nicki replied gently. She tugged up her pants to expose the tattoo on the inside of her ankle; "This is the symbol for J.R. Tolkien, my favorite author. I grew up hearing tales of magic from my grandmother and I've always wanted to believe in it." Nicki let the hem of her pants fall back down and sighed softly. "I want to believe that magic can be a part of life Alex, but I don't expect it to actually happen. I'm scared too."

"I'll think about fencing club," Alex promised her with a quick, uncomfortable nod.

"Okay," Nicki answered with a nod before stepping back from Alex. "See you next Sunday for practice?" It was more of a question than a statement and Nicki stood waiting for an answer.

"Yeah, next Sunday," Alex agreed with a nod before she walked out of the building.

When she stepped back out into the sunlight, Alex released a soft breath she hadn't realized she'd been holding. The entire walk back to her dorm room, she pondered the issue of fencing club, torn between avoiding Aiden and his uncomfortable habit of smacking his magic theory in her face and learning something she'd always wanted to. When she returned to the dorm room, she decided to delay making up her mind and set her phone alarm for the time of the first meeting to make up her mind then.

When the alarm for fencing did go off that evening, Alex was sitting at her desk and reading The Canterbury Tales by Chaucer for Literature class. Setting aside her book, Alex picked up the phone and turned off the alarm, but kept staring at it. She couldn't decide and the issue of spending any more time around Aiden and Nicki than necessary and finally learning to fence had been in the back of her mind all day. Then there was Nicki's offer to consider. Despite the strangeness of everything: the visions and now the similar nightmares, a part of her did like the girl.

Pulling a coin out of her wallet, Alex tossed it up in the air softly saying, "Heads go and tails don't." It landed on heads.

Fencing class met every Sunday and Wednesday night from 7 to 9 in the first-floor basketball court of the old gym. Alex stepped into the court to find several large mats already down and a small crowd of students waiting. A girl at the front door dressed in fencing gear and armed only with a clipboard and pen stopped her and asked Alex to sign in before allowing her into the room. Another group of students, all dressed in the familiar white fencing jackets and pants were moving about the room and setting up equipment. There was a range of years with several seniors and juniors, but a couple of younger students as well. It wasn't difficult to spot Aiden and Nicki as they set a rack of foils down to the side before picking up their face masks. A tall gentleman with dark brown hair that was starting to gray and a kind face heavy with laugh lines stepped forward and smiled at the waiting students.

"Welcome everyone," he called pleasantly. "I am Professor Leonardo Bosco, I teach chemistry here at the university, but in my youth, I was a fencing champion and greatly enjoy teaching it to others." Professor Bosco moved along the line of students looking them all over with a smile. "Now some rules, the fencing club offers you three days of participation to try out fencing and learn some basics. I'm afraid that beyond that there is a membership fee in order to pay for the insurance necessary to have you swinging metal things at each other. We have some equipment available for use during this trial period, but I strongly encourage all of you who gain a real interest in fencing to purchase some of your own."

After the introduction, Professor Bosco called forward two students that he introduced as seniors who had been in fencing club since their freshman year. While they both put on their masks and gloves, Professor Bosco explained that they were using foils and would be aiming to touch each other's chest area. Alex listened to the Professor ask them if they were ready and both moved into a slight crouch with their right feet forward and their foils raised in front of them.

The one on the right moved forward quickly, trading a few soft exploratory foil clicks with his opponent as the other retreated slightly. Then with a sudden burst, the left student advanced forward, pressing the student on the right back with quicker and quicker moves. They lunged, but the blow to the chest was deflected by the other's foil as they stumbled slightly. Both righted themselves and began once again with slower movements with their foils, testing the other. This time the right student pressed forward first, advancing with quick steps and putting the other on guard. The metallic clicking of the light foils hitting each other echoed as the advances and retreats continued for another minute before in a sudden burst of speed the student of the left lunged forward and struck the tip of his foil against the chest of his opponent.

Cheering erupted from the students dressed in fencing uniforms and from several of those watching as Professor Bosco stepped forward and awarded the point. Both students lowered their blades and removed their face masks, allowing the Professor to reclaim everyone's attention.

"A good demonstration," Professor Bosco congratulated the students. "You won't be moving like that in only a few lessons, but we can start you on the basics and with practice, you can become a skilled fencer as well."

Professor Bosco rubbed his hands together and asked who had fencing experience before he counted out the students into small groups. To Alex's relief, Nicki stepped forward to take the group that Alex was assigned to while Aiden took another group. They started with a short lecture about the different kinds of swords used in fencing while Nicki showed them one of each before she moved on to the different parts of the uniform. Alex tried to pay attention to Nicki, but her eyes strayed over to Aiden from time to time across the gym with his own small group.

Nicki pulled them forward one at a time and had them pull on spare jackets, gloves, and masks before she handed any of them a foil. Under her supervision, they settled into the en garde position with their knees right above their toes. It felt strange to Alex's body in comparison to the karate classes she'd taken when she was younger, but she soon adjusted her balance to settle into the position. They were facing the wall and Nicki moved swiftly down the short line, adjusted positions where needed.

In the next hour they mastered the en garde position and Nicki started teaching them how to move, advance and retreat quickly, but started losing their attention as several of the students with some experience started fencing to show Professor Bosco their skill level. When nine arrived, Alex returned the equipment she'd borrowed to the racks and turned her attention to Professor Bosco who delivered a quick farewell and reminder of the next meeting.

"Hi Alex," Aiden greeted walking up to her as the students began to leave. "Did you enjoy yourself?"

"Yes," Alex answered cautiously.

"That's nice to hear," Aiden told her with a smile as Nicki came up next to them. "How did she do?" he asked Nicki, turning to his friend.

"Pretty good," Nicki answered. "She had a chicken wing with the foil for a few tries, but she's straightened her arm out now and is quick on her feet."

"Well, soccer players tend to be," Aiden replied with a grin. "Anyway, hope to see you on Wednesday Alex," Aiden told her before he turned away to go help with cleanup, giving Alex the familiar small wave over his shoulder.

"That was weird," Alex observed with a raised eyebrow as Aiden moved away.

"What, a normal human interaction is weird?" Nicki teased with a smile. "I think he feels bad he upset you the other day."

"He told you about that?" Alex asked with a small sigh.

Nicki shrugged and answered, "We've been best friends since we were six. His Dad taught us fencing together since we were ten and we have dinner at each other's houses at least once a week so yeah he tells me stuff."

"Thick as thieves," Alex huffed in irritation.

"Usually," Nicki told her before sighing, "After I forgave him for stealing Sarah Thompson away from me." Nicki held up her thumb and forefinger close together, "I was this close and then they start dating."

"Uh, okay…" Alex replied slowly and a nod.

Nicki chuckled and gave Alex a pat on the shoulder before saying, "Well see you in class tomorrow, have a good night."

"Right," Alex agreed. "See you tomorrow."

As she stepped out in the quickly darkening campus, Alex smiled softly and chuckled. Waving to some of the other departing students, she headed north towards the lake and her dorm room feeling better about life in general. Aiden and Nicki were definitely strange, but she found that she liked them a little. Looking back over her shoulder, she caught a glimpse of the two of them leaving the building with Aiden's father and laughing. She shook her head and headed for her own home, pulling out her phone to call her mother and report on the general improvement of college life.

11

All Hallows Eve

Late October brought a chill to Ravenslake that even the joy of midterms being over couldn't overcome. No longer were students sunbathing in the afternoon sun, but instead, the first heavy coats were appearing. Alex and Jenny had fully settled into their dorm room with a thick blue rug between the beds, a hanging plant by the window and photos of their new friends along the walls. Alex's mobile phone was full of new numbers of those she'd met through intermural soccer, fencing, classes and a couple of parties. To the excitement of all the students, Halloween was on the coming Friday adding to the cheerful atmosphere on campus.

Professor Yates' office was a corner room with light entering from two windows on either side of his desk. Bookshelves lined the walls, filled not only with old looking heavy bound books, but trinkets from around the world. An elegant old world map hung by the doorway to the office and a small wooden table that matched the dark color of the desk stood next to the comfortable chair in front of the desk. It was all Alex could do to stay still rather than looking about wildly as she sat down for her meeting with Professor Yates to discuss the upcoming semester.

In the past month, Alex had gotten over her first encounter with the Professor and done her best to put vision and strange dreams at the back of her mind. She'd done well in his class with strong grades and compliments on her papers, but she hadn't realized until the October advising notices arrived that he was the professor assigned to her. Now that they were alone in his office and he sat looking over her current classes and her possible classes for spring semester, Alex felt all of her nerves return. Professor Yates hummed an unfamiliar tune softly as he read over the copy of Alex's current schedule and her draft schedule for the next semester.

"Well," Professor Yates finally said, looking up at Alex from the papers in front of him. "Everything looks in order. You're on the right track working on your general education courses now, but I'm pleased that you'll be taking a few English courses." Leaning back in his chair, Yates' silver pin caught a beam of sunlight making it shine. "I don't see any problems in your academic schedule, but make sure you select one or two backups just in case the classes are full."

"Yes, sir," Alex answered automatically, keeping her hands in her lap.

Her tweed-clad professor studied her for a moment and gave her a warm smile. "So how are you adjusting to university life?" Yates asked pleasantly.

"Adjusting?" Alex repeated a little surprised at the turn of conversation. "Alright, I guess. I like my roommate and my neighbors in the dorm are pretty cool."

"Good," he answered with a smile. "You're making friends?"

"Yes," Alex answered. "I've made a few good friends and have people I hang out with."

"Do you have a job or activities outside of school?" Yates asked before noting her discomfort. He laughed softly and leaned forward, "If I'm making you uncomfortable you don't have to answer Alex. I just like to know that my advisees are doing alright outside the classroom as well."

"Right," Alex replied with a soft blush. "Well I'm on an intermural soccer team and a part of the fencing club."

"Ah, then perhaps I saw you at last weekend's demonstration?"

"No," Alex told him with a shake of her head. "I'm still a beginner so I'm not doing any of the demonstrations yet."

"Well Professor Bosco is an excellent teacher so I'm sure you'll be joining in the demonstrations in no time."

"It's actually his son who is working with me," she told him on reflex. "Aiden Bosco."

"Yes," Yates said with a nod, "I've met Aiden at faculty events and his sister Aisling. He's not in any of my classes presently." Yates straightened up Alex's papers and schedule draft, handing them back to her. "Well, I am glad to hear that things are going well. If you need anything just let me know."

"Thank you," she answered with a soft smile as she took the papers from him and stood up. "I'll see you in class."

"One more thing," Yates added, standing up as Alex moved to the doorway.

"Yes Professor?" she asked turning back to him.

"Be careful on Halloween," Yates told her, a strange look of worry crossing over his face. "Make sure that you stay safe."

Blinking at the professor, Alex opened her mouth to ask what he was worried about, but the memory of the visions made her fall silent. Instead, she gave him a quick nod and quickly left the room. Shutting the door behind her, Alex leaned against the wall outside Yates' office for a moment to collect her thoughts. When she heard the professor moving inside the office, Alex took off down the hallway towards the stairs. She didn't slow down or think on the issue until she was outside and walking towards her dorm.

"I'm overreacting," she told herself softly as Hatfield Hall came into view. "He probably just wants to me be safe with alcohol and keep an eye on my drink."

That made sense, she decided. Professor Yates would have seen and heard about a lot of bad things due to parties and probably didn't want anything happening to one of his students. It had nothing to do with the hallucinations. Slowing down, Alex tightened her coat around herself as she dug into the pocket for her key card. As she unlocked the door, Alex decided that the Professor was right and that she just needed to be careful at the Halloween party she and Jenny had been invited to and put the warning out of her mind.

Halloween, All Hallows Eve, Friday night was a busy night on the campus of Ravenslake University. Small parties were taking place in numerous dorm halls and several large parties were raging amongst the Greek houses to the south of campus. In the dark sky hung a large waxing moon that illuminated the campus with a low haunting light. Only a few children remained out trick or treating with the youngest already tucked away in their beds.

The Delta Beta Alpha house was bright with lights and dance music burst out into the street with laughter and shrieking making it impossible to actually hear any lyrics. Costumed students danced on the lawn and mingled with friends, many already shaky on their feet. All the furniture of the living room had been pushed back against the wall leaving the wooden floor open for dancing. Food and drinks covered every flat surface except the floor with fallen streamers, fake spiders and shredded black paper scattered there. False cobwebs hung from the ceiling and the talking skeleton by the front door had long since run down its batteries.

Alex was standing at the side of the room in her light blue and white checkered dress with a basket on her arm which served as her Dorothy Gale costume along with a pair of silver shoes that she'd explained multiple times through the night as being faithful to the book rather than the movie. With Jenny's help, she'd styled her blonde hair into two braids with curled tips. Next to her was Lance in a crusader knight costume including a gray hood pulled up over his head and a helmet under his arm. His foot was tapping to the beat of the music, but he wasn't trying to talk to Alex over the music. Alex hummed softly as a new song she knew came on but kept her attention in the middle of the dance floor where Jenny as Cleopatra and Arthur as Marc Anthony were dancing. They were the center of attention for the party. Jenny in her long black and gold dress and her long hair styled around a gold headdress and Arthur in golden battle armor.

Sipping her beer, Alex glanced at the door and tried to hide a yawn. Suddenly, Alex shuddered and gripped the wall next to her as she fought back the chill rushing through her body. It passed as quickly as it had come and Alex relaxed, wondering if a window had been opened nearby. Another song started and Alex grinned as she started to sway to the beat. Lance chuckled and snatched her drink from her hand before giving her a quick spin. Alex let Lance lead her out further onto the dance floor. Jenny glanced over at them as they danced, a strange expression crossing her roommate's face that quickly vanished.

Another icy shiver rushed up Alex's spine as if an icy hand had brushed her neck. Looking over her shoulder, Alex searched for any sign of the source, but saw nothing only to have another cold spike in her arms and then her legs. She grit her teeth and kept dancing, trying to warm up in the rush of bodies and movement, but all she wanted was to curl up. Another shiver made her stop dancing and wrap her arms around herself.

"Alex?" Lance called, barely making himself heard above the music.

"I'm okay," Alex told him as loudly as she could between her grit teeth as she shivered again.

Despite her words, Lance gently gripped her arm and led her out of the living room and into the kitchen. The food on the kitchen island had long since been devoured and there were only a couple of people milling around the large room. Releasing her arm, Lance stepped back and checked her over with a worried expression.

"Are you alright?" he asked.

"I'm fine," Alex said as she set the basket down on the kitchen island, congratulating herself on her brilliance before she pulled a zip up hoodie out of the basket. "Just got a bit cold."

"Cold?" Lance repeated. "Really?"

"Yeah, cold," Alex defended with a frown. "Maybe I'm not used to alcohol," she suggested in a softer and slightly apologetic tone. "Only had it a couple of times in high school."

Lance nodded as Alex pulled on the gray hoodie and zipped it up. Her shivering eased only a little, but she did her best not to show any discomfort in front of Lance. He waited a few more moments before leaving the kitchen to return to the party. Alex rejoined the party after getting a drink of water and navigated through the crowd to find her friends. She spotted Arthur near the doorway, speaking with a teammate who was swaying dangerously on his feet. Arthur looked around and spotted her. He gestured to her to join them with a slightly frantic look on his face that propelled Alex forward through the throng of students quickly.

"Alex," Arthur exclaimed with relief as she stepped up next to him. "Look can you tell Jenny that I needed to drive some people home. I'm not sure when I'll make it back."

"Sure," Alex replied, looking over at the clearly drunk football player dressed up as a pirate. "That's a good idea."

"Yeah, and he lives across town with a couple others I need to round up," Arthur told her with a shake of his head. "Lance can probably drive you home."

"Okay," Alex agreed before she jumped back as the football player staggered on his feet. Arthur caught him quickly and slung the man's arm over his shoulders before lowering him to the sofa.

"I'd better collect the others," Arthur said with a sigh. "Apologize to Jenny for me."

"She'll understand," Alex promised him with a smile before she quickly darted away from the drunk man who looked ready to be sick.

Alex glanced back to see Arthur grabbing the arm of another unsteady student and taking him to the couch. Shaking her head, Alex looked around the living room but saw no sign of Jenny. Alex climbed up the stairs to the second floor and glanced around the first room which was a mess with a student snoring on the bed despite the noise from downstairs. Looking around the corner, Alex spotted Lance and Jenny in the hallway talking in low voices. Neither noticed her until she called Jenny's name, making her roommate spin to face her with wide eyes.

"Sorry I scared you," Alex apologized, "Arthur asked me to let you know that he's going to drive some people home."

"Oh," Jenny replied, straightening her headdress. "Is he coming back?"

"He wasn't sure," Alex admitted. "One of the guys is in pretty bad shape."

Jenny rolled her eyes but nodded in understanding. Lance frowned with a touch of concern flashing in his eyes before he looked over at Jenny.

"Don't worry I'll give you a ride home," he promised Jenny before he looked back at Alex, "You too, just let me know when you want to head back."

"Thanks," Alex told him cheerfully. "That's nice of you."

"Thank you, Lance," Jenny gushed, gesturing down at the high gold heels she was wearing. "There's a reason we drove in the first place." Jenny sighed softly and then smiled at him, "I'm ready to go home now since Arthur has left."

"Okay," Lance said kindly before looking at Alex. "What about you?"

"Uh," Alex hesitated, "I'll stay a little longer. This is Aisha's house and I haven't talked to her yet. I'll just walk home," she added with a small smile. "You don't need to make two trips."

"I'd rather pick you up later than have you walk home," Lance told her with a slight frown. He glanced at Jenny and then back to her. "I'll be back in an hour to pick you up, that okay?"

"That really isn't necessary," Alex insisted, but Lance gave her a stern look until she relented and agreed to meet him in an hour.

With Arthur gone, Lance escorted Jenny down the stairs with Alex trailing behind. She nearly tripped on the stairs when another shiver shook her body, biting back a curse. Then she heard a strange long howling over the music. Frowning, Alex looked out a window as she reached the foot of the stairs. There was another howl; it sounded closer than before, but she didn't see anything stranger than drunk students in the yard. A Halloween song started to play and Alex laughed softly to herself for mistaking a sound effect for a real animal. She gave a quick wave to Jenny and Lance as they left and went in search of Aisha.

An hour and a half later, Alex was standing out on the street as people around her staggered home and she tightened her hoodie. Pulling out her phone, she noted that it was past 3 in the morning and still no sign of Lance. She tried texting him again, but there was no answer. A sudden strange howl echoed through Greek row and made Alex spin around in alarm. She couldn't pinpoint which house it came from but convinced herself that it was just a sound effect again. Across the street, the last light in Delta Omega Alpha turned out. Sighing in surrender, Alex turned and started walking down the street towards the silent intersection.

The soft click of her low heels against the sidewalk echoed in the night as Alex passed by one of the old fashioned looking lamp posts that lined the walk between the library and the administration building. Glancing over at the commons, Alex was struck at how large and dark it was in the moonlight. She tightened her hoodie around herself, grateful for the warmth on her arms, but regretting choosing a costume with a skirt. Another shiver passed through her body and Alex allowed herself a soft pitiful whimper. Alex increased her speed and focused on the street up ahead as she mentally mapped out the fastest route back to her dorm room that didn't involve cold grass.

A howl echoed across the campus stopping Alex in her tracks. Looking around slowly, Alex did her best to stay calm. Maybe someone had gotten a loudspeaker and was playing a Halloween prank. That would explain the sounds she'd heard back at Greek row too. Professor Yates' advice about being careful replayed in her mind causing her stomach to tighten. She stood perfectly still in a pool of light from a lamp post and waited as her eyes traced the area in front of her.

Then there was the sound of footfalls to the right, past the Carlson building that were echoing in the darkness and coming closer. Alex turned sharply towards the noise and started to move forward while watching the edge of the building. Three figures came around the corner of the building, one of them holding a flashlight which was shining towards her.

"Alex?" the familiar voice of Nicki asked and the girl lowered her flashlight and moved closer to the lamppost.

Alex nearly laughed, Nicki was dressed as Glinda the Good and her soccer teammate grinned at her costume. She eyes went to the figures behind Nicki and she wasn't at all surprised to see Aiden and Bran looking towards her. Aiden was dressed like a 1950s greaser complete with a black leather coat, but his hair was a mess and Bran was dressed in some kind of steampunk outfit with a metal black cane instead of his regular wooden one.

"Hi," Alex greeted with a quick nod to her classmates. "How was your Halloween?"

"Good," Nicki answered as the trio approached Alex and joined her on the sidewalk. "We went to a party downtown, but our ride back to campus bailed."

"Mine too," Alex told them with a nod. "Uh, shall we?" she gestured up the sidewalk in the direction of the dorms. Nicki nodded in agreement and they all started moving again.

Everyone stopped when a long howl echoed between the large empty campus buildings. "There it is again," Aiden hissed as he spun around and peered out into the darkness. "That's got to be the fifth one I've heard."

Another howl ripped through the night, closer than ever, and Alex felt as if a shard of ice had been thrust into her chest. Gasping for air, she spun around, nearly knocking into Aiden who was looking about with worry himself. Another howl pierced the night only to be joined quickly by another.

"Oh god there's more than one," Nicki gasped next to Alex. "What are they?"

"Wolves," Alex suggested softly as she stepped backward towards Nicki, pressing them together.

"Not around here," Aiden whispered. "I've never heard of wolves coming so close to the city."

"It's got to be a prank right?" Bran added, sounding slightly out of breath, "A trick for Halloween."

"We should hurry back to the dorms," Nicki told them, grabbing Alex's hand and tugging her forward. "Just in case."

"Right," Aiden agreed and they all started walking at a faster pace towards the Administration building.

Bran moved a bit slower than the rest of them, but they stayed together in a small huddled group. The sounds of Bran's metal brace, the click of Alex and Nicki's heels and their increasing shallow breathing surrounded them. Then a low snarl made

them all jump and halt in their places in front of the empty
Fine Arts building. Nicki slowly lifted her small flashlight and
shined it around the area. They heard something large moving
in the darkness, avoiding the beam of light.

"Oh god," Nicki breathed, "There's something out here."

Growling erupted from the darkness. Someone screamed and
they all started to run back the way they had come. Behind
them the growling turned into a howl, followed by two more
howls and the sounds of something large rushing through the
grass after them. Bran gasped in pain next to Alex as he
struggled to keep running.

"The Kittell Building," Aiden shouted, changing his direction
towards one of the campus buildings. "We have to get out of
the open!"

Alex dared not turn around or speak as they rushed for the
brick building's main entrance. Nicki sprinted ahead, holding
up the skirts of her gown with one hand until she reached the
solid wooden doors and tried to pry them open.

"Locked!" she shouted, turning back to them before
screaming.

Aiden lunged forward and grabbed her hand, pulling Nicki
along with them as they followed the building's walls, hoping
to find an open window or doorway with glass they could
break. Instead, a sharp howl in front of them made them freeze
as something moved towards them from the front. Gasping,
Alex turned and saw something moving in the darkness behind
them.
"We're surrounded," she whispered, terror sweeping her entire
body.

Bran grabbed her hand and pulled her away from the wall of the Kittell building and they stumbled towards the Carlson building. Light gleamed out from a lamppost between the two buildings, revealing no doors on the Carlson building they could use and windows well over their heads. The snarling grew louder all around them, rumbling through the air like thunder. Beyond the light of the lamppost, the darkness itself seemed to be moving, twisting into animalistic shapes. Alex took a small step back, too afraid to breathe. The cold brick of the building pressed into her back contrasting with Bran's warmth as he huddled next to her in shared terror.

A long canine form stepped into the light of the lamppost, its long legs coming into view slowly. A soft gasp escaped Alex as the creature stepped into the light. Its pale fur shimmered in the light, almost translucent, revealing the bony form of its deep chest and wide shoulders as it took a slow step towards them. Pointed ears rose from its long head, pressed back as the creature growled at them exposing long sharp teeth. Its violet eyes flashed dangerously and it stalked towards them with slow deliberate movements. Two more joined it in the light, both growling and snarling as they slowly moved towards them.

"Oh god," Nicki whispered, turning her face against Aiden's shoulder.

The leader of the small pack paused and watched them, seeming to bask in their fear. Alex swallowed, trying to summon up a scream or a shout for help, but was unable to move her lips. Crouching, the canine's muscles tensed and Alex whimpered, gripping Bran's hand in a tight grip.

The Hound leapt forward, teeth bared and long claws stretched out towards Aiden. A scream exploded into the darkness and a flash of light lashed forward, colliding with the Hound. There was an animalistic cry as the Hound was thrown to the ground, a gaping wound in its side. The light lashed again, a whip of brilliance in the low light, striking another Hound. The third Hound snarled and turned from them, leaping into the darkness beyond the lamplight. It was thrown back a moment later by the swirl of light, impacting the sidewalk and skidding several feet. As the leader Hound rose to its feet, silver blood dripping from its wound and its side dissolving slowly Professor Cornwall stepped into the light of the lamppost.

Everything froze for a heartbeat. Alex gaped at her Professor in shock. The Hound leapt forward, leaving the ground in a burst of speed and shadow. Professor Cornwall lashed her right hand towards it and light burst forth in a graceful arc. They met in an explosion of shadow and light, the swirl of light engulfing the Hound which gave a long low cry of agony before dropping to the cold cement. Professor Cornwall reached into the pocket of her black overcoat and drew out a knife that glinted dangerously in the light of the lamp. Growls echoed off the walls of the building as the two Hounds crept towards the professor, flashing their teeth and stalking around her.

"Stay back," Professor Cornwall ordered calmly, not taking her eyes from the nearest Hound.

It leapt at her and the light whip appeared once again, slashing at the creature, but the second one lunged forward. There was a sudden rumbling in the ground beneath its feet before dirt and grass ripped upwards to grab the creature. A sharp snap made Alex flinch as the Hound was pulled to the ground by a twisting rope of grass, shattering its leg bones. A wave of dirt and rock surged up and over the creature's head, crushing the skull as the other Hound fell to the cement ensnarled in a pulsing rope of light.

Professor Yates stepped into the light, joining Professor Cornwall with a quick glance over at the students huddled against the building. With a smooth movement, he drew out a knife similar to Professor Cornwall's and knelt at the creature's side. Alex held her breath, only to flinch when he thrust the knife into the ribs of the Hound. She heard a dull cry from under the earth that had crushed the first beast's head. The body shimmered and dissipated like the mist in the sun.

Without a word to Yates, Cornwall plunged her own knife into the Hound at her feet and watched dispassionately as the body dissolved. She did not linger and stepped purposefully towards the pack leader that lay bleeding on the sidewalk. It snarled at her, snapping at her hand as she reached for it. Showing no fear, Cornwall gripped the beast's head and brought the knife across its throat. Alex watched the blood fade away from the sidewalk along with the body, leaving no sign that it was ever there. Yates made a small motion with his hand and the patch of the lawn that had risen up to trap the Hound smoothed out and the grass smoothed back out. Turning his attention to them, Yates stepped closer to them and studied them carefully.

"No injuries," he observed with a soft smile appearing on his features. "That is good, but we cannot linger. There may be more."

Professor Yates nodded to Professor Cornwall and gestured for the four of them to follow him. Aiden and Alex glanced at each other, but then Aiden took a shaky step forward and followed the professors with the others trailing after him into the darkness.

12

Changes Wrought

833 B.C.E. Snowdonia Wales

Clouds hung low around the mountains as the chill of winter began to settle over the land. Myrddin paid this little mind as he climbed the worn path up the mountain to the lake, his staff softly striking the rocks with every memorized step. A bag over his shoulder clinked softly as the small earthen jars he carried gently shifted as he moved. Stopping, he turned and looked down the mountain at the small village nestled amongst the foothills. From here he could see the small herds that dotted the landscape and the roundhouses huddled close together.

Much had changed in the year since his mother's death and while it remained a painful memory, Myrddin valued the lesson he had learned that night. Despite his fears, he had taken on the mantle of the priesthood and done his best to keep his people's connection with the Earth strong. He'd traveled throughout the region to meet others in the priesthood and kept the peace despite so many of them knowing what he was. Myrddin shook his head at the stray thought and turned his attention back to the path up the mountain. Yet he couldn't help but think of it. In the past year, Cyrridven had taught him much about the Sídhe, stories his mother had dared never tell him and he could understand their worry that one with the blood of a Sídhe held such an important station as a keeper of the connection between the Earth and the people.

Walking forward, Myrddin passed through the mists that were hanging over the mountain and allowed his feet to guide him. There was no sound on the mountain save the click of his staff against the ground each time he took a step. As the sun rose higher in the morning sky the mist began to disperse just as he reached the crest of rocks that nestled the mountain lake. Carefully, he navigated his way down the slope of the mountain and to the edge of the water.

The lake was calm as it was every third day when Myrddin made the climb. It was no secret in the village where he went, but all now gave the area a wide berth as none were certain what his business here was. Myrddin often amused himself imagining their reactions during the silent moments in his roundhouse when the absence of his mother weighed most heavily on him. Their avoidance was without a doubt a blessing as a frozen pillar of water stood in the center of the lake with a cauldron of ice resting on it as it had been for a year and day now. Pausing at the edge of the water, Myrddin examined the cauldron with a slight sense of unease. Mist rose out of the shimmering vessel as if it were an ordinary cauldron heated by flames, but he knew this was not the case. The potion that had been brewing for so long was fueled by something he had only gained the slightest understanding of. Magic.

Setting aside his bag, Myrddin gave himself a moment to study the cauldron at a distance. Cyrridven had explained only that the potion came to her in a vision early in her years in his world, but Myrddin now suffered some doubts. Breathing out, Myrddin raised his staff slightly off the ground and brought it down on the small rocks of the shore with a sharp crack. He repeated the motion twice more and watched as the water in the lake rippled. Once this had frightened and astonished him, but today he simply found himself wishing it did not take so long. Cyrridven appeared in a swirl of water and magic, smiling warmly at him.

"Good day Merlin," she greeted pleasantly.

Merlin was now the only name she called him and in the past year, Myrddin had found himself responding to the name more naturally. Myrddin gave her the small bow that had become their custom in the past year, his hand keeping his staff straight.

"Good day," he returned as he rose his head up and met her eyes.

Cyrridven's dark green eyes were warm but held concern in them. Myrddin believed it was for him, but they never spoke of such things directly. He doubted that they would start today.

"Is the potion ready?" he questioned, trying to keep his voice steady and leaning forward on his staff slightly with both his hands clasped on the staff near his face. It was a habit that his mother had hated, but it continued to this day.

Nodding, Cyrridven moved closer to the shore and gave him a careful look. "Are you certain you are prepared, Merlin?"

"Neither of us really knows what this potion will do to," Myrddin replied as calmly as he could. "Just that it will 'open me fully to the world', whatever that means," he added with a slight grumble.

"I wish I could tell you for certain," Cyrridven sighed, the water swirling around her faster in her agitation. "But I am not a child of the Iron Realm; my connection, my understanding is limited."

"Yes," Myrddin answered, he'd heard this before and gestured towards the cauldron. "Shall we?"

Cyrridven gave him another searching look, but turned gracefully and drifted over the surface of the lake to the tall pedestal. While she wasn't looking, Myrddin straightened up and took in a deep breath for courage, hoping to stop the slight shake of his hand. Looking up, he saw Cyrridven lift the ice cauldron from the pedestal with a spark of strange light. In an instant, the ice pedestal that had stood for a year on the surface melted away and flowed back into the lake, leaving no trace. He drove his staff into the ground next to him and released it slowly.

His eyes were fixed on the small cauldron as Cyrridven brought it to the edge of the lake. It shimmered in the sunlight, the small magical symbols he had learned in the last year etched into the ice around the rim dark with shadows. Taking another breath, Myrddin stepped forward, the water of the lake lapping at the tips of his shoes. He could just see into the cauldron. The long thin rod of ice that they had used to stir the mixture through the last year and a day was waiting for him to use it to collect a few drops of the thick liquid. It had no true color, shifting between muddy brown, spring grass green, stone gray and sky blue as he looked at it.

"Remember Myrddin," Cyrridven whispered, breaking the silence that had descended over the mountain. "The first three drops will open your spirit, but the rest is devoid of all magic and is a terrible poison."

"I'll remember," Myrddin promised as he carefully reached for the stirring rod. It was cold in his hands but did not melt or slip as he gently lifted it out of the cauldron. Several large shining drops gleamed and he cautiously brought the rod closer to his left hand. Myrddin held his left hand still and allowed three drops to fall onto his fingers before quickly bringing them to his mouth. He was vaguely aware of shoving the rod back into the cauldron and taking a step back as the droplets hit his tongue.

They were sweet, far sweeter than anything he had ever tasted. He braced himself, unsure of what to expect, but nothing happened. Looking towards Cyrridven, he saw a look of concern on her own face and she looked down into the cauldron at the remaining liquid which was taking on a reddish color.

"I don't think it…" Myrddin started to say before his knees weakened and he stumbled forward, his knees colliding with the small rocks of the shore.

He felt the pain sharply through his legs and a shudder rushed through him. Opening his mouth to speak, he felt choked as the smell of the nearby plants, the nearby animals, and his own body filled his throat. The air carried the taste of grass, leaves, and stone as it floated across his tongue. The chirping of the birds echoed into his ears along with the lapping of the lake and the shifting of the rocks. Grasping his head, Myrddin groaned in agony, unable to think, unable to separate the sensations flooding through him. He felt the fabric of his shirt too intensely, felt the breeze on his face too harshly and felt the ache in his knees all through his body. Then everything went black, silent and still.

Myrddin opened his eyes slowly as his mind returned to him, but found only darkness. He was lying on cool ground and inhaled the scent of the earth with caution. This time he was not overwhelmed, but comforted by the scent of moist earth and clay. Flexing his fingers, he felt the dirt give way to his fingers and brushed his thumb across a stone. Then he listened, but there was no sound of Cyrridven or the water of the lake. He blinked to check that he was truly in darkness, keeping a burst of fear in check by focusing on the feel of the earth in his fingers. Feeling by hand, Myrddin slowly rose to his knees and tried to see something in the darkness.

Then there was a flash of light before him and a small glowing orb appeared before him. It spun softly, wisps of light floating around it like small arms and the glow intensified. He did not look away from the orb of light, not even to see where he was. It radiated warmth and filled Myrddin with a surge of emotions, all coming too quickly for him to identify any of them, but he felt strong after the wave passed and had a lingering sense of joy.

The light dimmed and the wisps of light curled into the orb, creating a smooth perfectly round form. Myrddin watched in silence as the surface hardened and took on a gray color with a metallic shine, not unlike the one he knew from bronze. The strange metal orb hung in the air before him, still shining with a strange internal light. Red light began to creep over its surface, cracking the metal slowly and Myrddin gasped with shock as the orb turned red hot before his eyes, so bright it almost hurt to look at it.

Suddenly the orb was struck by an unseen force, causing a sharp metallic sound that sent Myrddin flinching back. He barely kept himself from rushing forward to prevent damage to the orb. Another blow struck the orb, producing the same sound that reverberated around Myrddin. The orb turned and Myrddin paused as he observed that the side of the orb had been altered and twisted into a new shape. Flame erupted around the orb, heating it back to a red-hot lump of metal. Then another blow struck the metal, altering the shape further. Myrddin stood transfixed, watching the flux of the light as the metal was heated and struck again and again. Slowly a new shape began to emerge as each blow was struck. Myrddin breathed out slowly as he recognized the form of a human stretched out in the air, floating and glowing with a soft light. Nothing happened for a long time until Myrddin took a cautious step towards the form, holding his right hand out towards it.

Gently, he lowered his fingers and the touched the indistinct face of the metal form. The metal was smooth to the touch, but heat still lingered as Myrddin studied the strange thing in front of him with curiosity and wonder. Then he felt it, a pulsing beneath his fingers, so similar to the beat of a heart. The pulse quickened and Myrddin felt something liquid touching his fingers, something warm and sticky. Drawing his hand back, Myrddin looked down at it with alarm. His fingers were red with blood dripping down the long lengths of his fingers to pool in the palm of his hand. Looking down at the metal form, Myrddin gave a shout of alarm as blood flowed over the human figure, covering it with a thick red skin. A flash of light blinded Myrddin and he slammed his eyes shut as a rush of magic forced the air from his lungs.

"Merlin!" an alarmed voice screamed near his ear as a hand grasped his shoulder tightly. "Merlin!"

Taking in quick breaths, Myrddin focused on the voice and recognized it as Cyrridven's. He could hear the water of the lake next to him and feel the rocks of the shore digging into his flesh. Forcing open his eyes, Myrddin found himself back on the shore of the lake, collapsed on his knees with Cyrridven leaning over him, one hand on his shoulder and the other gripping her cauldron. When his eyes met hers, she released his shoulder and drew back from him. Her dark green eyes dropped away from his eyes to his mouth and Myrddin felt blood flowing into the crease of his lips. Instantly, he licked his lips, tasting the metallic tang of his own blood and reached up to check his nose.

"Blood," Cyrridven whispered thoughtfully as she watched a drop of his blood fall to the shore and be swept into the lake by a small wave. Her eyes returned to Myrddin's as the flow of blood stopped and he lowered his hand. "What did you see?" she questioned.

"I saw…" Myrddin started slowly before he frowned and looked down at his blood covered hand. "I am not certain," he admitted. Gripping his staff, still driven into the earth, Myrddin pulled himself up. Ignoring the protests of his knees, he studied the blood on his hand and considered the vision he had been given. "I don't understand what I was shown yet," he told Cyrridven before tightening his grip on his staff, "But I will."

Cyrridven and Myrddin spoke no more on the matter but carefully poured the remaining potion into the small jars that Myrddin had brought. As the last drop fell from the lip of the cauldron into the third small jar, the cauldron began to crack in Cyrridven's hands. Seeing only her look of alarm, Myrddin reached forward to catch a shard of the cauldron before it fell into the water, but the shard vanished in a puff of mist just before it touched his hand. Holding the cauldron more gently, Cyrridven watched in amazement as the cauldron turned to mist in her hands and faded into the breeze. Exchanging a quick look with Cyrridven, Myrddin closed and sealed the last jar before wrapping it in fabric and returning it to his bag.

"What should I do with the poison?" He asked her, pulling the bag over his shoulder.

"Keep it safe," she answered simply, "A spark of magic is in everything in this world, everything except what is in those bottles." Cyrridven sighed and looked past Myrddin, "Who knows how it might be useful in the coming days."

"Against the Sídhe," Myrddin observed with a nod. "Very well, then I will keep these safe."

"What will you do now?" Cyrridven asked him with a cautious look. "I have done for you what I can. The magic of your world is not mine, not naturally, and I cannot help you any further."

"Yes you can and you will," Myrddin replied automatically before a look of confusion and surprise took over his features. "Uh… I am unsure why I said that."

Cyrridven considered him and then nodded. "I think that perhaps you speak the truth that even I do not yet know Merlin," she told him, folding her hands in front of herself. "It has been more than a thousand years since I entered your world. The crossing left me so weak and so pained that I hid myself in the waters of this world. I slept for so long and woke knowing a few truths that were whispered to me, and gifted with a small link to the magic of this world." A warm smile appeared on Cyrridven's face and she tilted her head, "I have tried to do what was asked of me, but I think that now that responsibility has been passed to you." Turning away from him, Cyrridven floated out towards the center of the lake, a peaceful expression on her face.

"Wait!" Myrddin called after her, "What if I need your help?"

Cyrridven turned back to look over her shoulder at him and warmly replied, "If you need my help Myrddin you shall have it, but the answers you need I cannot give to you. Only you can find them."

He opened his mouth to ask her another question, but she vanished into the waves of the lake and did not return to the surface even when he knocked his staff three times on the shore. Sighing softly, Myrddin rubbed his forehead and turned away from the water. He checked on the small jars of poison and with a final glance at the lake started for home, more uncertain than ever of what his future held.

13

Mages Gather

Alex kept glancing over her shoulder and into the darkness as they were led away from the Carlson building by Professor Cornwall. Bran was struggling to keep up with Cornwall's fast pace as they crossed the lawn between them and the Hamilton building. Nicki and Aiden were just ahead of her and kept looking back at Professor Yates who was at the back of the group. When Alex glanced back, she flinched at the cold and determined look on the Professor's usually warm and open face. Instinctively, she knew that the anger she saw there was not directed towards any of them, but she felt fear at the expression.

They followed the wall of the Hamilton building around to a side door and Nicki raised her flashlight at Professor Cornwall's command so she could pull out a small ring of keys. The professor looked around quickly before inserting the key and unlocking the door with a quick turn of her hand before shoving it open roughly.

"Quickly," Professor Cornwall hissed as she stepped into the dark building and led them straight to the staircase right beside the doorway.

Nicki's small flashlight gave them just enough light to see by, but Professor Cornwall didn't seem to need it as she easily navigated the stairs to the second floor and took a sharp right at the top. Stopping in front of a doorway near the end of the hallway that had a sign next to it reading 'history department', Professor Cornwall opened the door and gestured them inside. It was a small office with a desk and a long row of filing cabinets. Another door down the short hallway from the receptionist area was open with light spilling into the hallway. Professor Cornwall glanced backward as Professor Yates stepped through the main doorway and locked it behind him. He gave her a nod and Professor Cornwall gestured for them to follow her into the open office.

The office was reasonably large with a heavy wooden desk dominating the space near the window. Six framed old world maps hung around the window, stacked on top of each other as decoration. Bookshelves lined two of the walls, stuffed with a variety of books some new and some old and many small antique items. Most interesting, however, was the source of the soft light that filled the room. Jack-o-lanterns of varied sizes sat all around the room, two on the desk, several on the bookshelves, one by the doorway and three more tucked into corners of the office on the floor. A long sword lay in the center of the desk beside a strange polished metal disk. On the desk within arm's reach of the two chairs were two cups of teas, still steaming.

Alex glanced towards Aiden who gave a tiny shrug and moved further into the room so that Nicki and Bran could join them. Professor Cornwall and Professor Yates stepped in after them and locked the door. The professors moved around the students and sat down in the chairs that Alex supposed they had vacated when rushing to the rescue. Professor Cornwall picked up her tea and took a small sip before setting it back down to look at them. Professor Yates, on the other hand, took a sip and settled back in his chair still holding the cup between his hands.

No one spoke, Alex stood completely still between Bran and Aiden with Nicki on the other side of Aiden as all four of them gaped at the professors. After waiting a few moments, Professor Cornwall reached over to pick up the polished metal disk and held it up near one of the jack-o-lanterns on her desk. She studied it carefully before nodding to herself and saying something to Professor Yates in a strange language. Nicki perked up at the language, tilting her head curiously as she listened to the quick exchange. Professor Yates sighed and Professor Cornwall set the metal disk back down on the desk.

"What happened out there?" Aiden suddenly asked. "What were those things and how did you stop them?"

"Let us start with who we are," Professor Yates suggested with a soft smile. "Ambrose Yates is not my real name. The name of my birth is Myrddin, but I am much more famously known as Merlin. My associate Morgana Cornwall is better known as Morgana le Fey," he told them, watching their faces in interest.

Alex couldn't help it, she burst out laughing. Her lungs ached as her ability to breathe deserted her and she leaned back against a bookshelf, nearly shaking it with the force of her laughter. A nervous giggle erupted from Nicki, quickly followed by a frantic chuckle from Aiden. Only Bran remained composed, looking at the rest of them with mild alarm and then back at the professors. Neither Professor Cornwall nor Professor Yates said anything else as they waited for the nervous release of fear to pass. Alex recovered first, gulping in air and studied the two carefully and as casually as she could manage.

"Merlin and Morgana?" Aiden repeated when he had caught his breath. "Really? That would make you hundreds of years old."

"Those old stories are more than a bit displaced," Professor Cornwall answered with an elegant shrug. "We are both closer to three thousand years old, born during the Bronze Age of the British Isles."

Raising an eyebrow at the strange response, Alex glanced at Aiden for guidance in the strange situation. He blinked at them both with surprise but took a small step forward. Curiosity was evident on his features and Alex hoped that he wasn't leading them into even more trouble due to his fascination with magic and myths.

"Let's say that is true," Aiden suggested, "And that the two of you are Merlin and Morgana from the King Arthur legend… just earlier than most stories. I'd still like to know what those things were and why they attacked us."

"Those were Sídhe hounds," Professor Yates answered gently with a glance to all of them. Nicki let out a small gasp of alarm that made Aiden turn to look at her with worry.

"She hounds?" Bran repeated with a confused tone. "Like girl hounds?"

Professor Yates shook his head and turned his eyes towards Alex and asked, "Miss Adams, you referred to the Sídhe in your worksheet earlier this semester, did you not?"

"Uh," Alex glanced at the others, uncomfortable being the center of Professor Yates' attention. "Sídhe is an older Irish word for the Fae… it means people of the mounds," she answered hesitantly.

"Correct," Professor Yates told her with a kind smile. "I am afraid that those hounds were sent out to scout for their Sídhe masters. I suspect their orders were to track any humans with magic that they found. To them, we would have been far too dangerous to attack, but four young people all together would have made far too tempting a target."

"Magic," Alex repeated with a soft exhale. "Shit, this is really about magic." She looked at the two professors with wide eyes and asked, "Are you really Merlin and Morgana?"

"Yes," Merlin answered gently, setting down his tea and meeting Alex's wide and frightened eyes. "I am Merlin and she is Morgana, but the lives we have lived are quite different from the medieval stories that you are familiar with." When Morgana snorted behind him, Merlin added, "Especially Morgana's story."

"So when we first met and had those… visions," Nicki asked in a strong voice that quivered only the tiniest bit before she said the word visions, "That was magic."

"Yes," Morgana answered, "When two people with similar magical ability first meet or see each other after being apart for some time their magic reaches out to each other. It is often the first magical thing that a mage ever encounters. Mages have a special purpose in this world and the Connection, as we call it, serves that purpose by identifying mages to each other and giving them some basic information about each other."

"Wait," Bran interrupted, holding up a hand and giving it a small wave. "I get the feeling that there is a lot to go over, but you said that mages have a purpose. Let's start there and go onto the … Sídhe from there."

"Very well," Morgana agreed with a nod of her head, "Magic is a defensive system of this world."

Holding out her hand, Morgana curled her fingers slightly. A moment later a burst of light appeared, twisting in strange shapes in the palm of her hand. Alex drew up slightly from the sudden display, her mind returning sharply to the whip of light that had been used to strike down the Hounds. Morgana's light grew brighter and brighter before it burst forth, long twisting lines of light filling the room above them. They moved, grew and turned around each other until they settled into the form of a large tree growing from the professor's hand with the branches spanning above them.

"There are many worlds, each different and separate with its own properties," Morgana explained softly, her voice piercing the awed silence that had taken over the room.

Merlin now raised his hand, palm down and made a small graceful gesture. Tiny orbs of soft blue light appeared on his fingertips and he waved them towards the tree. He repeated the gesture as the orbs began to settle on the branches of the tree and a few in the trunk, creating glowing points of blue amongst the golden light of the branches.

"Earth is known as the Iron Realm," Morgana continued and Merlin made another gesture that caused the highest blue light in the truck to glow brightly for the students. "This name comes from the physical nature of the planet and the iron found in the blood of many of its species, particularly the sentient dominant species and the iron core of the planet."

Morgana gave the four gaping students a pointed look, but they didn't notice. Alex carefully reached up and brushed her fingers through one of the branches. It wasn't solid, but the light made her skin glow and danced across her fingers beautifully, causing a small smile to appear on her face and the knot in her stomach to loosen slightly.

"Other worlds have different kinds of life, different manifestations of energy or different physical laws so when they collide there can be ugly side effects," Morgana finished with a slight huff that made them all look back at her sheepishly.

Next to her, she heard Bran gasp softly and mutter something about proof of the multiverse. Merlin nodded and took over the explanation smoothly, giving Alex a sense that they'd given this lecture more than a few times before, which was an idea that managed to both calm her down and give her a greater sense of dread.

"When something enters the world that should not be here, more magic is produced and imbued in humanity to fight off the alien aspects that have entered the world," Merlin explained and the blue light of Earth pulsed again before dimming and the nearest light on one of the large branches by the Earth light started to glow. "The Sídhe are not of Earth; their home world is Sídhean, one of the worlds closest to Earth in the Tree of Reality."

Nicki held up her hand, passing it through the light of the branches by accident before blushing and lowering it. "Is this Yggdrasil?" she asked with a touch of disbelief.

"No," Merlin told her, "Yggdrasil is a mythological creation strongly based on the Tree of Reality, but the reality is a bit more complicated."

"You see children," Morgana told them, ignoring a glare she received from Aiden at the word children, "These worlds are links to the greater whole of reality, but each one exists in a different dimension of reality. When creatures of one world move to another, such as the Sídhe coming to Earth, it can cause problems. Magic is produced as a defensive reaction of the Earth to the presence of something alien coming here. Mages are born to combat these outsiders in order to ensure that the natural processes of Earth continue as they should without the physical laws, different forms of life or energy having too much of an impact."

The last sentence made Alex tense even as she felt a rush of excitement. Magic was real, that was a dream coming true, but Morgana's statement rang too much of violence and destiny, making her feel ill. Next to her, she saw Bran shift uncomfortable and risked a glance to see Aiden taking everything in with the most serious expression she'd ever seen on his face. Her eyes returned to the golden branches and the soft blue lights that hung like ornaments. There were dozens of them and her eyes traced back one of the branches to the light on the trunk that was apparently her home.

"Like white blood cells," Nicki suggested with a thoughtful expression, ending the silence that had descended in the room. "Mages are the white cells to fight an infection on Earth."

"Not an inaccurate comparison," Morgana agreed with a small pleased smile. "And just as the body always has white blood cells there is always some magic in the world. Mages are born into every generation, some more powerful than others and some never discover they have magic. Other times, like now when beings from other worlds enter ours, the Earth releases more magic for the use of mages to fight back the invaders."

"So magic fluctuates," Aiden verified with a small frown. "There is a limited amount available?"

"Not in the sense of a measuring cup," Merlin assured Aiden with a chuckle. "It is always there, but when there are lower levels of magic it is harder to access and you cannot do as much with it. However, I do not believe it possible to ever run out of magic in the world."

Aiden looked more than a little relieved at that statement and his excitement started to return, renewing Alex's urge to smack him. As it was her limbs felt too heavy to move and she kept telling herself to wake up. This wasn't the sort of revelation about magic she'd dreamed about while a little girl or imagined as a part of a game with friends. This talk of defending Earth and being born to be a mage was quickly dampening the thrill of magic and the beauty of the magical sculpture that filled the room.

"So, all of us are mages," Bran questioned slowly, "Four of us? Is that a lot in one place? I'm afraid I'm not sure of how to take this." Alex thought he sounded far too reasonable.

"Four mages is a large number," Merlin agreed with a nod to Bran. "There are usually very few of us at any one time. I believe the most I ever saw at one time was in India near the end of the Vedic period," he told them with a quick glance over at Morgana.

"Roughly 300 B.C.E.," Morgana supplied before taking another sip of her tea. "And there were seven mages then including us."

"But why Ravenslake?" Alex asked suddenly, crossing her arms. "Why Oregon?"

"Why not?" Morgana countered with a small shrug. "Magic is focusing here because this is where the greatest threat currently is. The Sídhe have managed after nearly three thousand years to build a new route into our world and it is near here." She looked at each of the four students carefully, "All of you were drawn here by the magic you were born with. Magic seeks magic and tries to connect in order to become stronger."

"So we're all there is?" Nicki questioned in a soft and astounded voice. "All the mages on Earth are in this room."

"Most likely," Merlin replied with a nod. "But there may still be a few more scattered out across the Earth. Usually in our experience when the Earth is reacting to a threat, it releases magic to create mages close to the problem." He chuckled and smiled more widely at their expressions, "After all why grant magic to those who are in the wrong place to use it."

"Alright," Alex interrupted with a frantic wave of her hand. "Let's say that magic is real and we're mages," she said the last word with some difficultly as her eyes darted up to the glowing tree. "What does it mean for us? What does it mean right now?"

Morgana actually nodded in slight approval to Alex's question. "I'm afraid that you don't have many options," Morgana told them. "You were born as mages in order to fight invasions into this world and nothing will change that. We will teach you to access and control magic and fight the Sídhe."

"What if we don't want to?" Alex asked, crossing her arms across her chest. "We can't even legally drink!"

"The Sídhe have many more Hounds," Morgana informed her with a raised eyebrow.

Morgana raised her hand again and the tree's magical form suddenly vaporized and all the light rushed back into Morgana's palm. The female mage gripped the glowing orb and smashed it in her fist, keeping her eyes on Alex before opening her palm to show her what looked like golden glitter. The particles swirled up from her hand and began to take on tiny shapes of humans, hounds, and mounted figures. Alex watched as many of the humanoid figures were attacked both by the Hounds and the mounted figures. Their light flickered and vanished and Alex flinched as the sounds of metal crashing on metal, screams and cruel laughter echoed in her head.

"They won't care that you don't wish to fight them. It will be enough that you have the power to," Morgana said seriously. "They will not leave you alone."

"Iron is one of the only things that the Sídhe fear and that can truly kill them when they are in our world," Merlin intervened with a quick glance at Morgana. "At the dawn of the Iron Age we had a war with them that sealed them out of Earth for 2,800 years, but our original protections are falling and the change of technology away from iron means that it is now easier for them to return. These Hounds were a test," Merlin told them seriously. "They will send more and they will find a world poorly prepared to face them."

"Come on," Bran argued suddenly, "Bullets and tanks! They could be stopped."

"They have their own form of magic," Morgana informed them, "Like us they can manipulate the world around them and they have the power to impact our world. I'm afraid that the metal of tanks would soon be crushed, missiles would be turned back and bullets would simply be vaporized." As she spoke the glowing particles in the air formed the various shapes she described and the fates of them. A glowing tank was twisted in on itself, a missile made a sharp turn in the air and the bullets just faded away.

"Strangely the more advanced that humanity becomes the harder these fights become if for no reason other than there is more that they can use against us," Morgana observed with a small sigh.

"So what do you suggest?" Aiden asked her as his eyes darted between Morgana and the fading light of her magical demonstration, "Swords and shields?"

"They won the first war," Merlin told Aiden with a small shake of his head. "But no, our suggestion is to learn how to control your magic. That is the starting point and we should have some time before the full force of Sídhe can enter the Earth. Their weakness to iron means that they have to use a complex magical process to survive in our world."

"Then why do they want Earth?" Nicki asked quickly.

"Power," Merlin answered with a sigh, "Sídhe politics are much more vicious than anything that exists on Earth. Our world would give them slaves, resources and access to more worlds. Sadly, Earth also links to more worlds than any other world in the whole Tree of Reality; from here they could launch a large-scale invasion of many other worlds."

"They're evil then," Nicki confirmed with a slight shudder.

"Not evil," Morgana replied with a dark look passing over her features, "Evil suggests a decision to be cruel and hurt others: the Sídhe simply don't care and don't think that anything else has value. A human can be evil, but people, in general, are not. With the Sídhe… they just honestly believe that their desires matter most in all of creation, no matter who it harms."

"And that's worse?" Alex asked with a frown.

"I've lived through some of the greatest acts of evil in history," Morgana said in an emotionless tone, "Genocides, wars, and torture. I've seen slavery, rape, and murders, but I still know that what the Sídhe could do to humanity and Earth would be far worse than anything we have ever done to each other."

"So not fairy tale creatures," Nicki joked only to swallow, looking a little ill.

"No," Morgana agreed with a shake of her head. "This is no fairy tale. I'm afraid that your best chance to survive to accept our training. Once you are trained, you will have enough power to be able to make a choice, but until then you are victims of destiny."

"That's it?" Bran questioned with a panicked expression. "Train or die?! We're just kids!"

"Not to us," Merlin told them as he stood up. "In the land of our birth, you are adults." A sad look passed over his face. "We had hoped that the Sídhe would not break through so soon, but that was not to be."

Exchanging one more look with Morgana, Merlin strode towards the door, collecting a brown trench coat from the hook beside it. Slipping it on, he gestured for them to follow him. "I will see you back to the dormitories tonight. It's late and you are undoubtedly feeling overwhelmed."

"Each of you take a jack-o-lantern," Morgana instructed from her desk. "I will provide you with the details as soon as we arrange a space for lessons."

No one moved from their spots until Morgana gave a small cough that clearly carried a note of her impatience. Stepping forward, Aiden collected a small jack-o-lantern from her desk. Alex and Nicki each grabbed ones from the shelf and Bran picked up the smallest one on a table by the doorway. Nodding in satisfaction, Merlin opened the door and said a few more words to Morgana in the strange language they had used earlier. As they went out the doorway to head for the dorms, Alex looked back over her shoulder at Professor Cornwall, only to find her already grading homework with her red pen.

14

Sahmain Ends

No one spoke as Yates or rather Merlin escorted them across the campus from the Hamilton Building towards the dormitories. Everything was still and quiet with no sounds of traffic or students. The moon had set, making the campus even darker than before and much more menacing. Ahead of them, Merlin was humming softly with his hands in his pockets. Alex tried to draw comfort from how calm he was but found she couldn't manage that feat.

A soft sigh of relief escaped Alex as they approached Michaels Hall with its bright exterior lights shining down on the lawn and parking lot. Nicki kept moving her light onto every car and truck that they passed in the parking lot and Alex realized with a twist of fear that something could be waiting. Whistling now, Merlin seemed oblivious to the fear in the students behind him. He stopped just in front of the largest entrance to Michaels Hall and turned back to them.

"I am sorry," he told them kindly, "Morgana and I assumed that the Sídhe would focus on us and not go after other mages." Merlin nodded to the jack-o-lanterns that each of them was carrying, "Samhain ends at sunrise and the Sídhe won't have as much power to cross into our world. Even so, I will make you some iron weapons before we start your magic lessons."

Alex opened her mouth to point out that she didn't live in Michaels Hall, but Merlin turned and walked into the darkness. The words died on her tongue and she swayed slightly on her feet from exhaustion. Aiden caught her arm gently and looked over at Nicki who was digging out her key to the building. Bran stepped up next to Alex and looked towards the Hatfield building. The lights stretched a far distance over the lawn, but Alex's stomach turned at the dark void between the lights from Hatfield and Michaels. Glancing over at Bran, she swallowed as she felt herself becoming physically ill. It definitely wasn't sunrise yet and the jack-o-lantern in her hand didn't feel like much of a protection.

"Come on!" Nicki hissed from the doorway where she was holding open the door of the building and glancing about with a frantic expression, her nails digging into the skin of the pumpkin. "I'm not staying outside."

Realizing that she didn't have to walk through the dark, Alex gratefully pulled away from Aiden and darted up the stairs. Aiden and Bran were right behind her, closing the front door with a solid clunk behind them. Everyone jumped at the sound and Nicki let out a nervous giggle before motioning everyone towards the elevator. The doors opened with a ding, but Nicki stayed still just looking into the small space. Alex swallowed as she realized the thought that Nicki must have had. Without a word, they all headed for the stairs, letting Nicki lead them up to the fourth floor.

The floor was quiet, with only a few stray sounds from the occasional doorway like music or snoring. Reaching a doorway in the middle of the hall, Nicki pulled out her key and unlocked it after handing her jack-o-lantern to Aiden. Easing open the door, Nicki snatched the small pumpkin back and shoved it into the room, waiting for a moment for any reaction. She poked her head into the room and hit the light switch with a sigh of relief. They piled into the room and Nicki turned on a lamp and placed her jack-o-lantern on the window sill. Alex took in the room, only half of it was occupied with the right half being devoid of any personal belongings.

"No roommate?" Alex asked before she really thought about the question.

"Not anymore," Nicki replied as she sank into the desk chair and kicked off her heels with a grateful sound. "My original roommate wasn't comfortable living with me and requested a different room."

"Oh," Alex responded before she sat down on the empty bed on the right side of the room.

Alex carefully placed her jack-o-lantern on the desk next to her. The basket still slung over her elbow knocked into her side and Alex finally remembered that she had it. Shaking her head slightly, she put it down at her feet by her dirty silver heels. Bran sat down next to her, releasing a soft groan before he rubbed his leg with gritted teeth. Aiden locked the door behind them and leaned against it, taking in a long breath. Frowning, Nicki reached for a bottle on her desk, grabbed a bottle of water sitting on top of the small fridge and handed them to Bran. He took the painkillers with a grateful smile and took two without a word.

"So," Aiden said slowly from the doorway. "Is the plan just to camp out until sunrise?"

"I don't think there was really a plan," Nicki admitted with a glance at Alex. "I'll admit I'm glad to not be alone."

"Yeah," Alex agreed with a quick nod. She reached out and loosened her shoes, but hesitated to take them off in case something else happened.

Nicki huffed and tried to adjust her Halloween gown before she gave up and climbed from her chair again. Stalking over to her dresser, Nicki pulled out some spare clothing and ordered Aiden and Bran not to look while she changed. To Alex's surprise, Nicki tossed her a t-shirt and pair of drawstring sweats to change into. Deciding not to argue, Alex tried not to show any embarrassment as she changed out of her checkered dress and into Nicki's clothes while the boys kept their backs turned. The pants were short on Alex as she was a few inches taller than Nicki, but they were serviceable and the t-shirt was large, probably used for sleeping and hung comfortably on her frame. A simple as it was, changing clothing helped Alex relax and start processing what had happened.

They all settled into the room, Bran leaning back on the empty bed with a pillow behind his back that Nicki had given him and his legs stretched out. He'd removed the brace from his right leg but had his cane leaning on the dresser right beside him. Deciding to give him room, Alex sat in the chair in front of the empty desk, pulling it out so she was seated next to Aiden who'd taken over Nicki's desk chair when Nicki had climbed onto her bed. Jack-o-lanterns had been strategically placed around the room, their flickering candles casting strange shadows on the walls that didn't help to put anyone at ease.

"Okay," Alex spoke up, unable to bear the tense silence. "Any clue where to start?"

"Magic is real," Aiden offered, failing to hide the fear in his eyes. "And it has some ugly strings attached."

"Figures," Nicki grumbled, "It couldn't be like in the stories now could it and of course fairies are evil."

There was weak laughter in the room that faded away awkwardly. Shifting in the desk chair, Alex looked around at the three other apparent mages in the room. She didn't think that any of them had ever met Arthur but decided that it couldn't hurt to ask.

"Have any of you had a …. Connection," she asked, remembering the word they had used after a moment, "With anyone else?"

Bran frowned in confusion and Aiden tilted his head slightly as he considered the question. Shaking her head, Nicki reached into her fridge and pulled out a pitcher of water before grabbing a couple of glasses from a high shelf over her desk.

"I guess not," Alex sighed in response to their silence. "There's this guy, Arthur Pendred and when I first met him… I saw a fire and heard I don't know maybe charcoal burning and there was this weird ringing noise like metal being struck. It was a lot like what happened with you guys except-" Alex cut herself off before she said: it didn't scare me.

Raising an eyebrow and giving her a knowing smirk, Nicki handed Alex a glass of water which she took gratefully. Aiden looked thoughtful and Bran just shrugged.

"Strange that Merlin and Morgana didn't identify him if he is a mage," Aiden murmured. "Don't you think?"

"Maybe they've never met him," Nicki suggested as she retook her seat. "We all have a class with at least one of them."

"I don't think Arthur is in any of their classes," Alex replied with a shrug. "But when we first met it really felt like a Connection."

"Maybe it was a different kind of connection," Nicki ventured with a smile.

Shooting her a quick glare, Alex tried to be irritated, but honestly, the bit of humor felt awfully good at that moment.

She shook her head quickly when Aiden and Bran looked over at her.

"Maybe you're wrong," Bran told her. "It might have been a smell trigger or something."

"Or maybe they just don't know about him," Aiden added with a quick nod to Alex. "We'll have to mention it when they contact us about magic lessons." He blinked and snorted, shaking his head. "That's gonna take some getting used to."

"There was a time when you have jumped at the idea," Nicki reminded him with a soft wistful smile. "Wasn't that long ago."

"And you were right there with me," Aiden replied with an equally warm smile towards Nicki.

Alex smiled as she observed the moment. It made her miss her brothers with a fierce pang in her chest that made her eyes tear up. She blinked to stop them, afraid that if she let herself start now she wouldn't be able to stop.

"So?" Aiden asked, turning back towards them. "As you may have noticed Nicki and I are major geeks and fans of fantasy. We've always wanted magic to real," he shrugged, "Be careful what you wish for and all that. Apparently, Alex had a potentially magical experience before we met each other. Has there been anything else?"

"Me," Bran answered, his head lowered slightly as the others turned to look at him. "I've always had a … sense of what to do to make things turn out alright for me," he told them softly. "Just little things like where misplaced items were, what route to take to avoid problems, standardized test guesses, that sort of thing." His hands shook slightly and he reached over to grip his cane like a lifeline, still not looking up from the floor.

"When I was fifteen my mom and I were hit by a drunk driver, that's how this happened to my leg," he explained gesturing to them. "The thing is that while I was in the car I… saw what was going to happen. I grabbed the steering wheel from my mom and jerked us mostly out of the way. The other car just hit my side and not badly enough to kill me. I think… I think if I hadn't had that vision my Mom and I would have died."

Swallowing, Alex looked over at Aiden and Nicki for some guidance, but both of them looked as lost as she felt. Alex looked back at Bran who was still clutching his cane and looking at the floor with a completely blank expression.

"Then magic is good," Alex announced trying to sound more confident than she felt and ignoring the tightening in her throat. "Maybe the source isn't what we all imagined and wanted as children. Maybe it is born from bad things happening, but maybe at the core of what it is, it really is good."

She risked a glance at Nicki and Aiden only to find them both smiling gently at her before they turned their attention to Bran. He shifted on his cane, leaning forward off of the bed to look at them. Giving Alex a small nod, he looked to Aiden and smiled.

"Well," Aiden sighed, "I guess then we'll have to worry about magic lessons."

"And learning to use iron weapons," Nicki added before looking at Aiden. "I think I owe your dad a huge thank you for letting me learn to fence with you."

"I don't think this was something he imagined," Aiden told her before looking over at Alex.

Shrugging, Alex said, "I guess all we can do is wait and see."

Nicki's stomach growled suddenly and she blushed before jumping to her feet. She pulled a box off one of her shelves and pulled out a couple of bags of popcorn.

"I can't offer you anything special without leaving the room," she told them as she opened the microwave, "But I can at least take the edge off."

The next hour and a half was passed with lots of questions about families, favorite books, reasons for majors and anything else that someone could think of to pass the time. It was clear that everyone was tired, but unwilling to sleep until the night ended and the sun rose. Two of the jack-o-lanterns had completely burned out with the last two nearing the end of their wicks when the first bit of sunlight poured into the room through the window.

Jumping to her feet, Nicki pulled the curtains open all the way and grinned as she looked towards the east. Alex quickly followed her to the window to look out at the reddish clouds glowing just over the horizon. Relief made Alex's legs shake softly and she quickly sat back down, turning her chair towards the sunrise.

"Good morning everyone," Nicki cheered with a beaming smile.

They gave it another twenty minutes before the need to sleep finally scattered the group, now armed with each other's phone numbers in case of emergency. Nicki promised to call her grandmother and see if she had any ideas for where they could get some iron horseshoes this weekend instead of waiting for Merlin's iron weapons.

Despite the sun beginning to shine across the campus, Alex and Bran moved across the lawn swiftly. Bran kept looking around even as he walked across the lawn while Alex made sure that she didn't rush ahead of him in spite of her own desire to return home and sleep. Pulling out her card key, Alex quickly unlocked the main door Hatfield and held it open for Bran.

"Thanks," Bran told her shifting on his cane. "I'm afraid the running last night is something I'm going to feel for several days."

"Will you be alright?" Alex questioned with a worried frown.

"Some sleep and pain killers will help for today and I'll be seeing my physical therapist on Tuesday," he assured her with a smile. "You get some sleep," he chuckled and looked down at the slippers she was still wearing. "And don't forget to return Nicki's clothes."

Alex watched Bran turn away and head down the corridor to his first-floor room for a moment. Once again, she decided against the elevator and climbed the stairs to the third floor. Already people were moving about and talking in the corridor, but everyone seemed to be keeping the noise level reasonable. Reaching her doorway, Alex unlocked the door with a strong sense of relief and stumbled inside, locking it behind her. She dropped the basket with her stuff on the floor and used her foot to shove it over by her dresser. Striding towards her bed, Alex kicked off the slippers and debated changing clothes. She decided it was too much work and collapsed into her bed. Alex snuggled into her pillow and clutched Galahad to her chest as she turned on her side. Inhaling the soft scent of the stuffed animal, Alex gratefully held Galahad to her face.

Her exhaustion faded slightly as the pure relief of being back in a familiar environment returned. Galahad shuddered in her arms as Alex's entire body began to shake from her conflicted emotions. Shoving her face into the stuffed toy, Alex wished he was a lot bigger. It took her a moment to recognize that she was crying softly, but she couldn't really understand why. Those Hounds tried to kill her, but she'd met Merlin and Morgana le Fey. Magic was real and she was going to learn, but it came at a price and terrible evil creatures were trying to take over Earth. Biting her lip, Alex stopped a hysterical laugh from escaping her and thought for a stray moment that she was grateful the breakdown was happening in private. Opening her eyes, she looked across the room to where she assumed Jenny was still asleep.

There was no one there. Frowning, Alex welcomed the distraction and looked around the room for signs of her roommate. Jenny's outfit from earlier on Friday was still draped across the bed and her shoes were on the floor. Her eyeliner and the magnification mirror she had used to do her Cleopatra look were on the desk where she had left them. There was no sign that Jenny had returned home at all. Worry replaced the mixture of terror, relief, and sorrow that has been churning in Alex's stomach. What if she was right about Arthur and he was a mage too? What if the Hounds had also attacked Arthur and Jenny was with him?

She sat up and crawled across her bed to reach for the basket that contained her cell phone. Suddenly the door opened and Jenny stumbled into the room, out of breath and a mess. Her dress was wrinkled and her makeup badly smudged. Alex nearly leapt off the bed to hug her roommate, but Jenny's sudden stop when she spotted Alex derailed the action.

"Alex?!" Jenny gasped, "Uh hi!"

"Hi," Alex returned with a confused expression. "Are you only just getting back?"

"Yeah, uh we… oh god!" Jenny exclaimed with a horrified expression. "Oh, honey I'm so sorry. Lance got distracted and …."

"It's okay," Alex assured her quickly, her entire body relaxing and the exhaustion returning. "I just got back… I met up with some other friends and lost track of time." Alex waved the phone she'd just retrieved. "I was about to call to make sure you were okay," she confessed.

Jenny shifted on her feet, looking oddly nervous before she moved to her bed and pulled the shoes off. Smiling at Alex, Jenny said, "I'm fine. I'm sorry about you not getting a ride. I'll make it up to you." Jenny stood up and grabbed her toiletries. "I'm going to clean up and get some sleep."

Alex blinked as her roommate all but rushed out of the room. She wondered if something had happened, but her eyelids were feeling extra heavy from her earlier crying. Instead of pondering Jenny's behavior further, Alex lay back down and curled under her comforter. Softly exhaling, she held Galahad to her chest, hoping that her childish belief of him repelling bad things was true.

15

Light in a Childe's Hand

824 B.C.E. The Sídhean

The long network of tunnels was all she had ever known. Each tunnel was circular in shape with smooth polished stonework that shimmered in the orbs of light that floated every three feet above her head. Sídhe magic rippled across the white stone, creating images of their home realm in beautiful soft colors. As she turned into another tunnel, a scene from a Sídhe story played out beside her on the wall with a glittering palace crafted out of mist rising above a rich violet forest and three riders with their Hounds rushing towards it. When she was younger she would have stopped to watch the images despite the summons, but now she had learned better and walked past with only a glance.

Ahead of her, a tall Síd woman with long white hair that shimmered in the lights was striding quickly down the hall. The train of her light blue robe trailed behind her and the girl was careful not to step on it. Her eyes went to the woman's pale hand where a scroll was clutched tightly. The lady's white gloves were accented with golden fingernail covers that were digging into the parchment, the only sign of her aggravation which only made the girl following her more nervous.

Moving quickly, they passed a circular doorway that led into a series of large rooms. Several young children looked at her curiously; one even looked out into the hallway to watch her as she approached the end of the tunnel network. Directly in front of her was a massive golden circular door engraved with interwoven curling designs. Two guards stood before the doorway, one on each side of it; she only recognized one of them. They towered over the girl as she moved closer to them, their violet eyes narrowing at the sight of her. Each was dressed in elaborate golden armor decorated with designs like the one on the doorway and armed with a sword. The one on the right outranked the other, indicated by the golden decorations on his gray horns that rose above his white braids and was unknown to the girl.

The woman stopped and gestured for the girl to go forward. Taking a few tentative steps towards the doors, the girl stopped and dropped to her knees, lowering her head down low with her hands placed flat on the floor. One of the guards stepped forward, but she did not look up at them. The Síd stepped on her hand, but she kept in the cry of pain. He chuckled and moved off her hand before placing the tip of his boot beneath her chin, pulling her face up.

"Aren't you a pretty one," he observed with a slow smile as his eyes traced her features. It was the higher ranking Síd so she did her best to stay very still. "Your name." She remained silent and the Síd's smile widened. "You may speak."

"I am called Morgana," she answered softly, keeping her green eyes lowered respectfully.

"And your age?" the Síd asked, reaching a gloved hand with golden coverings over his claw-like fingernails down to brush a strand of her long dark brown hair. The claw touched the skin of her cheek.

"I am six years of age," she told him, fighting down a rising sense of fear and dread. "In the care of the Lady Eolande," Morgana added hoping he would stop touching her and let her pass.

"Not yet seven then," the Sídhe guard sighed, "Your sort grow up so quickly and yet not quickly enough." He dropped his hand away from her face and took a step back. Now he turned his attention to the woman waiting in the corridor. "Is there an arrangement for this one yet?"

"There is not," the Síd woman behind her answered calmly.

"Then I shall be speaking with you," the guard told her with a smile. "I like ones who don't show pain easily." Morgana heard him move back to the doorway.

The second guard did not look down at Morgana and in a bored voice asked, "State your business here with the earth childe Lady Eolande."

Behind Morgana, Lady Eolande moved forward, her gown brushing Morgana as she passed her. Holding out the scroll, Lady Eolande announced, "This iron childe has been summoned to appear before Her Majesty. I brought her here immediately."

The guard accepted the scroll and read it quickly before he gave his superior a nod. Then, moving in synch, each guard gripped the large golden rings on each half of the door and pulled the golden doors open. Morgana looked up, unable to contain her curiosity as the space beyond the doors was revealed to her for the first time.

Beyond the golden doors that marked the end of the brightly lit white tunnels that she had known all of her life was a dark space. Gasping softly, Morgana scooted away from the door drawing a laugh from the guard with the golden decorations on his horns. Stepping away from the doors, he grabbed Morgana's arm and hauled her to her feet.

"Easy pretty one," he cooed as he dragged her towards the darkness. "You have the honor of entering the Crossing: where our realms meet and the Queen rules all."

Frightened even more by the darkness, Morgana tried to pull away. The guards both laughed and the one holding her wrapped his hand around her throat forcing her to be still. Leaning over her from behind her back, he put his lips next to her ear and whispered, "Not often your kind goes so close to Sídhean. I do hope you come back pretty one; it's been too long since I had the thrill of an iron childe. Just remember your place."

Picking her up roughly, he tossed her through the doorway and into the dark space. Her knees collided with a black floor painfully and she looked back just in time to see the heavy golden double doors closing. Darkness surrounded her and Morgana dared not move. There was always light and always someone nearby, if not Lady Eolande then one of the Sídhe assigned to educate her and the other iron children. Now there was no light and she was alone. Darkness and silence. Two words she'd heard of, but never understood. Now she did and they weighed on her, compressing her chest and locking her into her own mind with fear.

Morgana gripped her arms to reassure herself that she was still there in the darkness and not fading away into the nothingness that surrounded her. A cold chill began to creep over her skin, the white tunic dress she wore offering almost no protection. Curling into herself, Morgana closed her eyes and tried to calm down, but there was no glow of light on her eyes as there had always been. There was no soft chatter from the other iron children, no soft snores or breathing. Nothing.

A whimper escaped her, a sound she had been taught long ago to never make. Fear was consuming her and tears pricked at her eyes. Had she caused trouble? Lady Eolande had not seem displeased with her; in fact, her caretaker had been unusually attentive. Perhaps it was just a ruse, a trick and she'd been brought here to this horrible darkness as a punishment for some crime. She was going to fade away, she just knew it. What other fate could await her in such darkness?

A spark of anger ignited in her. She'd always been so good! She did what she was told, never cried, tried not to show her human emotions and always tried to please the Sídhe! How could they let her fade away into nothing? Maybe this was a test before she turned seven and her duty to the Sídhe was selected. Biting her lip, Morgana reached for the pain that told her that she was still there. She wanted light! She didn't know how to pass this test without it, but if it was a test then there had to be a way.

Morgana's eyelids suddenly brightened and her eyes snapped open to find a small orb of light glowing in her palm. It was a small orb like the ones that dominated the halls of her home. She stared at the softly glowing ball of light in her hand with a sense of relief, awe and confusion, unsure of where it had come from.

Then there was a musical laugh that echoed in whatever strange space she was in. Morgana could still not see and strained her eyes trying to peer beyond the reaches of the light. The orb glowed more brightly, illuminating the smoothly tiled floor all around her, the carved pillars inlaid with gold that lined the space leading up to a crowd of Sídhe who were all watching her. Morgana quickly lowered her head but was at a loss of what to do with the light.

"How precious," a high female voice cooed. "Just look at my little mage."

Morgana dared not look up even at the sweetness of the voice, far too used to such tricks being used on her in the past to test her behavior. There was the gentle swish of fabric moving and soft footfalls ahead of her as the Síd moved gracefully through the space. Around her, the hall brightened even as the light in her palm dimmed. A sense of exhaustion seeped through Morgana as the light flickered away.

"So precious," the female voice breathed, right in front of Morgana. Even with her lowered head, she could see a pair of blue slippers with elaborate golden embroidery. "My own little iron mage," she cooed once again. "Morgana," she called gently, "Look at me my little darling."

A command. One that chilled Morgana. The voice was too soft and gentle; even when they were ill Lady Eolande never spoke like that. She'd only ever heard such a tone from Brodie, a simple-minded girl who had looked after her years ago until the Sídhe decided to euthanize her. Slowly and carefully, Morgana raised her chin, waiting for a smack or another sign of displeasure.

Her eyes met a pair of large brilliant purple eyes with violet and black color around them making them stand out against her pale skin. Elegant features looked down at her, relaxed in a calm and pleased expression. Her lips, painted a dark shade of red, curled into a smile. Morgana stared in awe at the Síd before her who seemed taller than the others she had met and whose clothing nearly glowed with magic interwoven with the golden fabric of her gown and the white thick cape that hung over her shoulders. The strange woman's pale hair was woven around a tall golden crown with a glowing violet gem. Strangest to Morgana was that the woman wore no gloves: her long pale fingers with her long arcing claws at the tips were fully visible without decorative covers.

"Oh, how obedient she is," the woman praised and Morgana heard low voices all around them but dared not look away from the woman. "Eolande has trained you so well."

The woman turned from Morgana and she found herself watching the flowing white cape as the woman strode across the hall. The return of light meant that Morgana could now see that she was in a vast hall, filled with carved pillars and statues of the Sídhe. Long streamers decorated the arched ceiling, stretching from one side to another and accented by small orbs of light and jewels. Gold accented everything, even the tiles that Morgana remained kneeling on. But the centerpiece of the room was the throne, a solid golden chair on a raised dais at the far side of the hall with a white and golden cloth draped artistically over the arms. It was here that the strange Sídhe woman stopped, turning and lowered herself regally into the throne.

"Morgana, my childe," the woman spoke, her words echoing in the great space, "I am Queen Scáthbás, the liege lady of the Sídhe."

Morgana swallowed, she'd known of course that she was to appear before the Queen. Lady Eolande had told her that as soon as she had read the message, but there had been no time to think, no time for her to properly explain what it meant to Morgana. Now, Morgana could feel the weight of the moment, almost taste it in the air which was much sweeter than what she had always known and hear it in the hall which dwarfed the tunnels she'd grown up in. Her Majesty was watching her with fond amusement as Morgana tried to understand how she was supposed to react. Chuckling, Queen Scáthbás lounged in her throne and gestured a bare hand towards Morgana.

"Just look at her," Queen Scáthbás announced, "We take a child to serve us and find that we have one of the Iron Realm's mages!"

Laughter rippled throughout the room and Morgana frowned. The word mage was unknown to her, but it sounded a bit like magic, a force she knew only the Sídhe to possess. Unsure of herself, Morgana remained silent. Her eyes traced the crowd quickly, taking in the abundance of gold on their clothing and jewelry. Their clothing was more complex than the robes wore by the caretakers, but not like the armor worn by the guards. This was something completely new and like the stories that played out on the walls of the tunnels, but Morgana didn't understand which story this was. Slowly, the laughter died down and Queen Scáthbás studied Morgana intently before shaking her head.

"Oh, my poor little childe doesn't understand." Scáthbás motioned Morgana forward with a graceful movement of her hand, one of the long claws beckoning. "Stand up and come closer to me."

Standing up on shaking feet, her knees aching from her earlier collision with the floor, Morgana took a few steps forward. The Sídhe drew back from her, clearing a side path for her towards the throne. Whispers filled the space as they pointed and peered at her, turning into a blur of colors and purple eyes as she forced herself to keep moving towards the enthroned figure.

Morgana reached the steps of the dais and dropped back to her knees, setting her hands on the floor and leaning forward to hide her face once again. Strands of her long dark hair fell forward, pooling on the tiled floor in front of her. The whispers lessened and silence consumed the hall as everyone waited, including Morgana to see what would happen next. Then a few whispers started once again as Morgana heard the golden fabric of the Queen's robe shift. Soft delicate footfalls reached her ears and she sucked in a breath as Queen Scáthbás came closer and closer to her. No one moved and the whispers stopped as the Queen stood directly in front to Morgana.

She was so close; Morgana could feel power radiating off of the woman, so much stronger than anything she'd even felt from Lady Eolande or the other caretakers. Her palms were sweaty and she kept swallowing as her heart beat faster and faster, uncertain of what was going to happen and feeling almost more afraid than she had alone in the darkness.

Then a hand settled on the back of her head, stroking her hair gently. There was a collective gasp of shock from around the room and Morgana felt herself stop breathing. A brush of bare cool skin against her temple told her exactly why all the Sídhe had gasped: the Queen was touching her without gloves. Tears pricked at Morgana's eyes as the gentle gesture continued. No Síd ever touched a human without gloves except those who wished the thrill of the danger and she'd always heard whispers of them from the older children, the ones who hid in the corners before they were dragged away and handed to the Síd who had selected them. Only the other iron children had ever touched her skin.

Morgana trembled, her limbs shaking as tears welled in her eyes. Biting her lip, she sought to stay silent and contain the shudders of her body. Queen Scáthbás made a soft cooing sound that resonated in the silence of the hall.

"That's a good girl," Queen Scáthbás praised, "It's alright my precious one. You belong to me now. You have magic all your own Morgana and you will do great things with it."

A bare hand moved from her hand and traced gently down her cheek. Turning into the touch on instinct, Morgana sighed in delight when the hand paused to cup her cheek, a thumb carefully brushing away a tear. Tugging gently, the Queen's hand pulled up Morgan's chin and made the young girl look up at her.

"I don't understand," Morgana whispered as her green eyes met Queen Scáthbás' purple ones.

"You don't do you," the Queen replied with a small smile. "My sweet Morgana, seven days ago the magic weaver who serves in the Iron Realm keeping the tunnels lit grew ill and weak. As the lights dimmed, you were already asleep, but even in your dreams you sent forth your magic and made light in the sleeping quarters, making a small orb like the one you made today. Eolande informed me and I knew at once that you might be a mage. A simple test was all I needed to be certain," Queen Scáthbás smiled broadly at her. "And you passed it so perfectly."

"I have magic?" Morgana breathed in awe. Sídhe had magic, all of them carried at least some magic, but iron children like her had no magic.

"It is rare in your primitive poisonous kind," Queen Scáthbás agreed. "But in truly precious children such a beautiful gift may be found." The Queen smiled gently again and brushed a strand of Morgana's hair from her face, brushing the back of her finger over Morgana's forehead. "You'll use that gift to help me will you not my beautiful girl?" Queen Scáthbás asked as she gently cupped Morgana's cheek once again.

Morgana's eyes widened and she tried to speak but felt too overcome to form the words. The fear of her seventh year faded into nothing, the fear of the terrible touches of the guard ceased to be and the fear of the unknown fate that awaited her vanished. After so long, it all felt too good, too wonderful to be true and yet her mind could not have imagined such gentle touches from a Sídhe. A tear rolled down her cheek and she managed a tiny nod.

"Lovely my precious," Queen Scáthbás sighed happily. "You belong to me and no other now, none shall ever mistreat you." Morgana soaked up the promises with a blissful expression. She gasped as the Queen leaned down and pressed a kiss to her forehead. "Yes," the Queen cooed, "My little iron mage will serve me well. We shall bring all of your poor iron cursed kind into our light."

"Yes," Morgana cried softly, promised as the gentle caresses continued. "I'll do whatever you need me to do."

16

The Triskele

There was something very unsettling to Alex about walking through the side door of the Kittell Building Monday evening. Only a few days earlier she had been running around this building with the others to escape Sídhe hounds and the memory of their terrible echoing howls made her shiver. Most of Saturday had been spent sleeping, tossing with dreams of the long tunnels and strange music and nightmares of the Hounds lunging towards her. Alex's conversation with her family had been brief with her delivering one-word answers to questions before begging off early with the excuse that she was still sleepy from staying out too late on Halloween.

Despite the urge to tell her family everything, Alex had no idea of where to start with the explanation. Not to mention she had no idea of what would happen if she did tell them. When she opened an email from Professor Yates or Merlin, a falling sensation had overtaken her as Monday night was announced as their first magic class. Fear was mixed with excitement and awe as she realized that this was happening and she was actually going to learn how to use magic.

The surrealism of just getting up and going on with her life on Sunday as if something life changing hadn't occurred had thrown Alex off balance. In the books she'd read, Alex had always struggled to believe that people could just go on like nothing had happened. Now the realization that it was all she knew how to do was educating her first hand of just how true that storyline could be.

As she descended to the basement of the Kittell building where Yates and Cornwall had arranged to teach them, Alex jumped as someone approached her from behind. She relaxed when she turned to see Aiden smiling sheepishly at her, his book bag hanging over his shoulder. Alex smiled weakly at him; at least she hadn't been the only one to bring note taking materials.

"Hi," Aiden greeted as they fell into step next to each other upon reaching the bottom of the stairs. "Good fencing practice last night, sorry we didn't have a chance to talk."

"That's okay," Alex replied softly. "I didn't feel like talking anyway."

"I know what you mean," Aiden confessed as they walked towards an open door with the lights on. "All weekend I found myself trying to tell my family or talk to Nicki, but nothing would come out."

"You wanted to tell your family?" Alex asked with a surprised expression. "I thought about it, but never tried to…"

"We're close," Aiden explained with a small shrug. "And you may have noticed that I'm a bit of a geek: I get that from them. They'd probably believe me if I told them, but then they'd have to worry and I just… I don't know…" he trailed off and they fell silent.

It wasn't difficult to find the right room, only one door was open in the hallway with a light on. Without a word, both Aiden and Alex stopped just before they reached it, remaining silent and waiting for the other to take the first step into the room.

"Honestly!" Nicki's voice called behind them, "You cowards!"

The redhead strode past them, her own patchwork bag over her shoulder. Despite her words, Nicki slowed down for a moment before straightening her shoulders and stepping into the room. Exchanging a glance, Alex and Aiden followed her into the room.

It was a decent sized lecture hall with three different floor levels for desks. Tonight, however, the regular wooden desk and chair combinations were stacked at the back of the room with only four desks placed on the middle floor level, spaced out evenly. The lights at the back of the room were off with only the lights right above the teacher's desk and above their desks turned on. Despite the size of the room, it gave Alex the impression of an interrogation chamber.

Morgana and Merlin were waiting, dressed in their usual attire except that Yates had removed his jacket and had his sleeves rolled up. Sitting at the professor's desk and grading papers was Morgana, who looked up at them and gestured them towards the desks. Bran was already seated closest to the door, his cane leaning against the back of the chair. As he walked past, Aiden and Bran gave each other quick fist bumps. Nicki sat down next to Bran, Aiden next to her which left Alex furthest from the door. Everyone took their seats, pulled out their things nervously, unsure of what they needed for the lesson.

"Morgana," Merlin called, turning towards his counterpart.

Holding up a finger, Morgana did not look up from the paper she was grading. "We instructed them that we would start at seven, they are early."

Shaking his head slightly, Merlin chuckled and gave the waiting students a small shrug. Alex risked a glance over at Aiden who offered her a tiny smile before she looked back at Morgana. Professor Cornwall seemed completely calm, maybe even a little bored while Professor Yates looked excited and pleased to have them gathered together. His eyes met Alex's and he gave her a quick wink before looking up at the clock. Walking over to the doorway of the classroom, Merlin shut it and then raised his hand. Alex watched curiously as a soft blue haze covered the doorway, settling on the wood and giving it a gentle glow that lingered.

"Now it is seven o'clock," Morgana announced, capping her red pen and drawing their attention back to her. "Let us begin," she added as she stood from the desk gracefully. "You've had a few days to adjust yourselves to this new reality," Morgana said as she picked up a marker from the desk and strode to the large whiteboard that filled one side of the room. "We are going to start with the basics of magic. We have explained the source of magic and its purpose, but in order for the four of you to survive as mages, you must learn the basics of how to control magic and how to use if correctly lest you harm yourselves. To start, do you have any questions about what was discussed on Samhain?"

"Was King Arthur real?" Nicki asked suddenly, raising her hand high in the air.

Morgana sighed and set down the marker with a slight eye roll. Turning with a forced smile, she looked at Nicki and answered, "No, there was not a King Arthur or a Camelot."

"Oh," Nicki sunk in disappointment before brightening up again, "What about Excalibur? Was there a real sword that inspired the legend?"

Merlin stepped towards their desks, quickly, to intervene before Morgana replied. He smiled warmly at Nicki.

"Well that's a complicated question Nicki," he answered gently. "When I was young the Bronze Age was still in place and swords were created by pouring molten bronze into molds. In my case, the first sword I ever made was done with a stone mold. Once the metal cooled, I literally pulled a sword from a stone."

Alex blinked at that piece of information and Aiden gave a low whistle, clearly impressed. Merlin beamed at their expressions and when Morgana stepped forward to speak, gestured for her to wait. "And a part of my people's religion was returning items to the earth by burying them or placing them in water. Plus, there was a Lady of the Lake who taught me magic and dwelt in water. She inspired the mythology of King Arthur and several goddesses in the later Celtic tradition."

Bran leaned forward with a small frown, "So how did you two become associated with King Arthur? I mean the myths say that Morgana was his sister-"

"Anyway," Morgana interrupted, her eyes flashing dangerously. "As much as I appreciate your curiosity about history there are several things we need to cover today so you can start learning magic." She gave Bran a look and added, "And I'll remind you that modern retellings make me evil and incestuous."

Bran flushed slightly at her pointed remark and nodded quickly, shrinking back in his chair. Morgana shifted her green eyes to Aiden next, then Nicki and then Alex, silently reminding them that she was the professor and worse, the fully realized mage. Apparently, she was satisfied with their chastised expressions as she turned sharply on her heel.

Back at the white board, Morgana selected a black marker and uncapped it, making a sound that resonated in the now quiet room. Merlin chuckled softly, earning him a look from Morgana, but it didn't seem to bother him. Alex noted that he looked amused at Morgana's theatrics and wondered for a moment if they had stayed together all throughout their long lives. She frowned softly; the thought of just how long they had been alive raising new questions, but Morgana began to write on the board and Alex forced herself to pay attention.

In one long graceful movement, Morgana drew the triskele symbol on the board that matched her necklace and the pin that Merlin wore. A long line, three spirals all sloping in the same direction rotated outward from a shared central point. It reminded Alex of an optical illusion, standing in stark contrast to black on the white board.

"This is the triskele," Morgana told them, reverence in her voice. "It is a powerful symbol of the path that Merlin and I have walked for nearly three thousand years. It has been a symbol of the ways of our people since the Neolithic period." At the confused look on everyone except Nicki's face, she added, "The stone age. Within this symbol is a sign of the core of magic."

Examining the symbol, Alex tried to understand what Morgana was talking about but didn't have any idea what the ancient woman saw there. It sort of made her think of the trinity necklaces she'd seen from time to time, but she had a feeling that Christianity wasn't the answer here. Next to her, Nicki raised her hand slowly.

"Nicole," Morgana sighed, "You don't need to raise your hand here."

"Okay," Nicki replied with a quick nod, "I think it represents land, sea, and sky. I read that once."

"That's a largely Celtic interpretation of the symbol," Morgana agreed. "Not one that was at the core of our beliefs, but relevant I suppose." She paused for a moment, but when no one spoke up continued with the explanation. "The Triskele was also a symbol of life, death, and rebirth. Our people lived with the knowledge that we existed in a cycle within the earth that gave us strength. This was very important when we were confronted with the Sídhe."

"We had to be Children of the Iron Realm," Merlin added from his place by the desk. "Iron is one of the only weaknesses of the Sídhe and thus it was vital for our survival that humanity drew its strength from the earth and its iron. Our people joined the earth when they died and gave it the strength to help us stay strong in the face of danger." Merlin sighed softly, "It's also why in the Iron Age after the Sídhe were pushed back from this realm that funeral rites changed away from serving the community and strengthening the world to celebrating a person as an individual."

"Off topic," Morgana scolded Merlin, but her voice lacked any real anger or bite. Instead she sounded vaguely sorrowful but quickly recovered. "The triskele to mages holds a much more important message. It is a sign of balancing the forces of this world and the place of humanity within it. Any ideas?"

No one spoke. Alex would have guessed the classical elements, but there were four of those so that wouldn't work and Nicki had already talked about the sky, sea and land thing so she had nothing. Fortunately this did not seem to surprise Morgana, in fact, she seemed pleased at their silence and curious expressions.

"The three forces of magic are: science, nature, and the unknown," she told them before her index finger glowed and she reached over to tap the sign on the board. The black lines turned brilliant gold and floated off of the board in a shimmering movement of light. Hanging before them in midair, the glowing triskele symbol pulsed gently, each of the three spiral branches staying intact as the entire symbol began to rotate slowly.

"Science, nature, and the unknown," Morgana repeated as she walked around the glowing symbol. "They used to have different names, but that is how you would best understand them. I'm sure you are familiar with the views some hold of the roles of nature and science in the human experience, you may even be aware that some view these two forces as existing opposite to each other, but mages know better."

"What do you think we mean by nature and science?" Merlin asked them, speaking up once again.

Morgana returned to the board and picked up a marker, writing down science, nature and the unknown with space underneath each of them. The symbol of the triskele that hung between the students and the board faded from the air in a brief shower of shimmering gold. Without Morgana redrawing it, the triskele appeared plainly on the board once again, black against white.

"Well," Bran offered slowly, clearing distracted by a moment, "Science I suppose would be technology and the human pursuit of understanding how the mechanics of the universe work, like articulating the physical laws of gravity, mass, and forces."

Merlin nodded and wrote Bran's examples under science on the board as Morgana stepped calmly to the side, allowing him to take over the lecture.

"A good thought Bran," Merlin congratulated warmly. "So what about nature? If we put the understanding of the physical laws of the universe with technology under science then what could be meant by nature?"

"Maybe our instincts," Nicki offered slowly. "And how we relate to the naturally occurring world that we don't create and control," she finished in a rush.

Merlin nodded and took the marker from Morgana, writing down Nicki's suggestion. He also wrote the word knowledge next to science on the board.

"Knowledge used to be the word we used in place of science a century ago," Merlin informed them with a serious expression. "Humanity is distinct in the natural world. We are separated from other animals and the processes of nature by our consciousness: our sentience divides us from the rest of nature. Science is how we cope without the natural advantages that other animals have for their environments. Nature is seeking to understand not only how that natural world works, but how we as a creature separate from it fit into the world. This isn't something that can be broken down by science because it relies not only on the physical but the emotional. Our moral choices, our desire to either be harmonious with nature or ignore it and how we react to the scientifically understood processes of the natural world are at the core of how a mage must think about nature."

Tilting her head slightly, Alex considered the words as Merlin wrote them down on the board, her eyes moving back to the triskele which dominated the board. Everyone was quiet, giving Alex and the others a few moments to study the symbol and try and understand what was being explained to them.

"The unknown," Morgana spoke up as she moved to the front once more. "Is the undefinable, the things that science and nature do not answer." She opened her palm and a small orb of light appeared, twirling slowly in the air like a tiny spiral galaxy as she continued speaking in a softer tone. "Humanity since the dawn has always felt the unknown. In our long history, we have explained it as gods or spirituality. It is that feeling that draws you one way. That sense of something unseen, but felt; the connections we feel to those we have only just met." The ball of light vanished and Morgana considered them carefully. "Long ago, humanity lived in balance with these three aspects. The belief in magic was not primitive or just trying to explain the unknown, but a result of life being dependent on all three of these forces. Humanity is not just an animal; we have a distinct place in the world that grants us greater responsibilities and great abilities if we can put ourselves into balance with these forces."

"This is the challenge that you must face," Merlin explained as he joined Morgana in front of them. He held out his hand and a long twisted wooden staff appeared in his hand. The wood was old and worn smooth in many places with carving faded into the staff. He leaned on it slightly as he studied all of them. "As the world changes, each generation of mages faces different difficulties to finding this balance, but I have faith that each of you will manage."

"Once you have balance, you can tap into the magic that surrounds you," Morgana continued. "Magic is raw. It is in this world without true form, only effect. A mage gives magic form through their will. Once you have balance, the only limitations are the amount of magic present in the world and your imagination." She closed her hand and the ball of light vanished, darkening the room once more.

"So," Aiden asked slowly, "How do we do that?"

"We'll start simple," Morgana explained. "Mediation and focus: you must think about what we have told you and think on your place in the world."

Alex gaped at Morgana, completely thrown by her statement. It sounded so simple, but at the same time nearly impossible to wrap her head around. She glanced over at the others, noticing looks of concern and doubt on their faces.

"And now you understand why this was easier for earlier people," Morgana offered with a small chuckle.

"I personally find yoga helpful," Merlin added with a wide smile. "Close your eyes," he suggested. "And think about a happy memory, how it made you feel and how you feel right now in comparison."

Closing her eyes, Alex tried to conjure up the memory of her birthday last May just before the end of the school year. All of her friends had been together to celebrate with her, knowing that they'd all be going different directions soon. There had been a bittersweet feeling to the party, but an underlying gratitude and joy that they were together. Frowning, Alex compared the memory to the present. Frustration, fear, and worry were dominant now.

Her hands tightened in response as the churning in her stomach returned. She had no idea how to approach 'bringing balance' to herself. She enjoyed hiking and skiing, she recycled but had grown up in a decent sized city with the internet and a cell phone. Plus she'd only attended church for Christmas and Easter, and that had only been maybe every other year when she was growing up.

"Enough," Morgana called out, distracting Alex. "You all look ready to start hyperventilating."

"It takes time," Merlin told them as they opened their eyes. "I studied magic for over a year and had the benefit of a magical potion before I began to gain any significant control."

"But what if we're attacked again?" Bran asked, voicing their shared concerns.

Smiling, Merlin walked over to the desk and picked up a duffle bag from behind it. He set it on the desk with a heavy thunk before unzipping it. Humming softly, Merlin drew out several daggers in leather sheaths with symbols marked on them. Merlin placed four of them on the table before picking one up and carefully drawing out the dagger. The blade was a shining gray metal and symmetrical with both sides of it sharpened and glinting dangerously in the light.

"I've made for each of you an iron dagger," Merlin explained, holding up the dagger so they could see it, including the carved wooden handle that had some kind of metal on it. "They are ten inches long and very dangerous so be careful. Daggers are stabbing weapons. If you see a Síd, run. If they get close enough for you to use this, then use it and stab them as hard as you can. Iron is poisonous to them and in our world will cause them to almost instantly dissipate. I have burned into each of your sheathes a weak magical seal to help cloak your daggers, but I strongly suggest you try to keep them out of sight as magical crafting is not my greatest talent." He chuckled to himself while Morgana just shook her head. "Remember that you are just beginning to learn and avoid conflict with the Sídhe if at all possible."

Merlin sheathed the dagger and picked up the other three. Walking to each of their desks, Merlin handed one to each of them. When Alex's hand closed around the leather sheath, she made an involuntary shiver. Merlin gave her a soft smile and patted her hand gently before moving on to the others. Staring at the dagger, Alex couldn't think of anything to say in response. With slow and shaky movements, she used the metal clasp on the back of the sheath to fix the dagger to the inside edge of her book bag, considering ways to wear it on around campus.

"That's all for tonight," Morgana suddenly told them when Merlin stepped away from Bran's desk with empty hands.

"Rest up, take in what we discussed and we will meet again here tomorrow night, same time."

"I have a question," Nicki suddenly announced, looking towards Morgana with wide eyes and still clutching her dagger. "Do all mages live as long as the two of you? Will we?"

Alex looked towards Morgana and Merlin quickly, aware of the stillness that had taken over the room. Merlin slowly shook his head and Morgana cleared her throat before answering.

"No," she assured Nicki, "Merlin and I have trained many mages over our long years, that is a part of our purpose in this world. Our students have aged, had families and died of many causes over the centuries. Immortality isn't something you should be concerned with."

There was something in Morgana's voice that caused Alex to stare at the woman, feeling as if she was on the cusp of understanding something new about the woman and Merlin. But Morgana clapped her hands and gestured towards the door, reinforcing their dismissal and interrupting their thoughts. Packing up her things more slowly that necessary, Alex watched the others file out. Nicki glanced back at Morgana with a guilty expression. Alex brushed her fingers over the dagger she was now armed with and headed for the doorway. She reached the door and stopped, turning back to Morgana.

"Is it possible to have a Connection with someone who isn't a mage?" Alex questioned before she lost her courage as Morgana fixed her dark eyes on her.

Professor Cornwall frowned slightly and raised an eyebrow. "A Connection can only be formed between those with magic," she informed Alex simply. "It is impossible otherwise."

"Then I- I think there is another mage on campus," Alex managed, the knot in her stomach tightening. "His name is Arthur Pendred and when I first met him I had a vision of fire and some kind of hammering in the background," she explained in a rush.

"Merlin and I will check on this boy," Morgana told her firmly. "Do not speak with him about this. There are other possible explanations besides this boy being a mage."

"Like what?" Alex asked before she thought better of it. She swallowed when Morgana raised her eyebrow again, but then the professor chuckled slightly.

"Unless you wish for another two-hour lecture then I suggest you leave it at that. We will check on it, but I do not expect the boy to be a mage. We have already scryed the area."

"Scryed?" Alex repeated, "Like using magic with a bowl of water to see other things?"

Smiling softly now, Morgana nodded and added, "That is one method, though Merlin and I are a touch old fashioned and use polished bronze disks. That was the scrying method of our people." Morgana made a show of looking over at the clock and then back at Alex, "Surely you have homework to finish."

"Yes ma'am," Alex agreed with a nod, recognizing that a dismissal when she heard one. Straightening her bag, she stepped out into the hallway to find the others waiting for her. She smiled in gratitude, Alex joined them in taking the elevator up to the ground floor and heading for their dorms in companionable, exhausted silence.

17

Circles of Friends

Humming softly, Alex tapped her foot to the beat of the music playing through her ear buds. In front of her on the laptop screen was a word document with only a few lines of text and several bullet points. Alex huffed and leaned forward, resting her elbow on the edge of her desk as she reread the start of her essay about *Paradise Lost*. She had the basic points down, but absolutely no motivation to sit still and write. Nibbling on her lip, Alex toyed with the tips of her damp hair. She glanced out the window at the snow-covered lawn where a few students were taking advantage of the sunny Saturday morning to build something. It didn't resemble a snowman yet and with it being college kids Alex wasn't certain it ever would.

The door of the dorm room banged open and Jenny flinched at the noise in the doorway. Turning to face her roommate, Alex watched Jenny duck inside their room in her robe with a towel wrapped around her head. Jenny put her things away and snatched up her clothes to get ready for the day. Alex looked back at the screen and moved the cursor down to one of the bullet points to elaborate the short statement into a full sentence. It helped a little and she was able to add on another two sentences before the motivation vanished once again.

"That doesn't look like it's going well," Jenny observed casually.

Taking out her ear buds, Alex shifted in her chair to face Jenny who was pulling on a pair of long black boots over her blue jeans. As usual, Jenny already looked damn near perfect and hadn't even put on her makeup yet. Despite liking her roommate and being her friend, Alex did find it a little annoying.

"It's not," Alex admitted, "And it's due Monday first thing."

"It'll be fine," Jenny assured her with a shrug as she stood up and went to her dresser. "What's it for?"

"*Paradise Lost* for literature class," Alex told her, standing up from her desk and moving to the bed. Stretching out, she looked over at Jenny and watched her roommate put on her makeup. "So what have you got planned for the day?"

"Nothing actually," Jenny replied with a slight sigh. "Breakfast with the boys, but they have practice until this afternoon."

"How about we do something then?" Alex offered. "I've got nothing other than some homework today."

"Really?" Jenny questioned, turning to Alex with a raised eyebrow. "Nothing at all?"

"Nothing," Alex replied with a small frown at the doubtful tone. "Why?"

Jenny shrugged, showing a little embarrassment at Alex's reaction. She spoke as she turned her attention back to the mirror, "It's just that the last time we spent any real time together was Halloween and that was two weeks ago. You've missed lunch with us four times in the last two weeks and skipped out on dinner twice this week alone."

"I've just been busy," Alex offered, ducking her head slightly and giving a small shrug. "I've got fencing and study sessions, but soccer will be over after tomorrow's game." She reached for Galahad and squeezed him softly. "I'm just figuring out my schedule."

"I know…" Jenny shrugged uncomfortably, "It's just you've got study sessions Monday and Thursdays, fencing on Sundays and Wednesdays and soccer on Sundays. I feel like I never see you anymore," Jenny added turning back to Alex. Then Jenny shook her head and gave a small forced laugh, "Sorry honey, I guess I've just been missing girl time. I love the boys and I don't mean to be clingy."

Jenny's tone was light-hearted, but Alex still felt a stab of guilt. "I'm sorry," Alex said. "I don't mean to keep bailing on you and the guys, things are just in an adjustment phase."

"Did you blow midterms?" Jenny asked. She tilted her head slightly with a concerned expression taking over her face. "Is that why the sudden study sessions?"

"I didn't blow them," Alex answered. "But I didn't do great… Anyway, how about you and I do something this morning after breakfast and before the game. Go shopping or see if there are any good movies in town," Alex proposed.

A wide grin lit up Jenny's face and her roommate glanced over Alex's fuzzy slippers, sweatpants and old Disney t-shirt. "Sounds like a plan, but you'd better clean up first."

Rolling her eyes, Alex made a show of huffing as she released Galahad and reached across the bed to open her dresser. The sight of Jenny's smile made her feel a bit better, but she found herself making a promise to make sure she set aside time for Jenny. After all, her roommate had been her friend since she arrived and had made an effort to include her socially. Just because she was becoming friendly with Aiden, Nicki, and Bran and was taking magic lessons didn't mean she had to give Jenny up as a friend. As she brushed her hair, Alex smiled at the thought that maybe magic was an even better reason to have a least a few normal people in her life.

They met the boys for a quick breakfast before they vanished off to the land of football, which despite Alex religiously watching the games with Jenny she still didn't understand beyond the basics of offense and defense. Jenny had informed them all the plan was to meet up at Bookend Coffee before lunch and a movie once practice was over. Arthur gave Jenny an amused look at her decision but didn't argue.

Jenny's enthusiasm didn't fade even as they climbed out of Jenny's red car and into the chilly air of downtown Ravenslake. Despite it not being Thanksgiving yet, there were clear signs of Christmas preparation in the storefronts and along the street. A few of the street lights already had strings of lights hanging between them and the jewelry store across the street already had garlands lining the interior of the windows, framing the display of rings and necklaces. Grabbing Alex's hand, Jenny pulled her into the newest shop, a small boutique with a sign made of twisting letters that Alex could barely read. She smiled at Jenny's cheerfulness and did her best to keep up with the shorter girl as she stalked through the shop like a lioness on the prowl.

Over the course of the next two hours, Alex learned a great deal about Jenny that she hadn't properly realized before. Jenny loved wearing bright colors in the summer but favored darker jewel tones in the winter. She preferred silver over gold unless it was white gold. At the main street candy shop, Alex learned that Jenny was allergic to peanuts and shared her allergy to strawberries, but adored white chocolate. Their last shopping stop of the day before heading back towards campus was the Book Nook which Alex recalled as she stepped inside was the shop that Aiden's family owned.

For a moment she was back in her Connection vision with Aiden as the scent of books enveloped her along with a hint of old leather. Looking around, Alex noted the spiral stairs near the door that wound themselves up to the second floor which looked over the main entrance. All the walls were tightly packed with dark wooden bookshelves that reached the ceiling with a rolling ladder track curving around the square room. A small side archway led into another small room filled with shelves and an elevator was tucked into the back. Metal plates were fixed to the various shelves to mark them and wooden signs hung from beams in the ceiling declaring each section. The entire place seemed steeped in the scent of books and the sense that it had been here a long time.

Shaking herself back to the present, Alex followed Jenny up to the counter and smiled as her friend inquired about romance. An older woman with light brown hair with hints of gray in it pointed Jenny towards the archway into the side room. Alex's eyes were drawn to a metal plaque behind the woman on the wall with the Book Nook's name and the year 1921.

"Can I help you?" the woman asked Alex, startling her slightly.

"Is this store really that old?" Alex questioned, pointing to the sign.

"Yes, it is," the woman replied with a wide smile. "My grandfather founded it when he moved into the area in the 20s. The newest thing here other than books is the elevator we put in ten years ago to keep the second-floor open. "

"Oh, then you're Aiden's mother," Alex realized with a small smile.

"Yes I am," the woman told her before tilting her head and smiling. "I'm Shannon and you must be… Alex isn't it?"

"Yeah," Alex replied a bit nervously, but the woman just smiled warmly.

"Aiden has mentioned you and so has my husband since you're in his fencing club. He says that you've got a lot of potential and determination."

"Thank you," Alex answered, not sure what else to say. "It was nice to meet you," she added before heading off to search through the shop.

The second floor was much smaller, Alex discovered upon climbing the wooden spiral stairs with roughly half the floor blocked by a wall with a locked wooden door marked for staff only. Alex turned around to look out over the open space to the first floor. A wrought iron chandelier hung over the entrance and from her vantage point, Alex could study the sloping metal that twisted into curved designs holding the light bulbs. She wondered if Aiden looked at it differently now before she turned her attention to the nearest bookshelf where mythology and religious texts were displayed. Pausing, Alex considered the bookshelf carefully. She'd wandered upstairs to look around rather than looking through the fiction and literature section and now had a moment of surprise at her own course of action.

Her eyes were drawn to a paperback book with a pale cover and green lettering styled like old medieval letters that read: *Faery Mythology*. Alex pulled the book off the shelf and studied the cover before opening the book to a random page. It was a story about a knight being taken by the Fae and the actions of his sweetheart to save him while the Fae rode on a procession one night. Flipping open to another section, Alex was confronted with an image of a tiny creature with claws, sharp teeth and wings. Turning to the index in the back, she read through the entries that listed various stories from around the world that related to faeries. Closing the book, Alex headed for the staircase, trying not to overthink the purchase, but unable to shake the sense that it was important to get it.

Jenny was already at the checkout and texting on her phone while Shannon checked her out, three books stacked in front of her on the counter. Just as she reached the counter, Shannon was returning Jenny's card and slipping the books into a small bag.

"Hi Alex," Jenny greeted when Alex stepped up next to her and placed her own book on the counter. "The guys are done with practice and heading out to Bookend." Without looking at Alex, Jenny put her phone away and slipped the bag of books into one of her larger bags.

Shannon picked up Alex's book to scan it and blinked in surprise before looking at Alex. "Do you kids have a project?" she asked, "Nicki just bought this book."

"No project," Alex told her quickly, "Nicki mentioned it and it sounded interesting."

"Well good timing," Shannon replied as she rang up the sale. "We just got this in with Thursday's shipment to replace the one Nicki bought."

"Lucky me," Alex forced as she pulled out a twenty to pay for the book.

She accepted her change and slipped the book into her one bag. Giving Shannon a quick wave and smile, Alex moved quickly to the doorway where Jenny was waiting for her. As they stepped outside, Jenny shuddered at the sudden temperature drop.

"Coffee," Jenny muttered, unlocking her car, "Need coffee."

Chuckling, Alex climbed into the passenger seat and put her bags in the back with Jenny's as her roommate shivered and started the car.

"I thought San Francisco got snow?" Alex remarked.

"We do, just not this much," Jenny growled before pulling out into traffic. Alex bit her lip to keep from laughing at Jenny's expression.

They found a parking spot in the conveniently located campus parking lot just down the street from Bookend Coffee, but Jenny shivered all the way up to 7th Street. Arthur and Lance were both standing out on the sidewalk, chatting with smiles and seemingly unaffected the snow. Alex supposed after running around outside in the snow for a practice, a few minutes wouldn't bother them.

"Sweetie!" Jenny called as she carefully rushed up the sidewalk.

Arthur grinned and slung an arm around her, pulling her close and giving her a quick kiss. Alex averted her eyes quickly to Lance and blinked at the strange expression on his face, but it was gone a moment later as he nodded in greeting.

"How was practice?" Jenny asked, turning her eyes towards Lance with a wide smile.

"It was good," Arthur told her with a shrug before gesturing to the doorway. "Shall we?"

"Goodness yes," Jenny cheered as she moved for the door.

It opened outward and Jenny had to jump back to avoid being hit as another group came out of the coffee shop. Aiden barely managed to keep his coffee in its take-out container from spilling all over Jenny as he came to a sudden stop. Behind him, Nicki and Bran looked around him to see what the holdup was. Looking up, Aiden smiled as he saw Alex and stepped out of the way and onto the street. Nicki and Bran stepped out beside him, each of them carrying their own cup of coffee.

"Hi Alex," Nicki greeted with a smile before turning her eyes to the people with Alex.

"Guys," Alex said quickly, giving her roommate a quick glance. "This is Aiden Bosco, Nicki Russell, and Bran Fisher. My study group." Alex gave the others a stern look and stressed the last bit as she pointed to each of them in turn. She gestured to those around her one by one, "This is Arthur Pendred, Lance Taylor, and my roommate Jenny Sanchez."

Nicki grinned, shifted her coffee to her left hand and held out a gloved hand to Jenny who took it with a wide smile. Alex risked a glance at Arthur to see him watching Aiden with a hint of suspicion, clearly remembering when Aiden had made her cry. She smiled to herself, giddy that Arthur remembered.

"It's so nice to meet you, Jenny," Nicki greeted with a quick glance over Alex's roommate that made Alex chuckle softly. Jenny missed the meaning of the look and returned the handshake and smile.

"It's nice to meet you," she said pleasantly as she waved in greeting to Bran and Aiden.

Alex watched carefully as Arthur greeted them all and shook hands with Aiden and gave Bran a friendly nod for any sign of a Connection forming. There was nothing, none of the mages showed any reaction to Arthur, not even with physical contact. Her good mood faded as a sense of unease crept up on her. Was there something off with his magic or with hers? Was she wrong about him? Instead of dwelling on the question of why only she felt any magic from Arthur, Alex forced herself to focus back in on the introductions taking place around her.

"So," Jenny asked, looking at Aiden and Jenny, "How did midterms in Cornwall's class go for you?"

"Good," Nicki told Jenny cheerfully. "I love history and while she's intense I enjoy her teaching of lesser known aspects of history."

"Our tests went fine," Aiden assured Jenny, seemingly amused by Nicki's giddiness. "But the study group is helping, especially with Alex and my assignments from physics lab." Alex gave Aiden a grateful smiled over Jenny's shoulder before his phone beeped. "Excuse us," Aiden told Jenny. "I'm afraid we've got a game that is about to start." Aiden looked at Alex and grinned, "You could join us."

"What game?" Jenny asked him curiously with a small tilt of her head.

"Tabletop RPG," Aiden informed her with a small smirk already pulling at the corners of his mouth, already confident of the reaction he was going to get.

"That sounds fun…" Jenny answered quickly, "But we have plans."

"Well have a great afternoon, it was nice to meet all of you" Aiden replied with a nod to Arthur who was still watching him and a smile to Alex. "See you at fencing club."

Alex nodded to her other friends and gave a small wave as they hurried down the street with their coffees. Jenny gripped Alex's arm and tugged her into the warmth of Bookend Coffee as Arthur opened the door for them. Many of the tables were occupied with students and a few locals with cups of steaming coffee that warmed Alex just with the sight of it. The scent of coffee beans filled the space, but Alex could also detect a hint of the pastries baking in the back that made her mouth water as she and Jenny joined the line.

"They seem nice," Arthur said with a bit of hesitation. "So you have how many classes with Aiden and fencing club?" he asked, trying to sound uninterested.

"We're in physics class, physics lab, calculus, and history," Alex listed off before making a slightly irritated face. "Man I do see that guy a lot, but he's nice if a bit weird," she assured Arthur quickly.

"He's kind of cute," Jenny ventured with a teasing smile. "Unless he's with Nicki," she considered thoughtfully.

"He's not with Nicki," Alex promised with a little smile, "But I'm not into him."

"Too bad," Jenny sighed, "Double dating could be fun. Although he seems like a bit of a geek."

"Major geek," Alex verified with a nod. "How about letting me pass my first semester before you try and set me up."

"I make no promises," Jenny replied with a grin. Arthur laughed loudly behind them at her words while Lance pushed Alex forward gently as the line moved forward. Without missing a beat, Jenny cheerfully greeted the barista and placed her order.

By some miracle there was a free table in the loft, finally paying off Alex's habit of always checking. More than two months into school and Alex had never managed to snag a seat in the loft before so she rushed to the table and slid into one of

the chairs, barely managing not to spill her coffee. Jenny
followed much more calmly, sashaying over to the free chair
and sitting down gracefully. Lance and Arthur slumped into
their seats, already sipping from their coffees. Another pair of
students came up to check the loft, sighing in disappointment
before heading back downstairs which made Alex grin in
triumph. Arthur's eyes twinkled with amusement and he
snorted into his coffee while Lance just shook his head and
looked like he was considering pretending he didn't know who
they were.

"You do know we're not staying here that long," Jenny teased,
"Despite your victory. Coffee and then some non-campus
food."

"Have you sat in the loft before?" Alex questioned with a
raised eyebrow and a slight huff. "I haven't."

"I have a few times," Lance told her with a shrug and when
the others looked at him he added, "I wake up really early
some morning and like to get a coffee. This place is pretty
quiet at five in the morning."

"Which would explain why this is news to me," Arthur
remarked with a chuckle. "At five in the morning if I'm not at
an early practice I'm asleep."

"Me too," Alex agreed with a wide grin. "It's only on Sundays
that I manage morning runs, otherwise I don't run until the
afternoon."

"You people are weird," Jenny remarked before taking a sip of
her own coffee which was some super fancy thing that had
taken what had seemed like an eternity to order to Alex. "So
what should we do for lunch?"

"I feel like Mexican," Arthur suggested, "Outside the taco bar, there never seems to be Mexican food on campus."

Alex considered the statement. "You're right," Alex realized, "There are burgers, Chinese food, pizza and sub sandwiches but no Mexican."

"Sounds like it's Mexican for lunch," Lance observed with a glance towards Jenny who returned the stare for a long moment before snapping her attention back to Arthur.

Blinking, Alex studied Jenny for a minute, wondering what had just happened, but the cheerful conversation about classes and football had resumed. Alex picked up her coffee cup and took another sip, listening as the conversation changed to a lighthearted debate about what movie to see that afternoon. Jenny argued in favor of a drama while Lance was adamant they should see an action movie. Watching the interaction for a moment, Alex relaxed and glance at Arthur who merely winked at her, sharing her amusement. Smiling in return, Alex settled back into her chair and took another sip of her coffee, basking in its warmth and the moment of normalcy.

18

Changeling Child

822 B.C.E.

Morgana woke suddenly to the sound of a bell, her hair tangling around her face as she shifted in her bed. The white fabric with golden embroidery pooled around her legs as she rolled over and opened her eyes. A Síd in a soft blue gown was standing in the doorway of the small round room with a golden tray which held a golden chalice and a small golden bell. Climbing from the large bed, Morgana did her best to move gracefully to the doorway. In the light from a magical orb, the chalice gleamed brightly showing the tiny engraving that covered the surface. Morgana took the chalice gently in one hand and raised it to her lips.

The mixture was sweet, but thick and stuck to the inside of the mouth and throat, slipping down slowly. Refusing to show any distaste, Morgana drained the chalice and set it back on the tray. Giving her a nod, the Síd took a step back from her and then turned sharply to leave the room. Morgana waited for a moment before she pulled back the white curtain that divided her room from the outer chamber across the entryway. She quickly straightened the sheets and pillows of her bed, tightening them until they were free of any wrinkles before turning to the gold and stone wardrobe that dominated the far corner of her room beside a matching table.

Moving quickly and efficiently, Morgana changed out of the white gown she wore to sleep and dressed in the elegantly embroidered pale blue gown that was Queen Scáthbás' favorite. Morgana slipped her feet into a pair of pale blue slippers that matched the dress and selected a long golden belt with the sign of the Queen and draped it around her waist. Grabbing her brush, Morgana tended to her long hair and had managed to untangle the knots when the curtain was pulled back and another Síd entered. This one nodded a greeting to Morgana which she returned but did not speak with her.

The Síd came to Morgana's back and the girl saw a flash of long claws covered with golden protectors in the corner of her eye before the Síd gathered up her hair and began to style it into a braid. Morgana remained as still as she could, even when the Síd tugged much harder than was needed. Taking a few deep breaths, Morgana tried to calm herself and not show her excitement for the day.

"The Queen is waiting," the Síd told her, releasing her hair that Morgana could feel piled on top of her head in a series of braids.

"Understood my lady," Morgana replied, turning and giving the Síd a small bow.

Gathering up the fabric of her dress, Morgana moved quickly for the door and stepped out into the large white corridor. A guard was posted by her doorway but made no reaction as Morgana passed him. Keeping her head high and her shoulders back, Morgana walked down the long hallway towards a gleaming golden archway at the far end. Two more guards in golden armor stood at the ready, weapons drawn. One eyed Morgana with a hint of suspicion and a touch of fear as she passed between them. The other gave her a look she had learned in the past year was connected to lust and caused a flash of anger within her. Morgana did not fear his expression or his desires. She no longer feared the touches of the Sídhe who had come to take away the other children over the years: she had no reason to fear them. None would ever touch her without the consent of her mistress. She belonged to the Queen herself.

Despite her confidence, Morgana slowed as she stepped into the chambers of the Queen. Music echoed in the large domed space and the Queen's back was to Morgana, seated before a beautiful polished gold mirror. To her right was the Queen's bed, draped in a golden cloth with elegantly carved golden accented stone. Morgana's steps echoed softly on the white tiles as she approached Queen Scáthbás. The Queen's long pale hair shimmered all the colors Morgana knew in the light of the magical orbs, hanging down her back in gentle waves. Her tall golden crown sat on a small cushion on the vanity top before her. Creeping forward to Queen Scáthbás' side, Morgana bowed deeply and waited.

"My precious one," Queen Scáthbás greeted with a smile, reaching out a hand and touched the top of Morgana's head. "Did you sleep well, my beautiful girl?"

"I did Your Majesty," Morgana answered, closing her eyes and savoring the touch. "Did Your Majesty?"

"I dreamt of the beautiful world that we shall make the Iron Realm into," Queen Scáthbás sighed softly, removing her hand from Morgana's head. "I fear that dream shall never be."

Morgana swallowed, unsure of how to comfort the queen, but Queen Scáthbás picked up a golden brush and handed it to Morgana. Taking it gently, Morgana rose from her knees and moved around to the Queen's back and began to carefully brush her mistress' hair.

"What do you dream of precious one?" Queen Scáthbás asked softly.

"I do not remember often," Morgana confessed. "But I dream of the great stories that I have heard growing up. The Sídhe warriors, their magic and the worlds that were brought into the light of the Sídhe."

"My little mage," Queen Scáthbás cooed, "One day soon you shall be a part of those stories. Did I not tell you that we would bring your poor iron cursed world into our light?"

"Yes, Your Majesty," Morgana replied. "You did."

"I told you that the day I claimed you," Queen Scáthbás said wistfully, catching Morgan's hand with her own ungloved one. She pulled on Morgana's hand gently, bringing her around to the side of her. "I told you that you would serve me well, my little darling."

"And have I?" Morgana asked, dropping her eyes.

"You have worked so hard learning to use your magic," Queen Scáthbás told her with a smile, touching Morgana's chin to make her look back up at her. "And you are so well behaved, so obedient and quiet. My perfect little girl."

Morgana smiled at the praise, basking in the warmth of the Queen's words. Returning the smile, Queen Scáthbás looked in her mirror and then back at Morgana. "Finish my hair won't you, my little darling, use your magic."

Nodding, Morgana stepped back from the Queen and closed her eyes. She inhaled slowly, feeling the pulse of the magic around her building. Calling it forward, Morgana conjured an image in her mind of the Queen's long hair being styled into her favorite elaborate seven braids coiled around her crown. She opened her eyes and pushed at the magic, feeling it absorb her commands, her will and begin to work. Watching, Morgana kept a tight rein on the magic as the Queen's hair magically braided itself and began to weave into an elaborate style. On the cushion, the crown shifted unsteadily before rising into the air and settling on the Queen's head. Morgana released a slow breath as the braids finished weaving around the crown, securing it in place in a tall tower of gold and white.

"Lovely, my little darling," Queen Scáthbás praised, turning away from the mirror to look at Morgana. "Your control of your magic is becoming perfect. You have been taking your potion each morning?"

"Yes Your Majesty," Morgana answered eagerly.

"Of course you have my precious one," Queen Scáthbás replied with a gentle smile. "Then you're nearly ready for the great mission that I must bestow on you."

"Mission Your Majesty?" Morgana questioned in confusion. "I shall do whatever you ask of me," she added in a rush.

"I know you shall my darling," Queen Scáthbás answered, rising to her feet. "It is a great thing that I need you to do for me. You are the only one who can do it. The Fate of the Tree of Reality has favored us above all other realms by giving you to me. But you will have to be strong and true throughout your mission. You must be my sword, my voice, and my heart."

"I am not certain I understand Your Majesty," Morgana said carefully, watching the Queen's face for any sign of anger or displeasure. To her relief, Queen Scáthbás merely sighed softly and placed a gentle ungloved hand to Morgana's cheek. On impulse, Morgana leaned into the warm living touch, her eyes fluttering for a moment.

"My precious one," Queen Scáthbás whispered, drawing Morgana closer to her and wrapping an arm around her.

Gasping softly, Morgana leaned tentatively closer to the Queen's body and felt the arm around her tighten slightly, bringing them even closer. Queen Scáthbás cooed gently and

Morgana smiled, unable to hide her joy. The Queen chuckled softly and a hand brushed a strand of hair that had fallen from her braids behind her ear.

"Do you remember your promise to me?" Queen Scáthbás asked her softly. Morgana basked in the quiet shared moment with her Queen and looked up at her, green eyes meeting purple.

"I promised you that I would do whatever you wished," Morgana whispered.

"Yes," Queen Scáthbás answered gently. "Yes, you did my beautiful little one. I have kept you safe since you became mine haven't I."

"You have my Queen," Morgana agreed, bowing slightly to the Queen and glorifying in the moment the Queen tilted her chin back up towards her.

"No one has touched you have they?" Queen Scáthbás confirmed. "You always have food, water, light, clothing, and care."

"Always," Morgana rushed to reassure her Queen. "I have no fear and no wants in your service."

"And I have been good to you in other ways have I not," the Queen reminded her. "I have shown you the depth of my love and made the court understand that you are my beautiful girl. My precious mage."

Morgana felt tears rising in her eyes, but did her best to remain in control. Nodding, she struggled to find her voice, but whispered, "Yes, Your Majesty. I love you so much," Morgana choked out before looking down, unable to contain a few stray tears.

A warm soft hand brushed away the tears as the Queen knelt before her, bringing them face to face. Morgana's heart stopped and she couldn't breathe as the Queen leaned forward and kissed her forehead. The lips remained against her skin for a long moment before the Queen moved back from her and stood once again. She held out an ungloved hand to Morgana.

"Then come with me my precious one. The potion has done its work and given you the strength needed for the task ahead."

Without hesitation, Morgana happily took Queen Scáthbás' hand and allowed herself to be led from her chambers. Guards barely hid their shock as they strode past them. It was often that Morgana was seen with the Queen, but rare that Queen Scáthbás touched her iron cursed childe so freely in front of others. Morgana glowed in the moment, in the public display of Her Majesty's love and trust. Entering the Great Hall, Morgana walked as tall as she could, refusing to show any fear before the gathered Sídhe as she walked with the Queen. Many approached them slowly, but Queen Scáthbás waved them back and kept gliding towards the great golden doors that had brought Morgana to Sídhean almost two years ago. The guards before it dropped to their knees and Queen Scáthbás pointed towards the door.

"Through there Morgana are the tunnels we raised you in, the tunnels were other iron cursed childes we have rescued from a terrible existence are still being cared for so that they might repay our love and kindness. But beyond our tunnels is the Iron Realm. The tunnels grant us safe passage into the poisonous realm of your birth. By passing through the tunnels my Riders and Hounds gain the strength necessary to pass into the poisonous land and survive. Our magic pulses in the tunnels protects us and gives us power even in a cursed land."

"I understand Your Majesty," Morgana assured her quickly, clutching at Queen Scáthbás' hand as she gazed at the great golden door that still frightened her.

"When you were a babe my precious one, a Síd rescued you and brought you into our tunnels, but a magical being was left in your place so that the iron folk would not hunt for you."

"A Changeling," Morgana whispered a hint of awe in her voice.

"Yes, a Changeling and by a great miracle of Sídhe strength that changeling still lives," Queen Scáthbás informed her with triumph. "It never died in the iron cursed lands or was discovered by the humans, but lives among them." Queen Scáthbás frowned, "But it is not aware of the truth my little darling, it can use no magic and cannot help me. Morgana, we are in danger."

Morgana's eyes widened and she gasped softly. The idea of the great Sídhe being in danger was horrifying, they were powerful, beautiful and terrible. Nothing in any of the realms could harm them save the poison of the Iron Realm and their magic protected them there.

"How?" Morgana breathed, fear in her voice. "What could endanger you?"

"Something has happened in the Iron Realm," Queen Scáthbás breathed to her, speaking low and sharing a secret with Morgana. "It has created a weapon from the core of its magic, the pulse of its world and the dreams of its poisonous people. My Riders have heard that one of the earth mages is seeking a childe and my mages have long scryed for the weapon. Two moons ago, we found it."

Listening with baited breath, Morgana watched as the queen knelt next to her, leaning forward to whisper in Morgana's ear. "It is a childe Morgana, an iron childe more dangerous than any other. My magic had found it for me, but the Iron Realm seeks to protect its new weapon." Queen Scáthbás smiled, "But, my precious one, fate has favored me greatly, for this childe shares a home with the Changeling left in your place. You and this abomination share the same iron blooded mother."

Gasping softly, Morgana pondered the words but was aware of the Queen watching her reaction carefully. Morgana met her eyes with as much determination and courage as she could.

"Shall I kill or take the childe for you Your Majesty?"

Queen Scáthbás smiled at her, cupping Morgana's chin with her hand and leaning forward to kiss her lips gently. "My precious one," the Queen cooed, "I knew you would not let me down, but I have a different plan."

"What shall I do?" Morgana asked, straightening her back.

"I do not know the power of this weapon. I must know what defenses the poison realm can muster before I dare invade with my full force and bring the light to the iron people. My little darling, you must take on a great mission for me. You must return to the Iron Realm, to the home of your birth and watch this childe for me. Live amongst the iron folk and report their plotting to me so that I might stop them once and for all."

"Return…" Terror gripped Morgana at the words, "to the poison lands?"

"The potions I have been giving you have made you stronger," the Queen soothed her. "Despite the power, you carry from us, despite the blessings I have given you and the food you have eaten you are still an iron childe." Morgana teared up at the words, shamed once again by her iron blood. Queen Scáthbás brushed her cheek gently, "But, my precious mage, that will now serve me better than any Rider or Hound ever could. You will go for me where no others can." Queen Scáthbás paused and then asked, "Will you do this for me, my beautiful girl?"

Trying to stop her tears, Morgana nodded quickly and cried harder when the Queen tenderly brushed away the tears. "I shall do whatever you need me to do," Morgana promised, "Whatever you ask I will do."

Queen Scáthbás smiled in triumph and stood quickly, gesturing a waiting Sídhe named Murden who was watching Morgana with a dark look. "Murden, send a Rider and use the call to retrieve the Changeling. Prepare for the ritual, our childe is ready and I have waited long enough for my answers," she ordered sharply, sending several Sídhe scattering to obey. The Queen's long fingernails ran through Morgana's hair, loosening the braids into long waves. "This will be a glorious day in our history my little darling," Queen Scáthbás informed her. "The day that marks the beginning of the end for the Iron Realm and the beginning of our ascent to the throne of reality."

Morgana was taken from the Queen back to her chamber and given another goblet of the strange potion. Taking a moment, Morgana studied the liquid before drinking it down, marveling at the rich red tone and the slow waves on the surface. She did not remain in her chamber for long before a Sídhe tossed a thick bundle of clothing to her. A long tunic of off white fabric spilled into her hands and a pair of plain brown shoes of some kind of animal hide fell to the floor. The fabric itched against her hands and was much heavier than her usual bright and flowing gowns. Without compliant, Morgana slipped out of her gown and slippers and into the long pale dress and shoes. A dark red tunic with shorter shelves was pulled over the top of the longer dress and a thick length of twisted material similar to cloth was wrapped around her waist to hold everything in place. Morgana shifted uncomfortably in the clothes but remained silent about her discomfort as the Síd motioned for her to follow her.

Morgana felt out of place as she walked through the elegant halls of the Sídhe that had become her home in the clothing of the poisonous realm. Instead of walking with her shoulders back and her head held high as Queen Scáthbás had taught her, she wanted to fade into the shadows. The Síd led her to the doorway in the Great Hall where Murden stood waiting in his long white and gold robes, watching her with his usual expression of distaste. Unlike usual, today he had a large bag of white fabric slung over his shoulder and was wearing a heavy pale blue cloak. Morgana dared to look over her shoulder towards the golden throne where Queen Scáthbás sat, presiding over her great court. She smiled and nodded to Morgana, giving the girl courage as the golden doors opened.

"Come," Murden ordered, "Let us be done with this."

Morgana resisted the urge to rush back to Queen Scáthbás and beg her for a different way to prove her love and loyalty. All the tales of the Iron Realm she had been told as a childe rushed back to her, every fear growing within her. Then the doors were fully open, exposing the long white corridors. Murden stepped through the threshold and Morgana took a breath and followed him through, barely aware that four armed Sídhe were following her.

The white tunnels of her childhood greeted her with their cold stone. Morgana saw none of the magical images that had entertained her on the walls and no iron children could be seen. The large golden doors closed with a heavy thud behind her as Murden led her forward and Morgana glanced around through the archways lining the long hall, but she could see no one. She forced her fear back and walked with as much grace as she could muster even as the unfamiliar clothes weighed down on her as a reminder of where she was going.

Following Murden, Morgana's aggravation grew as the slope of the tunnels changed upwards and an engraved golden door came into sight in front of them. Four guards were posted in front of the door and Morgana stopped to watch Murden speak with them. She'd seen this door only a few times as a childe before being pulled away by the caretakers. This was a dangerous door, more dangerous than even the way into the Sídhe Realm.

Slowly, the four guards moved aside, creating a path for Murden, Morgana, and their escort. The door was pulled open by a single guard and Morgana caught sight of the outer image of the door. It was a fearsome sight with monstrous faces and weapons, a warning she realized. Beyond the doorway was a long dark tunnel carved in black stone with small light orbs hanging in the air every few feet casting a dim glow that served only to make the passage more frightening. Still, she kept putting one foot in front of the other, replaying Queen Scáthbás' words for courage.

"Wait," Murden ordered and Morgana paused in her walking, turning to look over her shoulder as their escort vanished into a side room.

Blinking, Morgana considered the open archway with a small frown, unsure if it had been there a moment ago. Under other circumstances, Morgana would have asked about the use of magic, but right now her mouth was far too dry to form a single word. Murden remained perfectly still and the guards stared straight ahead, not even bothering to look at her. A few moments later the four armed Sídhe returned, each of them leading a shimmering white horse that took Morgana's breath away. Swallowing, she closed and opened her fists, realizing that she was with four Riders. The final Rider was leading a fifth horse and handed the leather and golden reigns to Murden.

One of the Riders moved ahead of them with his horse, leading the beast through the threshold and into the dark tunnel ahead. Murden followed him and Morgana darted after him, aware of the three remaining Riders stepping into the tunnel behind her, flanking her on all sides. A moment later, the tunnel darkened as the golden door behind her closed.

"Which branch?" Murden questioned the Rider in the lead softly.

"Tunnel branch 13," the Rider replied calmly, it voice echoing in the passage.

Morgana was quiet, as they moved quickly through the long tunnel, ignoring many branching tunnels that headed into new directions, each of them darker than the last. Swallowing, she turned her eyes to the large steed to her right which shined slightly in the low light of the orbs. She was tempted to reach out and touch the beast but had been told the dangers of ever touching a Rider's steed.

Breathing deeply, Morgana became aware slowly of her aching muscles and the sweat that was gathering on her brow. She reached up and brushed the sweat away with her hand, feeling the moisture on the skin of her hand with curiosity. Sweating was a rare event for her, having lived her life in the Sídhe tunnels and Realm, but now she was uncertain as to the cause. Morgana took another breath, feeling how difficult it seemed to be with a jolt of alarm.

"It is the crossing," Murden told her, looking back at her over his shoulder with a smug expression. "The magic of these tunnels eases the transition between Sídhean and the Iron Realm. You have lived your life in our magic, in our power."

"Is it safe?" Morgana asked weakly.

"The potion has prepared your body for returning to the Iron Realm," Murden answered, a dark chuckle escaped him before he added, "Otherwise, the crossing would leave you weakened and aged."

The way he said the words made Morgana fall silent and look at the ground of the tunnel. They suddenly turned off the main path and down a branch tunnel. A chilly wind blew down the tunnel and Morgana peeked around Murden and the Rider to see darkness up ahead with the light orbs ending. She caught a strange scent on the rush of air that she struggled to identify, but seemed somehow familiar to her. Suddenly, all the Riders stopped moving as one and mounted their horses with Murden mounting his a moment later. Before Morgana could say or do anything, the Rider to her right reached down and scooped her up, bringing her onto his steed in front of him. She grabbed the saddle horn tightly and tensed up as the horse began to move forward.

Her eyes were fixed on the opening of the tunnel as the first Rider stepped through the threshold and into the beyond. A moment later the horse she was on followed and Morgana gasped. There were no ceilings or walls around her. Above her head was a dark canopy far beyond her reach with a full glowing moon that illuminated the landscape. The Rider gave her no time to gape at the strange world, spurring on his horse, but Morgana caught sight of a group of towering trees, small plants and rolling hills in the moonlight. Things she had only ever heard of and seen in the magical paintings of the Sídhe. As the horse began to gallop forward after the Rider's leader, Morgana closed her eyes and reminded herself to keep breathing as the speed and motion threatened to make her ill.

The rapid pace did not last long and as they slowed down Morgana could see a small hill free of trees ahead of them. Grass shimmered in the moonlight as the wind gently caused it to sway in a movement that fascinated Morgana. Breathing deeply, Morgana was overwhelmed by the new and strange scents surrounding her, some good and some bad. Above her head, the moon entranced her and the stars gleamed brightly, even in the dominating light of the moon. Her attention was only taken away from these new and exciting things by the sight of a fifth Rider appearing at the crest of the hill with a small figure in the saddle before him.

Riding to the top of the hill, Murden dismounted first with a small huff before straightening his cloak. Morgana was shifted off the horse by the Rider who dismounted next to her and put a firm hand on her shoulder, keeping her in place as the fifth Rider dismounted with the small figure and pulled back the hood of the figure's cloak

Eyes widening, Morgana stared in shock at the small girl of nine years in front her. They were perfectly identical with the same features, the same green eyes, the same long brown hair and even wearing the same clothing. The only difference was that this child's hands were bound and a gag was placed around her head, keeping her silent. Coming face to face with her own Changeling made Morgana's heart skip a beat and she could see the terror and confusion on the girl's face. A pang of sympathy rose in Morgana, startling her and she schooled her features into the calmest expression she could manage, feeling Murden's eyes on her. No one spoke and her duplicate struggled against the firm grasps of the Rider with no success.

Murden reached into his satchel and withdrew a long length of white cloth with golden Sídhe lettering sewn in it. Morgana gasped softly, recognizing the magic woven into the material with both awe and fear.

"Bind them together," Murden ordered the nearest Rider who carefully took the length of cloth in his gloved hand, the shifting of the metal of his golden gauntlet almost echoing in the stillness. The Changeling struggled against the Síd holding her, only to be grabbed roughly by another Rider who tugged her forward. The Rider met Morgana's eyes and beckoned her to come to him. Raising her chin, Morgana stepped forward and stood calmly while the Changeling was shoved against her, putting them back to back.

Soft muttered whimpers escaped from the gag, but Morgana willed herself to ignore them, reminding herself that this poor creature was a Síd who had been tainted by the iron folk. Two Riders held the Changeling still as the length of fabric was tied around them and both ends were carefully placed in Morgana's upturned hands.

Murden pulled out a golden chalice from his satchel and handed it to a Rider. Morgana watched as he withdrew several small vials and jars, mixing a potion in the chalice and did her best to ignore the shaking Changeling bound to her. Soft words rolled off Murden's tongue and Morgana closed her eyes as the magic became to build around them. It felt different, she realized with a frown, there was resistance to the normally smooth gathering of Sídhe magic. Morgana struggled to breathe as the magic encircled them, thickening around herself and the Changeling. Her skin felt itchy and slimy at the same time as if she was horribly filthy.

A wet claw moved against her forehead and Morgana's eyes snapped open to find Murden drawing symbols on her forehead with the potion and a look of intense concentration. He moved around them a moment later, leaving Morgana's skin to cool as the wind blew past her and chilled the Sídhe symbols. She could hear the Changeling crying behind her as Murden did something that Morgana could not see for several moments and felt the girl once again fight against the binding.

Tightening her grip on the ends of the cloth, Morgana refused to let it fall or loosen. Murden returned in front of with the chalice and a small satisfied smile. Bringing the chalice forward to Morgana's mouth, he tilted it up in a clear message even as the spell continued with his words. Obediently, Morgana opened her mouth and drank down the potion.

The second the first drop hit her tongue, fire flashed throughout her body and nearly made her choke. A tight grip on each of her shoulders kept her in place. Another set of hands tugged her head back, making it impossible for her resist drinking the potion. Tears escaped her eyes and Morgana couldn't breathe without gulping down more of the mixture. She could feel her tears running down her cheeks, doing little to ease the terrible burn that was consuming her body.

Screams muffled only by the Changeling's gag reached her and it was all Morgana could do not to fall to her knees between her own agony and the shaking of the girl at her back. A tight grip took hold of her waist, keeping her upright and Morgana managed a tiny sob around another painful gulp of the potion. Her vision blurry from the tears, Morgana could no longer see Murden, but heard his magical words and felt his magic tightening around her, pushing her closer and closer to the Changeling.

Suddenly the chalice was pulled away from her lips and Morgana swallowed the last of the brew on reflex. With her mouth clear she gasped for air and released a pained sob, tears flowing down her cheek. Her back ached and creaked as it was pushed against the Changeling. A sharp crack against the back of Morgana's head made her flinch and nearly drop the cloth as the Changeling's head collided with the back of hers. The backs of their arms were flush against each other and at some point, their legs had come together. Struggling to see clearly,

Morgana looked at Murden who was watching them with a look of triumph as he slowly reached into his bag.

Another burst of magic made Morgana scream as a bone snapped and the pain flashed through her, but the Changeling echoed the cry of pain through the gag. Despite the position, Morgana both saw and felt a Rider rip the gag from her, no the Changeling's mouth. Murden stepped closer to them, moving to their right. She felt him lower a hand to her hand and say another few words of a chant. Then a handful of dust was scattered over their heads. She was aware of no more.

19

Drops of Water

Bookend Coffee was a bustle of students from the University and professionals from the downtown area grabbing a quick cup of coffee on a chilly Thursday afternoon. The five employees were rushing between machines, registers, and the pastry cabinet as quickly as they could without causing a collision. Near the front of the line, Alex shifted on her feet impatiently with a relaxed Nicki. The front door opened once again, sending a blast of chilly air throughout the front of the coffee shop. Briefly, Alex wondered who had designed the interior set up.

"Wouldn't it make more sense to put the door by the people who already have their coffee?" Alex asked Nicki in a low voice, leaning over slightly to look at the front of the line to see how much longer she had to wait before placing her order.

"No," Nicki answered with a chuckle, "This way the people in line want coffee even more and don't leave even when the line is long."

"Too bad this is the closest good coffee," Alex grumbled even as they moved forward.

"Easy girl," Nicki told her, patting her arm, "You'll have your caffeine soon."

They made it to the front of the line and placed their orders with no fuss. The barista was cute and Alex wished there was time to flirt, but the line behind her curbed the desire. Instead, she dropped her change into the tips jar and accepted her steaming cup. Nicki tugged at her arm and directed her back to the main door and out of the crowded building.

"How far have you gone in the mythology book?" Nicki asked as they stepped outside Bookend Coffee, both of them clutching steaming cups in their hands.

"Not very far," Alex admitted with a shrug. "Last chapter I read was the Stolen Bairn story. Although I now understand a bit more about the Changelings we talked about in Yates' class."

"I'm almost done," Nicki informed her as they walked down the street back towards campus. "But I'm unsure about how the various kinds of fairy folk relate to the Sídhe."

"Maybe they are just myths," Alex offered with a shrug, "or maybe those little creatures like brownies were magical constructions?"

"Constructs," Nicki corrected automatically. "Maybe, Yates wouldn't tell us much about those."

"Cornwall just wants to make sure we can use magic without telling us too much about the advanced stuff. Probably so we don't try it on our own before we can control it," Alex observed before taking a sip of her coffee.

"But none of us of have managed anything," Nicki sighed. "How long do you think it will take?"

"Don't know, but I'd bet Bran does it first," Alex told her with a shrug.

"Nah," Nicki chuckled. "Aiden will be first, he's taking up meditation to try and find his balance," Nicki informed Alex, rolling her eyes she said the last word.

"I still don't get what that means," Alex answered, making a face.

"Me either," Nicki replied as they crossed the street. "But Aiden thinks it's about achieving some kind of peace and self-actualization."

"Does he even know what that means?" Alex teased with a grin, "or just reciting something from one of his role-playing guides."

"Don't knock it till you tried it," Nicki retorted smiling and glanced Alex. "Anyway I want to talk with Cornwall and see if she's willing to spend the session explaining some more about the Sídhe and what else we can expect to face."

Alex nodded and sipped her coffee as they reached the edge of the arboretum. There was a touch of snow over the ground and trees, but the sidewalk was clear and dry. They fell into a comfortable silence, sipping their coffees and enjoying the sunshine. A few students passed them either on their way to classes, going home or heading to the coffee shop.

"So…" Nicki said slowly when the dorms came into sight. "Are you enjoying magic lessons?"

Alex chuckled, "First time anyone's asked that question."

"And the answer?" Nicki questioned, glancing over at Alex.

"A little I suppose," Alex conceded. "Being able to see Merlin and Morgana use magic isn't something to take for granted, but I do find the lack of magic we do frustrating."

"Right there with you," Nicki sighed. "What I'd give for a holly and phoenix wand."

"You are such a geek," Alex teased, barely containing a laugh.

Nicki's response was lost in the ringtone which played a song that Alex didn't recognize, but thought might be an oldie song. With a look of mild confusion, Nicki pulled out her phone and raised it to her ear.

"Hi Gran," Nicki greeted pleasantly. "How are things?"

Alex took a few more steps and then stopped, realizing that Nicki wasn't beside her anymore. Turning quickly, she found Nicki standing in the middle of the sidewalk, completely still. Her face was pale making her freckles stand out sharply and her mouth was open in shock. Alex barely reached her in time to grab the cup from her shaking hand before she spilled coffee all over herself.

"Nicki," Alex called, worry filling her voice as dozens of possibilities rushed through her mind: from Nicki's grandmother was in the hospital to a Síd had managed to capture her despite it being daylight. "Nicki!"

"Uh," Nicki blinked at Alex, her eyes still wide. They were shining with emotions that Alex couldn't decipher, making her even more nervous. "Yeah Gran," Nicki said into the phone, but not taking her eyes off Alex. "I understand." There was a pause and Nicki's eyes closed tightly, a tear escaping to run down her cheek. "No, I don't want to…. No thanks. Yeah, I'll consider it. That's probably a good idea, I'll be home soon."

With a jerky motion, Nicki put her phone back into her pocket and bit her lip. She looked over at Alex and took her cup of coffee back, not meeting Alex's eyes. Without a word she started moving determinedly towards the dormitories, leaving Alex stunned for a moment before she recovered herself and hurried after her.

"Nicki!" Alex called, slowing down only when she was at her friend's side. It took only a glance to see, even under her coat and multicolored scarf, that Nicki was shaking. "Nicki are you okay? Is your grandmother okay?"

The question about her grandmother seemed to cut through the haze and Nicki nodded quickly, but her shoulders were tense and her lips pressed together tightly. Nicki didn't speak, but dug into her pocket for her phone and pulled it out with a jarring motion. Alex glanced ahead to check how close they were to the dorm only to realize that Nicki had changed direction, leading them towards the parking lot.

"Come on Aiden," Nicki whispered as she held the phone to her ear. "Damn!" Nicki hissed before taking in a quick breath and saying, "Aiden, it's Nicki. I really need you to come by my Gran's... I just... need you there okay."

The phone was returned to her pocket and Alex struggled to understand what was happening. "How about I drive you home," Alex offered tentatively as they reached the main dorm parking lot. "Probably better if you don't drive."

"I'll be fine," Nicki muttered, fishing out her keys.

Rushing after her, Alex stumbled for the right words. "Look, Nicki, I don't know what happened, but you're upset and I have no idea how to fix it. But please let me drive so I at least don't have to worry about an accident."

Nicki stopped and Alex heard her take in another breath before she nodded. Hiding a sigh of relief, Alex pulled out her own keys and gestured in the direction of her own dark blue car. Nicki said nothing as Alex unlocked the car and brushed the small dusting of snow off the windshield. Alex pulled out of the parking lot and into the gentle flow of traffic, grateful that she already knew the location of the Russell Gallery. It didn't take long to cross town, but it felt very long to Alex who had to contain all her questions. Instead, she stayed silent and turned into the small parking lot tucked at the side of the three-story brick building by the lake. Nicki climbed out with a word and Alex debated if it was better to leave her alone or follow her inside.

Opening the door, Alex climbed out of her car and followed Nicki to the side door that accessed the third-floor residential area. Nicki held the door ajar for Alex, not commenting on her continued presence. They climbed the stairs quietly and Alex tried to focus on the photographs of Nicki and her grandmother that lined the walls around them. The top of the stairs opened into a large living room with a slanted beamed roof and large windows. A large curved comfortable looking sofa dominated the space with a dining area set up behind the living area that connected to the kitchen with a breakfast bar creating a division. Alex noticed the various pottery pieces and paintings around the room for only a moment as Nicki shrugged off her coat and scarf, hanging them on a coat rack. Alex scrambled to do the same, hoping that Aiden would get Nicki's message soon.

"I've lived here since I was six years old," Nicki told her softly. "My parents brought me to town to stay with my grandmother while they went to Portland." There was a long moment of silence as Nicki stared at the living room, seeing something that Alex could not. "They never came back, until today. Gran refused to let them see me unless I agreed." Nicki sniffed and rubbed her eyes, "I bet they're already driving off again."

Without another word, Nicki turned and walked to the closest door on the right where a wooden plaque hung proclaiming it: Nicki's Room. Alex followed Nicki inside. A large picture window looked out over Ravens Lake, framed by artistically hung blue drapes that shimmered in the dying sunlight. A tall bookshelf dominated the wall next to the window filled with books, figurines, and small pottery pieces. On the other side of the window was a reading chair with upholstery that matched the drapes and the comforter on the bed. A dresser stood near the bed, covered with various cosmetics and hair accessories, but also a wooden and glass jewelry box and a small electric fountain that was gently flowing.

Nicki sank onto the bed, her hands trembling. Alex followed her after a moment of hesitation and sat down on the bed next to her, reaching over and placing what she hoped was a comforting hand on Nicki's. Only the soothing sound of the fountain kept Alex grounded and from stumbling for something to say. She studied the fountain as she collected her thoughts, it was a simple design with a large curving spout rising from the center and pouring forth the water. Watching it, Alex felt Nicki turn one of her hands and clutch Alex's tightly. Soft sobs reached her ears and Alex looked at Nicki who had turned her face down to hide the tears. Leaning forward, Alex brought her right hand around Nicki's shoulder and squeezed gently. Another sob escaped Nicki, louder than before. Pulling her friend closer, Alex allowed Nicki to rest her head on her shoulder and stayed still as her friend cried.

The grip on Alex's hand tightened, becoming painful, but she managed to hold in a soft sound of discomfort. Nicki wouldn't have heard it; her own sobs filled the room. Tears ran down her cheeks, wetting Alex's T-shirt more with each passing moment. Softly, Alex used her free hand to rub circles on Nicki's back and whispered soft words to her, promising everything would be okay. Over the next few minutes, the tears lessened and the sobbing eased, leaving Nicki leaning quietly against Alex, clutching her hand like a lifeline.

"I used to lie about them," Nicki told Alex, her voice thick and heavy in the room. "At first when I thought they'd come back I said that they were on important business in Asia, or sometimes I said they were in the Army. In middle school, I started to say that they were missing, some kind of tragic accident. I was always making up stories to explain to other people and I suppose myself why they left me here." A deep sigh escapes Nicki, "a few years ago I accepted they were never coming back. I said they were dead. No fancy story, just they were dead."

"I'm sorry," Alex whispered, loss of what else to say.

"Gran never talked about them," Nicki told her the short pain laugh. "It's funny, for years I wanted them to come back for me, I wanted to ask why, but now…"

"Now?" Alex asked gently.

Nicki exhaled, the sound loud in the small bedroom. "I don't want them here. I'm angry at myself for letting them make me cry."

Alex didn't speak, she continued rubbing circles on her friend's back and hoping that Aiden would arrive soon. As much as she wanted to provide more comfort to Nicki, she found herself at a complete loss of what to say, what to do or what not to do. Alex licked her lips and swallowed, trying to overcome her dry mouth. Nicki's breathing so ragged and tears were flowing slowly down her cheeks.

"I'm sorry," Nicki whispered. "I… I wasn't prepared for this."

"It's not your fault," Alex told her quickly, trying to keep her voice gentle and not reveal the anger that she felt towards Nicki's parents.

She felt a strange pang of guilt for her own family and wondered how Aiden felt every time Nicki came over to his family home. Swallowing, Alex dropped her eyes to her hand that was starting to ache from Nicki's grip. Minutes later, Alex frowned as she became aware that something in the room had changed. She looked up quickly towards the open door but didn't see any sign of anyone moving around. The silence in the room felt heavy and in a moment Alex realized that the fountain had stopped.

Alex glanced towards the fountain and gasped. It wasn't that the fountain stopped working, Alex heard the motor running. But the water was swirling out of the basin into three curving columns. As she gaped at the gently flowing water, the three twisting columns combined in the center of the fountain over the main spout and formed a small sphere balanced between the three flows of water. Exhaling, Alex swallowed and was preparing to speak to Nicki when the water froze. Alex could see water solidifying and expanding, an icy chill settling in giving the strange sculpture a soft blue tint in the light of the room.

"Nicki," Alex managed in a shaky voice, "look."

"What?" Nicki asked, raising her head to look at Alex, but still not releasing her hand. She blinked away her tears and stared up at Alex's face. In the absence of any words from Alex, Nicki followed her gaze the fountain and gasped.

"Oh my God!" Nicki shrieked, clutching Alex's hand.

At her alarm, the ice cracked and began to crumble back into the basin of the fountain. Both girls watched in stunned silence, listening to the soft plops as each ice chip hit the remaining water in the fountain until Nicki raised her hand and made a tentative gesture. Nothing changed and another chip of ice fell back into the basin.

Glancing at Nicki, Alex watched her friend close her eyes and let out a long slow breath. Alex didn't move or speak even as

Nicki tightened her grip. Nicki's free hand moved gracefully through the air in a brief gesture. Turning back to the fountain, Alex watched a small wave of water rise from the basin in short abrupt movements. Slowly the small streams of water wound up the remainder of the icy columns. In the corner of her eye, Alex could see Nicki's hand was shaking even as she continued to gently move it through the air.

"I'm… I'm," Nicki stuttered with wide eyes locked on the fountain in the water.

"Doing magic," Alex breathed, her eyes darting between Nicki and the water slowly spiraling out of the basin to reform the structure that had cracked.

"Gran taught me to make sculptures like this with me when she told me that my parents were coming back," Nicki whispered her voice raw. "I'd been here all summer and Gran wanted to enroll me in school, but I still thought I would be going back to Nevada." The soft, almost pained laugh escaped Nicki and she sounded on the edge of hysterical to Alex. "Funny that I think of that now."

Alex didn't respond, choosing to brush her thumb over the back of Nicki's hand. Neither girl spoke as Nicki experimentally waved her hand to move the water causing a small wave to form at the side of the basin before she moved her hand back releasing the water to rush back to level once again. Slowly, as Nicki breathed in and out, the water turned to ice once again.

"I'm doing magic," Nicki repeated, excitement and awe filling her voice. "Alex, I'm really doing it!"

"Yeah," Alex replied, her own volume raising in excitement, "You are!"

Nicki let go of Alex's hand, turned and hugged her tightly. Laughter erupted from them both and Alex looked over at the fountain to see the structure beginning to melt in the heat of the room, but not crumbling like before. Suddenly there was a rush of footsteps and both of them turned towards the door in alarm.

"Nicki!" Aiden's voice cried out as he rushed in. "Are you alright? Is your grandmother okay?!"

"I'm fine Aiden," Nicki cheered, "Look at what I did!" She gestured to the ice sculpture and when Aiden blinked at it in confusion, she raised her hand and let out a soft breath. Nothing happened and she tried again.

"You can do it," Alex whispered to her, leaning forward to watch the fountain and ignoring the confused look they were getting from Aiden.

Nicki lowered her hand and closed her eyes, taking in a long breath. Opening her eyes again, she waved her hand gently and grinned when a small wave of water rose out of the fountain and swirled around in the air.

"Holy smokes!" Aiden gasped, stepping up to the fountain. He poked his finger into the water and then ran his hand through the small spout. "Nicki!" he cheered, turning to her with a wide grin, "You did it!"

"I did!" Nicki nearly screamed, jumping off the bed and hugging Aiden. He lifted her off her feet and laughed. Standing up, Alex watched the water splash back in the fountain and smiled at the two friends, wondering if she should leave so that Nicki could talk to Aiden.

"You sounded upset earlier," Aiden told Nicki as he set her back down and studied her face. "You've been crying," he observed with a frown taking over his face.

"My parents came back," Nicki told him weakly, "I had Gran tell them I don't want to see them."

Aiden looked at Nicki for a long moment before he nodded and smiled, "And you used magic!"

"I know!" Nicki answered, her smile returning. "I can't wait for our magic session tonight! I can't believe I did magic first!"

"Well technically Bran still did magic first with his visions," Aiden reminded her only to get a sharp punch in the arm. Looking at Alex, he gave her a quick wink and a warm smile.

"You're a brat," Nicki pouted before she sniffed and frowned. "I'm going to clean up," she muttered uncomfortably before vanishing out the door.

Aiden's eyes returned to Alex and his smiled faded softly. "Thank you," he told her, "I saw your car outside, you drove her here?"

"I was with her when she got the call," Alex offered with a small shrug. "She seemed too upset to drive."

"Thanks for that," he told her with a serious nod. "And thank you for staying with her."

"Course," Alex answered, feeling uncomfortable in Aiden's gaze. "She's my friend."

"Yes she is and you're ours," Aiden agreed before his easy-going smile returned. "Now we just need to convert you to the ways of the geek."

"I'm geeky enough already," Alex argued with a roll of her eyes.

"No such thing," Aiden argued with a wide smile, his eyes glinting. "That's just modern mainstream stuff, but there is so much more."

"I think I'll settle for magic lessons and college right now," Alex answered, trying to keep her own smile contained.

"Suit yourself," Aiden answered, "But you're always welcome."

Alex was about to thank him for the warm sentiment when an excited shriek from elsewhere grabbed their attention.

"Guys!" Nicki called, "You should see what I can do in a bathtub!"

Aiden sighed and looked up, muttering something under his breath before he turned and headed out the door. Despite having no idea where the bathroom was, Alex stood up to follow and see what Nicki had managed. Glancing at the ice sculpture she'd made just using the fountain, she guessed that it would certainly be different.

20

The Monomyth

A textbook on physics sat propped open in front of Alex and her tablet lying next to it on the large library table was showing a series of equations that she was supposed to be reviewing. However, Alex's attention was on the smaller book open on top of the textbook, *Faery Mythology*. Reaching into a bag of chips, Alex considered the author's interpretation of the story that made up the first part of the chapter. This story had presented the Fae, or the Sídhe, as Alex corrected in her head, as living in vast magical caverns under special hills. From her history class with Professor Cornwall, she was aware that most of the 'faery hills' were actually the work of Stone and Bronze Age humans, but Merlin and Morgana had mentioned that the Sídhe did use tunnels.

At least the small study room off the main stacks section of the library gave Alex privacy to read and mutter about faeries and Sídhe without getting strange looks. Through a glass window, she could see the rows of bookshelves and occasionally looked up as other students passed by. On the other side of the small room dominated by the one large table surrounded by chairs was a white board with a series of math problems that someone else had been working on along with a doodle of a rocket.

Popping a chip into her mouth, Alex muddled over the mythological question and wished that Morgana had given into Nicki's request for a serious question and answer session on the mythology and history surrounding the fight they were now in. Sadly, Merlin and Morgana had been completely focused on Nicki's newfound connection to her magic. Alex understood the excitement and the urgency, but Nicki had been swept out of the room by Merlin for practical use lessons leaving Alex, Aiden, and Bran alone with Morgana who was more determined than ever that they learn how to access their magic.

All of which was why Alex was in the library on a Friday night doing more mythology reading rather than working on the homework assignment that she'd been putting off for nearly a week. Sighing, Alex looked back over at her tablet as the screen went dark and tapped it once again to keep it awake. An alert for power flashed and Alex groaned. Digging out the charger, Alex located the outlet in the wall of the room and plugged the tablet in. She closed the mythology book and set it to the side, forcing herself to focus on the physics information in front of her.

Her mechanical pencil scratched the paper of her notebook softly, but it sounded loud in the quiet library. Alex drafted a list of bullet points for her part of the physics lab report and figured that she'd need to call Aiden in the morning to go over them before they finalized the report. The sound of footsteps out in the stacks made Alex pause, but they were paced normally so she went back to work. A knock on the open door of the study room a few moments later made her look up.

Arthur was standing in the doorway with a small smile and his backpack slung over one shoulder. He gestured to one of the free chairs and asked, "Can I join you?"

"Sure," Alex agreed quickly, pulling her things out of the center of the table.

Alex looked down at her books, but glanced up to watched Arthur shrug out of his coat and stretch after setting his backpack on the table. Forcing back a smile, Alex reached for her tablet and started typing up her part of the lab report for physics. Across from her, Arthur reached into his bag and pulled out a thick political science book with small plastic tabs sticking out on all three of the unbound sides. They settled into their work in silence, only talking briefly when Alex offered her bag of chips to Arthur and he pulled out a few with a smile. Yet, Alex could see some tension in Arthur's shoulders every time he moved. He kept running his hand through his hair and his jaw was clenched. She considered asking him directly what was wrong, but her stomach churned uncomfortably as she internally debated whether it was any of her business.

"Uh…" Arthur started slowly, his eyes rising to meet Alex's as she looked up. "Has Jenny said anything about housing next semester to you?" His jaw was clenching and unclenching with every breath he took.

"No," Alex replied automatically, feeling a hint of dread from Arthur's tone. "I assumed the plan was still for you two to move in together."

"She's renewed her place in the dorm with you," Arthur informed her, forcing an almost painful smile. "I figured she must have talked with you about it."

Despite his efforts, Alex could see the conflict on Arthur's face. He ran his hand through his hair again, making the already erratic blond hairs stick up in unnatural directions. Alex shook her head and bit her bottom lip slightly, dropping her eyes to her books as she tried to figure out what response to use.

"She's angry with me isn't she?" Arthur sighed what felt like an hour later, slumping back in his chair and fiddling with his hands. "I'm not sure why and she's acting normal when we're together, but… I don't know. It is strange that she changed her mind about living together."

"Maybe she's just enjoying the roommate experience," Alex offered with her own forced smile and a casual shrug. "You know, regular college stuff or... maybe she decided it was too soon for moving in together." Alex paused and rushed to explain her statement, "I mean, I know you two have been dating for years, but living together can be a pretty big step and maybe Jenny just wants to hold it off a little bit longer."

Arthur paused and straightened up a bit, clearly considering her remark. Slowly, he nodded and visibly relaxed. "You're probably right," Arthur agreed with a small and more natural smile. Then his smile turned sheepish and he added, "I should talk to her about it rather than her roommate and make sure she knows that whatever she wants is fine."

"Good plan," Alex agreed, giving a quick nod and looking down to hide a blush as Arthur beamed at her.

"Thank you," Arthur laughed gently. "You're the only female friend I've got other than Jenny of course and I can't imagine trying to talk that out with the football team."

"Lance probably would have listened," Alex offered with a little smile.

"Yeah, he would have listened and smacked my shoulder as a sign of solidarity and sympathy before figuring out some exit," Arthur replied with a chuckle and a more relaxed shrug.

"Arthur," Alex scolded lightly, trying to keep herself from smiling too widely as a genuine smile lit up Arthur's face.

"He's a good friend," Arthur assured her, "But he's not the chattiest guy if you haven't noticed."

"I've noticed," Alex assured him. "But then Jenny probably thinks I'm quiet too because she's a bit of a chatterbox."

"That she is," Arthur agreed with a smile. "Honestly it's one of the things I like best about her, just listening to the strange tangents that she can go off on and the things she thinks of."

Alex smiled softly at the description. She honestly found Jenny's rambles on fashion irritating, but her observations on recent events and news stories could be interesting. The biggest problem was when she wanted to talk about movies while they were still watching them and her tendency to yell at the television when one of Arthur's out of town games was on.

"You should hear her when she's watching one of your games," Alex told him with a teasing smile.

"I've heard her from the stands often enough," Arthur informed Alex with a slightly raised eyebrow. "So I can imagine."

Silence descended again and both returned to their work while nibbling on the bags of snack food between them. Their hands brushed once when they both reached for the chips and she was grateful that he didn't look up and see her blush. Arthur left for a few minutes and returned with bottles of water from the first floor vending machines. More than half an hour had passed since their conversation when Arthur started shifting around in his seat again.

"So literature?" Arthur questioned, glancing at the mythology book with interest before he looked back at Alex. "I've never asked, but what do you want to do?"

Alex opened her mouth and then closed it in hesitation. "I thought I'd teach," she admitted finally with a shrug, "But now I don't know what I want to do anymore."

"Are you going to change majors?" Arthur asked, tilting his head slightly and leaning on his hand as he studied Alex with a spark of curiosity.

"I don't think so," Alex told him. "But I think that I might shift my focus more to mythology and folklore. Maybe I'll take some anthropology classes," Alex said, smiling at the thought.

"Why?" Arthur asked and Alex could see real curiosity in his eyes.

"Well," Alex reached for the faery mythology book, "I started reading this because of... studying Shakespeare and my professor told us about how faeries were viewed in Shakespeare's time versus the vision of small people with wings that we have now. I guess it told me that as wonderful as stories are, that it can be really important to look at how meaning can change. According to my friend Nicki, studying how stories change and affect a people can be a real important part of understanding humanity."

Arthur was giving her a look of serious consideration and Alex fought back a blush, refusing to expose her silly little crush to him as much as possible. Slowly, he nodded and leaned back in the chair.

"That's interesting," he told her. "I remember one of my high school teachers talking about the monomyth, the idea that humanity keeps telling the same story over and over with similar elements."

"Yeah," Alex agreed with an energetic nod, "It's the pattern that we give our heroes as they confront something and cross the threshold between the known and the unknown." Alex considered the book in her hand for a moment before realizing that she was being far too quiet and added, "Of course what kind of job could I get except university professor. What about you?" Alex asked, "What do you want to do?"

"Not football," Arthur muttered with a chuckle, "I'm ready for the season to be done." He fiddled with his hands for a moment before looking back at Alex to answer the question. "I want to go to law school and study constitutional law," he admitted. "If I could do anything with my life, I'd love to be a part of an effort to reevaluate the Constitution and update it."

"Isn't that Congress' job?" Alex asked, leaning forward on her hand and delighting in the way that Arthur's eyes were lighting up.

"Usually," Arthur agreed, "But over two hundred years a lot of things have changed. Did you know that Senators were originally selected by the legislatures of the states and not a popular election?"

"No, I didn't know that," Alex told him.

"Yeah," he said, talking with his hands more than Alex had ever seen him, "Originally representatives were for the people and senators were for the states in order to help protect state governments and their powers. Obviously, that isn't the case anymore which is one of the reasons for the consolidation of power at the federal level."

"And you don't agree with that?" Alex asked with a hint of surprise.

"I'm not sure," Arthur admitted, "I just think that's an example of why it should be critically looked at beyond just a singular issue at a time which is how all changes are done now." It was Arthur's turn to blush slightly and he leaned back in his chair. "Sorry, that went on a bit."

"You sat through me discussing the pattern of the hero in human stories," Alex reminded him. "And for what it's worth I think you'll do great in law school."

"Thanks," Arthur told her with a wide smile.

His phone beeped with an incoming text and Arthur gave her an apologetic shrug before reaching into his pocket. Alex was silent and went back to her work as Arthur pulled out the phone and checked the message. A moment later the phone was returned to his pocket and Arthur reached for his backpack.

"That was Jenny," Arthur told her in a cheerful voice. "She wanted to see if I was free for dinner." He was beaming now and Alex forced a smile.

Arthur finished packing up his things in a rush of motion and pulled on his dark coat. Swinging, his bag over his shoulder, he reached across the table and caught Alex's hand. He gave it a squeeze and beamed at her.

"Thank you, Alex," he said warmly. "I'll talk to Jenny tonight."

"You're welcome," Alex managed, giving him a wide smile of her own. "Have fun!"

With one last grin over his shoulder, Arthur vanished out the doorway and through the rows of shelves. Sighing, Alex folded her arms on the table and lowered her head down to rest on them. A soft giggle escaped Alex and she muffled those that followed against her skin.

"Alex," she told herself with a sigh, "You really need to get over this crush."

She gave up on homework, knowing that she wasn't going to be very productive and packed up her things. Turning out the light, Alex adjusted her bag over her shoulder and headed down the stairs to the first floor. She paused to zip up her coat and then stepped outside into the cool evening. There was still snow in patches across the grass, but the first snow of the season was quickly retreating and Alex was able to enjoy a calm walk home.

Her dorm room was dark, unsurprising given that Jenny was out with Arthur. A note on her desk explained that Jenny didn't expect to be home until Saturday morning. Sighing, Alex deposited her bag on her desk and sat down to begin organizing her school things once again. When she pulled out the mythology book, Alex tossed it onto the bed with a huff. Leaning forward, Alex switched on her lamp and leaned back in her seat, allowing herself to get lost in her thoughts.

After several minutes of sitting in silence, Alex rose from her chair and returned to the doorway to turn off the main light. The room dimmed and only Alex's desk lamp provided illumination. Alex toed out of her shoes and released her hair from the ponytail. Climbing onto her bed, Alex moved the mythology book and crossed her legs. Taking a deep breath, Alex let her eyes fall closed and breathed like Professor Cornwall had instructed them for mediation purposes. But behind her eyelids, Alex saw only flashes of Sídhe hounds, Nicki controlling water and Arthur's smile.

21

Almost Human

822 B.C.E. Northern Cornwall

Her eyelids felt far too heavy was the first thought that Morgana was aware of when she began to stir. Much too heavy, she realized as she struggled to open them. Then she became aware of the woven material beneath her fingers that was far too rough to be her bed in the Sídhe realm. Her muscles ached in an unfamiliar way and there was the sound of a soft and warm female voice nearby that felt familiar and pleasant to Morgana. The strangeness of what she was feeling and thinking began to alarm her and Morgana struggled against the blackness in which she was trapped.

Suddenly there was a warm hand against her cheek. It was too warm to be the Queen's and the fingers that brushed her skin were callused, but the gentleness of the gesture soothed her and the blackness began to recede.

"Morgana," the soft and warm female voice called. "Please wake up," the voice begged.

The hand moved to her hair, brushing fingers through the long strands. Keeping her eyes closed, Morgana tried to make sense of what was going on as memories of the Queen's request and the strange ceremony trickled back to her. An overwhelming sense of fear rushed through her, causing her body to tense before she could control the reaction. The hand in her hair stopped and another hand came up to brush her cheek.

"Oh my child," the voice whispered. "Morgana? Can you hear me?"

Then there was another voice, further away and deeper, a masculine voice which called out, "How is Morgana, Eigyr?"

Eigyr; the name was familiar and Morgana struggled to understand why but kept her eyes closed while willing her body to relax. The hand resumed stroking her hair and the other hand slipped down to grasp her hand. Warmth flooded through her body at the gesture and Morgana barely held in a sigh at the skin to skin contact. A thumb traced the back of her hand, rubbing in a motion that was soothing, familiar and alien to Morgana all at once.

"She is still asleep," Eigyr answered softly, her voice sounding distressed and tired. "Oh Uthyrn, I wish I knew what happened."

Footfalls echoed strangely in the room, sounding muffled compared to the sharp sound of feet against stone that Morgana had grown up with. Another, much larger hand was lowered to her head for a moment before it was removed, leaving a trace of warmth on her forehead.

"She'll be alright Eigyr," Uthyrn promised in a gentle tone that rang with affection. "Just be patient."

"But what if what the men saw was true? Sídhe Riders were nearby? What if they-"

"The Sídhe take the children," Uthyrn interrupted, his tone more forceful and commanding before it eased. "It is possible that they were preparing to take her, I will not deny that, but they left her. They ran out of time before dawn and Morgana is safe at home."

It was all Morgana could do not to frown as more of the blackness faded and her senses returned to her. She risked taking in a deep breath only to nearly cough as strange smells assaulted her nose. There was the musty smell of the dirt of the Iron Realm, mixed with a sweeter smell coming from the woman and a distant smell of something that Morgana thought might be food. She could hear the woman stroking her hair humming a soft tune, the man pacing nearby with his feet scuffing the ground and other sounds that were blended together in an unfamiliar mess.

Moving only the tiniest bit, Morgana tried to get more comfortable on the strange bed and dispel the last of the blackness that was clouding her mind. She remembered the Changeling and how they had been bound together. Remembering the pain as their bodies crashed together during the ritual made Morgana's aches intensify. The memory the fiery potion, the screaming of the Changeling and her own tears crashed over her. Whimpering, she squeezed her eyes shut and pulled away as the woman Eigyr tried to hold her still.

Images flashed through her mind, alien and wrong. Smells and tastes that she'd never experienced took on meaning. Words never heard and with meanings that she could not comprehend began to organize themselves neatly in her mind, like one of the queen's scrolls. Too much and too strange. Tears slipped out of her eyes and a sob was ripped from her mouth. Another sob echoed hers, but Morgana did not believe it came from her and tried to roll away from the hands seeking to comfort her.

"Morgana," Eigyr cried, her voice breaking through the confusion. "Morgana, my baby!"

She was crying, Morgana realized, startled by the notion. Had she been struck when she tried to pull away? Morgana did not think that she had lashed out so why was she crying. She stopped moving but did not open her eyes. Tremors continued to rock her body, but she gripped the fabric beneath her tightly and breathed in the strange scent. Everything here was different, but it was real. Morgana breathed in again and listened to the woman's crying even as she felt her hands rubbing her back through the clothing that the Sídhe had given her.

The bed shifted as another figure knelt on it. Another pair of hands, Uthyrn's hands, grasped her gently, holding her still, but not holding her captive. Staying still, Morgana kept focusing on the smell and feel of where she was, pushing away the strange images and sounds that were echoing through her mind. The small hands of Eigyr ran through her hair, rubbed her neck and gently wiped away the tears on her cheek. Uthyrn's larger hands rubbed circles on her back and ran gently up and down her exposed arm. Despite the confusion, Morgana could not help but relax into the bed as the gentle touches continued, warmer and more comforting than anything she'd felt before.

Time moved without Morgana having any sense of its passage as she enjoyed the warmth of the embrace. Eigyr's crying softened and faded and Uthyrn's hand vanished, although Morgana could hear him pacing nearby. Now that she could think, she could feel the small weight of a bag inside her dress and wondered what Murden might have left with her. Slowly, it became more and more difficult to be still and the rising noise levels around her made it impossible to slip into sleep, no matter how comfortable it. Morgana gathered her thoughts and braced herself for the worst, reminding herself that this was all for the Queen. Opening her eyes slightly, Morgana shifted to give the illusion that she was waking.

"Morgana," Eigyr's voice gasped with delight and relief.

Warm hands returned to her face and arms and Morgana found herself carefully being raised to a seated position. She held back her pleasure at the gentle touches, sternly reminding herself of her mission and purpose in the Iron Realm. Morgana opened her eyes fully and focused on the woman next to her, only to softly gasp.

Staring at the woman, Morgana's mouth hung open in surprise as memories flitted through her mind like leaves on the breeze. The woman, Eigyr, had long dark brown hair like her own and facial features that were so much like the ones Morgana saw in the mirrors of her chambers. A pair of warm brown eyes, moist with tears met her own green ones as a hand reached for her.

"Morgana?" the woman questioned. "Are you alright? Were you injured?"

"Mother," Morgana breathed as the tentative hand brushed her cheek, the word springing to her lips unbidden. Stray tears gently ran down her cheeks as she drank in the sight of the woman, her heart beating quickly and a tightness in her chest making it difficult to breathe.

Smiling at her, her mother shifted forward and wrapped both arms tightly around her, cocooning Morgana in warmth. She did not tense back from the touch, surprising herself, but instead relaxed into the warmth of the woman holding her. Long gentle fingers stroked her hair. There were no claw protectors scratching her, no whispers around them about her poison blood and no quick end to the contact. If anything, the woman's arms became tighter around her and her mother began to gently rock her.

"Eigyr," Uthyrn called, "Let the girl breathe."

The grip around her loosened and Morgana found her lungs quickly taking in a deep breath that she hadn't known she needed. Yet, the arms remained around her and the woman turned slightly, bringing Morgana flush to her side. She could now turn her head to see more of the place she was in. It was a large room of some kind and circular with a sloping roof of branches and other materials that Morgana did not recognize. The floor was trodden down dirt which she had to still the impulse to wrinkle her nose at and the doorway was covered by thick animal pelts. She was on a primitive bed with a lumpy mattress and coarse fabric underneath her. Aware that she was perhaps observing the room too much, Morgana turned her attention to the tall man, Uthyrn who was watching her.

Uthyrn was broad shouldered with a thick unruly head of light brown hair worn in a long braid and brown eyes hidden under thick eyebrows. His clothing was crude to Morgana's eyes with a simple woolen tunic and belt over thick legging and leather shoes on his feet. The only things of note to her were the bronze brooch that fastened the red woolen cloak that hung over his shoulders, the jet beads that hung around his neck and the golden decorations at the end of his long braid. As she looked at him, a strange feeling of sorrow welled up in her that she was at a loss to explain.

"Stay with her," Uthyrn told Eigyr as he studied Morgana. "She is not acting like herself."

"She'd had a fright," Eigyr replied, brushing a soft kiss to Morgana's cheek. "She'll be alright."

"Yes," Uthyrn answered with a nod, walking towards the doorway. "But best that she isn't alone. I will make sure that the patrols have gone."

Eigyr chuckled as Uthyrn vanished past the pelts and pulled Morgana gently until her head lay against the woman's shoulder. The hand at her back kept rubbing gentle circles and Morgana felt a soft kiss pressed to her forehead.

"Your step-father," Eigyr muttered. "As though I'd leave you. Arto will be fine with Caoimhe for a few hours."

Both names echoed in her head; Morgana groaned and turned her cheek further into the warmth of the woman, her mother. The word sent a thrill through her, it was a word known to her only by explanation of reproduction. She'd never truly given the word any thought while she lived in the Sídhe Realm although on occasion families appeared before the Queen. Morgana froze and her body tensed, the Queen. She was surely betraying her Queen by allowing this ... iron creature to touch her so. But she was also to live in place of her Changeling self, live in the iron realm in order to observe her Queen's enemies.

"Morgana?" her mother called, shifting so she could lift Morgan's face up towards her. "My child are you alright?" Her mother's eyes became moist and Morgana wondered if she would cry again. "What happened Morgana? Did the Sídhe....?"

Fear. It was all Morgana could hear. The fear in the woman's voice despite her attempts to control it. She was so afraid, but of what? Staring at her face, Morgana tried to understand why the woman said the name of the great Sídhe with such fear? Surely she had to know that the Sídhe rescued children, surely she should have been saddened that Morgana had not been taken. Why was she so afraid?

Suddenly Morgana could hear crying and screaming around her. She could hear worried voices whispering nearby and children whimpering. Warnings echoed in her mind, so many warning about the Sídhe. The days to avoid leaving her village, warning to be home before dusk and never leave before dawn, but she'd been careless. She remembered the howls of the Hounds and the Sídhe Rider grabbing her away from the field she'd been in only the day before. Morgana could feel the bruises on her arms, could remember being taken to the hill where…. where she'd seen herself arriving with a group of Sídhe.

"No," Morgana crocked. "No, they… started to take me, but dawn came before we got to the tunnels," she managed.

"I'm so sorry," her mother whispered, wrapping her in another hug. "I'm so sorry you had to face that. The moment we knew you were gone Uthyrn took the guard out to search for you. I could barely believe it when they brought you home. I hoped, but-"

Tears, Morgana realized as few drops hit the top of her head. Her mother was crying. A dull pang hit her chest, feeling like a hammer had struck her. It was hard to breathe and hard to think of anything but those tears. There was a wrongness to it that Morgana did not understand, but was certain of. She shivered, fear creeping into her mind at the alien feelings that she had towards this woman. It should not matter, Morgana told herself fiercely as she shut her eyes tightly and focused on the face of Queen Scáthbás in her mind's eye.

"I love you, Morgana," her mother whispered, the words muffled by her hair, but still reaching Morgana clearly.

Her hands shook and she had to close her eyes tighter as another wave of unfamiliar images flashed through her head.

She could hear singing, sweet and natural nearby. Her mother's face leaning over her as a hand cupped her cheek. Soft whispers that she was loved. Laughter nearby. Her face hurt from smiling. There was a tall man who scooped her up and held her. He said that he loved her, but there was grief. That man was gone, her father was gone. Mother was still here and mother loved her.

"You're shaking," Eigyr sniffed, pulling away slightly from Morgana to study her.

"Just…." Morgana trailed off, tears slipping from her own eyes. "I love you," she croaked, the words painful and heavy on her tongue, but the need to say them was too strong. It was urgent, she'd die if she didn't and worse yet, they felt true.

Smiling gently, Eigyr brushed a strand of hair behind her ear. Movement in the corner of her eye made Morgana turn her head quickly towards the door. Eigyr moved off the bed in a fluid motion and Morgana's eyes landed on a small child that her mother moved towards. He looked roughly two years of age with light brown hair and Uthyrn's brown eyes. The boy was looking up at Eigyr with an expression of adoration, Morgana noted with a frown. Her mother's hand moved to the boy's head and brushed several long strands of hair from his face in a gentle fashion that made Morgana tighten her fists.

"As you can see Arto," Eigyr said happily, "Your sister is safely back with us."

Morgana's frown deepened as she considered the words. If this was her brother, then this was the weapon of the Iron Realm and the threat to the Sídhe. This was her mission. Another wave of images and sounds crashed through her mind. More prepared for it, Morgana tensed and kept breathing through the rapid flashing of her Changeling's memories as they tried to settle into her own mind.

Her father was gone, but then Uthyrn came into their lives. He was a leader, a protector of the bronze routes to the southern lands and strong like her father had been. She did not like him at first, taking Father's place and taking Mother, but Mother smiled again. Then Mother had become heavy with child and the boy had come. So small, so helpless and so trusting. He reached for her, he laughed and smiled at her. So many memories of holding him and playing in the grass with him as Mother and Uthyrn looked on. Her brother, her little brother. So many emotions tied up in him, more than with Mother. Protectiveness, irritation, anger, selfishness, amazement, gratitude and love.

Taking a shaky breath, Morgana eased the tight grip she'd made on the bed without realizing it. Arto was still gazing at Eigyr, but he turned his head to smile at Morgana. She lowered her eyes but forced an uncomfortable smile. Her stomach turned and her chest hurt, there was just too much. How could the Queen expect her to survive this? There just too much of everything up here? She had no distance from these iron creatures, no shields and she was alone. How could she do this?

"Gana?" a small voice called just before a tiny hand was placed on her knee. "Gana?"

Morgana's hands shook, but she forced herself to look at the boy, Arto. Green eyes met brown and then there was something, a rush of magic so different from that which she had grown up with in the Sídhe Realm. It surrounded them, it linked them and Morgana was overwhelmed with images not from the mind of her Changeling, but from the boy.

Red hot flames danced before her and a strange metal orb glowed in their heat. Its surface cracked, spilling orange molten tears to the surface of a smooth stone. She inhaled the scent of fire, of charcoal and metal. A heavy metallic ringing echoed around her, once, twice and thrice before it all vanished.

Crying filled the roundhouse as Arto stumbled back from Morgana, tripping on his own feet and falling back against the floor. Eigyr moved forward, but Morgana pushed herself off the bed and dropped to her knees in from of Arto. Without hesitation, she gathered him in her arms and held him close, feeling his heart beat against her chest. He sniffed softly in her arms and burrowed closer to her. Feeling soft hair in her fingers, Morgana realized that she'd begun stroking his hair without meaning to.

"Gana?" the boy cried softly, weeping tears against her upper chest.

"It's alright Arto," Morgana whispered gently, astonished by her own words. "It's alright."

His crying eased and Morgana realized that Eigyr was kneeling next to them, her hand gently resting on Arto's head. Slowly releasing the boy, Morgana watched as Eigyr gathered him up and rocked him. Her mother made soft cooing noises before rising to her feet, Arto still snug in her arms.

"He must be exhausted," she observed in a low voice before turning her eyes back to Morgana. "Will you be alright by yourself while I take him back to Caoimhe?"

"Certainly Mother," Morgana answered, her eyes still fixed on Arto. Her heart was still pounding and the scent of fire and metal filled her nose. If she hadn't known better, she would have believed that smoke filled her lungs. "I'm tired as well," she continued with a small yawn. "I should sleep more."

Eigyr nodded slowly and Morgana's heart ached again as she realized that the woman hesitated to leave her. Giving another yawn, Morgana sat back down on the bed and stretched out, lying her head down so she could see her mother and brother. Smiling gently, Morgana sighed and closed her eyes, but focused on the sound of Eigyr moving towards the doorway with slow hesitate steps.

"I will leave you to rest," Eigyr told her from the doorway. "Perhaps Uthyrn has news."

For several minutes after her mother left the roundhouse, Morgana remained still on the bed with her eyes closed. Strange faces danced in her mind, connected to memories just beyond her reach, but flashes of strange emotions came with them. There was so much… joy, but there was also fear connected to the Sídhe. Her fingers twisted in the fabric as an image of a Rider with a Hound crashed forward in her mind and Morgana felt the crippling terror that her Changeling self had gone through. Breathing deeply, Morgana did her best to shove the images away. One breath and then another and another to regain her balance and sense of purpose.

Despite years of training, it wasn't a simple task. She was alone in the roundhouse and yet still felt surrounded by those the Changeling had known as family. Their scent was in the air around her, their things scattered nearby on the tables and shelves and she could feel their presence in the wood of the house itself. Morgana moved slowly, watching the doorway and carefully moved her dress enough to retrieve the bag that had been hidden beneath her belt against her body. It was a small smooth bag that her fingers rejoiced to feel after nothing but the coarse fabrics of the iron realm. A small drawstring was tied tightly and Morgana needed a moment to loosen it. Once it was open, she dared not look inside for several minutes before she grew angry at her own fear.

Tilting the bag gently, Morgana held her breath as a small smooth metal disk fell into her hand. Gasping softly, she set the bag to the side and brushed her fingers over the metal with some hesitation. She closed her eyes and breathed to connect to her magic. Morgana flinched, the connection had twisted and felt so weak, but she pushed the magic forth and into the metal.

A chill rushed over her body at the effort, but Morgana continued the effort until the surface of the disk began to shimmer softly. The smooth surface was cloudy, but the face of the Queen was distinct and well known to Morgana. Guilt sunk into her as she gazed at the face, but Morgana wasn't certain of the source. Was it guilt for her enjoyment of the iron woman's touch or guilt for the falsehood she was committing against the Iron folk. The thought was disturbing and Morgana had to fight it back.

"Morgana my darling," the Queen cooed, her voice cool and musical, but it no longer seemed as comforting. "How goes your mission my precious one?"

"I have been accepted by the iron folk in the place of the changeling," she said clearly, gratified that her voice did not quake.

"And the weapon?" the Queen asked urgently. Morgana did not need to see her clearly to know that she eyes would be gleaming.

"It is here," Morgana answered, minding her voice and tone. "It is very young. I do not believe it has any knowledge…. but…." She was going to speak of the strange burst of magic when she met the boy's eyes, but the words would not form.

"But?" The Queen pressed, her voice taking on a cold edge that Morgana was familiar with when the Queen scolded her enemies, but the Queen's voice gentled a moment later. "What is it my darling?"

"But I shall need to observe it more carefully," Morgana assured her. "This may yet be a trick. I will need to watch all the iron folk and observe how they treat the weapon. The answer may be there."

"My clever darling," the Queen praised. "Indeed the weapon may not know what it is, but the iron folk must know something. Watch and be vigilant my precious one. This is the day when our glory truly began! You, my perfect girl, shall be the greatest of heroes and all the iron folk will be brought into the light so they may rejoice in your name."

"Yes Your Majesty," Morgana whispered with as much awe and reverence as she could muster.

Her response satisfied the queen and the metal disk returned to normal as the magic was withdrawn. Sighing in relief, Morgana dropped it on the bed, rubbing her hands together in a desperate attempt to warm them. Her body's aches were worse than before and her mind felt muddled. Magic had not been so difficult for many months, but she felt as though she had just cast her first clumsy spell. Picking up the metal disk, Morgana slipped it back into the bag and hid it once again under the dress. She lay down on the bed; this time feeling true exhaustion and this time grateful for the blackness that became overtook her.

22

The Tree of Reality

She was dreaming, Alex knew that she had to be dreaming, but she couldn't wake up. The darkness of the tunnel stretched out before her and the small light of her phone barely improved visibility. Cold stone met her fingers as Alex reached out to trace the wall and once again tried to force herself to wake up. Far behind her, she could hear musical voices whispering and laughing, the sounds echoing down the tunnels and distorting. Taking another step, Alex kept the light down so she could see her feet and the stone beneath them. The air was chilled and stale, making it difficult to breathe.

A whimpered echoed down the long tunnel and resonated all around her, followed by a muffled sob. Stopping, Alex listened to the sound and her stomach tightened painfully as she recognized that someone was crying. The noises behind her grew louder, their words were indistinct, but the tone had shifted. A shiver rushed down her spine and Alex resisted the urge to stop and look back, knowing that she wouldn't see anything.

She stepped forward, shining her low light forward. There, just ahead the tunnel turned and widened. Alex took a few more steps forward and looked around the turn. A sudden blast of fresh air met her nose and she inhaled deeply. The air rushed over her skin which felt raw and frozen in the icy breeze. Swallowing, Alex continued forward, minding her footing as the tunnel sloped upwards towards the surface. Up ahead Alex could see the moonlight and the stars shining into the dark tunnel, making the black stones shine. For a moment Alex couldn't move and the knowledge that this was only a dream faded away. Desperately, she reached forward, letting go of the wall and nearly dropping her phone. A few steps more was all it took before she was looking up towards the night sky.

A scream ripped up the tunnel. Spinning, Alex stared back down into the darkness, holding her phone out in front of her, desperate for some light. The screaming died down, but shattering sobs echoed around Alex a moment later. The whispers in the distance were louder now and Alex caught a few stray words in the darkness: kill, slave, iron childe, and blood. Heavy in the air, the words knocked around Alex's mind and a creeping doubt that she was dreaming began to take hold. Gripping the wall once more, Alex stumbled backward towards the opening. On her back, she could feel the chill of the wind through her sweatshirt and the smooth floor gave way to sharp rubble beneath her tennis shoes.

She was going to climb out of this, Alex reminded herself. This was a dream and if she got out of the tunnels, she'd wake up. The sobbing was weakening in the distance, accented by whimpering. Then a small and simple word rang down the tunnels to Alex's ears.

"Mommy!"

It was a child's voice. With shaking hands, Alex turned her light back towards the turn and took a shaky step towards it. The crying softened further, but the whispers were louder than ever. A few more careful steps brought Alex back to the narrow tunnel. Raising her phone higher, Alex shone the light away from her feet only to gasp.

A pair of purple eyes stared out at her from the darkness, glowing softly with glee. Her phone fell from her hand and cracked against the stone, the light vanishing from the tunnel. Whatever was in front of her chuckled darkly and reached for her.

The blaring of her cell phone alarm brought Alex sharply back to reality. Her eyes flew open as she gasped for air, turning her head away from her pillow. Disoriented as she was, Alex blindly reached for her phone and turned off the alarm before slowly sitting up in bed. She was in her dorm room and Jenny was seated over at her desk, giving her a funny look over her shoulder.

"You okay sweetie?" Jenny questioned with a touch of worry in her voice.

"Nightmare," Alex answered quickly, rubbing the back of her neck. "What time is it?"

"Six o'clock," Jenny replied. "Dinner time before your study group. We're meeting the boys in ten minutes."

"Right," Alex agreed with a little nod as the word came back into proper focus. It was Monday; she'd been tired and took a nap after literature class. "Food and then studying," Alex repeated to herself as she found her shoes next to the bed and slipped into them.

"Go splash some water on your face," Jenny suggested with a soft smile. "Might help you wake up a bit."

"Good idea," Alex answered quickly, shoving her keys into her pocket.

She stopped by her dresser long enough to comb the tangles out of her hair and tie it back before heading for the bathroom. Without looking in the mirror, Alex splashed some water on her face and rinsed out her mouth. Then she studied herself in the brightly lit mirror. She looked tired. The nightmare was occurring more and more regularly for her while Nicki had admitted she hadn't had it for a while. Alex just hoped that the theory it was linked to hearing about the Sídhe was accurate and it wasn't an omen of some kind.

When she got back to the dorm room, Alex grabbed her coat and wallet as Jenny touched up her makeup and picked up her purse. Neither of them spoke as they followed the sidewalk over to Michaels Hall. Lance and Arthur were waiting in the hallway by the main door of the cafeteria. Lance gave them both a smile and wave while Arthur stepped forward and greeted Jenny with a kiss on the lips. Then he surprised Alex by kissing her cheek quickly.

"How was your day darling?" Arthur asked as he took Jenny's hand.

"Not bad," Jenny answered with a wide smile. "Busy certainly; I'll be glad when Thanksgiving break arrives."

"Yeah, I can't wait to go home, even if only for a few days," Arthur agreed as they headed inside.

Michaels Cafeteria was already busy with lines of students at the salad bar and the drinks station while others darted between the different food stations. Rather than join the line, Arthur headed for a small square table in the center of the dining space which was still empty and Alex, Jenny and Lance split up to select their preferred meals. Alex finished first with a slab of lasagna and a salad and sat down at the table with a smile at Arthur as he stood and went to get his own meal. She only had to sit for a few moments alone before Lance slid into the seat next to her with a full tray and a smile. Jenny was only a few steps behind and smiled at them both.

No one said anything of significance until Arthur sat down and then Jenny launched into a story about her journalism class. Alex tried to focus on her friends and the story, but an odd sense of something hung about them making the air seem a bit thicker and heavier than it should. Lance was quieter than usual, which for him meant that he only said five words during the whole meal and two of them were simple yeses to agree with something Arthur said.

"Are you feeling okay?" Alex asked Lance softly when Jenny and Arthur left the table to grab some desert for them.

"Fine," Lance answered quickly with a rather forced smile. "I think I have a touch of a cold or something," he added with a shrug.

"Okay," Alex replied uncertainly. "Just don't get too sick before Thanksgiving."

"Oh I don't know, if I go home ill then Mom will make me chicken and rice," Lance observed with a slight smile.

"She'll probably make it anyway," Alex remarked. "You've been away from home for a while now. I remember when Matt came back home for the first time. Mom had his favorite things stocked up and made him his favorite meals, plus she did his laundry." Alex grinned and added, "I guess it's my turn now."

Lance opened his mouth and started to speak when Arthur and Jenny returned with four small plates with chocolate cake on them. Smiling, Jenny set a piece down in front of Lance while Arthur handed a plate to Alex. The conversation changed once again to the wrap up of football season for Lance and Arthur along with Jenny asking Lance when he was going home. It was the beeping of Alex's phone that reminded her of her magic lessons and she regretfully stood up.

"Sorry guys," she apologized as she pulled on her coat and collected her bag. "I'll see you later Jenny."

"Right," Jenny replied, her face falling before she replaced it with a smile. "Well, have a good study session hon."

"Probably not, but thanks for the hope," Alex answered, giving her friends a little wave and grabbing her tray.

Stopping long enough to deposit her tray at the dishwashing station, Alex pulled on her gloves and headed outside. The onset of autumn meant that magic lessons started after dark and since Halloween, she'd become more than a little hesitant about being out after dark. Her hand slipped into her bag and rested gently on the hilt of her iron knife. It felt warm to her touch and Alex relaxed slightly. As she crossed the lawn, she noticed Nicki, Aiden, and Bran a little ways ahead of her.

"Nicki," she called, "Aiden! Bran wait up."

The trio stopped and Aiden turned to look over his shoulder at her as Alex rushed up the sidewalk to join them. Grinning, Nicki reached over and gave her hand a quick squeeze. Returning the smile, Alex squeezed her hand back and then dropped it as they started to walk towards the Kittell Building.

"My parents sent me a letter," Nicki told them as they passed under a street light.

"Oh," Aiden replied sounding uninterested, but Alex noted him watching Nicki carefully in the corner of his eye.

"I sent them a response," Nicki continued, "Gran read it for me to make sure it didn't come off too bitter or angry."

"So you told them…." Bran trailed off, glancing at Aiden in search of guidance.

"I told them that I'm grateful for the chance to have closure, but I'm not interested in having them be a part of my life,"

Nicki answered, looking up at Aiden with a sad smile. "I think Gran was happy with that."

"She loves you," Aiden replied with a shrug. "I doubt she'll ever forgive your mom."

"I kind of wish she would," she sighed, rolling her neck slightly. "Honestly, I've forgiven them now and I feel... just so much better."

"Plus magic," Bran added, making them all chuckle.

"The magic is good too," Nicki admitted with a grin before looking at the others. "So any of you have a great truth that needs admitting to find balance?"

"Not me," Aiden remarked, "You know me, pretty much an open book."

"An open geeky book," Nicki muttered, linking her arm through his and shaking her head.

"I'm not sure, but if it is something like that then it'll probably be about my dad's death in Iraq or Mom's guilt over the accident," Bran informed them, shifting the tone back to heavier subjects. "But the meditation seems to be helping so maybe I'll find my balance soon."

"I hope so," Nicki huffed. "Honestly, working one on one with Morgana is every bit as intimidating as it sounds."

Aiden bumped Nicki's shoulder with a laugh. "You're not really motivating me to find my balance," he told her playfully.

The Kittell Building loomed over them, almost completely dark save for the main hall lights. Across the lawn, the commons still had a few lights on and down the sidewalk the library was still brightly lit, but there weren't many students out. Aiden pulled open the front door and gestured everyone inside with a small bow. Nicki patted his head as she passed and Alex barely contained a snort at his look of indignation.

Professor Yates and Professor Cornwall were waiting for them in the room, speaking by the desk in low voices which stopped the instant that Nicki strode into the room. Everyone took their seats and Nicki braided a small lock of her hair while Bran maneuvered into the desk.

"Good evening," Merlin greeted them with a smile. "Today we'll continue working on your meditation practices so you can keep working on it over Thanksgiving break."

"Professor?" Nicki called, holding up her hand.

"Yes Nicole," Merlin asked patiently.

Nicki ignored the use of her proper name and tugged at the small braid she'd made to unravel it. "I've been reading up on faery mythology and I was wondering how the other creatures matter. I mean," she stumbled slightly, "Are they real and if so what's the connection? Are they weak to iron? Do they help the Sídhe?"

"I'm not sure that's the most pressing thing to teach you," Merlin began to say.

Bran jumped in, leaning forward in his desk, "But sir, we're not getting anywhere just doing meditation. Surely we also need to know more about what might be coming after us."

Merlin and Morgana exchanged a look that spoke of just how long they'd know each other because without a nod or any sign of agreement, they both raised their hands and golden streams of light sprang forth. Despite being comfortable or mostly comfortable with the existence of magic, Alex watched in awe as the streams of magic formed a large tree in front of them. Soft blue balls of light were casually tossed by both Merlin and Morgana onto the tree, causing certain parts of the golden trunk and branches to pulse.

"The Tree of Reality," Aiden observed as he studied it more critically than before. "Which ones were Earth and Sídhean?"

Smiling at the question, Merlin pointed to a pulse of blue in the gold near the top of the trunk where the branches began to spread. "This is the Iron Realm, Earth," he reminded them.

"And all of these worlds are in different… realities?" Bran questioned he studied the tree intently.

"No," Morgana told him, "In many cases the worlds on the same branches are in the same reality, separated by space, but metaphysically linked by the Tree of Reality due to the presence of sentient life."

"So is this all the worlds with life?" Alex asked, looking at Earth which was alone.

"I don't know," Morgana told her, earning a startled expression from Alex. The usually elegant teacher simply shrugged and continued to explain, "We don't know everything. Our knowledge extends to the thirty-nine worlds that make up the tree, but why those worlds and if there are any beyond it is something we have no answer to."

"That would take the fun out of being alive," Merlin added with a chuckle, lightening the mood a tiny bit. "My personal theory is that the Tree of Reality is an energy system to ensure the continuation of the universe in some form. It links different realities, perhaps to keep them connected for the next Big Bang."

Bran grinned at the idea and Merlin gave him a quick wink while Morgana huffed and shook her head.

"Regardless," Morgana began again, "These are the worlds that have the potential to affect and even end life on Earth. Due to Earth's position at the base of all branches, it is a crossroads in the tree of reality."

"Do you have a theory?" Bran asked, his eyes still locked on the tree.

Morgana sighed, but answered, "I favor the idea that someone with too much magical power got bored one day and thought it would be fun to link a bunch of worlds together that shouldn't have ever met in order to see what would happen." Her crisp tone made them all freeze uncomfortably and Morgana turned her attention back to the tree.

She moved around the tree calmly and pointed at a pulsing point near the one Merlin had indicated was Earth. "And this is Sídhean," she announced before shifting her hand and gesturing to the branch that the Sídhean world was on. Looking at the branch, Alex noticed it split into another branch near the Sídhe world with three more glowing lights on one side and four on the other branch.

"Sídhean is a cross road world much like Earth," Merlin explained, "It sits at the split of two branches and shares traits with both. Earth is not the first world that Sídhe have sought control over. The sad fact is that those seven worlds and their peoples are already under the power of the Sídhe."

"All of them?" Nicki repeated in shock. "Seriously, seven whole worlds?"

"The branch that Sídhe naturally sits on joins those who have certain traits in common, mainly a weakness to iron. To answer your question about the different mythological kinds of faeries, this is the reason for the variety of creatures and their shared weakness. All the different types of faery folk are members of peoples who have been conquered by the Sídhe. As you can see they can go no further in their quest without first taking Earth."

"And then they'll have access to all the other branches," Nicki murmured as worry settled on her face. "That does answer my mythology question."

"And because Earth is in the way, none of the other worlds can fight the Sídhe."

"Like Earth, many of these worlds have their own problems," Merlin told them, shaking his head. "There are those who don't worry about the Sídhe and many worlds just like Earth are largely unaware of the Tree of Reality that links them to potential hostile peoples."

"And others assume that the Sídhe weakness to iron means that they can go no further," Morgana added with a look at the branches. She waved her hand and the small glowing balls of light that marked the worlds around Sídhean all turned blood red. Shuddering slightly, Alex dropped her eyes and looked at her hands, aware of the silence that had settled into the room. "Sadly," Morgana continued a moment later, "The protections that were created on Earth will fail soon and humanity has forgotten much."

"Plus plastic has taken over," Aiden sighed, leaning on his hand. Alex snorted softly despite herself and looked up at the tree.

"That doesn't help," Merlin agreed while watching Morgana for a long moment as she stared at the glowing red worlds. Then he waved his hand and the tree vanished in a shimmer of gold, blue and red. "Now it is time to turn your attention back to learning your magic."

"But-" Nicki began to protest.

"Nicole," Merlin said firmly, stopping her. "I appreciate your curiosity, but Morgana and I are thousands of years old. We could never tell you everything and knowing it is not what will save you when the Hounds return. I suggest we return our focus to your magic lessons."

23

Of Dreams and Visions

Staring up at Hatfield Hall from the parking lot, Alex tried to prepare herself for the return to school after Thanksgiving break. While at home, she'd found it frighteningly easy to forget about the Sídhe and magic. It had been simple to hug her parents when she arrived home, tease her younger brother Eddy and be teased in return by her older brother Matt. Mom had spoiled them all with home cooked meals and doing the laundry. Sighing softly, Alex hoisted on her backpack and picked up the folding laundry basket that was now filled with clean and folded clothing.

She closed the door of her car with her foot and headed for the building, trying to remember which pocket of her backpack she'd hidden her dagger in. The realization that she wasn't certain made Alex inwardly flinch at her own negligence while another little voice inside of her pointed out that nothing had happened in a month. December started the next day and the only magical event in November had been Nicki gaining control of her powers. Alex huffed, that wasn't true anymore. Aiden had apparently succeeded in lighting a candle with his powers during mediation the day after Thanksgiving according to Nicki's excited phone call yesterday.

Alex had no doubt that Morgana would be testing him at Monday's session. And Bran had already had magical visions for years even if he couldn't control them. She swiped her key card with more force than was necessary and set down her laundry long enough to pull the door open with a hard jerk.

If Aiden had gained control then she was falling behind the others. Shaking her head, Alex stepped into the elevator and took a breath to calm down. Her hand dropped to the top of her laundry basket where Galahad was placed for safe keeping and she pet the plush fur to calm down. She was being silly and worrying too much. There were people milling about all through the hallways as students said hello and unpacked their things. Alex greeted Mary and Tiana through their open doorway as she headed for her own room.

Setting her laundry down and shrugging off her backpack, Alex closed and locked her door with a grateful sigh. After the drive from Spokane, her back hurt and she was sure that she must have been gritting her teeth through the flurry outside of Portland. Rubbing the back of her neck, Alex toed out of her shoes and sat down to pull on a pair of fuzzy socks. She ignored her clean laundry in favor of unpacking her laptop and tablet, taking a moment to call her mother to let her know she'd arrived safely. On her phone was a text from Jenny letting her know that a travel delay would result in her getting home late, but that everything was fine.

Soon Alex was more relaxed, her laundry was put away and she was considering doing some meditation exercises, hoping that if they helped Aiden she'd have some luck with them too. A knock on her door grabbed her attention and Alex opened it to find Bran standing in the hall.

"Bran?" Alex half greeted, half asked. "Hi," she quickly amended. "It's good to see you."

"Welcome back," Bran greeted her with a small smile before gesturing into her room with his free hand. "Can I come in?"

Pushing down the urge to sigh, Alex stepped to the side and made room for Bran to walk into the room. His cane tapped loudly against the tiles as he moved to Jenny's bed and sat down. He huffed slightly and set his cane to the side making Alex wonder if the cold made things harder for him. She considered asking, but Bran looked up at her with a strange expression, his green eyes almost calculating.

"So?" Alex questioned, "What's up?" Chuckling, Alex tilted her head and added, "I have a feeling that you didn't show up just to welcome me back."

"No, I didn't," Bran admitted with a nod. "Nicki called you right?"

"Aiden has control over his powers, yeah she called me," Alex assured him.

Bran snorted and at her surprised expression explained, "Control is saying a bit too much. He lit a candle during mediation and then yesterday he set a blanket on fire. Luckily Nicki was there and put the fire out."

Eyes widening, Alex couldn't help but smile as the scene played in her head. She had no doubt that Nicki was going to be lording that over Aiden for at least a week.

"I guess it's good that she found her magic first," Alex offered and was pleased when Bran's lips twitched into a real smile. They were quiet for a moment and Alex noted Bran pulling at a thread on his jacket cuff. "So, what else do you want to talk about?"

Bran raised his green eyes to Alex's and acknowledged her with a tilt of his head. "Nicki said you've been having the nightmares," Bran informed Alex. "Aiden had it a few times too. The dark tunnel and the strange voices in the distance."

"It's not surprising," Alex remarked with a quick shrug, trying to sound calm at the sudden focus of the conversation. "We've all been told that the fate of the world is depending on us gaining control of our magic and the Sídhe use special magical tunnels to enter our world."

"But all of us having the same nightmare?" Bran pressed.

Sighing, Alex sank onto her bed, grateful that Jenny wasn't due back for another few hours since their flight out of San Francisco was delayed. She didn't want to risk anyone walking in on this conversation.

"Maybe it's just about the Connection we formed," Alex offered, rolling her shoulders which suddenly felt very tense and uncomfortable.

"Maybe," Bran conceded with a small sigh. "I'll go with that explanation, but has your dream differed at all from the dark tunnel and the voices?"

"Differed...." Alex said slowly, her mind instantly jumping back to the child she heard scream and cry. "Nothing major, but..."

"But?" Bran pressed, leaning forward a little bit. "But what?"

"In the last two weeks," Alex stumbled, biting her lip before she forced herself to continue. "I get to the end of the tunnel."

"You get to the end?" Bran asked in surprise, "Nicki and Aiden said they never made it to the end."

"Yeah," Alex mumbled, "But then I hear a little kid scream and cry so I turn around and go back into the tunnel. I usually wake up around then, but I can see the stars and I turn back."

Bran was studying her with a slight frown, but he nodded slowly. "My dream differs too," he confessed. "Except I don't find the exit, but a path that leads further down. I hear metal hammering so I follow the sound even though it takes me deeper."

"And?" Alex questioned, "What do you find?"

"I wake up just as I'm coming around a corner, every time. I can see this bright light that illuminates the cave walls in front of me, I can smell smoke and feel the heat of a fire, but I haven't been able to turn that last corner," Bran told her, his eyes distant. Alex didn't' have to wonder what he was seeing.

"And you think it means something?" Alex asked him softly, tucking her feet under her as she felt the chill of the tunnels settle over her skin. Her mind went back to when she'd first met Arthur. A fire wasn't so unusual, but the metal clanging was a shared detail that made her heart beat faster.

"Yes," Bran answered shortly, "I think it is very important. My theory is that it is the magic of Earth trying to warn us." As he spoke, Bran was toying with a paperclip that he'd drawn out of his pocket.

"Of what?" Alex asked in a quiet voice that sounded weaker than she wanted. "We already know that the Sídhe are getting stronger. The dreams might be useful if they allowed us to map out the tunnels," Alex argued before frowning as she considered the idea. "But then again the tunnels don't really turn much."

"No, they don't," Bran agreed, looking a little amused despite the serious expression on his face. "But I just can't shake the feeling that the dreams are important. We're supposed to learn something from them."

"Have you talked with Cornwall and Yates?" Alex asked, shifting on her bed and tapping her fingers against her knee.

"I tried," Bran replied with a shrug. "They did that evading thing they're so good at."

"I've noticed that," Alex muttered before adding, "Perhaps they don't know either."

"They said that it isn't unusual for mages to have vivid dreams and remember them," Bran explained, but the worry lines between his eyes didn't ease.

"Maybe that is all it is," Alex suggested, playing with her hands before fisting them in her comforter to stop, not wanting to show her nervousness to Bran.

"Maybe," Bran sighed, "Anyway, welcome back." Bran climbed to his feet with the aid of his cane and headed for the door surprising Alex more than a little.

"Uh okay," Alex stumbled, "I'll see you tomorrow."

"See you tomorrow," Bran answered as he reached for the doorknob. He paused and turned back to Alex and added, "Will you tell me if your dream changes again?"

Alex hesitated but nodded. "Sure," she promised. "If you really think it's important."

"I think everything is important now," Bran informed Alex with a small shrug and he took another step through the doorway. "I'm sorry to spring this on you, but I wanted to talk you about it since I've had a chance to talk with the others already. I just…" Bran paused and sighed, "I saw you out my window and just I had a feeling that I needed to talk to you." He started to move again out the door.

"Bran, wait a second," Alex called, reaching a hand out towards Bran for a moment before she started fiddling with them in front of her. "I think there is something else."

Turning back to Alex, Bran nodded and closed the dorm door. He didn't move back to the bed but leaned on his cane as he watched her try to collect her thoughts.

"My friend Arthur," Alex started to say slowly. "Arthur Pendred, when I first met him I had a vision just like when I met you and the others," Alex told him in a rush.

"Are you sure?" Bran questioned, his face twisting with worry and a hint of doubt. "Really sure?"

"Yes," Alex assured him. "There was this metal banging sound and I could smell smoke and feel the fire. Like-"

"Like my dream of the tunnels," Bran finished with a strange expression. "Does he have classes with Cornwall or Yates?"

"No," Alex answered with a shake of her head. "But none of you guys felt anything or reacted to him."

"That's true," Bran muttered, tapping a finger against the head of his cane. He gave Alex a searching look. "Why haven't you mentioned this before?"

Shrugging, Alex tucked a strand of hair behind her ear and fought the urge to lower her eyes. "I thought... I don't know, but since no one else got anything from Arthur I thought that it was just me or that I'd imagined it."

She was getting really tired of the way that Bran was studying her until he chuckled. "You've got a crush on him haven't you?" She didn't respond and Bran rubbed his forehead. "But if you're right… then there could be something really big happening here too."

"Like what?" Alex pressed, crossing her arms over her chest defensively. "What could this have to do with Arthur? Why would the vision I had when I met him be like your dream."

"Question," Bran interrupted, stopping Alex from building up a good rant. "In the vision did you see him or was it just the smoke and fire."

"I could smell smoke, see fire and hear the metal pounding," Alex answered, "But no I didn't see him. When I learned about the Connection I was really surprised that Arthur wasn't one of us."

"I have a hard time believing that Morgana and Merlin didn't find him if he is a mage," Bran told her thoughtfully. "But what else could it be?"

"I told Merlin and Morgana about him last month," Alex told him, "After you guys had left, but Morgana said that they'd check on him."

"And she hasn't said anything since?" Bran asked, almost urgently.

"No," Alex replied, shaking her head. "Morgana said that there were other possibilities, but didn't elaborate. I put it out of my mind," Alex admitted with a sheepish shrug.

"That's strange," Bran muttered, biting his bottom lip for a moment. "I hate to speculate when there is so much that we don't know. But I have a hard time thinking this is a coincidence."

"Any ideas what the metallic sound is?" Alex asked him, trying not to move her hands around.

"Not at the moment," Bran confessed. "I'll need to do some research, but when I first heard the sound I actually thought of a blacksmith. I guess that could make sense with the fire, but there has to be more to it than that."

"Maybe you'll see more when you have the dream again," she encouraged him, making Ban smile a little. "You are the one with the visions after all."

"If that is my power then I could live with it, just so long as it becomes a bit more useful and consistent," Bran told her.

The sound of a key in the lock made them both pause and Bran reached back to grasp the knob and open the door. Leaning to the side a little, Alex was able to see Jenny standing in the doorway with her bags and a snow-dusted coat.

"Jenny," Alex greeted, moving forward past Bran while she smiled at her friend.

Bran tensed up when Jenny looked over at him but gave her a smile. "I'll leave you to get settled," he told Jenny quickly before looking back at Alex. "We'll talk more later. See you tomorrow."

"Yeah," Alex agreed quickly with a nod. "See you tomorrow Bran." She closed the door behind him as Jenny walked over to her bed and locked the door.

Turning to her roommate, Alex waited for her to speak as she shrugged out of her coat and hung it up. Able to see Jenny's face, Alex frowned. Jenny looked awful. Instead of appearing refreshed from their week break, she had bags under her eyes and her body language betrayed her exhaustion.

"Hey," Alex greeted gently with a soft smile. "Was the flight that bad?"

"The flight?" Jenny repeated, looking at Alex with wide confused eyes. "Oh no, the flight was fine and the drive here was fine. I just didn't get much rest at home."

"I'm sorry to hear that," Alex replied softly. "Did something happen?" she asked tentatively.

"No," Jenny answered as she hoisted her suitcase onto her bed. If she noticed that Bran had been sitting there, she said nothing. "Dad took time off and we did Thanksgiving with Arthur and his mom. It was nice. I just didn't sleep well." Jenny gave her a painfully forced smile. "I guess I'm still adjusting to living away from home."

"Oh," Alex agreed, forcing a small smile. "I'm sure you'll feel better soon." Alex's eyes went to Jenny's suitcase and computer bag. "Do you need any help?" she offered, "You know so you could go to bed earlier."

"No," Jenny answered, turning to her suitcase and unzipping it. "I can get it, but thanks."

"Okay," Alex moved back to her desk and sat down. "Uh, have you had dinner? I could run out and get you something."

"Arthur and I swung through a sandwich shop before we left Albany," Jenny assured her, before looking up and adding, "But thanks, honey."

Jenny's use of 'honey' made Alex feel a little better so she gave Jenny a nod and turned her attention back to her computer. There was no doubt in her mind that something was bothering Jenny, but then again Alex really didn't have room to point fingers, she reminded herself. Of course, it could be argued that she couldn't tell Jenny the truth about her study group or other group of friends without risking a future of therapists and medication, maybe even an asylum. Despite her darkening mood, Alex chuckled at the strange way her mind worked.

She pulled up her school email and double checked her homework list as Jenny put her clothes away. They both stayed silent, but after a few more minutes the silence became less tense and Alex was able to put both Jenny's quiet behavior and her conversation with Bran out of her mind, at least until she tried to sleep that night.

Then the dream returned and she found herself once again following the sounds of the child crying, but also listening for the sounds of metal being struck.

24

The Wandering Priest

817 B.C.E. Northern Cornwall

Morgana's long brown hair whipped over her face as another gust of wind blew over the hill where she stood watching over Arto on the slope below her. It had been a warm summer day with a clear sky so Morgana could not begrudge her brother for leaving the village to have some fun, but the sun was sinking low in the sky. In front of her, completely oblivious to the lateness of the hour, a seven-year-old rushed after a dog who was barking playfully. Brushing her hair from her face, Morgana fixed her dark green eyes on her younger brother and her hand crept to the small bag tied to her belt where the bronze disk that connected her to the Sídhe was kept along with a few other precious items that she'd collected over the years to avoid suspicion.

After five years no one questioned her about the night she'd been taken. Her powers had become weak to the point that even using the disk was a great challenge. Morgana paid it little mind, despite the moments that fear of her own treacherous thoughts crept over her. The last five years had granted her control over her Changeling's memories and a chance to make her own in the Iron Realm. She'd grown tall for a girl her age and already Uthyrn was speaking of what marriage match would best benefit their family's control of the bronze trade. He'd suggested a match with the lords of the peninsula copper mines to the north to compliment his control over the regions tin mines. No matter what he suggested for the future, Morgana's attention remained on Arto at all times.

"Morgana!" Arto called, waving to his sister and pulling here out of her thoughts. She chided herself even as she waved to her brother for losing focus. The boy's wide smile made her heart beat faster, but her hands turn cold as the weight of the disk around her waist increased.

"Arto," Morgana scolded half-heartedly as the boy reached her. "You're filthy, what will mother say?"

"She'll shake her head and sigh," Arto answered with a giggle.

Their dog, a brown long-legged creature rushed up to them, coming to stop at Arto's side. Morgana met the dog's intense brown gaze and saw its lips draw back to growl at her. Stepping back, she gave Arto a small smile and gestured him towards their village in the distance.

"Come along Arto," Morgana sighed, glancing at the dog as it bared its teeth at her once again when she reached to ruffle Arto's messy dark blond locks.

"Down Alano," Arto scolded the dog with a frown before he looked up at his sister. "I'm sorry," he apologized quickly, "I don't know why he is like that around you."

"Perhaps he knows that I am Sídhe touched," Morgana offered with a reassuring smile. "Dogs are very perceptive to the unnatural."

"There isn't anything wrong with you," Arto protested sternly. "You are not unnatural."

A smile tugged at Morgana's face that she did not seek to fight. Reaching over, she brushed a strand of Arto's hair from his face. Ignoring Alano, Morgana leaned down quickly and kissed her brother on his forehead.

"Not all believe that," Morgana reminded him gently. "But it seems that enough time has passed that they know I am not going to change into a Sídhe myself."

"You're thinking about that priest's test aren't you," Arto observed with a scowl. "You shouldn't Morgana. The priest was a fool to think you were a Changeling. That was months ago."

Forcing a smile for the young boy, Morgana replied, "You're right Arto, but let's hurry home. Caoimhe was in quite a state looking for you." She tried to give her brother a stern look, but he merely beamed in response, certain that she was not truly angry.

Sighing, Morgana held out her hand and smiled in satisfaction when the seven-year-old grabbed it, twisting his fingers around hers. It didn't take them long to reach the outer wooden wall of long poles driven deep into the ground that protected the large village from those seeking to cut into the region's bronze trade. Down at the shore, Morgana could see loads of bronze goods being loaded onto the shallow wooden ships and goods from the continent being unloaded. She wondered if there would be anything new or just more wine. Probably wine from Rome, she decided; Uthyrn was extremely fond of it and his control over the region's bronze production meant he had it as often as he wished.

They turned to enter the great gate of the village and both stopped suddenly in their tracks. Caoimhe stood only a few feet in front of them, her gray hair tangled and giving her a fierce look made worse by her dark brown eyes being fixed on them. Her arms were crossed over her chest and her thin lips had nearly vanished with the sternness of her expression. Even Alano whimpered at Arto's side and ducked his head behind his young master's back.

"Arto," she called sharply, "What were you thinking child?"

"I just went to play," Arto protested, puffing up with courage that Morgana found rather foolish and knew would only earn the boy a longer punishment.

"Without any warning," Caoimhe demanded with a shake of her head. "This was not the time child. The wandering priest Myrddin arrived only moments before you slipped off and your sister went after you. Uthyrn and Eigyr were not happy to find that both of their children were missing."

"Who is Myrddin?" Arto asked when Caoimhe's rant eased and looked up at Morgana.

"I haven't heard much of him," Morgana admitted with a slight frown. "Is he important?"

"Myrddin has great power," Caoimhe said in a softer, hushed tone as she stepped closer to the children. "He calls himself Merlin now, but the rumors say he even has the power to strike down a Sídhe Rider without losing his life. Apparently, he has wandered the islands for many years and faced many dangers. Him being here to speak with your parents is an omen of some sort."

Morgana's chest tightened as a rush of nervousness nearly overwhelmed her. Releasing Arto's hand, Morgana grasped at her mirror bag for a moment before putting her hands together as Caoimhe studied her filthy younger brother.

"Well, Arto you had better come with me," Caoimhe huffed with a shake of her head. "Honestly, on such a nice day you manage to get mud all over yourself."

The seven-year-old boy beamed in triumph, completely unaware of his sister's warring emotions. Forcing a smile,

Morgana watched Caoimhe grasp Arto's hand and tug him further into the village.

Looking over her shoulder at Morgana, Caoimhe added, "Myrddin is already meeting with your parents so do not interrupt them. If it goes on too long then come to my roundhouse for something to eat."

"Of course," Morgana answered quickly. "Thank you Caoimhe. I am sorry for the trouble."

Watching Caoimhe walk away, Morgana tried to move her heavy limbs as a rush of fear and excitement pounded through her. She was starting to get a few looks from the other residents of the village as they moved through their daily activities and finally managed to start walking towards her family's roundhouse.

Their village was built on a large hill overlooking the coast where the locals could keep a close watch on the production and trade of bronze. It enjoyed high status in the trade network of bronze and the locals were wealthy with almost everyone possessing bronze, jet, and items from as far away as Rome. All around Morgana people were moving animals on the pathways, packing loads of copper and tin away for the night and showing off bronze pieces cast that day. There was a sense of excitement and fear in the village and Morgana could hear bits and pieces of conversations that all seemed fixated on the strange man who had come to their settlement. Everything from if his name was Myrddin or Merlin if he had really destroyed a Sídhe tunnel entrance on the western island or theories of why he was here were being discussed.

Keeping her expression neutral, Morgana moved through the network of paths between roundhouses until she came to the path that led the rest of the way up the hill to where her family's large roundhouse stood. Glancing around, Morgana made sure that no one was paying attention to her before she stepped off the path and raced towards the back of the roundhouse.

Resisting the urge to peer into the roundhouse and see the stranger, Morgana moved carefully around the large structure until she was out of sight. She scooted up against the roundhouse wall and pressed her ear to the rough texture of the side, straining her ears to listen to the conversation. At the moment everyone in the roundhouse was silent and she could hear the fire crackling in the hearth and Uthyrn pacing.

"Can you be certain?" Eigyr questioned suddenly, breaking the silence. Morgana flinched at the fear in her mother's voice. "If you are wrong Merlin...."

"I fear my lady Eigyr that there is no mistake," the stranger, Merlin, replied gently. Morgana frowned at his words, her hand dropping to the bag around her waist. "Your son has a great destiny; he was born with a special soul."

"And what is your role in all of this?" Uthyrn demanded in his gruff voice, his pacing pausing.

Morgana shuffled even closer to the wall, no longer worrying about her dress being ruined or the poke of the uneven wall against her skin.

"I am a mage," Merlin answered calmly and it was all Morgana could do to stay quiet. This was one of the queen's real enemies, but her expected fury and righteous anger did not overcome the worry for Arto that was filling her. "Many years ago I was given a vision by the raw magic of our world and with that vision, I was given the task of caring for this special soul. I am afraid that Arto has the vital task of protecting our world from those who invade it."

"Invaders… you mean the Sídhe?" Uthyrn asked, his voice far weaker and more frightened than Morgana had ever heard. "No," her stepfather hissed, "Not my son, not my child."

"I am sorry," Merlin replied and Morgana could hear him moving in the roundhouse. "This has nothing to do with Arto being your son, this is about the soul within his body and the power he carries because of it."

"But the Sídhe," Eigyr whimpered, her voice barely audible to Morgana. "What can he do against them? Weapons don't work and they are becoming more and more militant with every passing year."

"I understand your fears," Merlin assured them and Morgana longed to hit the meddling fool. "There are ways to fight the Sídhe, even ways to destroy them."

Nearly jumping in alarm, Morgana blinked blankly at the wall and became aware of the tight grasp she had on her mirror disk. She took a long slow breath and focused on the conversation.

"I can remain here for at least a few years and train Arto, but it will soon become unsafe for the boy to remain anywhere for any length of time."

"You are suggesting that we just hand our son over to you!" Uthyrn demanded his voice gruff and angry. "He is only seven years-"

"I am aware of his age," Merlin cut in smoothly. "And I do wish that this was not necessary, but the magic of our realm has already warned me that the Sídhe know of the boy and his presence here."

A small pained cry escaped Eigyr, but she recovered enough to ask, "If they know then why have they not attacked? Why haven't they come after him?"

"They may be waiting to better understand the threat the boy could pose to them," Merlin answered, as calm as before. "The current ruler of the Sídhe, Queen Scáthbás is not a rash creature, she does nothing without certainty of success."

His tone held enough respect, even if only begrudging, that Morgana puffed up a little in pride at the words about her queen. It had been so long… Morgana shook her head and strained to listen.

"Perhaps…" Uthyrn's voice trailed off.

"What is it lord Uthyrn?" Merlin questioned, his tone both calming and yet leaving no room for silence.

"Five years ago our daughter, well Eigyr's daughter from her first marriage, was captured by the Sídhe. We recovered her, but-"

"Uthyrn!" Eigyr snapped. "How can you suggest such a thing! She was tested not even a year ago by one of the priests. She is not a Changeling and Morgana would never harm Arto, she spends all of her time with him."

"Too much time with him," Uthyrn counted, his tone irritated. "She is fourteen years old and watches the boy like a hawk at all times."

Merlin interrupted the brewing argument by asking, "Were they always so close?"

"She always loved him to be sure," Uthyrn admitted. "Arto was only two when Morgana was taken, but her behavior changed after that and you cannot say that it didn't Eigyr."

"Morgana was taken by Riders," Eigyr replied in a sadder tone. "It must have been terrifying, she has always refused to speak about it."

"I see," Merlin said slowly and Morgana frowned at the tone. "I am sorry that your child had to endure such a trial, but Arto is my primary concern. For the sake of our world, he must be protected or we will be yet another people put under the yoke of the Sídhe."

Biting back a hiss at the harsh words, Morgana drew back from the roundhouse as the adults inside began to move about the structure. Her hand already scrambling for her mirror before her mind caught up with the action. Forcing herself to take a deep breath, Morgana let go of the bag and started walking quickly but calmly down the hill. She avoided the path until she'd reached the bottom of the hill and stepped out onto a side path as smoothly as she could.

No one paid her much attention as everyone was settling down for the night. With each passing moment, more and more people were vanishing into their roundhouses as the long summer's day came to a close. Morgana picked up her pace and glanced around as she approached the gate. A few men were standing in a circle talking about the wandering priest which only served to enrage Morgana even more. Quietly, she slipped past them and outside the wooden wall of the village.

With the sun sinking, the gentle rolling grasslands around the village were dotted with long shadows. The almost full moon was already rising in the sky promising Morgana at least some light. She walked along the wall for a few moments before veering off to head for the nearest hill. Glancing over her shoulder, Morgana noted with relief that no one was following her and there were no sounds of alarm. With luck, she could complete her business and slip back to Caoimhe's for dinner.

Morgana reached the hill and followed the slope down until the village was out of sight. Opening her bag, Morgana's fingers brushed the small jet carving that her mother had given her a few years ago and a small gold coin that had been brought back from Rome before she located the large round metal disk at the bottom of the bag. Pulling it out, Morgana released a long slow breath and ran her fingers along the edges of the metal.

Closing her eyes, Morgana struggled to connect to her weakening magic. The connection had crumbled in the last few years and now she felt as if she was seeking to draw water with a bucket filled with holes. All her energy and former power just slipped away. Cold seeped into her body and her fingers felt frozen to the metal as she pushed every spark of magic that she could muster into it. Her entire body shook, her breathing became labored and her legs gave out under her. Crashing to her knees, Morgana held back a cry and instead used the rush of pain to force more magic into the mirror. The metal surface clouded only in the center, but it was enough and Morgana felt a burst of triumph.

"Morgana my darling," Queen Scáthbás cooed through the mirror. "It has been so long since you have sent news to me my precious."

"I am sorry," Morgana gasped out, "My magic… it is fading more and more by the day."

"Your magic… oh that cursed Iron Realm," the Queen snapped, her musical and gentle tone falling away to anger and urgency. "It only proves each day why it must be brought into our light, does it not my precious one. Perhaps it is time to bring you home to me, at least for a brief time."

The thought of returned to Sídhean made Morgana's heart race, but she wasn't certain if she was happy or frightened by the idea. Queen Scáthbás smiled warmly at her and stroked the surface of her mirror as if reaching for Morgana's own face.

"You are becoming so lovely my darling," the Queen sighed. "I curse the fact that you are needed in the Iron Realm and cannot be at my side."

Tears welled up in Morgana's eyes and her throat felt tight. She nodded quickly and sniffed as she struggled to control her reaction to the Queen.

"I have news," Morgana managed to say and Queen Scáthbás' kind expression cooled into a regal one.

"Then report," her Queen ordered, looking at Morgana with intense violet eyes that were clear even if the rest of her face was not.

"A wandering priest named Myrddin who calls himself Merlin arrived today and told my pa- the Iron folk leaders that the child Arto is a weapon against the Sídhe. He plans to train the boy in how to fight you."

"Merlin is there!" Queen Scáthbás hissed, her tone low and harsh. "Damn that abomination!"

"Who is he?" Morgana asked before she thought better of it.

"He is the abomination," Queen Scáthbás answered, no longer even really speaking to Morgana and just venting her anger. "His mother was an iron folk priestess who one of my soldiers enjoyed and allowed to live not knowing that by terrible iron magic trickery she carried a babe. By some horrible accident he was born with our power, but tied to the Iron Realm. For many years now he has thwarted many of my military expeditions across the land."

"But he cannot stop you," Morgana replied quickly. "I mean, he can't possibly have enough power."

"No not on his own," the Queen muttered thoughtfully. "I had wanted to know the powers of the weapon before it came to this, but there is now no choice in the matter."

"What will happen?" she questioned urgently, leaning closer to the mirror.

"Return to the iron folk," Queen Scáthbás commanded Morgana, not answering her question. "I will consider if we have continued need of you in the Iron Realm or if I shall send a Rider to bring you back to me."

Before Morgana could say anything else, the magical link was cut by the queen. Gasping, Morgana dropped the mirror on the grass and struggled to breathe as the last of her magic was pulled from her in a violent burst. She did not know how long it was before she regained control and carefully picked up the mirror. It was a struggle to stand, but she managed it and looked up. The sun had set and only the moon provided any light to her.

Closing her eyes, Morgana breathed in deeply and tried to calm her warring emotions. She might be returning to the queen, but… what was going to happen to Arto? Merlin could die, but hopefully, her iron family could be kept safe. It would be hard for them to accept Sídhe rule, but Morgana would have a powerful position. She could protect them and help them understand. Yet, the thoughts did not comfort her as they usually did and the mirror in her hand felt icy cold and heavy.

"Morgana," a soft timid voice called. "Morgana are you alright?"

Gasping in surprise, Morgana spun to see Arto quickly coming up behind her. "Arto," she called, hiding the metal disk behind her back. "What are you doing out here?"

"Something strange is going on," her brother informed her. "Mother came to fetch me, but she'd been crying. I asked her what was wrong, but she wouldn't say. I – I thought something had happened to you because of that new priest that came to town. The last one thought you were a Changeling-"

Dropping to her knees, Morgana placed one hand on her brother's shoulder and shushed him in a gentle voice. She gave him a soft smile and chuckled before she assured him, "I am fine Arto. I was just… just a bit bored waiting for Mother and Uthyrn to finish with Myrddin or Merlin or whatever it is he calls himself."

"Mother called him Merlin," Arto offered, relaxing slightly and giving his sister a smile.

"Merlin then," Morgana muttered before she looked over her brother's shoulder back towards the village where the glow of fires could be seen. "Did you really rush off on Mother?"

The boy flushed and Morgana barely contained a laugh. Darkness was beginning to settle around them and even in the moonlight, it would be a difficult walk without a torch. Standing up, Morgana dusted off her dress and tightened her shawl around her as the heat of the day was quickly fading.

A howl ripped through the cooling air was dusk settled over the hills. Morgana straightened up and listened to the wind as it rushed past her, wondering if she had merely imagined the noise. Then another howl echoed down the valley and her heart jumped in her chest. Her time on Earth had not dimmed her memories of that majestic howl, of the baying of the Queen's Hounds. She'd seen them so rarely, but the memory of them was fixed in her mind.

"Morgana?" Arto called, shivering in the cold and looking nervously in the direction that the howl had come from.

"It's alright Arto," Morgana promised with a pleased smile. The Sídhe were returning for her.

"But, that doesn't sound like a dog," Arto protested, reaching over and grabbing his sister's hand. "What if it's a wolf?"

"It isn't," Morgana assured him, but the boy began to tug her in the direction of home.

She stumbled every time that she tried to look around in hopes of seeing one of the Hounds. In the moonlight, she imagined that it would look truly magnificent.

"Morgana," Arto called, giving her hand another tug. "Hurry!"

Another howl sounded through the hills, much closer than before and Morgana froze as she heard rapid footfalls behind them. Pulling her hand away from Arto's, Morgana spun to look behind them where the moon was casting shadows with every rock and tree. The lean canine form stepped out of the long shadows and into sight, its fur glistening in the moonlight. Gaping in awe, Morgana relaxed at the sight of the beautiful creature as it moved closer with smooth steps that displayed its powerful and graceful form. It wasn't until the whimpers of Arto reached her that Morgana felt any worry. A snarl erupted from the Hound and Arto stumbled back as the creature approached him. The small boy's eyes were wide in terror, shining with unshed tears of fright and Morgana was frozen in place. The Hound's ears slanted backward and it bared its sharp teeth.

The Hound stopped, sniffing the air and turning to look directly at Morgana with flashing violet eyes. It considered her for a moment before turning its head back towards her brother. Arto was in danger, Morgana knew, but the Hounds could only be sent forth by the Queen's command which meant that this was her will. As the Hound stepped closer to Arto who stumbled away from it, Morgana was frozen with indecision. Her brother was real, she cared for him, but the mere memory of her queen made her heart race and filled her with a deep gratitude. She couldn't move, she couldn't think straight and couldn't decide.

The Hound leapt forward, teeth bared, long claws poised to slice Arto to ribbons and a snarl ripping through the night. There was a rumble and the ground shook, sending Morgana crashing to her knees as a pillar of earth rose up in front of Arto. Crashing into the wall, the Hound fell to the ground and snarled, twisting back to its feet. Before it could take another step, the wall of earth crumbled down around the Hound in a swirl of rock and dirt. Snarls turned to whimpers in a split second as the earth closed around the creature in a thick layer of dirt. The sudden small cocoon rumbled and contorted violently. Even through the sound of the shifting rock, Morgana could hear the cracking of bones before the earthen structure crumbled away leaving no trace of the Hound.

Arto's eyes were wide and the tremors of his shaking were visible even in the low light of the moon. Reaching towards him, Morgana found herself unable to move her legs and stand.

"Arto," she called gently, crawling forward a tiny bit. "Arto."

"Do not," a stern male voice commanded with barely contained anger.

Twisting to look over her shoulder, Morgana's breath fled as Merlin strode past her, his staff thudding against the ground with every step. He did not look at Morgana. As he approached her terrified brother, Morgana found the strength to climb to her feet but swayed unsteadily.

"Easy child," Merlin said gently and Morgana realized that he was speaking with Arto.

The small boy was still shaking, his wide brown eyes locked in a gaze with Merlin. Sighing softly, Merlin reached forward and placed a hand on Arto's head. The boy's eyes slid shut and he slumped forward into Merlin's waiting arms. Adjusting his grip, Merlin swept the child up, carefully balanced on his forearms with his staff still poised for battle. Instead of turning towards the village, Merlin shifted to face the opposite direction and began to walk, passing Morgana without a word.

"No!" Morgana cried, lunging towards Merlin to grab Arto's hand. "Don't take him!"

Cold brown eyes met hers and Morgana gasped as a rush of magic surged through her. It was a warning, cold and distant. Her limbs stopped moving, her grip on Arto's hand loosened. Merlin tightened his grip on the boy and drew him away from Morgana.

"Stay back," Merlin ordered his voice icy and barely veiling his anger. "I feel grief for what was done to you Morgana, but you cannot serve two worlds with any sense of truth."

"But," Morgana gasped, trying to think of words to defend herself, to explain.

"Do not protest to me," Merlin hissed, drawing Arto further away from her.

"I haven't told them anything important," Morgana promised, stumbling forward on shaky legs. "And they already knew about Arto that is why…"

"Why they did this foul magic," Merlin finished, his brown eyes taking her in sharply. "Yet you made contact tonight. I felt your strained magic calling out to them. Had you not done so then perhaps I could have allowed the boy to remain here longer, but you have confirmed his importance to them. I will not risk it."

"Please," Morgana begged, her legs giving out completely as she gazed at Arto. "Please don't take him."

Merlin stepped further away from her, cradling Arto gently and shook his head. "No," he answered simply. "He will be taken care of Morgana," he promised, his tone softening. "I will protect him."

"I could protect him here!" Morgana protested. "I am a mage like you!"

"And yet your powers were barely enough to contact the Sídhe," Merlin countered. "You are of no use in protecting the boy."

"My powers are strong," Morgana argued, trying to force her icy limbs to move, to allow her to stand and steal her brother from Merlin. "I was taught by the Sídhe Queen, I…. I would protect him."

"Even from your queen?" Merlin asked and when she didn't answer he nodded. "That is the truth you chose to ignore, child. This boy is a threat to the Sídhe and they will destroy him, especially now that they know I have taken an interest in him. He is no longer a curiosity or a potential threat, he is a true danger. The Sídhe are not the benefactors of humanity, but nothing more than slavers. And deep down, you know that, don't you?"

"I would protect him," Morgana told Merlin weakly, her chest tightening at the thought of the Sídhe ever laying a hand on her precious brother, even the queen.

"No," Merlin said, his voice sorrowful, "No you would not. I waited longer than I should have tonight to see if you would, but you did not move. You did nothing. I do not doubt that you love your brother and others in our Iron Realm, but you still obey the Sídhe. You have never left that part of you behind. That is why you have so little magic left child. You are torn between worlds and you have no truth. The magic of both the Sídhe Realm and the Iron Realm has abandoned you."

A cry ripped from Morgana's throat as Merlin turned away from her, his talismans jingling and his staff dragging slightly on the ground with each step he took as he carried away her brother. Unable to look away or move, Morgana watched as the mage vanished over the hill with Arto and passed out of sight. Collapsing forward into the dirt, Morgana sobbed and clawed at the ground. She reached into her pouch and drew out her small mirror, clutching it to her chest as her only lifeline.

25

Alignment

Alex placed her hand on Bran's shoulder as she leaned over him with a mixture of excitement, anticipation, and dread as her fellow magic student focused on the small stone that was slowly moving across the top of the table on its own. Alex grinned as the stone floated into the air and slowly turned three times. She pulled back her hand from Bran's shoulder and clapped it against her other hand, tangling her fingers together in an effort to stay still. The stone clattered to the table and Bran released a long puff of air, slumping forward.

"Well done," Merlin congratulated loudly from in front of Bran. "I told you that meditation would help you find your center."

"Telekinesis," Aiden cheered from behind Alex. "I'm jealous, that's way more useful than setting things on fire."

Turning to look back at Aiden, Alex noted his wide smile and Nicki barely containing her own excitement next to him.

"It is likely that you all will be able to move objects with magic in the future," Morgana informed them calmly from the front of the room where she was erasing the white board. "At your current level magic manifests in you in the fashion that is best suited and natural to you. Once you grow stronger and have more control you'll be able to bring forth magic in other forms."

Merlin turned to look at Morgana and shook his head before looking back to the students. "I think that is enough for now.

Well done Bran, you will find it easier now to access your magic having managed it once."

Alex could feel Merlin's gaze turn on her and quickly returned to her desk to pack up her things. Doing her best to stay calm, Alex could feel her excitement slipping away as it sank in that now she was the only one who hadn't accessed her magic yet. For a moment she really hoped that Bran was right about the dreams being some kind of magic of their own, but then remembered his warning theory and shoved the thought away.

"Wait," Nicki called from her own desk, "Professor Cornwall I have a question."

Alex glanced up to see Morgana sigh and put down the eraser. "Of course you do," Morgana muttered before she looked over at Nicki. "What is it?"

"Uh, Christmas break starts in only a couple of days-"

"Yes I know," Morgana interrupted, "Just keep up your meditation exercises and if you practice your magic then be careful, especially you Aiden. We'll skip magic class this Thursday since you have finals and will meet again the first Monday back."

"Uh yeah," Nicki replied with a sheepish look, "But actually I wanted to ask about the winter solstice? Are Sídhe going to come through then? Will we be safe?"

Morgana looked over at Merlin and asked, "You didn't tell them?"

"I assumed that you had," Merlin countered with a shrug of his own and a nervous chuckle. "Oh well, Nicki caught it."

"When is the winter solstice?" Bran asked Nicki with a look of worry.

"December 21st," Nicki answered quickly before looking back at Morgana and Merlin. "So…"

Merlin gave her a gentle smile. "A very good question Nicole, but the solstice is an alignment day along with the equinoxes. On alignment days the magic of our realm is strongest and the protections around Earth are at their best. In 2,800 years, the Sídhe have never tried to enter our realm on any alignment day, even when their tunnels and doorways into our realm were at their peak."

Everyone relaxed a little and Alex let out an audible sigh of relief. Morgana stepped forward and added, "Of course the opposite is true on seasonal days which are days that the protections between realms are thin because of the change taking place from season to season. On Samhain, Imbolc, Beltane and Lùnastal when the power of Earth is focused on the transition to the next season, it is easiest for the Sídhe to come into our realm."

"The next season day is Imbolc on February 1st," Merlin explained, smiling at them.

"But it is possible that the Sídhe are gaining enough strength to come through before that," Morgana added sharply. "So keep your iron daggers with you at all times. The Sídhe's new gateway is near Ravenslake, but Hounds can go a great distance in one night if their masters command it."

"Why only one night?" Nicki asked as she raised her hand. "Do they have to return to their realm within a certain period of time?"

"The Sídhe don't like our daylight," Merlin told her with a glance at Morgana. "It doesn't harm them, but their natural environment is much darker. That is why even when they have a foothold in our world they stay underground. But as far as I know, a Sídhe could stay in our realm for many years if they could avoid iron."

"So we're safe on December 21st and during the daylight hours," Bran confirmed with a nod. "Good to know and now I'm looking forward to heading home."

Alex nodded in agreement and pulled her coat on, suddenly feeling colder than she had before. Glancing at the others, she met Aiden's gaze and he gave her a soft encouraging smile. Giving him a small nod of thanks in return, Alex managed a tiny smile.

"I think that is enough for tonight," Merlin said as Nicki's hand started to go up again. "Study hard for your finals and travel safely if you are leaving Ravenslake." He looked directly at Nicki and Aiden, "And if the two of you want, I have some iron filings that I can give you for your homes. Old iron horseshoes are also very effective."

"Noted," Aiden remarked as he swung his backpack up onto his shoulder. "Have a good….uh happy holidays professors," he decided on tentatively.

"I love Christmas," Merlin assured Aiden with a laugh. "Although Morgana remains rather traditional."

"I enjoy the winter solstice," Morgana huffed, "And most of the Christmas traditions are based-"

"If you don't want a lecture about holiday traditions being stolen from pagans then I suggest that you kids get moving," Merlin said loudly earning him a glare from Morgana.

They filed out of the room, two by two with Bran and Aiden leading the way and Nicki and Alex following.

"So doing anything special for the holidays?" Aiden asked Bran as they began to work their way up the stairs, everyone slowing down for Bran without any awkwardness.

"My mom's sister is visiting us this year," Bran remarked with a shrug. "That will be nice for my mom even if Aunt Haeun is kinda crazy."

"Haeun?" Alex repeated in surprise.

"I'm half Korean Alex, my grandparents came over with my mom and aunt when they were kids," Bran explained with a chuckle. Seeing her confused look he added, "I look more like my dad than mom. It happens."

"What about your dad's family?" Nicki questioned without missing a beat. "Will you be seeing any of them?"

"My paternal grandparents died a few years back and dad was an only child," Bran answered with a slight shrug. "What about you guys?"

"We're doing Christmas dinner with Aiden's family," Nicki informed him with a wide grin. "Gran loves the annual reading of The Dead."

"The Dead?" Alex repeated with a raised eyebrow.

"Yeah, my granddad Conner is stubbornly Irish," Aiden replied with a laugh as Nicki chuckled. "The Dead is by James Joyce is sort of the Irish version of a Christmas Carol. He reads it every Christmas. And on my Italian side, we sort of celebrate the Feast of Epiphany with another round of gifts in our stockings on January 6th which traditionally is when the witch La Befana delivers gifts."

"I've never heard of that before," Bran remarked as Aiden pulled open the main door and gestured for everyone to go through.

Alex shivered as they stepped out into the dark night, but the steps had been cleaned of snow and the sky was clear.

"I'm not surprised," Aiden said, replying to Bran last remark as he joined them outside and pulled on his gloves. "It's never really taken off in America. My dad only does it because his parents did."

They stayed together, chatting a little more about the upcoming holidays and their finals. Alex joined in on occasion, but her mind was unsettled by the stress of finals and the looming question of when she'd ever connect properly to her magic. Despite the sidewalks mostly being clean, she had a small layer of snow on her shoes by the time they reached the dormitories from kicking at the snow burs along the sidewalks. Aiden once again gave her an encouraging smile before he and Nicki vanished into the Michaels building.

"You'll get it figured out," Bran suddenly said as they crossed the snow covered lawn between Michaels Hall and Hatfield. "Don't worry so much."

"I'm not worried," Alex automatically defended before she caught the look Bran was giving her. "Okay, maybe I am a little. Being the last one to find the connection isn't fun. You at least had visions even before all of his started."

"As I recall you weren't particularly interested in magic in the first place," Bran teased gently.

Giving him a look, Alex huffed softly before answering, "That was before we were ambushed by the Hounds." She shivered at the memory. "I just… I want to be able to protect myself."

"It will come," Bran told her firmly, "I don't doubt that. You shouldn't either."

They finished the trek in silence, their feet crunching against what little snow had not already been trodden down and the metallic shift of Bran's brace. When Alex stepped into the warmth of her dormitory she sighed in relief. Bran gave her a small wave and wished her luck with her finals before he headed for his own room. Climbing the stairs, Alex pulled off her gloves and tried to shift her brain back to school subjects, but the nagging feeling of disappointment remained.

An hour later Alex was slouching forward on her left elbow and scrolling through her notes with a vacate expression as her free hand tapped on the desk. Her dorm room was quiet, blending in with the entire still floor of her dormitory as everyone buckled down for their final tests. A knock on the door made Alex jump and turn to look at it in surprise. Blinking at the door, she tried to bring herself back to normal life outside of physics problems. There was another knock and she jumped up from her chair, tugging a strand of loose hair behind her ear before opening the door.

It was Arthur, standing with his hands in the pockets of a black winter coat. He gave Alex a small smile that didn't reach his eyes before looking over her shoulder into the room.

"Jenny's not here huh," he said, looking to Alex for confirmation.

"No, she's been gone all evening as far as I know," Alex apologized before side stepping so he could come into the room. "Didn't she answer her phone?"

"No," Arthur told Alex with a sigh, running a hand through his hair in agitation. He looked back at Alex and asked, "Has she said anything about being mad at me? It's like she's been avoiding me for weeks now and I can't think of anything I've done."

Swallowing, Alex took in the information with a sense of surprise. Her magic lessons had kept her busy almost every evening for the last six weeks around fencing club and her soccer intermural team and she was often working on homework during meals with them. A sense of guilt rushed through her at the thought she'd been neglecting her first friends on campus and wondered if Jenny's more and more distant responses had been her fault

"I'm sorry Arthur," Alex replied softly. "She hasn't said anything, maybe she's just busy and losing track of things."

"Like you," Arthur questioned, tilting his head slightly to look at her. "We haven't really talked lately either."

"Yeah," Alex admitted with a shamed look, "That's my fault. Sorry."

"Don't be," Arthur told her quickly. "I shouldn't have mentioned it; I'm the one who had his life ruled by football for months. I can't talk and maybe that's all this is. Jenny got used to doing her own thing and now that football's over I'm overreacting."

He didn't look completely convinced, but his shoulders were squared and his eyes were lighter. Smiling in return, Alex felt her heart pound a little harder in her chest but shoved the feeling away. Rather than staying any longer, Arthur simply asked Alex to let Jenny know that he'd stopped by and apologized for interrupting her study session. Closing the door behind him, Alex leaned against with a sigh and let her mind wonder where Jenny was.

Thinking back on the last month, Alex recognized that her roommate had been coming home at odd hours, often not returning until after nine when Alex was already home from magic lessons. Jenny had seemed happy when she and Arthur had gone back to California for Thanksgiving but had been agitated upon her return. Shaking her head, Alex returned to her desk and tried to focus on her notes for her final.

A few more minutes passed and Alex's mind would not settle. The image of Arthur's downtrodden expression was burned into her brain along with the enduring disappointment of the evening. Leaning back in her chair, Alex took in a low and slow breath as her eyes slid closed. The room was too hot, too stuffy and feeling smaller with each moment. There was a twitch in her body, a need to move or scream that was itching its way up her spine. Gripping the desk, Alex took another deep breath and tried to center herself. She had a final test the next day at 10 AM and needed to review at least a dozen more things. Her brain intellectually knew this, but the itch at the back of her head was growing worse.

Standing up with a huff of frustration and defeat, Alex toed out of her slippers and pulled on her boots before grabbing her coat and gloves. She pulled a black knit hat with the university's logo over the top of her head and bundled up. Alex collected her bag, locked the door and headed for the stairs.

Outside Hatfield hall almost everything was quiet, a few students were moving between the buildings or towards the parking lots. She stood on the front steps and looked up at the sky for a few moments, but the light of the dorms meant that the stars were dim. Sighing again, Alex stepped away from the main entrance and headed for the arboretum path.

Snow crunched softly beneath Alex's boots as she followed the path out towards the lake. The lampposts cast a soft glow over the area, making even the week old snow look fresh and white. Alex enjoyed the silence and breathed in the chilly air, appreciating the freshness of it, even the tang of ice that it carried. There was no one around in any direction, but her hand slipped into her bag where her gloved fingers touched the soft leather of her dagger sheath. Up ahead was a bench that was clear of snow and ice looking out towards the lake through the bare trees of the arboretum. Alex sat down on it, tapping her foot against the cement base and watched her breath on the air for several minutes.

Looking around, Alex withdrew her hand from her bag and removed her glove. Her skin tingled in the cold night air, but Alex ignored it. Taking a long deep breath, Alex tried to calm her thoughts and connect to her magic. Nothing happened, but she let her eyes slide closed and tried again. Morgana's soothing voice from their second magic lesson returned to her and she tried to follow the instructions for meditation. Her heartbeat was too loud and the taste of the wind on her lips was too distracting. Sighing, Alex opened her eyes and looked down at her hand with despair.

"It will come," Morgana's voice suddenly spoke up from her right.

Standing up, Alex spun to the right with wide eyes only to find Professor Cornwall standing behind her in a long black double breasted coat with a blue knit hat. She was watching Alex with a strangely soft look of amusement and concern. For a moment neither of them moved until Morgana gestured to the bench.

"May I join you?"

Alex blinked at the question but nodded as she slowly relaxed. She stayed standing until Morgana had walked to the bench and gracefully sat down on the bench. Swallowing, Alex pulled her glove back on and wondered if she was going to be scolded for attempting magic in public. Of course, the question of how did Morgana know she'd be outside nagged at her.

"I come out here when I need to think and get out of my office," Morgana offered in a gentle voice as she looked out towards the lake. "The light here is calmer than in the city proper and the sight of the lake takes me back."

"To simpler times?" Alex questioned without thinking.

"No," Morgana answered, "Just different times." Her professor turned her attention to Alex, her green eyes studying her. "You have magic Alex, you need not feel any doubt about that. Building a connection is an individual challenge that is always distinct. You are special amongst the people of this realm, you have the power to protect it."

"I'm nothing special," Alex insisted, looking at her hands and twisting them nervously. "I'm pretty average. Reasonably smart and athletic, pretty and tall, but I've never been one of those girls."

"Those girls?" Morgana questioned and Alex could hear the raised eyebrow without looking at her professor.

"Really smart, really athletic or really pretty," Alex offered with a halfhearted shrug. "Except for my height I'm average and I'm okay with that," she added with a rush. "I'm not cut out for this magic thing!"

"I thought you liked the idea of being a mage?"

Alex shrugged again, still not looking at Morgana and focusing on the ice slowly cracking underneath her foot as she pushed down. She collected her thoughts for a few moments before responding to the question.

"I did sort of," Alex replied softly. "I grew up on magical stories that had me looking around corners for something magical for years. But this isn't just saying a spell or waving a wand. There isn't one evil person leading an army, but a whole other world that wants to invade us with other beings from other realms. And there are only six mages, not an entire hidden subculture to turn to." Alex took in a much-needed breath before shrugging again, "It just hasn't been what I imagined and I suck at it."

Laughing softly, Morgana reached over and squeezed Alex's shoulder gently. "Feel better?" the older mage asked.

Slumping back against the chilled bench, Alex sighed softly feeling both embarrassed and a little relieved at her rant. "I guess," she admitted, drawing some comfort from Morgana's unusual gesture of concern. "But maybe I shouldn't keep doing magic lessons with the others."

"Since they can use magic now and you can't," Morgana observed with a nod. "I can understand that. Watching them start studying magical techniques while you still can't connect would be frustrating."

That remark didn't help Alex's mood. Of course, it was accurate, but it made her sound like some kind of quitter.

"It's not just that," Alex added quickly. "I don't want them trying to make me feel better and not learning what they need. Maybe I have a bit of magic, but I don't think I'm really a mage."

"Why?"

"Nicki is doing ice sculptures and controlling water," Alex sighed, nibbling at her lip. "Aiden can make fire in his hand now, not to mention light candles at a distance and Bran not only has his visions but now he can move things with his mind. He's been feeling his connection getting closer and closer for three weeks now, but I can't feel a thing. It's finals week and I've got nothing."

"As I said, finding a connection is a very personal thing," Morgana reminded her before falling silent for a long moment. "You are special Alex, but you've led a very ordinary life until now. You have a loving family, a nice home and have never been challenged beyond high school drama." Morgana shook her head and released a deep breath that froze on the air. "Challenges not only help form a person but allow them to experience deeper levels of themselves. Nicole lived through being abandoned by her parents only to recently come to terms with the fact that she does not want them or need them anymore, Bran lost his father to a war and suffered an injury that would have left many bitter, but for his mother's sake has done his best to remain brave and positive through it all."

"And Aiden?" Alex asked softly, watching her professor's expression.

"Have you met Aiden's younger sister?" Morgana questioned without looking at her.

"No," Alex answered with a shake of her head.

"Aisling Bosco was diagnosed with bone cancer when she was six years old, Aiden was twelve and saw his sister undergo chemo and fight for her life. He saw his parents struggle to be brave and look after him even when facing one of the greatest horrors a parent ever can."

"I… I didn't know that," Alex said softly, scuffing her boots against the broken up ice below her feet.

"I do not believe he talks about it, but when one faculty member is facing such a thing it doesn't stay a secret at the university," Morgana explained with a small shrug.

"Is she alright?"

"Oh yes, the cancer was beaten when Aisling was ten. She can't play contact sports, but from the few times, I've met her at faculty functions she is a sweet and lively girl. But if you need a reason why you are struggling with magic Alex, then that is it. Aiden, Nicole, and Bran have all already faced challenges that have helped them learn who they really are and what really matters to them. They know their personal truths and that gives them the strength they need to find their connection."

"I see," Alex managed around a tight throat. "But maybe you should still focus on them. They can help you fight the Sídhe. I can't."

"You might be right," Morgana told her and Alex forced herself to nod. Her throat felt tight and tears prickled at her eyes, but she reminded herself quickly that this was for the best. She wasn't getting anywhere with magic and would only slow down the others. "But then again, I had to relearn magic when I was about your age," Morgana added, regaining Alex's attention.

"Relearn magic?" Alex repeated in confusion, turning to look at her professor.

Morgana dropped her hand from Alex's shoulder and looked up into the night sky, a sad wistful smile on her face.

"Yes," Morgana replied. "I first used magic when I was about seven years old, but it was… a slightly different kind of magic. More artificial and the truth that connected me to it fell apart over the years. It was a challenge and I even gave up on magic until someone I cared about needed me. Then everything clicked into place and I was able to do what I needed."

"I don't understand," Alex said slowly.

Sighing, Morgana looked down at the snow in front of them. "No," she answered, "I suppose not." Morgana was quiet for a long moment before she exhaled slowly. "I'll tell you why Merlin and I are still alive even after all this time."

"I thought you were chosen to teach other mages or something like that," Alex offered with a shrug.

"That is what I inferred," Morgana admitted, "But it isn't actually true." Morgana turned to face her and Alex forced herself to remain still as Morgana studied her. "Merlin and I are both half Sídhe. He was born that way and I became that way."

"How?" Alex gasped softly peering at her teacher in surprise and wonder. "I thought they couldn't… I mean the iron in humans?!"

"Merlin's creation was allowed by Earth through magic: he was brought into existence for a reason. I… I was a changeling," Morgana admitted in a soft and low voice, but her eyes didn't leave Alex's. "I was raised by the Sídhe and I served them for many years. In a way, I was Merlin's enemy in the early days of us knowing each other like the mythology now suggests. It took me a long time to let go of my loyalty to the Sídhe and recognize that they have no right to this world."

"And your magic?" Alex questioned, almost afraid to breathe.

"I first used magic in the Sídhe Realm," Morgana explained. "I was an earth mage, but growing up there had infused my magic with Sídhe energy as well. When I came to Earth on a mission for the Sídhe, I was out of balance with the forces of this world. I couldn't use magic and I couldn't connect for years. It bothered me," Morgana admitted. "I didn't fit in on earth and I couldn't even use the thing that had made me special and important to the Sídhe. In fact, I gave up on relearning magic, I did my mission and passed information to the Sídhe, but over time they didn't need me. In time I tried to put magic and Sídhe behind me when I accepted that I would never return to the Sídhean Realm. I married a man that I cared for and tried to live a human life."

"What happened?"

"That is a long story," Morgana told her quickly, her expression closing as she gave herself a tiny, almost invisible shake. "The point is Alex that magic will come when you need it. You may not be able to connect now, but you will when you need to."

"Okay," Alex replied, unsure of what else she could say.

They sat on the bench in silence, Alex brushing the tip of her boot over the ice and cement. Morgana was exhaling slowly and Alex realized that the mist of her breath was forming tiny animals that rushed off into the night. Chuckling softly, Alex smiled at the small display of magic and leaned back against the bench.

"Do your regret magic?" Alex asked Morgana softly. "And living so long. I mean… your husband is long gone right?"

"He is, but he was gone before I realized that I wasn't aging at a normal rate," Morgana answered, sounding tired and potentially regretting the entire conversation. "Regret isn't the right word since neither Merlin nor I ever had a choice in our lifespans. We just were like that and that was all there was to it."

"Must be hard," Alex muttered as she looked back at the stars. "Almost three thousand years of history. All the horrible things that have happened and not being able to change it, even with magic."

"Magic is to confront that from outside this world," Morgana told her, slipping into lecture mode.

"Not to confront that from within," Alex finished, remembering their fourth magic lesson. "Still, must have been hard."

"I am often appalled by those who make history but inspired by those who do not," Morgana answered as she stood up from the bench. Alex blinked up at her, but her teacher merely nodded to her. "Get some rest and do well on your finals. I will see you for your final on Thursday."

Morgana strode away, leaving Alex alone on the bench with her muddled thoughts.

26

Howls in the Dark

A suitcase thudded loudly against the tiled floor of Alex's door room, followed by a soft thump as a backpack was shrugged off onto the bed. Alex's laundry basket was already by the dresser with a load of clean laundry to be put away. Glancing over to Jenny's side, Alex noted that her roommate had a new tablet set up at her desk and a few unfamiliar pieces of jewelry scattered over the top of the dresser. Alex spotted a bright green sticky note on her desk shelf. She pulled off her coat and hung it up by the door before toeing out of her moist sneakers. Slipping on a pair of fuzzy slippers, Alex snatched up the note.

Hi Sweetie, I'm back, but I've got a lot to do so don't wait up. I'll see you later. Hope your holidays were great. Hugs and Kisses - Jenny

Shrugging, Alex tossed the note into the small plastic trash bin strategically placed behind the microwave on top of the fridge. Slumping down in her chair, Alex sighed and made no move to unpack her things. She closed her eyes and tried to relax, using the meditation techniques that Morgana and Merlin had taught them while straightening her back and easing her shoulders into a more natural position.

During winter break she'd spoken with the others almost every day, trying to learn details of what meditation techniques had worked for them and how they'd felt when they'd gotten close to their magic. Nicki was no help on that front as her magic had come after a sudden revelation, but Aiden and Bran had both used mediation. Yet the feelings of clarity, alertness, and inspiration were all still absent. Instead, all Alex felt was frustration, boredom and a hint of insecurity.

She hadn't been able to lose herself in her family like she had at Thanksgiving, even with three weeks away from Ravenslake. Almost every night she dreamt of the tunnel and every time she made it to the exit she always heard the child and turned back. There was a growing sense of urgency that Alex couldn't shake and couldn't explain.

Her parents had noticed her distraction, even her brothers had seemed worried within the first few days home. Alex had acted as normal and upbeat as she could and claimed that she was missing her friends and nervous about second semester whenever her energy was too low to keep up the pretense. In a terrible way, she had been grateful when she left her family to return to school, while she missed them deeply it was easier. Yet, while she regretted the distance that she was building between them she saw no other viable options until she could prove that she wasn't crazy.

Her phone beeped, breaking the silence and forcing Alex out of her frustrating thoughts. Picking it up, Alex sighed softly seeing it was a text from Nicki to see if she was back in town. After a moment of hesitation, Alex texted back that she had arrived. A new message popped up to see if she wanted some dinner and Alex's stomach rumbled loudly at the thought. She had just enough time to pull on a pair of dry sneakers before another text arrived saying that Nicki would meet her at Michaels Cafeteria in five minutes.

Fumbling around her room, Alex moved her iron dagger from the small purse she had used over break back to her school messenger bag and made sure that she had her student card before pulling on her coat. She considered leaving a note for Jenny but figured her suitcase and laundry would be a clear sign that she was home. Alex was almost out the door before she remembered to quickly make sure that her more personal laundry was in the dresser in case Arthur came over with Jenny.

The sun had set and there was no sign of Bran coming out to walk with her. Since Eugene was much closer than Spokane, she guessed that Bran was already with the others. Alex told herself that she'd be fourth walking across the lawn by herself; she'd gone out alone during finals week. Despite her self-reassurances, her muscles tensed up and she moved awkwardly across the lawn, irritated at herself for being afraid of the dark. Then again, she reminded herself as she kept close to the lamp posts, it wasn't the dark she was afraid of. It was the things in it.

Michaels Hall loomed overhead, the lights all around it casting a welcoming glow to Alex as she stepped out of the last shadows between the buildings. A few students were carrying suitcases and baskets of laundry inside and others were standing in small circles to smoke. Alex passed them quickly, pausing only to hold the door open for a girl carrying two bags. The girl gave her a grateful look before disappearing into one of the corridors that led to the dorm rooms.

"Alex!" she heard Aiden call her name and stepped into the building.

Just ahead of her were the wooden double doors that led into the cafeteria. Aiden was standing with his hands in the pockets of his coat, Nicki was leaning against the wall next to him, but pushed off the wall when she saw Alex approach. Bran was supporting himself on his cane and looked more at ease than Alex had ever seen him, even giving Alex a full welcoming smile.

Opening her coat, Alex strode forth to join the others with a smile of her own. Nicki stepped forward first and held out her arms for a hug. Chuckling warmly, Alex embraced her friend for a moment before accepting hugs from Aiden and Bran.

"How were the roads?" Nicki asked as they turned to head inside, pulling out their student cards.

"Not too bad actually," Alex replied as Aiden's card was swiped at the front register. "The worst part was just south of Spokane. It got better through the day." She handed over her own card to be swiped and glanced around. "Not too busy, I was afraid they'd be hit hard."

"It's only five thirty," Aiden remarked with a shrug as he started leading them towards a table near the salad bar. "Some people probably aren't back yet."

"True," Alex conceded as she pulled off her coat and slung it over the back of a chair. She eyed Aiden and Nicki's coats. "Why do you have your coats?"

"We just helped my roommate bring in some of his stuff," Aiden explained. "Didn't bother to take them upstairs."

Shrugging it off, Alex joined the others in grabbing trays and worked her away around the cafeteria booths to collect a slab of meatloaf, some mashed potatoes, a salad and a slice of chocolate cake. They all made it back to the table about the same time except Bran who had to carry his tray with one hand. By unspoken agreement, no one started on their dinners until everyone was around the table.

Dinner was calm, the daily communication meant that no had big news on the magic front to report and her friends were making a point of not saying anything about her continued failure to make a connection to her own magic. While it bothered Alex that the effort was necessary, she was grateful at the same time for it. Instead, she listened to Nicki happily telling Bran about a pottery series she had done with her grandmother and how pleased she was with how the set had turned out.

"Oh," Nicki suddenly gasped, looking around at them all. "What are your schedules? We never talked about that."

"Gee, it's not like we had more important things to talk about," Aiden teased over his plate of spaghetti.

Nicki just rolled her eyes and stuck her tongue out at Aiden before turning to Alex. "Do you have your schedule?"

Shrugging, Alex pulled out her phone and with a few clicks accessed the saved copy of her schedule. She was aware of the others doing the same and handed her phone to Nicki.

"Let's see," Nicki said thoughtfully as she inspected Alex's phone. "Well we're in the Epic with Professor Yates together as planned." Nicki gave Alex a wide smile. "You've also got…. Seriously Alex, World Mythology?"

"So?" Alex huffed, tensing up as Nicki rolled her eyes.

"I'm in that too," Nicki informed her with a shake of her head.

"Uh," Aiden called with a smirk, waving his phone in front of Nicki. "So am I."

"I signed up for that class as well," Bran remarked with a shrug while Nicki stared at them.

"I'm the actual anthropology student," Nicki muttered, crossing her arms and mock glaring at Aiden.

"And I'm the electrical engineering major who has to take a certain number of humanities credits," Aiden countered. "If it makes you feel better I'm in calculus with Bran."

Nicki shivered dramatically at the mention of math before turning her attention back to the rest of Alex's schedule.

"Spanish, World Art, and Culture?"

"Jenny's idea," Alex told her with a shrug. "We're in it together and you know, humanities credits," she added with a glance towards Aiden. He raised his soda in a silent toast, barely holding back a grin.

"And Personal and Exploratory Writing," Nicki finished, ignoring the exchange. "Aiden let me see yours." He dutifully handed over his phone while Alex put hers away. "Aiden's got calculus, electrical engineering, world mythology," Nicki glanced over at him before continuing, "Intro to American history and reason and critical thinking."

"That last one sounds awfully familiar," Alex remarked lazily, leaning onto her elbow.

"One of those lovely classes that nearly everyone takes," Aiden answered as he accepted back his phone. "I can only handle so many writing classes to meet my communications requirement."

Bran handed his phone over before Nicki even asked for it and silently continued to work on his salad.

"And Bran has got: the dreaded calculus, theoretical physics, world mythology, Spanish and modern physics."

"See, it's good that we all took world mythology," Aiden told Nicki with a wide smile. "Between us, there is almost no crossover otherwise."

Nicki ignored the statement and pulled out her own schedule, "And I have-"

"World mythology," Aiden announced, "And the Epic, whatever that is."

"It's an English class," Alex informed him quickly.

"That I already guessed from Yates being the teacher," Aiden teased earning him an eye roll from both Alex and Nicki.

"As I was saying, I have language and culture, an anthology class for an anthropology major." Aiden chuckled and slouched back in his seat, gesturing for Nicki to continue. "Intro to stats and intro to sociology," Nicki finished with a smile before putting her phone away. "And we'd still see each other a lot with a study group."

"So is Cornwall teaching U.S. history?" Bran asked Aiden as he set his fork aside.

"No, some other professor. I don't remember the name, but it wasn't her."

"That's not surprising," Alex told them with a shrug as she pushed her dinner plate to the side and pulled her slice of cake to the front of her tray. "I think she mostly teaches the upper-level history classes."

"I can believe that," Nicki agreed. "She scared off a lot of kids in our class."

"So no one is in any of her classes this semester," Bran said thoughtfully before he shrugged. "Hopefully she won't take offense at that."

Everyone around the table paused and glanced at each other. Chuckling softly, Alex shook her head and turned her attention to the slice of chocolate cake, figuring that it wasn't worth worrying about at this point. Besides, she had a sneaking suspicion that Morgana didn't worry about such things nearly as much as they thought she did.

Dinner ended soon after as more students poured into the cafeteria to get food and see their friends. As the noise level climbed higher, Alex and her friends pulled on their coats and returned their trays. Alex fell into step next to Bran and headed for the main door only to realize that Nicki and Aiden were following them. Turning to look over her shoulder, she raised an eyebrow at Aiden who just made a small nod towards Bran. Nodding in understanding, Alex silently agreed with the two other mages escorting them back to Hatfield Hall. After all, she mentally conceded, Bran's ability to run was limited and she had no magic, a thought that stung. They stepped outside and Alex tightened her coat around herself as a harsh chill shot up her spine.

"Man it's getting cold," Nicki huffed as her breath misted in the air.

"Yeah," Aiden agreed, pulling on a pair of fleece gloves as they slowly moved down the path. "If it gets much colder, it will be too cold to snow."

"Too cold to snow," Nicki mumbled. "That just sounds wrong."

"Wrong, but possible," Aiden answered as he shivered. "Come on, let's just get moving."

The crowd of students around Michaels was small with everyone moving inside as quick as they could, but Alex still saw plenty of bags and baskets of laundry going inside. Snow crunched only a little under their feet as they stepped off the sidewalk and onto the lawn between Michaels and Hatfield. Glancing down at the snow, Alex noted that it was almost completely trodden down from students, but frowned as she saw the impression of dog tracks.

"Alex," Nicki called with a hint of shivering in her voice. "Come on."

Without a word, Alex dismissed the tracks and picked up her pace as another chill shot through her body. They were halfway across the lawn and back into the outer edges of Hatfield's lights. Suddenly a high pitched howl echoed through the night making Alex and her friends stop in their tracks. No one moved except their hands all cautiously dropped to their bags or in Aiden's case to the back of his jeans. Alex's fingers felt warmer as she touched the hilt of her iron dagger and carefully drew it from the sheath, but left it concealed in her bag.

"Where did it come from?" Nicki asked in a low voice as they all looked around slowly.

"Not sure," Aiden answered in a low voice.

"We'd better keep moving," Bran muttered nervously.

"Back to Michaels or on to Hatfield?" Alex questioned, her eyes darting forward to Hatfield.

"Fall back to Michaels," Aiden decided after a moment of heavy silence.

Another howl erupted, this time closer and from behind them. Spinning, Alex looked towards Michaels, but saw something moving fast between the distant lamplights in the parking lot. She couldn't see it clearly, but the speed and size allowed for no doubt in her mind.

"No!" Alex snapped, "Hatfield, it's in the Michaels parking lot."

They broke into a run, as fast as Bran could manage as he awkwardly lunged forward, using his cane to support his leg the best he could. Looking over her shoulder, Alex could see the Hound closing on them. She could now clearly see its quadruped shape and the flash of its fur whenever it passed a light. In the distance, she could hear shouting and some screaming as the Hound tore after them.

"Call animal control!" someone screamed behind them as the students rushed towards the entrance to Michaels.

Another howl made Alex's heart jump as she turned to see a second Hound racing after them from near Rhodes hall, heading straight for their left side while the Hound behind them continued to gain. Snarling echoed in her ears and she was vaguely aware of Aiden shouting something, but she couldn't hear him. Aiden grabbed Alex's hand, pulling her sharply to run at a steeper angle and faster speed. Another rush of fear gave her legs extra strength to run faster towards Hatfield. Aiden dropped her hand and turned his attention to helping Bran increase his speed.

The steps of Hatfield were just ahead of them and Alex let go of her dagger in order to pull out her student card, nearly dropping both in her haste. Students ahead of them were dropping their things and fleeing inside, screaming as they spotted the Hounds. Alex was trying to rush to the front of the group with the card ready when another snarl erupted to the right of them. A girl on the inside shoved the door open and gestured for them to hurry.

A Hound leapt in front them, landing directly in front of the door and baring its teeth as they all came to a sharp stop. Behind it, there was a scream and the door closed. The lights of the building made its fur glow and illuminated the sharp curves of its rib cage as it stepped towards them. It snarled at them, taking a slow step towards them as it blocked the entrance. Aiden pulled Alex back from the Hound, flinching as the first Hound caught up with them. Behind them the low growling of the first Hound rumbled through the air, soon joined by the third Hound. The snarling grew louder and Alex spun, horrified to see another pair of Hounds stalking out of the shadows of Hatfield hall to join the one on the steps. She fumbled for her dagger as the Hounds formed a semi-circle around them, moving towards them slowly.

There were shouts from the building and screams in the distance, but Alex could barely hear them over the pounding of her heart. Ten cold violet eyes gazed at them as the Hounds lowered their ears and growled together. They were waiting Alex realized with a pain jump in her heart. Waiting to see what they would do, gathering information for the Sídhe. Her stomach churned and her body felt frozen as her sweat chilled and her breathing grew shallow.

"What do we do?" Nicki asked softly, not taking her eyes off the three guarding the doorway. "There are too many people around to use magic."

"Alex, can you get away?" Aiden questioned in a low voice.

"I don't think so," Alex replied, trying to ignore her trembling hand as she clutched at the sleeve of Aiden's coat in an attempt to regain control. "Sorry," she added in a whisper.

"The lakeside," Bran muttered as he took a few careful steps to the right where there were no Hounds. "There's a path just around the building. There's water there that Nicki could use."

"Maybe," Nicki agreed with hesitation. "We're too hemmed in here."

"One… two…" Aiden said as they all started to shift towards the right side of the building. "Three!"

Around and above them, Alex could hear screaming and shouting despite the snarls of the Hounds as they started to run. There were howls echoing around them as they rushed along the building, out of sight of the front lawn. Bran's pace was the slowest and Alex turned to look over her shoulder as one of the Hounds snapped at his legs. Spinning clumsily on his cane, Bran shoved his hand out towards the Hounds and swept it towards the building.

The first three Hounds which were almost upon him were suddenly pulled off their feet and thrown into the bricks of Hatfield Hall with a crash. Bran moved his hand again, not waiting to see their condition and tossed the three Hounds upon the remaining two who were gaining ground. The tangle of silvery fur snarled loudly and began to right itself. Reaching back, Alex grabbed Bran's hand and pulled him as hard as she dared to get him running again. A howl only a few seconds later told her that the Hounds would be upon them soon enough. Up ahead, Aiden led them off the sidewalk, trusting them not to trip in the snow as they headed further away from the buildings and into bare trees.

Snow covered the ground and a hint of ice hung on the trees as the lamplights caused the scene to almost glow. Above the lake hung a crescent moon that at the moment looked to Alex's frightened mind like a claw in the night sky ready to slice her open. Aiden stopped suddenly in a small clearing and spun back around, grabbing Alex and pushing her behind him as the first Hound erupted from the trees after them with a vicious snarl.

Fire burst forth in Aiden's hand, turning his fleece glove to ash as a fireball formed in his palm. Thrusting his arm forward, Aiden pushed the fireball directly into the face of the first Hound. Flames exploded out at the contact, licking at the air and sending a blast of heat across Alex's face. The smell of singed hair filled Alex's nostrils, making her stomach turn. Pained cries filled the air, but Aiden created another fireball and threw it at the Hound which was reeling back from them.

Digging into her bag, Alex struggled to find her dagger. A quick glance up told her that the Hound Aiden had blasted with fire was down, but two more were nearly upon them. A sharp cool pain in her hand made her flinch before giving her a sense of triumph as her fingers closed around the blade of her dagger. Ignoring the pain, she tightened her fingers around the blade and pulled it out of the bag. In the low light, she had just enough time to adjust the dagger with her hands so she was holding the hilt before the four remaining Hounds began to advance on them.

Staring into the violet eyes of the Hound around Aiden's shoulder, Alex forced herself to breathe, clenching and unclenching her free hand and bringing up her dagger in front of her. Morgana's promise that she'd have her magic when she needed it echoed in her mind and she waited, praying silently for a burst of inspiration telling her what to do. There was a moment of utter silence and stillness as neither Hound nor mage moved.

Bran moved first from beside Nicki at the far side, sweeping his hand forward again. Three of the Hounds bounded out of his way, but the fourth was shoved back into a tree. Closing his hand, Bran panted with a pained noise and glared at the

Hound. Alex glanced towards the Hound to see it caught in midair, hanging off the ground as its body twisted into an odd shape. She looked away quickly as the snapping of bones began to fill the air.

There was another blast of fire from Aiden, but the Hounds dodged it, leaping around and then forward as they rushed for Aiden. Beside Aiden, Nicki glared at the Hounds, bringing her palm up in front of her chest and sweeping it forward. As the Hounds launched themselves off the ground towards Nicki, snow rushed up from around Nicki like a wave of water, mixing with a spark of icy blue magic glowing forth from Nicki's hand. The air grew colder and there was a strange creaking noise followed by animalistic cries of pain that made Alex's heart stop. Her eyes adjusted and took in the sight of two Hounds impaled on a sloping wall of icy spikes less than two feet in front of them.

The final Hound growled at them, sweeping around them with a burst of speed and snapped at Bran. Fire swept past Bran, forcing him to turn his head away, but forcing back the attacking Hound. Alex heard the Hound Bran had trapped crash to the ground and dared a glance to see if it was moving. The creature stumbled to its feet, its body crushed on one side and limping badly, but it snarled at Alex meeting her gaze. Less than three feet away, Bran dropped to his knees with a pained gasp for air, shaking badly.

Nicki and Aiden turned as one to hold back the Hound that lunged for Bran. A wave of snow rose up from the ground which the Hound dodged, only to move directly into the path of a fireball. A growl behind her, made Alex turn back to the injured Hound which was making its way towards her. Holding up her dagger, Alex watched a drop of her lamp lit blood run down the blade and tried to keep her hand steady.

It lunged, releasing a terrible cry of pain, but baring its teeth as it jumped. Alex lashed out, kicking the beast as hard as she could in the upper chest as soon as it came into range. A dull pain swept through her leg, but the Hound was forced back from her body. It caught itself on three legs, skidding on the ground and growling. She couldn't hear what was happening with the other Hound behind her, the growling and her own beating heart overwhelmed her. The Hound crouched, watching Alex and breathing hard and then pounced. Her arm moved out, sweeping the iron blade forward on reflex. The red drops flew off the dagger, hitting the skin of the Hound with a hissing sound just before the flesh of the beast gave way, spilling out luminous blood from the Hound's neck.

It fell to the ground, struggling to stand, but fell to the side as its silvery blood seeped out. Alex lunged forward and buried her iron dagger into the throat of the beast, falling to her knees next to it. A gurgling growl turned into a keening cry of pain before the Hound's body dissolved into the air. Tightening her grip on her dagger, Alex climbed to his feet and spun to check on the others.

Bran was back on his feet, but leaning against a tree and breathing hard. The Hound that Nicki and Aiden had been fighting was crying in pain as its fur burned. Another fireball crashed into it and Alex could barely see as the body dissolved. Her eyes found Nicki who was stabbing the two Hounds impaled on the ice with her own iron dagger. Aiden turned to look at Alex, sweeping over her quickly with his eyes before he turned to Nicki and Bran to check on them.

"That's all of them," Nicki breathed in relief, slightly out of breath and not putting her dagger away.

"Bran?" Aiden called, moving over to his friend in two long strides. "You okay?"

"I'll be fine," Bran hissed as he moved. "Just… too much running, my leg feels like it could start burning at any moment."

Nodding in understanding, Aiden ducked under Bran's right arm to support his bad side. "Let's get inside," Aiden told them as he helped Bran step away from the tree. "Nicki, call the Professors, we need to know how to deal with what people saw." Bran huffed in pain as they moved. "And see if we can do anything for Bran."

Nicki nodded and pulled out her cell phone, falling into step behind Aiden and Bran as they moved back to the sidewalk. Alex moved next to Nicki as they started to follow the path up to Hatfield Hall, listening to Nicki quickly tell Merlin what had happened. Looking down at her dagger, which she was still clutching in her hand, Alex swallowed and held back her tears as the terrible question of what would have happened if Nicki and Aiden hadn't been so determined to walk them home entered her mind. Biting her lip, Alex slid her dagger back into its sheath and shoved her injured hand into her pocket as she tried to hold back a sob.

27

Song on the Wind

811 B.C.E. Somerset Levels

Morgana stared out pensively over the watery landscape
before her from her spot atop the tall tor that rose sharply out
of the gently sloping hills and waters that made up her current
home. The flooded valley with small islands linked with
wooden causeways stretched out towards the sea. A hint of
salt was carried on the wind along with the thick smell from
the marsh below her high perch on the hill. Down the grooved
path that Morgana and others had carved over the years,
Morgana could see the buildings of the village where she lived
now and studied it thoughtfully for only a moment. The wind
swept her hair around her shoulders, gently jangling golden
hair decorations scattered throughout her long brown locks as
a sense of unease settled over her.

Frowning, Morgana's fingers brushed the bronze brooch that
fastened the long blue cloak around her shoulders securely.
The metal felt warm to her touch with a gentle rhythm of heat,
almost like a soft pulse, but there to her sensitive fingers. She
traced the pattern of the metal working carefully, the brooch
had been a gift from her husband when she'd come north to
marry him almost two years ago. At the time Morgana had not
been pleased with the arrangement Uthyrn had made to ensure
their family continued to control bronze production, but Airril
had proven himself to be a good man.

She'd been prepared after Uthyrn's anger over Arto's
disappearance with Merlin to be saddled with some distasteful
brutish iron man. She'd tried to ready herself for the harsh
treatment of a Sídhe male that she'd grow up hearing whispers

about, but none had ever come. The greatest sorrow that she suffered here was missing her mother, the continued mystery of Arto's fate and the loss of her magic. Airril had not been what she expected, a diplomatic leader who oversaw much of the northern coasts copper mining with an easy grace. He wasn't afraid to smile, it was Morgana's favorite thing about him and even his less tolerable younger brother Sionn had made her feel welcome.

Dropping her hand, Morgana clutched the fabric bag which hung from her belt. The familiar smooth shape of the metal disk met her hand as her grip tightened around it automatically. It felt cold to her touch, sending a chill up her arm. Despite the warm thick cloth it was wrapped in, she could feel the chill radiating from it. The contrast deepened Morgana's frown.

Ever since the day Merlin had taken Arto there been no contact from the Queen. The Sídhe had sent no messages, no signs and no offers to return to the realm she had been raised in. Her fingers traced the shape of the metal disk as she brought her left hand to her brooch, gently tracing the curved design that adorned it. Everything had changed, but she felt no more certain or settled than she had almost six years ago. Most of the time she could ignore it, but a weight had settled in her stomach over the last few days and every little thing seemed to remind her of the past.

The howling of the wind increased suddenly and Morgana lifted her right hand to shield her eyes from the blowing dust. It took a moment to realize that she could hear voices on the breeze. Focusing on the voices, Morgana gasped softly as sounds familiar to her childhood reached her ears. She swallowed thickly, struggling to breathe and clutched tightly on the metal disk through the bag. When she regained control, Morgana loosened her grip enough to slip her hand inside the bag.

She could feel the chill of the metal disk even before her fingers touched it, sending shivers through her entire body. Pulling her hand away from the disk, Morgana tightened her cloak to fight off the chill. Standing still, Morgana listened to the soft music that drifting through the air, fighting back a sudden swell of memories from the tunnels. The caretakers had sung songs like this one, humming softly or playing a pipe while another sang in a haunting and sweet voice. Those had been the sweeter moments of her very young life. Wrapped up in blankets, in the perfect warmth of the white tunnel rooms with soft lights overhead, she had felt safe and content. There had been no fear or doubt, just a sense of belonging with those who cared for them and her fellow children in those moments.

Swallowing, Morgana held back her tears and gripped her hands together even more tightly. She'd given no real thought to the others she'd been raised with. None of them did. Once a boy or girl was claimed and taken away they were never spoken of, not even in hushed whispers when the caretakers were occupied. Only on occasion were they seen again and the stories they told…. Morgana unclasped her hands and tugged the cloak tighter around her as the chill in her body intensified to a bone aching cold. Of course, then there had been the whispers amongst the children of the role they played and how they served the Sídhe. While it had always sounded good to serve the Sídhe, even then the descriptions of the service had frightened her and now…. Morgana fought back a wave of nausea as her hands began to shake.

The song seemed louder and Morgana looked out across the valley, her eyes tracing the rolling distant hills that blocked the sea from view. Somewhere out there was a new tunnel opening with the Sídhe celebrating so loudly that they could be clearly heard. They'd ride tonight, Morgana realized as her entire body tensed. The Riders would storm out of the tunnels on their great steeds, the Hounds baying by their sides and villages throughout the area would feel their might. Queen

Scáthbás' quest to bring light to the iron folk and add the Iron Realm to the Sídhe collection of worlds would continue. Tonight it might even be her own village; they were located right next to the water and would be easy prey for the Riders. Perhaps the damage would be mild, Morgana told herself, only a few houses burned and a few children… Her stomach turned and her body shuddered.

Forcing herself to breathe, Morgana straightened up and turned her gaze back to her village. With slow steps, she began to follow a trail down the steep slope, keeping a tight grip on her cloak as the wind continued to whip around her. She could warn Airril, she decided. It was known that she had seen the Hounds when they attacked Arto and had been saved by Merlin, she'd told her mother that much. If she could just convince the priest that she heard their songs and the howling of a Hound then maybe they could prepare enough defenses for the Sídhe to go to another village. It was a treacherous thought that filled Morgana with dread and guilt, but she forced herself to move faster towards her home in order to see it through.

She found her husband just inside the wooden gates, speaking with one of the local metalworkers. His posture was relaxed and a cheerful smile was on his face. He laughed at something and Morgana felt calmer as she strode up to him.

"Airril," Morgana greeted with a soft smile. "I must speak with you."

Airril smiled widely at Morgana, the dimple on the right side of his face coming into view. His brown eyes gleamed with excitement as he took her hand and guided her further into the village. "My darling," he breathed, "The wandering priest Merlin arrived while you were gone."

"Merlin!?" Morgana gasped, coming to a halt and making Airril turn back to face her with a confused expression. "Merlin is here?"

"Indeed Morgana," Airril informed her, his eyes searching her face. Stepping closer, he squeezed her hand gently and raised his free one to cup her cheek. "What is it, Morgana? What did you need to speak with me about?"

Swallowing, Morgana tried to find the words to explain, but Merlin was in the village. She'd seen him destroy a Hound with his magic. Either the Sídhe would not come, to avoid facing him directly, or they would come and focus on him. It no longer mattered what they did to protect the village. She decided quickly that this was better for her, the danger would surely be discussed by Merlin and she need not expose her own knowledge.

The memory of the last time she'd seen Merlin swept through her and before she could think about the question Morgana asked, "Is there a boy with him?"

"A boy no, a young man. Perhaps thirteen," Airril informed her, still looking at her in confusion. "Merlin introduced him as an apprentice." When she said nothing in response, Airril stepped even closer and implored, "Morgana, please tell me what is wrong."

"Merlin and I.... we have history," Morgana explained simply. "He vanished many years ago with my brother Arto."

"And you think this boy might be your brother," Airril finished slowly with a worried expression. Nodding resolutely, he asked, "What would you like me to do? Merlin is a priest and we must not harm him, but perhaps-"

"No," Morgana interrupted as tears pricked at her eyes at
Airril's offer despite the political issues it could cause. "No, it
will be alright Airril. My parents were always certain that
Merlin had good reason for taking Arto and if the boy is my
brother… then this is a good day."

As they walked deeper into the village, Airril remained firmly
at Morgana's side until they reached the hill on which they
lived. Morgana only just kept her composure as Merlin came
into view, but swallowed when a boy stepped around him to
join in the conversation Merlin was having with their local
priest Ronis. She stopped moving and Airril gave her a long
moment before his hand moved to her back and gave her a
gentle push forward.

"Is it him?" Airril asked in a low voice as they approached.

"Yes," Morgana whispered, shocked at how weak her own
voice was.

"If you're not ready-"

"No," Morgana replied quickly, pleased at the strength
returning to her voice. "I will be fine."

It was only a few more steps, Morgana kept her head up and
hoped that she looked calmer than she felt as she and Airril
came to a stop. Merlin had barely changed, his clothing was
still loose and long, talismans hung around his neck, but a new
bronze triskele clasp held his cloak around his shoulders. But
Morgana knew that under that calm, drifter exterior was a
dangerous mage capable of striking down Sídhe Hounds.

"I greet you, Merlin," Airril greeted formerly with a nod of his
head. "Tales of you have often enthralled us."

"I thank you for the welcome," Merlin answered with a nod of his own, looking over at them. His eyes flashed with recognition, but he did not seem alarmed by Morgana's presence at Airril's side. The boy at his side, however, darted forward with wide eyes and a hopeful smile.

"Morgana?" he questioned in a voice that was just starting to change. "It's me Arto."

"I know," Morgana confessed, trying to keep her emotions in order. "Welcome little brother."

Merlin turned his brown eyes on Morgana, studying her in silence. She felt his heavy gaze even as she opened her arms to Arto and allowed the boy to wrap his arms around her waist. He was so much taller, she observed with a sense of awe and loss as she looked down at him when Merlin made no move to intervene. Arto must have been about twelve years old, nearly thirteen, she realized as she added up the years and already beginning to show signs of the man he would become. There was no doubt now that he greatly resembled Uthyrn, although his features were softened by their mother's looks. Gently carding her fingers through his darker brown hair, she remembered the lighter locks of his youth that had darkened. A rush of anger surged through her as she cataloged all the changes she and her mother had missed.

Arto released Morgana and stepped back with a wide smile still shining brightly. It was his turn to study her, taking in the changes that the years had wrought. Her face has lost most of her youthful baby fat and slimmed down, strengthening her resemblance to Eigyr, but her shoulders were broader like her father Kenwyn. Over the years she'd been told that she had his temperament and wit. Today, however, Morgana remained still and silent to give Arto the time he needed to study her. Carefully, she looked past him at Merlin and met the brown eyes firmly.

The action only amused him and Merlin chuckled, his shoulders relaxing visibly as he leaned forward on his staff. His eyes dropped to the bag on her belt and Morgana felt a strong desire to hide it away, certain that he knew what it contained. She resisted the urge to move away, raising her chin slightly in defiance. Next to her, Airril shifted uncertainly.

"Morgana," Arto called, drawing her attention back to him.

Her brother was frowning, having turned slightly to glance back at Merlin and then back to her. He had caught the silent exchange, Morgana realized with a flush of embarrassment and irritation at Merlin.

"I'm afraid that unlike mother and your father, I was not happy when Merlin vanished into the night with you," Morgana explained, looking back at Merlin with a challenge in her eyes.

"Sadly, there was no alternative," Merlin assured her, taking a few steps forward, his staff thumping on the compressed dirt with each step. "I sent messages when I could to your parents."

"Only to say that he was alive and well," Morgana protested, moving forward and placing a hand on Arto's shoulder. "Surely you are not so detached from humanity that you fail to see how lacking those messages were."

The amusement was gone from Merlin's eyes and he frowned at Morgana, leaning forward on his staff once again, but this time he gesture radiated power and impatience, not serenity.

"It is odd to hear you speak of detachment from humanity," he observed in an even tone.

Morgana's breath caught in her throat and she could barely contain her anger. Tightening her grip on Arto's shoulder, she steered the boy forward on the path while forcing a sweet smile.

"Well, the past cannot be changed, but Arto you must stay with us tonight."

Before anyone could argue with her, Morgana half-escorted half-pulled her brother up the path to their roundhouse at the top of the rise. It was the largest in the village with a steeply sloping roof and wood piled all around the walls under the cover of the thatch. The first thing a person saw when they entered were the stone shelves at the far side of the room where Morgana's jet necklaces, bottles of perfume, small vases of wine and golden trinkets, but Arto unlike most visitors paid no attention. Instead he quickly sat down on a stool by the hearth and looked up at Morgana.

"I am sorry that I could never visit," he told her softly. "Are mother and father well?"

"I have not seen them for some time myself," Morgana confessed as she gracefully sat down near her brother. "But the news from the south is that they are well and your father's trade continues to be beneficial to him."

"And you are married now? To Airril?" Arto asked with a glance towards the doorway, but Airril and Merlin had yet to follow them inside. A jolt of fear made Morgana shift with nervousness, wondering if Merlin would tell Airril about her history with the Sídhe. "Morgana?" Arto called, "Is Airril your husband?"

"He is," Morgana replied with a forced smile as she looked back at Arto. "He is a good man, our marriage came about when his father died and Uthyrn wanted a stronger partnership with the northern copper regions."

"Do you love him?" Arto questioned and Morgana stumbled for an answer. She was saved to her relief and horror by Merlin entering the roundhouse with Airril, smiling at Arto and barely glancing at Morgana.

"Well my lad, have you questioned your sister about your parents?" Merlin inquired as she sank onto a stool of his own.

"I have, Morgana, says that they are well," Arto answered with a small smile as he looked to his teacher.

"That is good," Merlin agreed with a nod before he looked at Airril. "You see, we have been traveling on Inisfail."

"The western island?" Airril sought to confirm. When Merlin nodded, Airril smiled and added, "I fear that I have never traveled that far myself."

"It was important that Arto sees the sacred sites there," Merlin explained calmly. "He spent a great deal of time studying with the priests."

"Ah," Airril began with a quick glanced towards Morgana. "Then Arto is your student, will he be a traveling priest like yourself or take over a particular region?"

"I suspect that he will travel a great deal as I do," Merlin answered and Morgana frowned at the answer, glaring slightly at Merlin.

She glanced back at Arto, who was alternating between looking around the tent with mild interest and studying Airril with a thoughtful expression. Rising from her seat, Morgana gave them all a smile and moved towards the door.

"Please excuse me, I will see about having something special for supper tonight," she explained quickly before pulling back the animal pelt. She could feel Merlin's eyes on her but ignored her discomfort in favor of a new rush of anger. Slipping around the roundhouse, Morgana moved down the hill towards the wooden wall that protected the village from the elements. Morgana stopped a few people long enough to arrange for some fresh meat and produce to be delivered to her roundhouse before she found a quiet space out of sight behind an empty roundhouse.

Pulling out her metal disk, Morgana fought back the urge to shiver and breathed in and out slowly for a moment. Then she closed her eyes and sought her connection to magic. It had been so weak the last time she had attempted this, but now she was scrambling in a void of nothing. There were mere wisps where her bond to magic had once been. Gasping softly, Morgana opened her eyes as the metal disk fell from her fingers. She distantly heard the thump as it hit the dirt. Her fingers trembled and her mouth was painfully dry.

Swallowing, Morgana closed her eyes and tried to calm herself, but the urgency of panic was already overwhelming her. She fell to her knees and wrapped her arms around herself as the fight to breathe continued. Her fingers moved to her brooch on their own volition. Morgana stopped moving, allowing the subtle warmth to flow into her body. The tightness of her chest eased and Morgana took in a shaky deep breath. Lowering her eyes, Morgana stared at the metal disk in the dirt, trying to understand, but failing.

28

Healer's Touch

Alex and her friends moved with fast, but cautious motions as they stumbled back to Hatfield Hall, all the while looking around for more Hounds. Students at the doorway were looking around with curious expressions and Alex overheard them talking about the Hounds and animal control. As Aiden helped Bran up the stairs as casually as he could, Alex caught a remark about the pack of greyhounds that someone's neighbor had seen. Pulling out her keycard, Alex unlocked the door, trying to ignore the gossiping students and held it open for her friends.

Aiden didn't need any direction, heading straight for the elevator and pressing the second-floor button. Bran leaned against the back of the elevator, releasing a labored breath and Nicki glanced down at the phone she was clutching in her hand.

"What did Merlin say?" Aiden asked when the door closed and the elevator began to move.

"Merlin is calling Morgana, they'll call us when they are together at his house. But he said that we should be safe. A pack stays fairly close together so there probably aren't anymore."

Aiden nodded, but his hand went to the dagger he'd concealed once again in the back of his jeans. Alex barely noticed her own hand dropping down to her own dagger. The blood on her hand was rapidly turning sticky and Alex shuddered as the wound throbbed with pain. Nicki made a move towards her, but the elevator opened and they all piled out.

Following the others down the hallway, Alex was reminded that she'd never been to Bran's dorm. They usually just said goodbye in the entry. His door was only two down from the elevator with the RA on the far side of him. Bran pulled out his key, making a small hiss of pain that caused Aiden to hold out his hand. Without a word, Bran handed him the keys and waited while Aiden got the door open before stepping back. Bran moved into the room with sharp movements that favored his left side, dropping onto the bed without even bothering with the lights. Reaching into the room, Alex found the light switch and flicked it as she and the others entered the room.

The room's layout was identical to Alex's own with two beds, two desks, two dressers and one large window. One of the beds was fairly bare, with a blue corner sheet and scattered books on it along with video game boxes. On the shelf above it was a fairly good sized flat screen TV that made Alex pause with appreciation. Bran was seated sideways on the other bed on the much more decorated side of the room. A large periodic table poster dominated the far wall along with a Star Wars movie poster.

Walking past Bran, Aiden strode into the room to the small fridge and opened it to retrieve a bottle of water. Nicki went to one of the dressers and picked up a bottle of painkillers. Alex stepped back and silently waited as Bran took one of the offered pills and swallowed it with a gulp of water. He took a few long breaths before easing himself back on the bed and hauling his leg up. With careful, but practiced movements he loosened the leg brace and removed it from his right leg.

"How are you doing?" Aiden asked, taking a seat at the desk.

"I've been better," Bran admitted, closing his eyes and leaning back against the piled up pillows. "But we're alive."

"Yeah," Nicki sighed, pulling her phone out once again and placing it on the desk between Aiden and Bran. She glanced at Alex and then looked down at her hand. "Alex, we'd better take a look at that."

Allowing Nicki to lift her hand up for inspection, Alex flinched as she saw the long, but thankfully swallow wound across her palm and on the inside of her fingers. Nicki reached for the water bottle and a roll of paper towels before pulling Alex over to the free bed. They shoved the games and books aside and sat down at the edge with the paper towel wrapped around Alex's hand. Nicki gently poured out some water and started cleaning away the blood.

"You may want to get stitches for this," Nicki observed with a deepening frown. "It looks shallow, but I really think something like this will scar. Plus I bet it hurts like hell."

Alex opened her mouth to reply but ended up only shrugging. "Not really," she admitted softly. "I'm not... not really feeling anything now."

"We're all alive," Aiden reminded her.

"But I didn't-"

"We're alive," Nicki repeated sternly to Alex. "Everything else is secondary."

"But so many people saw the Hounds this time," Alex argued with a shake of her head. "We can't ignore that."

"We aren't going to ignore it," Aiden agreed, the tone of his voice made her look over to him. His foot was tapping nervously against the floor, but he seemed calmer and met her eyes evenly. Nodding, Alex swallowed and looked over at Bran who was breathing more normally now but still tensed up. Bran's fingers were drumming a pattern on the comforter beneath him with sharp and jerky motions. As if sensing her gaze, Bran looked over at her and forced a smile.

"Hey Alex, it's not like I did a whole lot either," Bran told her in a forced cheerful tone. "I just don't have the strength and energy I used to have."

"I'm beat too," Aiden told them. "I feel really cold. That was pure adrenaline."

"Me too," Nicki agreed, glancing up from Alex's hand. "I'm pretty pleased with that wall of ice trick."

"No kidding," Aiden chuckled with a shake of his head. "Your powers are awesome. Both water and ice."

"I wonder if I could do steam," Nicki asked thoughtfully as she carefully dabbed up the blood closer to Alex's cut.

Alex glanced down and flinched, with the blood cleaned up she could see the dark red streak across her palm with raised edges of skin along both sides of it. Biting her lip, Alex pushed down her dinner and snapped her eyes shut.

"Bran?" Nicki called, "Do you have bandages?"

"Uh, there should be some gauze and antibiotic pads in the top drawer of the right dresser," Bran answered, gesturing towards the dresser next to Alex and Nicki.

"Thanks," Nicki replied, releasing Alex's hand and going to the dresser. Taking in several more slow breaths, Alex tried to stay calm. Nicki returned a moment later and Alex kept her palm still while Nicki wiped the wound with a gauze pad and then spread cool ointment over it. Alex hissed at the sting but didn't pull her hand away. A moment later she felt the light bandage being laid across her hand. Nicki was carefully wrapping her palm when the phone rang.

Snatching up the phone, Aiden answered it and turned on the speaker.

"Hello, Nicole," Merlin's voice greeted. "Is everyone there?"

"We're all here," Aiden answered, cradling the phone in his palm and holding it out so everyone could hear. "And we're mostly alright," Aiden added.

"Good," Merlin sighed gratefully. "That is a relief to hear."

Morgana's voice broke in with a hint of urgency, "There were five Hounds, correct?"

"Yeah," Alex managed, flinching in pain as the bandage caught on a tag of rough skin at the edge of the wound. "We killed five."

There was an audible sigh of relief on the other side of the line and then Morgana said, "Good. When I scryed that was how many I saw. You should be safe tonight and able to return to your rooms."

"Should be safe tonight?" Aiden asked with a hint of anger. "What happened to the seasonal days?"

"Indeed," Merlin cut in smoothly, "We were not expecting more Hounds until February 1st, Imbolc, the next seasonal shift day. The arrival of these Hounds means that the Sídhe have successfully created a tunnel system into our realm once again."

"The Sídhe tunnels are magical constructs, built of stone from their world and earth of ours," Morgana explained, sounding very tired to Alex's ears. "Passing through the tunnel is a magical and metaphysical act that gives the Sídhe and their creatures' greater immunity to our world. Iron still kills them, but this is what allows them to enter our world even on days when our realms defenses are still intact. They will now be able to come through when they wish."

Alex looked over at the others, trying to hide the fear that was churning in her stomach. She felt both relieved and even more frightened when she saw Aiden swallow thickly, Bran tense up and grit his teeth and felt Nick's grip on her hand tighten. There was silence in the room for several long and uncomfortable moments as Morgana gave them time to take in the news.

Bran spoke up first, "So on February 1st there'll be a lot of Hounds?"

"Most likely," Merlin answered, sounding far too calm for Alex's tastes. "And unfortunately it is likely that several Sídhe warriors will come with them. They are known as the Riders."

"Riders," Aiden repeated slowly before chuckling darkly, "Simple yet ominous."

"It is likely that their mission will be to kidnap children," Morgana explained, ignoring Aiden's comment. "Therefore you shouldn't have to deal with them, the Riders will be ignoring mages in favor of normal humans. They will leave you to the Hounds."

"Taking humans, you mean like Changelings?" Nicki asked, looking over towards the phone.

"I doubt they will bother with leaving one of their constructs in place of a human," Morgana replied in a sharp tone. "They have after all been without human slaves for nearly three thousand years and Earth blocks their access to any other worlds. I suspect that the labor population has decreased drastically unless the Sídhe have learned to take better care of their conquered worlds." Her tone was doubtful and angry in a way that sent a shiver up Alex's spine.

She could see that Nicki wanted to ask for more information, but remained silent. Alex assumed that it was the same fear of what she might hear that was keeping her quiet. Glancing over at the boys, Alex noted that Aiden looked pale, but had a stern look of determination. Bran's breathing was still labored and he shifted slightly, only to hiss in pain and grip at his right hip.

Jumping up, Aiden moved over to Bran and helped him shift into a more supported position. Merlin and Morgana were quiet over the phone and Alex wondered if they knew Bran and her conditions. They hadn't asked what mostly alright meant, Alex realized with a cold pang in the stomach. Her hand ached and she flexed her fingers as far as she could around the simple and bulky wrapping that Nicki had done. She could feel the torn skin stretching and contracting, a bit of blood still oozing. Giving her a stern look, Nicki stilled her hand and tightened the bandages slightly.

"What about healing magic," Aiden questioned suddenly, frowning and giving the phone a hard look. "Is it possible to heal injuries with our magic? Our own or another's?"

"How badly are you injured?" Merlin questioned, worry now filling his voice. "We didn't need to have this talk right away."

"Alex's hand is sliced up," Nicki informed Merlin, glancing away from the bandaging and towards the phone, pausing in her first aid.

"Plus Bran-" Aiden started to say, looking over at Bran who had an oddly closed expression on his face.

"Healing magic is not something to use lightly," Morgana interrupted through the phone, her voice carrying a chill. "It is a dangerous use of magic. Even Merlin and I only use it the gravest and desperate circumstances."

Bran shifted on the bed, barely holding back a groan of pain, but visibly flinching. Rolling to the side, his arm shook as it supported his weight, but in a clear voice Bran asked, "Why is it dangerous?"

"Healing magic requires the caster to put their energy and magic into the body of another," Merlin explained in a calm voice.

"But we release our energy as magic in fights," Aiden countered. "What is different about this?"

"Healing requires you to channel their own magical energy into another without harming them. For instance Aiden, your fireballs impact the body of another and cause damage, not just because of the element they are made out of, but because it is the raw energy of another, different being," Merlin explained gently, his voice sad and wistful. "Healing magic allows the user to pour magical energy into the target's wounds, which then is converted into the victim's own life energy and as such they become healed. Transforming your own energy into that of another is a difficult and draining process. The act of healing a simple cut becomes more draining than an entire battle with the Sídhe. It will leave you weak and vulnerable."

"By extension," Morgana added in a tight voice, "Trying to save another from a deadly wound will most likely kill the magic user and fail to save that life. Energy is lost too easily and wasted too frequently for healing magic to be a viable way of using your powers."

Silence took over the room again and Alex made a point of not looking at Bran's face. The hint of hope that had appeared on his voice, even momentary before Merlin's words told her a great deal. He never talked about the vision that had made him grab the steering wheel in the car from his mother or about what his life had been like before the injury, but his expression had been revealing.

"How do you make the conversion between your own magical energy and the life force of another?" Alex asked, surprised to hear her own voice. "How is it done?"

"You don't need to know that," Merlin answered gently, giving a forced chuckle.

"How is it done?" Nicki echoed, giving Alex a quick look out of the corner of her eyes.

"Children-" Merlin began to argue.

"How is it done?" Aiden repeated, leaning forward. "You've explained the danger, Merlin," Aiden added, looking at Alex and the others. "We understand that, but magic, this destiny of ours has taken a lot of choices from us and put us at risk anyway. Give us something that is our choice to use or not to use if the time comes."

Heart beating faster, Alex felt herself smile with pride at Aiden. A glance at Nicki revealed a wide and proud, but watery smile on Nicki's face. Bran's face was blank of expression, but his eyes seemed brighter than they had been a moment ago.

"Nicki," Morgana's voice called through the phone, warm and resigned. "You have the most control and ability to visualize… if you really want to learn this then you are the best choice to demonstrate."

Shifting, uncomfortably, Nicki glanced between the phone and Alex's hand. The layer of bandages was tinted red as the wound continued to ooze blood at a slow rate. By this time, the active pain had eased to a dull throb that Alex figured had more to do with her brain ignoring the pain than it did with the wound actually improving. She was tempted to encourage Nicki to take the offered magic lesson while also fearing the words of their teachers.

"Nicki," she whispered, trying to make sure that the phone wouldn't pick up their conversation. "It won't kill me. I'll go to the hospital and have it checked. It's easy enough to say that a kitchen knife slipped and I tried to catch it on instinct."

"A double bladed kitchen knife?" Nicki teased, not hiding the fear in her voice very well. "I've never seen one of those. That is the reason it is called a dagger and not a knife. Knives have a single cutting edge while a dagger is recognized in modern times as having two cutting edges." Nicki swallowed and shook her head, "And I'm rambling."

"Nicole," Merlin's voice called through the phone. "You don't need to learn this and certainly not now after a battle."

"But this is when we are most likely to need it," Nicki countered, raising her chin in a show of bravery. "Injuries will raise questions and I'm sure the campus gossip mill will be all about the strange dogs that were running loose on campus. I just hope they headed straight for us and didn't hurt anyone else."

"Very well," Morgana conceded, "Are you next to Alex? It is easiest if you can face one another."

Nicki climbed all the way onto the bed, folding her legs under her. Mindful of her hand, Alex shifted to copy the position in order to fully face Nicki and held out her hand.

"One second," Nicki told them through the phone. "I probably need to remove the bandage, don't I?"

"Indeed," Merlin replied calmly. "Contact with the injury and being able to see it are key to successfully healing someone."

As Nicki gently unwrapped the bandages, careful not to tug at the damaged skin, Aiden stood up and moved over towards them with the phone and his chair. He stopped and sat down in the chair after checking to make sure that he wasn't blocking Bran's view and held the phone out closer to them.

"Okay," Nicki said as she set the bandages aside on the bed, careful to fold them so the blood wasn't touching any of Bran's things. "We're ready."

"Close your eyes and breathe," Morgana instructed smoothly, her voice taking on a hypnotic quality. "Inhale slowly and exhale slowly."

Nicki obeyed, her eyes sliding closed and taking in slow breaths. Morgana repeated the words several times and Alex could see Nicki's shoulders easing slightly. The room was still and the noise of people in the halls and in other rooms seemed muted. Looking down at her wound, Alex found her revulsion fading slightly and barely noticed when Nicki brought her hands back up to cradle her hand. Alex closed her own eyes and took in several long and slow breaths, urging herself to relax.

"Connect to your magic," Morgana commanded gently, keeping her voice calm and even. "Find it Nicki and hold it close." The instructions confused Alex, but she heard Nicki release a soft sigh and remained still. "Gather it together, allow your magical energy to form an orb in your mind. Don't bring it forth into the world, keep it inside," Morgana instructed in her hypnotic voice.

There was only the sound of Nicki's slow breathing in the room as everyone, including Alex, had softened their own breathing. All other sounds were so far off and Alex felt like she was drifting away as she sank into herself, the ache in her hand easing with her disconnect from the pain.

"Now, reach for Alex's energy," Morgana told her, shattering the silence, but not the stillness that had taken hold of the room.

Alex braced herself, coming back to reality a bit at Morgana's words, but she felt nothing. Taking another slow breath, Alex wondered if there was something she was supposed to be doing. Then there was a tingling over her skin. She shivered slightly, trying to stay still and reclaim the calmness, but the tingling sensation increased. It wasn't quite a tickle, she felt no need to laugh, but a sense of discomfort was spreading over her body. Her skin felt a little too tight and there was a feeling like a feather being brushed over her skin very gently, just enough that she could feel it. Swallowing, Alex forced herself to stay still and resisted the urge to rub her arms and scratch her nose. She heard and almost felt Nicki exhale in front of her.

Opening her eyes, Alex gasped, the air rushing from her lungs. A light blue glow was surrounding Nicki, illuminating her red hair and making her freckles stand out sharply. It shimmered around her, pulsing gently with Nicki's breaths, shifting between a lighter and darker shade of sky blue with each inhale and exhale. Alex had a strange instinct to reach for the light, to gather it up, but forced the impulse away. Taking a shaky breath, Alex felt her hand begin to itch and tingle. She shifted it, but Nicki's grasp on it tightened and the glow intensified.

The itching and tingling increased rapidly as the light around Nicki grew brighter, losing some of it blue color and shifting towards white with sparks of blue floating around her. Gritting her teeth, Alex fought to keep her hand still and ignored the instinct to pull her hand away from the aggravation. Dropping her eyes away from Nicki's concentrating face, Alex looked down at the wound in her hand.

A sharp stinging pain made Alex flinch and gasp for air as the stinging spread through the center of the wound. Her eyes widened in astonishment as the dark red tissue began to ooze blood slowly, but the bright red color quickly faded into a soft bluish color. Alex fought to breath as the sting grew stronger, but the urge to pull away was gone. Seeping through the wound, the bluish blood began to slowly reattach and connect the sliced tissue fibers before her eyes. Blue sparks of magic danced through the wound, sending tiny jolts of hot and cold up Alex's arm.

The rough edges of the torn skin were changing color now, taking on the soft blue of Nicki magic as they seeped in her energy. Swallowing thickly, Alex struggled to breathe as the stinging sensation faded and the itching sensation became almost unbearable, but the feeling was lost as the skin began to shift and stretch before her eyes. The blue color around her hand intensified and two pieces of skin that were shifting stretched out across the wound and fused together in a spark of blue magic. More skin unrolled itself from around the wound, shifting and stretching to link with other bits of skin, growing and glowing softly.

"Wow," Aiden breathed nearby, but Alex couldn't look away as the small blue sparks of magic danced over her palm.

"Is it working?" she heard Merlin's voice ask, sounding far away.

"Yeah," Aiden answered, sounding out of breath. "It's working."

Gasping in pain, Alex fought to stay as quiet as possible, watching as the skin finished reforming. It took her a moment to hear the soft pained noises that were escaping Nicki. Looking up in alarm, Alex saw Nicki was gritting her teeth, her eyes clenched tighter as her body shook.

"Nicki!" Aiden called, moving over to them quickly.

"Aiden!" Merlin shouted through the phone, "Be careful. Nicole is connected to Alex's life force. Pulling her away is dangerous."

The words caused panic to rush through Alex as she stared at Nicki, unsure of what to do. The energy field surrounding Nicki was starting to swirl tighter around her, no longer focused on her hand. Sparks of blue and white, jumped around them both and Alex opened her mouth to call to Nicki, but found herself unable to speak. Closing her eyes, Alex forced herself to take a deep breath. She could feel the energy creeping over her skin, seeking other injuries to heal and slipping away from Nicki. Alex tried to visualize the blue tinted energy being pushed away from her skin, being pushed back at Nicki. She imagined a force field around her skin, protecting her from any more of the energy and pushed the idea as hard as she could towards Nicki.

There was a sharp gasp, the sound of something large falling to the ground and the energy stopped. Alex groaned, falling forward onto the bed, catching herself on her hands and gasping for air. Around her, she heard sounds of someone moving and voices, but couldn't understand the words. Someone touched her back and guided her back into a seated position, leaning her back against some pillows. Slowly, she reopened her eyes, fighting back a haze that was tangled with her thoughts. Aiden was leaning over her, a look of worry and relief mixed together on his face.

"Hi," Alex greeted softly, confused by the expression even while knowing that she shouldn't be.

"Hey," Aiden replied, the corners of his lips tilting up slightly. "Welcome back. Nicki's okay."

"Nicki?" Alex repeated in confusion.

"Nicki healed your hand," Aiden reminded her and she felt him take her hand. He raised it up and turned it so that Alex could see her palm. There was a thin white line across her palm and another line running across the insides of her fingers.

"And she's okay?" Alex questioned, the haze beginning to lift slightly. She could remember the pain in her hand and the light around Nicki.

"Yes," Aiden answered patiently. He leaned back and stepped back from the bed so that Alex could see Nicki sitting on the floor, her back against the bed and sipping some water.

The other girl looked over her shoulder at Alex and gave her a tired smile. "Hi Alex," she greeted in a weak voice. "Thanks for the push."

"Push?" Alex questioned, frowning again.

"I felt you push me away," Nicki explained with a growing smile.

Merlin's voice broke into Alex's confused thoughts. "You should be grateful that Alex managed to stop you," Merlin told them. "That is the danger with healing magic. Once you start to give your energy to another it is difficult to stop. It requires perfect control."

"Could that have killed Nicki?" Aiden demanded as he knelt at Nicki's side, placing a protective hand on her shoulder.

"No," Morgana informed him. "We would not have risked it. At your current magical level, your bodies will shut off the flow of energy before it kills you as magic hasn't become an encompassing part of your being yet."

"Yet," Bran repeated making Alex look over at him. He has a thoughtful expression on his face that she thought might be important, but couldn't decipher.

"The more you use magic, the more it becomes a part of you," Morgana explained calmly. "Once you reach that point, giving its energy to another is more and more of a risk as your body won't cut you off automatically."

"So it could kill you," Nicki murmured from her place on the floor. "I understand."

"It should not be used lightly," Merlin told them all firmly. "I trust that none of you will attempt it on your own."

"No," Aiden agreed with a sad expression. "I don't think you have to worry about that."

"Good," Merlin replied and Alex could hear the satisfied nod in his voice. "Try to get some rest. You all have classes in the morning."

The line went dead and Nicki groaned softly. Aiden helped her to her feet and led her over to the chair. He looked back at Alex and frowned before walking over to her.

"Come on," he muttered, holding out a hand to her. "I'll help you up to your room and then take Nicki home."

Nodding, Alex crawled off the bed and let Aiden support her. He glanced at Bran who nodded in understanding and shifted on the bed to be closer to Nicki. Alex flexed her hand, looking down at it with a sense of bemusement as Aiden collected her coat and bag from the floor.

"This was a bad night," Alex muttered to herself. "And my head feels like it was dumped in clouds."

"Dumped in clouds," Aiden repeated as they moved out into the hallway and towards the elevator. "That's a new one. I'll have to remember that."

"I really hate those Hounds," Alex told him with a huff. "I mean really, really hate them."

"I completely agree," Aiden replied as he helped her inside. "Come on Alex."

Alex leaned against Aiden and tried to connect the stray thoughts in her head together, but they were prancing around with no regard for her wishes. The elevator stopped and Aiden walked her out into the hallway, ignoring the looks they were getting. She barely managed to get her keys out of her bag, nearly dropping them twice before Aiden took them.

Her dorm room was dark and empty. It was probably a good thing that Jenny wasn't home. Aiden helped Alex to the bed and let her collapse on it. She heard him chuckle softly before she felt him tugging off her shoes.

"Nicki looked really pretty," Alex declared as she looked up at the ceiling, noticing an old hole where someone had hung a plant. "Surrounded by blue and glowing. Really pretty."

"She was glowing?" Aiden asked, giving her a confused look as he hung up her coat. "Really?"

"Yeah, glowing blue," Alex told him with a sigh as she settled back against her very soft pillows. "Then the blue sparks made my hand feel better, but it hurt too."

Aiden made a thoughtful noise and looked at Alex for a moment before he nodded in understanding. "You must have been able to see her magic when she connected to you," he observed with a smile as he picked up Alex's phone and pressed a few buttons on it.

"But I don't have magic," Alex reminded him, a frown taking over her features.

"Yeah you do," Aiden told her as he moved to the doorway. He flicked off the lights and stood in the light of the open door. "I set your alarm just in case. Let us know how you feel in the morning, Alex." Then in a softer voice, he added, "And you do have magic, you'll find it Alex. I promise."

29

Revelry

The music wasn't particularly interesting, a constant heavy percussion beat with barely audible vocals and the room was starting to stink of sweat along with the thick smell of beer. Holding back a sigh, Alex took a sip of her bottle of water that she'd settled on for the evening and glanced around the room. This weekend's frat party hosts had pushed back all the furniture and turned off the regular lights in favor of a few black lights and colored bulb lamps scattered throughout the room making looking around a headache.

She spotted Jenny and Arthur on the makeshift dance floor across the large living room and a couple of girls she knew from elementary Spanish on one the sofas up against the wall. Turning her attention back to the guy she had been talking to, Alex did sigh when she saw that his attention was already elsewhere as he shouted to another guy coming out of the kitchen. As the second man came up, Alex quickly stepped away and moved closer to the wall, feeling very hot and claustrophobic. With a practiced movement, she pulled out her phone and checked the time just to make sure that she hadn't missed her alarm in the noise, but was only 10:13, less than ten minutes since the last time that she'd checked.

"Something wrong?" A familiar male voice asked behind Alex. Turning quickly, Alex relaxed when Lance walked up to her with a small smile. "You keep checking your phone? Are you expecting a call or watching the time Cinderella?"

"Guilty of the second," Alex admitted with a sheepish smile and a small shrug. "I've got to leave early tonight by eleven so Cinderella isn't too far off."

"Any reason in particular?" Lance questioned casually as he leaned against the wall and looked around the room. His eyes settled over Alex's shoulders, watching Jenny and Arthur as he sipped his beer.

"I've got to be up early," Alex offered smoothly, making a mental note to do just that. Even if she didn't want to be out before morning on Imbolc, she could maybe go and stay in Bran's room for a few hours. Do some studying and put out the iron horseshoes that Merlin had given her around herself.

"Too bad," Lance replied with a shrug, sounded distracted before he shook his head a little and looked back at Alex. "You don't seem to be having much fun."

Shrugging, Alex took another sip of her water and let her foot tap lightly to the music. She had to concede that letting Jenny talk her into coming hadn't been her best idea. February 1st began in just a few hours with the potential of not only Hounds attacking, but the mysterious warrior Rides of the Sídhe as well. Alex took another sip to moisten her suddenly dry mouth and looked over to where Arthur was spinning Jenny around. They were both laughing and grinning like fools. The tension in her shoulders eased a tiny bit. Things had seemed tense between them lately, it was nice to see them having fun together.

She watched for a short length of time and pulled out her phone, making Lance snort behind her. It was only 10:21 and her shoulders slumped slightly. Behind her, Lance placed a hand on her shoulder and squeezed.

"Hey," he called, "You're not having fun Alex. Just head home and get some sleep." Alex turned to face him, trying to think up an excuse, but unable to. She had so little normal time anymore that didn't have to be spent on college work that it seemed wrong to ditch her friends. "Do you need a ride home?" Lance asked her, pressing the issue.

"No," Alex replied with a shake of her head. "I drove my own car, I'm parked up around the corner."

"I'll walk you," Lance said, taking her arm and steering her towards the front door.

Alex wanted to argue, to insist that she could stay another forty minutes, but it didn't seem worth the effort. Her mind was on the Hounds, the Riders and the potential havoc that would break out come February 1st. Then there was also the strange sense that she had forgotten something. She hadn't spoken with the mages since Friday when a stern warning had been given by Merlin to take care not to be out on Imbolc and Alex couldn't put her finger on what she was forgetting.

Stepping outside brought a rush of fresh air into Alex's lungs, and the chill in the late evening air caused her to perk up a little. Lance paused and waited for her to gesture in the direction of her car. He released his gentle grip on her elbow and they started moving up the shoveled sidewalk. Alex's hand dropped to her bag, ready to pull her dagger automatically. There had been only a couple of attacks since her return from winter break, all of which Morgana and Merlin had handled before they reached the school, but Alex's paranoia remained high.

"So, if you didn't really feel like a party tonight why did you come?" Lance asked, breaking the silence in a low voice.

Shrugging, Alex glanced around for anything out of place, but it was a Saturday on Greek row so the kids dashing in between houses and the loud noise filling the street wasn't unusual.

"Jenny asked me," Alex answered calmly, relaxing as they turned the corner and she spotted her car parked up the street by a large snow berm. "We haven't had much time to hang out lately except meals. When I agreed on Monday, I thought I'd be more upbeat."

"I get that," Lance replied with a small shrug of his own. "I didn't feel like coming, but Arthur was looking forward to it."

"Yeah," Alex muttered as a response. They reached her car and Alex carefully stepped over the bank of snow between the sidewalk and the road. She gave Lance a wide smile and small wave. "Thanks, Lance, I'll see you Monday for breakfast."

Lance nodded in agreement but stood on the sidewalk waiting calmly. Smiling, Alex pulled out her car keys and unlocked the door. She was about to climb in when a high pitched howl tore through the night and a painful ice cold shiver ran up her spine. Looking around with wide eyes, Alex struggled to control her breathing.

"Shit," Lance growled. "Not more of those wild dogs. My mom freaked out when she heard about the first time."

"Maybe they won't come into town," Alex managed in a weak voice that made Lance frown and give her a concerned look.

"Alex? Are you okay?" He asked as he took a step towards her. "I can drive you-"

"No," Alex snapped quickly before she forced herself to calm down. "No thank you, Lance, I guess I'm just a little freaked out by those dogs. The report about them running across campus was kind of scary. I'll just get home and settle in. I'll be fine."

Lance looked torn, but he nodded and stepped back onto the sidewalk. Forcing a smile and giving him a small wave, Alex climbed into her car. She turned the key with more force than necessary and locked the driver's side door. Propping up her bag, Alex didn't remove it but adjusted the dagger so that she could reach it if necessary. Lance was still watching as Alex pulled away from the curb. Glancing into her rearview mirror, Alex sighed in relief as he turned and started walking back to the party.

"Just get home and settle in," Alex told herself. "It's not February 1st just yet." Her grip on the steering wheel tightened and she swallowed as another cold shudder racked her body. "Maybe one of the others wouldn't mind a temporary roommate," Alex muttered softly as she made the turn to the north onto Meadow Street, hoping to avoid having to stop for wandering students.

It was a quiet night Alex observed, glancing at the mostly dark residential houses that were lined up neatly on the driver's side. The athletic fields and stadiums were dark with empty parking lots. Her fingers tapped nervously on the steering wheel as another howl resounded through the night. She couldn't tell if it was closer, not fully trusting her senses. Taking a slow breath, Alex resisted the urge to speed up as the bridge intersection came into view ahead of her with a green light beckoning to her before turning to yellow and then red. She was nearly home, with the Kelly Apartments just a right turn away and her parking lot just beyond.

With a sigh, Alex came to a stop and glanced around the intersection carefully for any signs of traffic. There wasn't anyone else out at the moment and she was about to make the right turn when sudden movement off to the left caught her eye. It was gone in a moment, but Alex could vaguely see several shapes moving in the darkness beyond the intersection.

She turned left before she thought better of it as fear of the Sídhe and worry for someone out too late warred in her stomach. At first, there was nothing and Alex was ready to dismiss the movement as a dog that had gotten out. Peering out the passenger window, Alex could only see the slope of the riverside park that went down to the water and the vague shape of trees in the low light of lampposts. Then a woman rushed under one of the lights, grasping the hand of a child while carrying another smaller one in her arms. Even with the low light of the lamp and the distance, Alex clearly saw terror on the woman's face.

Slamming on the brakes, Alex turned in her seat to look over her shoulder as the woman vanished into the darkness. A howl sounded in the night and Alex tensed, gripping the steering wheel tighter. Cold shivers ran up her body and her chest tightened. Alex put her foot on the gas and rolled forward. With a sharp turn of the steering wheel, Alex pulled to the side of the road, her wheels smacking the curb as she came to halt.

An even colder shudder shook Alex's body, her hands were shaking and every instinct was screaming for her to head for her own home and her stockpile of iron horseshoes. She was almost ready to give into the voice when movement in the darkness to the left of the car down at the riverside reminded her of the present threat. Alex didn't get out of her car, straining her eyes to see into the darkness. Carefully, she unbuckled her seat belt and pulled her dagger out of her bag, still in the sheath. There was more movement as a human form stumbled into the light of one of the riverside trail lamps. Moving before her fears could stop her, Alex climbed from the car and ran towards the disturbance. A muffled scream reached her ears, desperate and muted against a gag of some kind. Her feet slipped in the mud and snow that covered the slope down to the water, but Alex kept moving. A sharp aborted cry gave her a burst of speed and she stumbled onto the cement walkway and into the light.

The sidewalk was mostly covered in dirty snow with bits of dried leaves poking through, but now a vivid stain of red was seeping down towards the water. Frozen, Alex stared at the still form of the woman she had seen who was lying on the ground with blood oozing forth from a wound on her head. Limbs were tangled around each other unnaturally and Alex couldn't see if the woman was breathing. Stunned, she didn't move until a thick high laugh rolled out of the nearby darkness accompanied by gentle whimpers.

A figure stepped out into the light, its eyes already locked onto Alex. Gasping, Alex stumbled back as she stared in awe and fear at the towering figure before her. The Rider was taller than any man she'd ever seen in person, just over seven feet tall. Golden armor gleamed in the low light and teamed with his pale skin made him seem to glow. A pair of large white horns rose from his head, twisting and curving out into two branches each. Golden rings decorated them and his long white hair was styled in long braids that were spun around the horns. He was not dressed as a warrior, despite the armor and weapons, Alex realized. He was dressed in celebration, ready for a party and a good time. The thought made her sick and she trembled, shivering not from the cold, but from terror.

Luminous purple eyes watched her, taking in her reaction with glee. Thin white lips curved into a smirk and the Rider took another step towards her. Lowering his sword, he reached out a hand covered with a golden gauntlet with vicious looking nail covers visible towards her. She took a reflexive step back which only made the Rider's smile widen. Alex tried to scream, but the Sídhe waved his hand and only a small croaking squeak escaped Alex's mouth as her throat and lips tingled. Her skin itched and an icy sensation across her mouth made her begin to shiver uncontrollably.

Stalking forward, the Rider closed the distance between them. Alex's feet slipped in the mud as she tried to get away, but too afraid to take her eyes off of him. The Rider's free hand dropped to his belt where a long golden cord hung coiled around a golden clip. As his long fingers closed around it, the cord pulsed dangerously and an almost crippling shock of cold hit Alex. Spinning away from the Rider, Alex fought her way up the hill, back towards her car, using her hands to gain extra traction on the slick slope.

There was a sharp crack in the air behind her that nearly made Alex turn back. Pain jolted through her arms and back along with a burst of cold that made her fall to her knees in shock. Trying to move, Alex found her entire left arm and her upper right arm pinned to her sides. Looking down in confusion, Alex gasped as she found the glowing cord encircling her upper body. A sharp fast tug from behind pulled Alex off of her knees, sending her rolling down the side of the hill and back towards the Rider. Grunting in pain, Alex tried to maneuver her arms to make the fall less painful as sticks and rocks jostled her body.

When her brief but painful fall ended, Alex whimpered and looked up. She was at the feet of the Rider who was coiling up excess cord with a satisfied smirk. Breathing shallowly, Alex swallowed and slowly moved the free portion of her right arm towards the bag that was half twisted around her. The Rider didn't notice and studied her face. In a fast movement, he kicked Alex in the ribs and laughed at her muffled cry of pain. Kicking her again, the Síd pulled harshly on the cord, dragging Alex up to her knees. There was a sharp metallic hiss as the Rider sheathed his sword above her.

"Pretty thing," he observed, reaching towards Alex and tugging at her blonde hair. "And sensitive to pain." The Rider moved forward, leaning over Alex and causing the tension in the cord to loosen slightly. "I like that," the Rider breathed his face right above Alex's.

Dread welled up in Alex, but she couldn't move. She could barely breathe, feeling the icy breath of the Sídhe Rider wash over her face.

"Do you know how long it's been since I had an iron folk?" the Rider questioned with a dark chuckle, bending down on one knee. His clawed hand running up her left arm slowly, using the sharp points of his nail guards to cut into her coat sleeve. "Felt that boiling heat and danger?" The Rider placed his cold lips against Alex's ear and murmured, "Almost three thousand years. Damn the lords and their orders, I may not even wait to get you back into the tunnels."

Fear jolted her into action, the fingers of her right hand slipping into her bag. Gripping the hilt of her dagger, Alex summoned up every fiber of courage and willpower that she possessed and pulled it forth from the bag. Feeling the sudden movement, the Rider pulled back from her sharply. The Rider's eyes widened, but Alex slashed forward. The dagger scratched against the golden armor as it impacted, but Alex kept the movement going. Her hand jolted when the dagger slipped over the rounded decorative neckline of the armor. Pushing forward, Alex put as much force against the dagger as she could manage just as it connected with the smooth white flesh of the Rider.

There was a dull roar that turned into a gurgle. Alex opened her eyes, not even aware that she had closed them. Silvery blood burst forth, glowing like a shower of light in the lamplights. Falling forward, the Sídhe covered the wound, choking as he struggled to stay on his knees. The cord stopped glowing and loosened around her body. Jumping to her feet, Alex shook off the cord and kept her dagger up, hesitated as the Sídhe struggled in front of her. It looked just human enough to make her pause and her fingers clenched uncertainty around the dagger.

A snarl erupted from the shadows, a burst of light blasted forth. Alex had only a second to realize that it looked a lot like one of Aiden's fireballs before it collided with her chest, sending her crashing backward to the ground. Her chest ached and tiny sparks of bright yellow magic were sending jolts of pain down her arms and legs. Every breath was a struggle, but instinct and adrenaline helped Alex shift up onto her elbows despite the pain. Her eyes met the stormy violet eyes of the new Rider and she swallowed back tears of fear.

The second Rider was dressed in more gold than the first with golden beads and silvery gems woven into his long hair around a golden circlet. In his right hand, he held a glowing golden cord that stretched out in the darkness behind him. As he stalked towards Alex, he tugged the cord. There was whimper in the darkness and Alex could see a small shape by the dim light of the cord.

"No," she whispered as the Rider tugged on the cord again, already certain of what was at the other end.

The Rider pulled the cord tighter, winding it to his belt and the small child that had been with the woman came stumbling into view, the infant balanced in its arms. The golden cord was wrapped around one leg, up around the little boy's chest and tight around his neck. His mouth was covered in a translucent golden glow, only allowing small fearful whimpers to escape.

Stepping up next to his struggling comrade, the Sídhe Rider glared at Alex and his eyes went to the dagger that she was still clutching in her hand. Raising his hand, Alex tried to scream as a bright golden glow gathered in his palm, but the sound was muffled. As the Rider released the ball of light, Alex could only manage a tiny whimper before the world went black.

30

Blood on the Tor

811 B.C.E. Somerset Levels

Merlin hadn't even glanced her way when Morgana returned to her roundhouse. A potent mixture of anger, shame and fear brewed inside of her, making Morgana hesitant to speak even to her husband. To her relief, a few of the items she had requested had already been brought to the roundhouse and after giving Arto a forced smile, Morgana busied herself with slicing vegetables and placing them in the bronze cauldron near the hearth.

Airril kept the conversation light, asking Arto about some of the places they had visited while Morgana added more to the cauldron as everything arrived. Other villagers lingered as they delivered their produce to hear about the far northern islands where homes were made completely out of thin stone slabs or the great ancient sites on the western island. Morgana said nothing but found herself calming in the gentle flow of words from Arto that alternated between exciting memories and boring recollections that needed Merlin to add details. She felt envious of everything that the boy had seen and turned to watch as he presented several small treasures from a bag on his belt. There was an elegantly cast bronze axe head, a carved bone comb from the Roman lands and a bronze armlet. At Airril's urging, he also showed each of the three talismans that hung around his neck. The triskele carved into a smooth rounded stone was his favorite and matched one on Merlin's neck.

Dinner was one of the more elegant affairs they'd had since winter solstice's traditional slaughter. Their village had not seen many visitors of note so Morgana felt no hesitation in presenting roasted pig and stew to her guests. But it was Arto's eager acceptance of the food and the cheerful way he dug his way through it that brought a real smile back to Morgana's face. Airril noticed the change and reached over to gently brush her hand with his before turning his attention back to Merlin.

A howl interrupted the conversation as dusk was beginning to settle over the village and Morgana froze. Her breath caught in her chest and she looked towards Merlin with wide eyes. In her distraction overseeing Arto, she had all but dismissed the potential Sídhe threat.

"Morgana?" Airril questioned, reaching for her and placing a hand on her shoulder.

Merlin said nothing, setting aside his bowl, picking up his staff and rising from the small chair on which he'd been seated by the hearth. The talismans around his neck jangled softly and he spared Morgana a glance before gesturing to Arto.

"Are they here for us?" the boy asked as he jumped to his feet. His smile was gone, a serious expression taking its place.

"Possibly," Merlin answered with a nod as he moved towards the door. "Airril, keep your people close to their homes and stay with the children."

"What are you going to do?" Airril demanded as he climbed to his feet, reaching for the bronze sword by his bed that was so rarely used. "Can you truly kill them?"

"Some of them," Merlin replied calmly, drawing the animal hide cover of the roundhouse back. He did not look back at them, but added, "Thank you for the meal. It was excellent."

Climbing to her feet, Morgana's hand dropped to the bag at her side, clutching the cold disk. She barely noticed Airril move, but the next moment her cloak was thrown over her shoulders and he quickly clasped the brooch.

"Morgana," Airril called, finally gaining her attention. "I must go and gather the men to protect the walls, please stay with the women and children."

She gave him a small nod but did not speak or move from her spot by the hearth as he rushed out the doorway. Another long howl made her tense, but she managed a shaky breath. It was closer than before, no doubt closing in on the village with Riders nearby. Her village was on the northern bank of the water and the wooden wall wouldn't stand up for long against the Riders. Morgana did not notice her feet beginning to move, carrying her from the roundhouse and down the hill.

Airril's alarm had already spread. Women were gathering up their children and rushing up the hill towards Morgana's roundhouse. She grabbed the arm of one of the women and told her to make sure to grab extra blankets. Morgana began to move towards one of the roundhouses to help transport supplies up to her home but paused. Her eyes were drawn towards the village gate and out into the gathering darkness. The last rays of the sun were fading quickly and soon the only light would be from the moon and the stars.

Arto was out there, Morgana realized with a twist in her stomach. Merlin had taken a boy out to fight the Sídhe Riders. Maybe he had protected Arto for a few years, but now he was placing him directly in front of the Sídhe. Her hands tightened into fists and Morgana stalked towards the gate, determination and anger rising through her faster and stronger than any rational thought could. Another howl distracted the guards, making them look towards the East and Morgana caught sight of Airril before she slipped through the gate, feeling a tinge of guilt.

Tightening her cloak around herself, Morgana searched the horizon for any sign of Arto and Merlin. Just down the slope of the hill, the marsh water of the valley lapped gently at the shore of the river. A few shallow boats bobbed gently on the water. Wind rushed over the marshland beyond the river, a whistling sound filling the cooling air. Morgana took a slow breath and looked around carefully for Merlin and Arto.

Another howl howled, the sound echoing down from the tor. Turning sharply, Morgana looked up at the high rock and saw a flash of light, like a torch in the darkness. Without thinking, she began rushing away from the wall and towards the tor. To the east, the moon was rising higher and higher, casting more light across the moor.

As she reached the tor, Morgana could hear snarling, whimpers and words being carried on the wind. Stumbling forward, Morgana ignored a shiver of cold that rushed down her spine and looked towards the top of the tor where another flash of light illuminated the area. In the distance, she could hear the rumbling of hooves and swallowed back the urge to run.

At last Morgana reached the final slope of the long side of the tor, her chest aching and her legs beginning to shake. Up ahead a pair of Hounds were circling Merlin and Arto carefully. The rising moon glinted off of their coats and made their bared teeth gleam. Merlin's staff was raised in front of him as he watched the two Hounds carefully. Arto was behind his teacher with too calm an expression for Morgana's taste. Moving forward slowly, she slipped to the right and hoped to pull Arto back from the Hounds and the battle. One of the beasts howled, throwing its head back just as the other lunged.

Merlin's staff slammed into the ground with a resounding crack and a spark of bright light. Beneath Morgana's feet, she felt the earth rumble for a split second before a burst of rock and mud rose from the ground, catching the Hound around the torso only a foot away from Merlin. The mage made no move to step back or remove his staff from the earth. As the other Hound snarled and began to move, Merlin made a lazy gesture.

The mound of earth holding the first Hound shifted, dropping its weight on the second and binding them both in the rock and mud. More earth rose up to surround them, piling over them and muffling the snarling and gagging cries. Gasping softly, Morgana watched the mound sink back into the earth, taking the Hounds into the ground. A moment later the rock and mud became solid once more in front of Merlin and he calmly removed his staff from the ground. He held his palm out in front of him and a small glowing orb of light formed, similar to the one Morgana remembered making all those years ago. Raising it up, Merlin placed it on the top of his staff where it pulsed and made a field of light around the two.

"Riders are coming," Arto shouted. A long smooth slope up the side of the tor would make an easier path for the Riders.

"Indeed they are," Merlin replied with a small smile, patting Arto on the shoulder. "What do you think Arto?"

Arto didn't answer right away and glanced to the side, down towards the moors below. "I'd like to try the protection spell," he answered a moment later. "My sister lives nearby."

"Yes she does," Merlin agreed slowly, hesitation in his voice. "I am not sure that you are ready for that spell."

Hoofbeats were growing louder and Morgana forced herself to start moving closer to Arto and Merlin, using the light of

Merlin's staff to navigate. Her mind stumbled over what to say
to Arto to convince him to leave Merlin; the boy was talking
about magic, she had no doubt of that. But if he left now he
could settle into a quiet life. He'd never have to be a threat to
the Sídhe and they could leave him alone.

Two Riders came charging to the top of the tor, both mounted
on tall glistening steeds with swords drawn. Freezing in place,
Morgana couldn't breathe as one of the Riders slowly
approached Merlin and Arto.

"Surrender Merlin," the Sídhe demanded, but his eyes were on
Arto. "This is a pointless war. The Iron Realm cannot stand
against the might of Queen Scáthbás."

"I believe that you have enough worlds already," Merlin
answered calmly, allowing Arto to move up next to him. "You
cannot have this one." Merlin added darkly, "Of course I
would strip you of those worlds if I could."

"Curse the day you were sired," the Rider growled.

"If your kind didn't commit such crimes my siring would not
have occurred," Merlin returned fiercely.

"Enough," the second Rider snapped angrily. "The Weapon is
the priority. Deal with the blood traitor second."

Morgana shivered as the wind suddenly picked up. Arto's
mouth moved slowly and softly, testing unfamiliar words that
were too quiet for Morgana to hear. Both Riders drove their
steeds to action, charging towards Merlin and Arto. The boy
did not hesitate, staring at the Sídhe Riders around him with
calm and confident brown eyes. His unruly brown hair
blowing in the wind as he slowly dragged the blade of the
dagger across his palm. She shouted a warning that went
unheard as the wind howled more fiercely around the tor.

Closing his fist, Arto held it before him as his words were lost to the wind. His closed fist began to glow, softly at first, but brighter with each step the Sídhe took towards him. They were slowing, Morgana realized with relief as she risked a glance towards the two Riders. Her legs ached as she moved closer to Arto, nearing him just in time to see the boy tip his hand, sending red blood dripping to the ground before him.

Thunder echoed through the valley and lightning flashed across the sky, summoning forth a storm from the clear evening. The glow that had surrounded his hand, exploded outward, illuminating the dusk with the brilliance of the sun. Morgana felt a force hit her chest, sending her crashing onto her back. Pain jolted through her arms and legs from her chest making it painful to breathe. But she could still hear words being carried on the wind from the spell and with a cry of pain, Morgana pushed herself up onto her elbows and looked towards the Riders.

One of the Sídhe steeds had reared, catching the blast in the chest and released a frightened cry as the luminous flesh of its hide began to turn to dust. The Rider shouted and waved his arm, only to crash to the ground as its steed dissolved. The ground was glowing red and Morgana looked down in amazement to see the few drops of blood flowing freely down the slope of the tor like a brook, glowing with power. The Rider on the ground tried to move away, but the magical liquid touched his leg. Morgana flinched at his cry, but couldn't look away as the magic glow traveled up his body and it turned to vapor, blowing away in the stormy wind.

The second Rider tried in vain to steer his horse around the blood, but a mere glance revealed that the Rider's left arm was dissolving and the horse's legs were collapsing underneath it. Gasping softly, Morgana watched in shock as the second Rider and steed fell, vanishing into a cloud of dust before they hit the earth.

The glowing red liquid flowed all around her, following the slope of the tor and leaving soft pulsing sparks of magic behind it. Morgana watched one small stream come towards her with curious fascination, wondering at the magic behind it. Arto had not bled so much, that much she was certain of. She assumed that this spell used the iron in his blood and perhaps pulled iron from the earth itself.

Huffing in pain, Morgana rolled onto her knees and took a long deep breath to fight back the pain of the magical shockwave that Arto had released. She was almost ready to stand when the trickle of blood reached her and touched the fabric covering her knee. Morgana's whole body convulsed, her mouth falling open in a silent scream. Her blood was boiling, her lungs were tightening and her heart began pounding faster than she could bear. Falling forward onto her hands, Morgana whimpered in pain as an icy blast in her limbs met with a rush of blazing heat in her heart. Her body quivered as she struggled to breathe, her ears full of her own heart beat and her vision blurred by tears and fear and pain.

"Morgana!" she heard screamed nearby, the cry distorted by the wind.

"Arto, do not touch her," Merlin's voice commanded.

"But she's hurt," Arto argued, worry clear in his voice before it took on a tone of anger. "You said that the spell couldn't harm a human."

"It cannot harm any creature that belongs to the Iron Realm," Merlin explained patiently and in a sorrowful tone as the voices came closer.

There was a small hand on her shoulder, warm and comforting against the chill that clung to her bones. Taking a deep breath,

Morgana closed her eyes and focused on listening to the voices.

"But Morgana-" Arto's voice started to say.

"Is part Sídhe," Merlin interrupted. "Your sister was taken many years ago before you were even born Arto. Once the Sídhe knew of your birth they fused the child they had stolen and the Changeling together to be their spy and soldier in this world. To watch you and report to them."

Arto pulled his hand away and Morgana clenched her eyes tighter, waiting. Silence followed Merlin's words and she softened her breath, trying to verify that they were still standing by her.

"She's my sister," Arto told Merlin. His voice lacked the power that had resounded through the air with his spell and instead sounded like the small child she had cared for all those years ago.

"She is," Merlin agreed, "But she also belongs to the Sídhe."

"You're part Sídhe," Arto reminded Merlin suddenly, hope in his voice. "The spell didn't affect you, why?"

"I carry the blood of a Sídhe," Merlin agreed gently. "I am not loyal to them. My entire self, my soul and my magic are in the service of the Iron Realm."

"Can't we help her?" Arto asked, defeat creeping into his voice.

"The changes to what your sister is cannot be undone," Merlin told the boy. "And only she can change the bonds of her loyalty."

There was silence again, a horrible condemning silence. Slowly, Morgana opened her eyes and studied the blades of grass blowing in the wind before her. She made no move to reach for Arto and they gave no sign of knowing that she had been listening.

"Come, Arto," Merlin finally called. "You are ready."

"Ready?" Arto repeated, his voice beginning to drift away as Morgana listened to the footfalls of the two. "Ready for what?"

She did not hear Merlin's response or even if he made one as they moved further away from her. The chill finally faded and Morgana raised her head with difficulty. Dragging herself to her feet, she stumbled forward and looked down the slope of the tor. They were not yet too far ahead of her, Merlin walking with his stick in one hand and his other on Arto's shoulder and moving quickly towards the distant hills. She swallowed as her eyes dropped to the softly glowing lines of blood on the ground. Raising her chin and narrowing her eyes, Morgana hiked up her dress a few inches and began the climb down the tor after Merlin and Arto, following the still glowing light on Merlin's staff.

31

Prisoner of the Sídhe

Her chest ached and her arms were tingling with little jolts of pain as Alex struggled to open her eyes. Alex was sprawled on her back, but the surface was hard, smooth and chilly. The realization that she wasn't in her bed penetrated the haze around her mind, but fear and panic did not yet set in. She must have rolled off her bed in the night by accident, that would explain the pain and the tiles underneath her would explain the chill. Her fingers brushed the surface beneath her lazily as a slight moan escaped her lips. The surface was cool to the touch, cold even, but felt almost slick. Besides, she remembered with a frown, she and Jenny had a large rug between their beds.

Alex's mind began to clear and she could hear strange melodic voices in the distance. She stopped moving and could barely breathe as she recognized the sounds from her dreams. The memory of the Riders hit her hard, knocking the air from her lungs in a pained gasp of fear and rising panic. Keeping her eyes shut as naturally as she could manage, Alex struggled to slow down her breathing and appear asleep. She couldn't hear anything other than the voices which sounded distant making her believe that maybe she was alone.

Barely keeping her hands from shaking, Alex slowly opened her eyes. The smooth domed white stone ceiling that looked like it was made from one solid slab was about eight feet above her. Three small glowing balls of light hung in the air just below the ceiling granting Alex illumination. Twisting her head slightly, Alex looked around the room which was round in shape with more smooth white walls. To the right of her was an arched doorway with a heavy looking black door with golden metal accents and a small window.

Still taking long and slow breaths to hold her panic at bay, Alex carefully sat up. She was still in her jeans, shoes, and shirt; only her coat and bag were missing. Her body ached and protested at the movement as her hand went to her chest, feeling for any sign of injury. There was no blood or torn skin, making Alex wonder just what the blast the Sídhe Rider had used on her had done. She shivered as the memory of the first Rider's threats rushed to the forefront of her mind. Harming humans directly wasn't what they were after, she realized, even those too old to be changelings. Alex's stomach turned and she closed her eyes tightly to hold back the tears prickling in her eyes. Wrapping her arms around herself, Alex shuddered from the cold and from fear but kept tears from falling. Several soft dry sobs escaped her despite her efforts, but the sound of movement outside forced her to quiet.

Lying back on the floor, Alex turned her head carefully towards the door and tried to appear asleep. Her ears pricked up and the sound of her own heartbeat echoed loudly in her ears as the sound of a key being turned in a lock nearly echoed in the stone room. Breathing as slowly as she could, Alex resisted the urge to open her eyes as the sound of footfalls indicated that someone was entering the room.

They stopped, less than a foot from her. She could feel cold almost radiating from the figure and into her sprawled arm. Suddenly, they moved and pressed their foot onto her lower arm, pressing down on it. With a cry of pain, Alex's eyes flew open and she rolled onto her side as she tried to free her arm. A golden accented boot held her arm pinned and increased the pressure, making Alex hiss. Raising her eyes, Alex swallowed as she looked up at the second Rider who had hurt her.

"You killed a Síd," he announced in a cold, but beautiful voice. Had Alex not been afraid, she may have found the voice charming and calming. "Iron poisoned," he hissed, grinding his foot down on Alex's arm. "Your fate would have been to serve, to obey and pleasure. To produce more iron folk for our needs, but now you shall suffer true torment until I and all my comrades are appeased." He lifted his boot off of Alex's arm and kicked her in the chest, knocking the air from her lungs and causing her to flinch back. "And I have never been satisfied by the heat of an iron folk body," he growled, pulling his foot back to strike again.

With strength and speed born of desperation and fear, Alex rolled away from him just in time to avoid the strike. Pushing herself up onto one knee, Alex braced herself to move quickly and stared at the Rider. His sword hung at his side, but he made no move to draw it. Instead, he smirked at her, his violet eyes still glowing with rage. He was between Alex and the door, and she knew that simply running past him would never work.

"Your kind is a disease," Alex hissed, letting her pain and anger seep into her words. "A plague, a pestilence. Something to be put down like a wounded hound."

The amusement faded from the Síd's eyes and he bared his teeth as a growl echoed in the room. Rising slowly to her feet, Alex waited for his move, trying to guess what it would be. Professor Bosco's explanation of fencing attacks echoed in her mind as she glanced down at his feet for a hint of movement. Sliding her foot forward on the smooth rock, Alex centered her balance and waited.

The Síd stalked towards her, twisting his golden covered hand before his body, preparing to strike her. When the attack came, Alex shifted back; dodging the blow and hearing a snarl escape the Síd's lips. She lunged forward, under the Síd's arm to grab at the hilt of his sword. As the Síd twisted to grab her, Alex let her left side go limp and allowed gravity to help roll her to the side.

A slow metallic ring echoed in the room as the blade was pulled from the scabbard awkwardly. The sword nearly hung up on the scabbard as the Síd's body prevented the scabbard from shifting further, but a final desperate tug sent Alex crashing to the floor with the sword. Scrambling to her feet, Alex tightened her grip on the longsword. It weighed only a few pounds, but the blade was thicker than the fencing equipment she had used previously. Dismissing the differences, Alex brought the blade up in front of her just as the Rider turned and glared at her.

"You think you can kill me with that?" the Rider demanded harshly. "In my own realm! You have no power here. Your iron blade was left where it fell!"

Hands shaking, Alex sidestepped towards the door, fighting to keep the blade stable. She watched the Rider reach for the golden cord still hanging from his waist and tensed. A slow smirk crossed his face as he lifted the cord from the hook on his belt and began winding it around his hand. Glancing towards the door, Alex wondered for a moment if she could make it. But then what would she do.

The Síd snapped the cord in the air, smiling as Alex flinched at the sound. He took a step towards her. Swinging the sword, Alex flinched as the blade clanged off the metal of his armor and swept across his cheek. A thin line of silver blood appeared, but the Síd just laughed. Less than a second after the wound appeared, Alex saw the silver line vanish as the white skin knitted itself back together.

"You have no power here," the Síd repeated, snapping the cord in the air again and laughing coldly.

Bringing the sword up once again, Alex swallowed and released a slow breath. A hundred tiny bits of thoughts were running through her brain, all of them screaming iron to her. But her dagger was gone, she had nothing except herself and the Sídhe blade.

She moved before the idea finished forming in her head, moving the sword up her own left arm. The slice of her skin made her grit her teeth in pain, but her eyes were locked on the Rider's as his own widened. He backed away as red blood oozed out of the slice on her upper left arm and over the smooth metal of the blade. Releasing a breath, Alex swung the sword away from the wound, sending drops of her iron based blood through the air. They hissed as they collided with the Síd's face making him scream in pain. His golden covered hands rose to protect his face, but Alex swung back, bringing the tip of the blade slicing across the Síd's cheek.

This time she didn't hesitate, pulling back the blade as the Síd clawed as his own face to stop the corrosion of the blood. Thrusting forward, she drove the tip of the sword into his throat and grunted, shoving it forward a little more. The screams stopped instantly and the Rider's hands fell away from his face to his sides. Eyes widening, Alex was frozen in place as the flesh of the Rider dissolved before her eyes, turning to dust. The armor crashed to the floor of the room, clattering so loudly Alex expected an army of Sídhe to come bursting through the door. Then there was silence, leaving Alex alone and staring at the armor strewn about her with a sword dripping with red blood still clutched in her hand.

Catching her breath, Alex stared down at the armor and listened for any sound of movement outside the door, but everything was quiet. In the distance, she could still hear the haunting voices, but the tone had not changed. It took a moment for the rush of adrenaline to slow and Alex to be able to move again. Moving to the door, Alex peeked out carefully.

The room beyond was the same domed shaped as her cell, only much larger with multiple black doorways in the wall and a hallway leading away. A round white stone table with chairs stood in the center of the room with weapons spread across it and Alex's bag half dumped out. Creeping forward and listening for any sounds or movement, Alex went to the table and picked up her phone. She wasn't surprised when a no signal indicator appeared but quickly gathered up her things, checking to verify that her dagger wasn't present. She slung the bag over her shoulder and peered through the windows of each of the black doorways. All the other cells were empty.

Alex was still, debating the best course of action as she stared into the long dark tunnel stretching out before her. The haunting voices and the black stone tunnels were straight out of her dream, reminding her of Bran's warning theory. Pulling out her phone, Alex checked the battery and turned on the flashlight, preparing to move forward into the darkness. As she passed her cell, the glint of the golden armor caught her eye.

Glancing back into the tunnel, Alex darted inside and picked up the breastplate of the armor. It was large on her and most of the pieces wouldn't fit her, but the slight built of the Sídhe meant that while it was long on her, it wasn't too bulky. Everything else was too fitted and long for Alex to use, but having something protecting her vitals made her feel a tiny bit better. She picked up the belt and tightened it around her waist, hanging the cord on its hook, but not sheathing the sword. Alex collected the small ring of golden keys from the pile and carefully moved everything to the side of the cell in two trips.

Stepping outside the cell, Alex checked that there was nothing in view before locking the door and slipping the keys into her bag. She returned to the table and picked up one of the longer Sídhe daggers. Bracing herself, Alex raised it to the cut on her arm and pressed it down to aggravate the wound. Blood oozed out around the dagger blade, giving it a light red coating. Alex checked the sword, noting with a frown that the blood on the blade seemed to be seeping into the metal, giving it a reddish tint with small cracks appearing on the surface. She sheathed the sword and adjusted it on the belt as best she could before picking the blood coated dagger from the table. The dagger was light in her hand and more comfortable than the larger sword, not inferring with her movement as she pulled out her phone and turned on the flashlight. Taking a deep breath, she began to walk into the tunnel following the dim light of her cell phone.

The dark hallway stretched out before Alex with a gradual curve. Her right hand, holding the dagger, reached up and brushed a finger along the wall. It felt solid even as Alex told herself to wake up. She knew she wouldn't, that this time it wasn't a dream, but the tunnel was just like the one she had walked through so many times. Far away, she could hear the musical voices whispering and singing, echoing through the tunnel to her ears. The air was thick with a chill and far too stale. Glancing down at her feet, Alex watched for a moment as her sneakers stepped over the black stone floor. Every detail was like she had dreamed, except for the sudden branch in the tunnel up ahead.

Coming to a stop, Alex glanced carefully down the long black tunnel that her path intersected with. To the left, it sloped down slowly and Alex could hear the voices more clearly. A sudden burst of fresh air made Alex turn to the right and breathe in gratefully. Snarls echoed down the right tunnel and Alex tensed up, bringing up her dagger. She lowered her cell phone as she drew back against the black wall. Light began to fill the tunnel, making Alex slip further back the way she'd come.

Turning off the flashlight, Alex shoved the phone into her pocket. She transferred the dagger into her left hand and placed her right hand on the hilt of the sword. Blood was pumping through her ears, but Alex managed to take slow breaths as footfalls came closer and closer. They were slow and punctuated with only the occasional bestial growl. As slowly as she could manage, Alex drew the sword from the scabbard, flinching every time the metallic sound reached her ears.

But the pace of those coming closer did not change and more light filled the tunnel, spilling into the intersection. Holding her breath, Alex pressed herself against the wall more tightly and waited. A few moments later a Síd in golden armor, much lighter and less elaborate than the Rider's, walked past with a Hound at his side. The Hound stopped and sniffed the air with a low growl, drawing the attention of the Síd.

Leaping forward, Alex slashed the sword at the Hound and brought the dagger down awkwardly in the Síd's back. The Hound whelped in pain, turning sharply towards Alex as the Síd collapsed to his knees. Stumbling back, Alex brought the sword up in front of her, watching as the wound in the Hound's side widened and the flesh began to dissolve. Gripping the sword with both hands, Alex raised it high, glaring at the beast. It lunged and Alex brought the sword down as hard as she could. The blade sliced into the Hound's skull, the head dissolving in an instant. Bits of red tinted metal fell from the sword as small flakes leaving a jagged edge.

Just ahead of Alex, the Síd was raising a horn of some kind to his lips. Reacting, Alex jumped toward and swung the sword down at his unarmored neck. There was only a moment of resistance and Alex slammed her eyes shut. Taking a shaky breath, Alex heard the horn and armor fall to the ground before she opened her eyes.

The armor was in a pile along with a horn and sword. There was no golden cord with this Síd, but just ahead of the armor pile was a small glowing stone that was illuminating the tunnel. Stepped over the armor and glancing down the tunnels, Alex sheathed the damaged sword and reached for the stone. She touched it with one finger before quickly drawing it back and studying it. There didn't seem to be any effect to touching it. Carefully, she tried again, touching it a little longer before checking her hand. Alex repeated the process twice before she finally picked up the stone and held it carefully in her hand.

Alex breathed in the sweet air coming into the tunnels behind her but looked off towards the direction of the voices. She was waiting, she realized. Another gust of wind brought more fresh air into the tunnels from the surface; the opening she'd dreamt about was close. There were guards clearly, but she could get to it. She was armed and strangely, she knew the way. Still, she waited.

Then she heard it, a scream echoing down the tunnel followed by the musical laughter of a Síd. The scream died down, replaced with muffled sobbing. The whispers in the distance were louder than ever, words like: kill, slave, iron child and blood resonating down the tunnel. Tightening her grip on the stone and the dagger, Alex straightened up and took a deep breath. Her hands shook and her mouth was dry as she took her first step down the left passage, following the crying of the children, just like she always had.

32

Rebirth

Alex's hand shook as she crept down the sloping tunnel, using the glowing rock to light her way. She kept the light dimmed with her hands, fearful that at any moment another intersection was going to appear and a Síd would attack her from behind as she had done to the guard. Up ahead the musical voices of the Sídhe changed as some of the distinct voices vanished from the flow of words. She could hear them more clearly now: several Sídhe were arguing about ages. It made little sense to Alex, but the gradual reduction in the number of voices made her hopeful that an army wasn't waiting down the tunnel.

Around her, the rock color was beginning to slowly lighten from the dark black to a softer gray. The floor was no longer a worn down solid piece of rock, but instead carefully fitted pieces of ever lightening gray stone with swirls of white. Above her were more of the glowing orbs of light, hanging in the air every few feet and filling the tunnels with a golden glow.

Slowing down, Alex tried to listen for any more sounds from the children, but the crying was barely audible now. Alex both hoped the child kept crying to let Alex know they were still alive and fearing that it would anger the Sídhe. She also conceded that surely after so long without stolen children, perhaps the Sídhe would be more careful with the ones they now had. Yet the memory of the Rider's almost gleeful and crazed eyes filled her with dread.

The stone was almost completely white around her now and the tunnel made a sudden sharp turn up ahead. Pressing up against the wall, Alex careful sidestepped to the corner and peeked around, the dagger at the ready. She slid the light stone into her bag and placed her hand on the hilt of the sword.

Just ahead was a pair of guards in golden armor standing on either side of an arch doorway of carefully fitted white stone. The walls around the doorway were white and shimmering with flashes of colors and images that Alex ignored. She could now hear the words of the Sídhe clearly and stayed as still as she could to listen without them discovering her.

"It is against the laws," a female voice insisted. "The boy is no more than five years old."

"I make the law!" A male voice snapped, sounding harsh and gruff despite the natural smooth quality of his voice. "I want them both!"

"Milord," the female voice replied more softly. "Please think on the reason for the seven years law. Iron folk are so fragile. These are the first we have had in thousands of years; damaging them due to impatience would not sit well with the rest of the princes."

There was a growl in the room and both guards straightened up a little, making Alex creep back around the corner a bit more.

"I want the boy," the male voice repeated. "I want him now, not in two years! Give him to me Lady Eolande or you may find yourself stripped of your title."

"Milord, please," the female voice argued. "There are still more Riders out, these were brought by only the first two to return. Surely there will be at least a few more to come tonight."

The growling eased only a little at the words, while Alex's stomach turned at the thought of more Riders in Ravenslake. She silently wished that Merlin and Morgana could stop the others.

"Yes, I heard," the male managed to say, the temperature dropping at his tone. "In fact, I heard that an Iron folk killed one of them with iron."

"I was not aware," Eolande told him. "I only take the children; adults are untrainable."

"This adult isn't marked for training," the male growled again. "The Riders claimed her under the Spilt Blood law for torture. It is a waste! There are plenty of mine who would take a dangerous Iron folk over none at all; some would even enjoy breaking it."

"That is not for me to say, milord," Eolande responded once again. "But please my prince, I cannot violate the laws nor can I aid another in their violation. Perhaps after the Riders return and report, you and the other princes will evaluate the laws."

"Very well," the male huffed, his voice regaining a hint of courtesy. "I leave you to your new arrivals, Lady Eolande. Prove that I've allowed you to live for a reason."

Alex glimpsed a tall Síd dressed in elegant rich blue and golden clothing that looked like it was from the Renaissance period stride from the room as she ducked back behind the corner. Listening carefully, Alex stayed still and didn't breathe as the man and at least one other moved away from the doorway. Alex cautiously peered around the corner and smiled. Both guards were gone and the footfalls of the three Sídhe were fading in the distance.

Stepping out slowly, Alex scanned the rest of the tunnel quickly for any signs of another Síd, but there was nothing. Ahead of her, the tunnels turned again sharply out of her sight making her nervous, but also assuring her of some privacy. As she moved towards the door, Alex's hands started shaking again and she fought to keep her breathing under control.

Reaching the doorway, Alex leaned to the side and glanced in quickly. There was only one Síd, dressed in a long pale blue gown and carrying the baby towards the side of the room. The little boy was watching the Síd carefully with wide eyes and hiccupping around his soft sobs. The Síd, Lady Eolande, Alex gathered paid him no mind and set the infant down in a small cradle. Alex pulled back when the Síd turned towards the boy and started to move towards him.

"That is enough crying," the woman commanded coolly, sounding uninterested. "You must learn to behave yourself or there will be consequences."

"I want my Mommy," the boy hiccupped. "Where is Mommy?"

"I suspect that she is dead," Eolande informed him. "The Riders are not known to leave survivors and if she was alive I have no doubt they would have brought her here to serve as a breeder. You and your sister will not be fulfilling that role for some time."

Anger threatened to overwhelm Alex, but she fought it down, trying to think of a plan. It would be simple to enter the room and kill the Síd, but the child made her hesitate. There would be no body, but still the thought of killing the Síd in front of him made her feel ill. Taking a deep breath, Alex knocked her foot against the stone wall, just enough to make a noise.

"More Riders," Eolande announced. "Now be silent, you may have company soon and I will not have you encouraging bad behavior. I am finally reclaiming my position," the Síd muttered as she moved towards the door.

Raising the dagger, Alex exhaled slowly and waited. Her heartbeat echoed in her ears, but her palms weren't sweaty like she thought they would have been. Instead, the fear was being replaced with a calm for which she was both grateful and found frightening. Eolande stepped into the tunnel and Alex moved in one smooth action, driving the dagger into her throat, shoving her against the far wall and covering her mouth. A brief cry was muffled as Alex stared up into shocked purple eyes. A moment later the Síd dissolved and her gown fluttered to the floor.

Stepping back, Alex took a deep breath and checked down the tunnel. She heard nothing and scooped up the dress, shoes, and jewelry as one bundle. Alex stepped into the room and held up a finger to sign quiet to the little boy as she tossed the bundle to the side.

"Who are you?" the little boy asked, climbing to her feet and wiping his eyes. "You look normal."

"I'm a human," Alex assured him quickly; uncertain of how much the five-year-old would understand. "I'm going to take you home."

The boy hesitated, a frown on his face. "Not supposed to talk with strangers," he muttered.

"I'm Alex," she said gently, moving forward slowly and crouching down, trying to remember her babysitting days in early high school. "I know you don't know me, but I'm one of the good guys. You don't want to stay here."

"What about my sister?" the boy asked pointing towards the infant.

"Her too," Alex promised, "But I'll need your help in getting her out of here."

"Okay," he agreed softly.

"What's your name?"

"Ryan," he answered softly, his voice gaining a little more strength.

"Nice to meet you, Ryan," Alex told him, standing up and moving over to the side of the room to collect his sister.

The infant stared up at her with little teary blue eyes. She was wrapped in a blue fleece blanket with stars that made Alex smile softly. Glancing over her shoulder, she checked Ryan over. He didn't look injured and had normal clothing on, his right shoe was untied. Alex returned to Ryan and handed his sister to him before retying both of his shoes with double knots.

"What is your sister's name?" Alex asked gently.

"Amy," he replied, rocking her slowly which seemed to calm him down.

"Ryan do you have a coat?" Alex asked him as she glanced around the room. It was domed with small beds lining one side and cradles on another with a large table in the center. A chest stood near the door with a heavy lock on it.

"They took it," Ryan informed her, looking down at his shoes. "Sorry."

"That's not your fault," Alex told him before reaching for Amy. "Ryan, I'm going to carry Amy for a little bit, we may have to run. If I give her to you in a hurry then take her quickly." The boy nodded and gently handed his sister over. "And if I tell you to do something then you need to do it right away," Alex added seriously.

Ryan nodded again and Alex hoped that he really understood. She drew the dagger from her bag with her right hand, carrying Amy clutching to her chest with her left. Checking the hallway, Alex breathed a little easier at the silence and set a slow pace back the way she had come, mindful of Ryan's small strides.

They soon left the brightly lit section of white stone, sliding into the gray area without a word spoken between them. Alex carefully balanced the dagger in her left hand, careful not to touch Amy in order to pull the light stone from her pocket. Hesitant to put the weight of the infant on the small boy, Alex handed Ryan the light stone and relaxed as his eyes widened with excitement. It was comforting to know that some childlike wonder had survived the night. Ryan followed Alex's instructions, keeping the stone partially covered in his hands and holding it low. Due to his height most of the light was focused on the ground as they began to slowly climb the sloping tunnel floor.

A sudden growl up ahead made Alex freeze in her tracks and hold her breath. Bending down quickly, she handed Amy to Ryan and snatched the light stone from his hand without speaking. Alex raised the dagger and stepped forward slowly in front of the boy.

"Stay quiet," Alex ordered in a low voice as they crept forward.

The curve of the tunnel meant that Alex didn't see the Síd guard until he and his Hound were almost on them. Light filled the corridor as the guard's light stone illuminated the tunnel as he came around the bend. The Hound leapt for her, Ryan screamed behind her and Alex drove the dagger forward into the Hound's chest as it impacted with her body. Crashing backward to the ground, her head colliding with the stone, Alex grunted in pain. Her eyesight blurred and she gasped as the Hound dissolved above her.

"Alex!" Ryan cried, his terror and desperation piercing the haze.

Rolling to the side, Alex focused on the small boy as the guard turned his attention to him. There was a ball of light in the Síd's hand, Alex realized, followed by the certainty that it wasn't a good thing. Her eyes moved to Ryan, his face was pale and he was clutching a bundle tightly to his chest. Amy, the name registered in her mind.

The guard threw the ball of light towards Ryan and Alex raised her hand towards it. She might have shouted no or stop, but she wasn't certain. There was a tug in her stomach and her heart suddenly beat faster; she couldn't breathe. The ball of light stopped in the air inches from Ryan.

Stumbling back, the small boy pressed himself tightly against the wall, trying to move away from the pulsing orb of light. Alex gaped at it, feeling sparks jumping between her outstretched fingertips. Her eyesight was still fuzzy around the edges, but there was a faint glowing connection between her hand and the orb that shimmered like dark silver. In her fingers, she could feel the magic of the orb brushing against her palm and when her hand twitched at the odd feeling so did the orb. With her attention on the orb and mind still clouded, Alex barely noticed the guard reaching for the horn of his belt, but saw the movement in the corner of her eye.

Turning her head quickly, Alex spotted the horn and tried to roll to the side and climb to her feet. The orb followed her movement, shifting away from Ryan and closer to the guard. Eyes widening, the guard began to lift the horn to his lips. Alex pushed her arm forward, using the connection to shove the orb of magic at the guard. A sharp note escaped the horn. The orb collided with his chest, knocking the horn from his hands and forcing him to stumble back.

Gritting her teeth, Alex pushed herself to her feet, drawing the sword in a clumsy movement. More of the golden metal cracked off of the blade, but she hoped it was still sharp enough. The guard gripped the wall behind him and shook his head. Surging forward, Alex thrust the sword forward, throwing all of her weight behind the attack. There was a moment of resistance from the armor, but a sharp high pitched metallic sound followed as the armor crumpled around the blade tip. Groaning and gasping, the guard struggled against Alex. She didn't look up at his face, keeping her eyes on the hilt of the sword as she tugged it to the side. A sharp groan of pain reached her ears before it stopped just as suddenly.

The guard's body slowly dissolved, still struggling to push her away until its hands turned to dust. Alex released her grip on the sword and let it crash to the floor of the tunnel with the chest armor plate. Taking a shaky breath she reached into the pile of gear and pulled out the guard's sword. She glanced down at the wound in her arm that was beginning to clot and rubbed her hand over it. The blood began to ooze slowly out and with a cautious glance at Ryan; Alex lifted the sword to the wound and watched her blood ooze over the blade. Once again the metal began to take on a red tint and she knew it was only a matter of time before this blade fell apart. She repeated the process with her iron dagger.

She turned towards Ryan, the boy's eyes were closed tightly and his face was partially buried in his sister's blanket. Amy's little hands were touching her brother's cheek and tugging at his hair. Swallowing, Alex slowly stepped towards him and called his name. He didn't respond the first time and Alex moved closer, trying again. Raising his chin up, Ryan met Alex's eyes and gave her a watery smile. He was shaking, still clutching the stone and Amy. When Alex moved to take Amy from him, his grip only tightened and his sister gurgled in response.

"Okay you carry Amy," Alex told him, rising to her feet and looking down the tunnel. "We have to keep moving Ryan."

The boy didn't argue and when Alex started walking, he trailed along just behind her. The light source was brighter now without Ryan covering it, but stealth was no longer the issue. Breathing slowly, Alex tried to calm down and ignore the throbbing at the back of her skull. Sheathing the sword, she reached back and gently touched the source of the pain. There was already a large bump starting to swell, but an examination of her hand revealed no blood.

They walked in silence, Alex had no idea of the time that had passed or the distance they had covered. Her mind was a jumble as stray thoughts like worrying about more guards, Ryan's emotional health and the fact that she had used magic all competing for attention. She flexed her fingers around the hilt of the dagger, trying to remember what had happened with the orb exactly. But it was a blur of pain, confusion, and fear for Ryan. Those orbs didn't kill, that much was clear, but they were probably what the Sídhe used to keep prisoners under control and Ryan was so small, not to mention it could have hit Amy.

Alex shook her head, trying to snap herself out of stray thoughts, only to get a rush of pain from the concussion she'd suffered for the action. Taking a slow and deep breath, Alex tried to relax her muscles and focus on the goal rather than the gradual increase of pain she was feeling.

The blasting of a horn behind them made Alex want to scream and curse; the soft gasp it caused Ryan to make kept her focused. Her hands were shaking; feeling heavy and awkward as Alex took another step forward. At her side, Ryan slowly followed, balancing his sister in his arms while keeping the light clutched tightly in one hand.

Another horn bellowed down the tunnel, but Alex hesitated to look behind her. Up ahead was the intersection, complete with a small pile of armor. A burst of fresh air sent a rush of strength through Alex and cleared her head.

"We're almost there," Alex murmured.

Ryan's steps gained more speed and she heard the boy greedily gulping in the air. Amy giggled softly in his arms, almost making Alex smile. The sound of horns behind them was growing fainter, but Alex thought she could hear voices and Hounds snarling. She risked a glance down at Ryan, but the boy had his gaze locked forward. Looking behind them, Alex studied the curving tunnel but could see nothing beyond the light of their stone.

The fresh air may have given Alex a boost of strength, but her shoulders were beginning to ache from the strain of fighting and the weight of the armor. Pain at the back of her head was now a constant throb that she could almost, but not quite ignore. A stronger blast of air rushed down the tunnel, this time accompanied by a soft whistle. Alex's heart jumped in her chest as a memory of seeing a cave in Washington once with her family and the sound the wind made of the entrance came to mind.

Swallowing, Alex tightened her grip on the sword and once again said, "We're almost there."

A howl ripped up the tunnel from behind them, followed by another and another. Spinning around, Alex caught sight of beams of light coming up the tunnel and three shapes rushing towards them around the curve. Air rushed from her lungs and her limbs grew heavy as three more Sídhe guards ran up the tunnel towards them.

Alex raised the sword and dagger, trying to ignore the pain threatening to overwhelm her and the chill sinking into her bones as the Hounds approached. Behind her Ryan screamed, frightening Amy who howled and wailed. One Hound rushed ahead of the others and lunged. Alex swung the sword across her body, connecting to the side of the Hound with the fleshy smack. The iron-tainted blade met its flesh a sickening hiss. The Hound fell to the side, but Alex fixed her eyes on the two who were now on her.

The next Hound dodged her swing and snapped at her arm, almost catching it in its jaws. Lunging forward, Alex buried the dagger in its neck. Pain jolted through her left leg is the other Hound clamped its jaws around it. Her scream drowned out the Hound whimpering in pain as her iron blood spilled into its mouth.

A guard rushed forward, creating one of the glowing orbs in his hand. Groaning, Alex stumbled forward as the Hound dissolved, freeing her bleeding leg. Her eyes locked on the orb and she raised her hand. Trying to remember the lessons, Alex attempted to calm down, but the pain of her leg, head, shoulders and arm all crashed down on her. The ball of magic sparked violently in the Síd's hand, the golden color darkening to dark silver and growing larger. Frantically, the Síd moved to throw the orb, but it exploded in a burst of three streams of

magic, each one plowing into the chest of a guard, twisting
and sparking like bolts of lightning.

Alex couldn't look away as all three Sídhe seized up, their
mouths open in silent screams. Their bodies' natural pale color
darkened to the same metallic shade of the magic for a
moment before all three crumbled to dust. Gasping for air,
Alex stared at the piles of armor and weapons for a moment
before bending down to retrieve the dagger. She hissed in pain
as her leg throbbed and couldn't ignore the feeling of blood
seeping down her leg underneath her ripped jeans.

"Alex?" Ryan's frightened voice called from behind her.

Taking a slow breath, Alex turned and gave the boy a tiny
forced smile. Amy was still crying, but her wails were
beginning to soften, something Alex's pounding head was
grateful for.

"I'm alright," Alex managed to assure Ryan before she
gestured down the tunnel. "Let's go."

Each step hurt; the cold air of the tunnel not helping her
wounded leg and the stone floor making each step jarring.
Alex resisted the instinct to check the wound, too afraid of
stopping. She had her phone: when they got out she could call
for help and get the kids somewhere safe. The memory of their
mother still on the ground hit her hard and Alex had to grit her
teeth to keep from losing the shaky control that she still had.

Another gust of air hit their faces and the whistle was louder
than before. Panting, Alex looked down at Ryan, the boy was
clearly tiring and moving slowly, but his grip on Amy was
protective and he was speaking softly to his sister. Suddenly
there was a rumble up ahead of hooves and the snarls of
Hounds. Alex came to a stop and listened as Ryan stepped
behind her with a small whimper. The din of hooves and

snarls was quickly joined by crying, muffled screams, and high-pitched laughter.

Gritting her teeth, Alex bent over and used the dagger to cut at her torn jeans, exposing the wound fully. She slid the dagger over the wound, allowing the seeping blood to cover the blade with a thick red sheen before she raised it in front of her. After a moment of consideration, Alex slid the sword into the sheath and transferred the dagger to her right hand.

Breathing deeply, Alex tried to focus on how to call her magic. It had worked against the last few guards and now it sounded like she had a small army coming down the corridor. Flexing her fingers around the hilt of the dagger, Alex tried to remember how the others had described it. They visualized what they wanted, but they had elements or telekinesis. They just had to picture the water moving or ice or fire or how the object moved.

Alex exhaled and pushed the thought away, trying to focus on something that wouldn't lead to panic. The orbs were like light, but when her magic touched that last one it had turned darker, almost like silver. So it wasn't light that she could control, but what was it?

Uncertainly, Alex closed her eyes and tried to ignore the approaching sounds of Sídhe revelry and tried to envision the magical bolts that had destroyed the guards. Her fingers twitched and she felt a small shock travel up her right arm. The feeling grew stronger, her arm tingled and Alex turned her palm up and opened her eyes. Small dark silvery sparks of magic were dancing in her palm. A small laugh escaped Alex as she watched the sparks of magic zip between each other and connect, forming tiny dark lightning bolts.

"I've got it," Alex breathed, a smile taking over her face. "I am a mage."

"Alex?" Ryan called from behind her, backing away as the sounds of the Sídhe came closer and closer. "What do we do?"

"Stay back there and keep Amy close," Alex ordered, tightening her sparking hand into a fist. "I've had enough of this place. We are going home," she growled.

The magic in her hand flared at her words and Alex opened her fist once again, a shining metallic colored orb that pulsed with magic forming. Light poured down into their part of the tunnel as the Sídhe descended the long tunnel and Alex put her hand out in front of, ready to throw the orb.

A Rider appeared first, leading a tall pale horse with one hand and holding a golden cord in the other. Alex's eyes narrowed as the Rider's widened in surprise as she took in the young girl bound by the cord. Alex pushed her arm forward and visualized the bolts of magic striking the Rider down. To her surprise, the orb vanished from her hand, not being tossed through the air and instead a bolt of dark lightning sprung straight from her fingertips.

The Rider screamed, his body convulsing for only a moment and the golden cord falling from his hand before his flesh turned to dust. Two Hounds burst forward around the little girl who whimpered under the magical gag. Screaming, Alex pushed her hand forward and twin bolts of dark lightning erupted from her hand. The Hounds were instantly vaporized, letting Alex catch sight of three Riders pulling their swords and moving towards her.

The first one, dressed in the most gold with the longest horns glared at her and placed his hand in front of his body. The other two Riders waited on either side of him as a large glowing orb of magic formed in front of him. It sparked and had a strange green tint to it that distinguished it from the ones used on her earlier. The Rider released it, sending it shooting through the air at Alex. She raised her hand instinctively and felt the pulse of the magic. Grabbing that feeling, Alex commanded it to stop and it did.

The orb hung in the air sparking in front of Alex for a moment before its color began to darken. Laughing in triumph, Alex pushed her magic in the orb, imagining the entire thing darkening. Her legs shook and tingled as a drained feeling began to take over her body. She heard the Riders shouting and the slick metallic sound of swords being drawn, but didn't let it distract her. Exhaling slowly, Alex felt the orb finish transforming and mentally pushed against it, breaking the stream of magic between herself and it. Closing her eyes, she heard the Riders charging and commanded the orb to destroy them.

A wave of pressure hit Alex's chest as the orb burst into tiny bolts of dark lightning, striking the Riders and the horses. She didn't have to open her eyes to see their bodies changing colors and start to turn to dust. Slowly, Alex breathed in and opened her eyes.

Before her were piles of armor and weapons and just up the slope of the tunnel were several golden bridles and saddles. Alex took a slow step forward, panting softly as her legs and arms shook. The dagger fell from her hand and clattered to the stone floor of the tunnel. Alex ignored it and stumbled forward, following the slope until she reached the first little girl who was already shaking loose the cord. Behind her were three more children ranging from four years old to a young teenager.

They were all looking at her with wide eyes. Saying nothing, Alex moved around to help them tug off the golden cords. Then the questions started, first from the young teenage girl and then down. Clutching her head, Alex tried to keep her focus.

"Enough!" she shouted, her voice echoing off the walls of the tunnel. "Not now. First, we get out of here!"

Alex stumbled forward, gripping the wall to keep from falling before looking back to see Ryan dashing forward. He stopped just behind her, waiting for her to keep walking. The others shifted uncomfortably but had fallen silently. Swallowing thickly, Alex took another step and then another, following the rise of the tunnel as quickly as she could manage.

She wanted to drop: Alex would have taken a nap on the hard and cold stone floor had it not been for the footfalls behind that reminded her what she was doing. Soft cries and sniffing echoed softly in the tunnel and made Alex wish she had the energy to be comforting. Her fingers gripped at the stone walls which became rougher with each step. She could smell real dirt now, breathing in the scent of real earth and not just stone. Another burst of fresh air breezed down the tunnel which Alex inhaled greedily. The cold air made her skin feel raw, but Alex ignored the discomfort.

Then the tunnel evened out, creating a small smooth landing just before a tall cave opening. Beyond it, Alex could see snow and a few ice covered trees in the earliest light of dawn. Whispers and small cheers rose up from behind her as Alex reached the opening. She put one foot outside and looked to the east just in time to see the first hint of the sunrise above the horizon. Stepping towards it, Alex closed her eyes and felt the warmth of it on her face, listening as the children rushed out of the tunnel behind her. They were shouting and cheering and saying all kinds of things that Alex couldn't hear anymore.

Alex barely felt the weight of the armor vanish as it turned to dirt and crumbled around her along with the Rider's belt and sword. A few flecks of the dirt fell into her hands before she allowed them to fall to the earth. Her legs gave out and she fell to her knees, too tired to even hiss in pain as her wound hit the snow. A moment later, a warm hand was on her shoulder.

"Alex," a familiar feminine voice called gently. Something heavy and warm was wrapped around her shoulders. "Welcome back." The grip on her shoulder tightened and the voice added, "Happy Imbolc."

33

Cave of the Sword

811 B.C.E. Somerset Levels

The slow rising of the sun was a relief for Morgana as she trekked after Merlin and Arto across the moor and over the rolling hills. Even behind thick gray clouds, the light was a welcome addition, helping Morgana navigate over the terrain. Her knees were sore and her dress was filthy from every tumble she had made trying to follow them without the benefit of Merlin's magical light. They had turned north soon after leaving the tor, making Morgana uncertain of their destination. While she was breathing hard, there was no sign of Merlin or Arto slowing down. The only change was that the light on Merlin's staff was slowly fading away.

She had no notion of how far they had walked, but her body was aching at the abuse of hiking all night without any rest. Another spark of anger at Merlin rose up in her at his rough treatment of Arto, but then she saw the boy make an excited jump up ahead of her. They slowed down and Morgana ducked down, letting the long grasses of the plain disguise her presence.

Up head were the limestone hills, Morgana recognized them by the sharp outcropping and sighed in relief that at least she recognized where they were. Glancing over her shoulder, she could see the tor rising above a sea of early morning mists. Worry for Airril made Morgana bite her lip, but she quickly looked back towards Merlin and Arto in time to see them moving again. Merlin pointed towards the west and they began to follow the side of the limestone hill. Morgana frowned as she glanced the direction that Merlin had indicated: they were heading for the gorge.

The sun was still quite low when they reached the mouth of the gorge, and Morgana looked up uncertainly at the high cliffs that rose on either side of the small valley. Almost no light was reaching the bottom of the gorge, casting darkness over the path ahead. Merlin paused and created another orb of light which he once again placed on the top of his staff. Humming softly, he stepped into the long shadows with Arto at his side. Morgana huffed but followed them from a safe distance using the trees to hide.

Each step Morgana took along the narrow valley felt painful as her legs protested. Only the light of Merlin's staff illuminating the sides of the gorge allowed her a distraction from her exhaustion. She took in the pale stone as it rose far above her head, all the while wondering where Merlin was leading them. A quick gesture from Merlin had Arto climbing up a slope towards a cliff face with Merlin right behind. Morgana paused behind them and waited for a moment before following them up the incline.

Then they were gone and Merlin's light vanished from her sight. Morgana panicked for a moment before spotting a wide opening in the rock. She had to duck down to slip inside but was able to see the glimmer of Merlin's light ahead of her. Crawling forward, Morgana focused on taking deep breaths and tried to push away thoughts of the Sídhe tunnels.

Thankfully, the passage soon grew larger and Morgana was able to stand. She had to carefully move through several narrow sections but was able to keep an eye on the glow of Merlin's light up ahead, now terrified of losing it and being left in total darkness. Her foot slipped on the moist limestone and Morgana barely caught herself on a nearby stalagmite. Ahead of her Merlin paused but didn't turn around. She heard a soft chuckle echo up the passage and grit her teeth. He knew she was following them; he'd probably known since she had taken her first fall in the dark. The desire to hit him rose up once again, but Arto began moving through the narrow passage again.

The passage suddenly widened into a large cavern. Stalagmites and stalactites joined to form pillars of stone around the entrance with a small bank of slick shining stone before a large pool of water. The light of Merlin's staff glinted off the still surface and made the rocks shimmer with hints of green and orange along with flashes of black and pure white.

"It's beautiful," Arto breathed ahead of Morgana, coming to a stop at the edge of the water. As he turned, Morgana pressed herself against the passage wall, just outside the reach of Merlin's light.

Walking forward to join Arto, Merlin placed a hand on his shoulder and squeezed gently. "It is beautiful," he agreed warmly. "Shall we?"

Nodding, Arto pulled a bronze dagger from his belt and knelt, lowering the blade into the water. Then he lifted it up, pulled his arm back and tossed it. The dagger hit the smooth surface of the pool with a heavy splash, sending ripples outward. Water lapped at the shore and Morgana raised an eyebrow, wondering if Merlin had only brought Arto to this cave for an offering.

The water rolled outward from the impact, but gaining height and speed rather than calming. The height of each ripple grew higher and higher, surging out of the previously still pool. Gaping, Morgana stepped away from the wall, watching in awe as small streams of water rose gracefully from the surface, twirling together. The shimmering streams wove around each other forming a tall figure, cloaked in a veil of water. Then the water settled, solidifying the figure.

It was a woman or looked similar to one, Morgana amended quickly in her mind. This being was as different from humans as the Queen was. Long black hair hung across her shoulder with small braids adding texture and a circlet of glowing water droplets illuminated her face. Curving blue and black designs highlighted her large green eyes and made her bronze colored skin seem aglow. A beautiful smile took over the being's face as she beheld Merlin and Arto standing on the shore.

"Merlin," the woman greeted her voice warm with a strange echoing quality. It soothed Morgana and made her long to sink to the floor and sleep. "Arto."

"Lady Cyrridven," Arto greeted with a small bow that made Cyrridven chuckle.

"Oh sweet child," Cyrridven cooed before she returned her gaze to Merlin. "Then you are prepared."

"It is time," Merlin told her with a firm nod.

Cyrridven nodded and looked around the cave with a small frown. "An interesting choice of location Merlin, but it will do."

"I am hoping that the cave may conceal our actions from the Sídhe," Merlin explained with a hint of worry. "This will take some time."

"Indeed," Cyrridven agreed before raising her arms in front of her. Water swirled up from the surface and settled in her arms for a moment before washing away leaving a heavy looking rolled animal skin in her arms. "I have protected this as you requested."

"My thanks to you Cyrridven," Merlin answered with a small bow before he stepped into the water to take the burden from her.

Leaning forward, Morgana tried to understand what she was seeing as Merlin set down the large bundle and began to unwrap it. Arto blocked her view as he moved to help the older man. The young man sidestepped a moment later and set a large smooth topped stone to the side with a grunt. Then he lifted the stone onto a nearby stalagmite that had a wide base and twisted the stone to grind it down. The limestone slowly gave way until Arto had a level base.

Brushing off his hands, Arto checked the stone's position and tried to shift it, but it had settled enough not to move. Neither of them spoke as Merlin began to light a fire in one of the holes in the floor, putting the flames at a lower level while Arto set up a pair of bellows and began connecting the airways to the fire pit. Merlin then picked up a smaller pelt wrapped package and set it down by the stone that Arto had positioned.

Turning his attention back to the larger pelt, Merlin reached over and rolled it out, revealing piles of small rough rocks, many of them with streaks of red. Swallowing, Arto knelt down at the edge of the skin and reached out to touch the first rock.

"These are the purest in the heart of this realm," Cyrridven informed them, her words making Morgana frown with confusion, but clearly meaning something to Arto and Merlin. "I have purified them already to the best of my abilities."

"I can feel it," Arto breathed, his eyes sliding closed. "It's… it's like a heartbeat in the stone."

"It is the blood of this realm," Merlin told Arto in a low and gentle voice. "It does not flow on the surface, but if you can make it take shape for you then you will have power over the Sídhe."

"And this process will help me do that?" Arto questioned, glancing between Merlin and Cyrridven.

"I have observed mortals in other places use such a method," Cyrridven replied gently. "But you have powers they do not. Arto, there is no need to fear."

Swallowing, Arto nodded and set his hands on his thighs, breathing deeply and slowly. Morgana crouched down and moved closer just in time to see Arto's hands begin glowing a brilliant pure white as sparks of magic danced over his fingers. In a smooth motion, Arto reached out his hands over the large pile of stones.

Everything was still, the air thick and nobody breathing. The rocks shuddered and moved as the white sparks encircled them all. Spots on the rocks began to glow bright red and flickered to a dark metallic color. Pieces of the rocks began to crumble away as white sparks rushed over them, leaving glowing and pulsing stones of red and dark gray behind. The cavern was aglow with white sparks which swirled around the stones like a dust devil, tossing away the dust and fragments of stone. The glowing pieces of red metal began to rise into the air, carried by the white sparks of magic. They twirled around each other, crashing together with sharp metallic sounds and bursts of heat that made them glow like molten bronze.

Crash after crash brought more of the pieces together, increasing the size of the molten orb hanging in the air. Narrowing her eyes, Morgana was nearly blinded even as the glowing white sparks of magic began to fade away. She heard Arto exhale as the last piece joined the glowing molten orb, the cave falling silent. Her brother's hand shook as he raised them and reached for the metal orb. Morgana began to open her mouth to shout a warning but merely gasped as Arto's hand stopped just above the surface. He released a small hiss at the heat, but slowly drew his hand back and beckoned with his fingers. The molten material followed his hand, flowing forward through the air and shifting from an orb into a long glowing rod.

"Well done," Merlin said, breaking the silence in the cavern. "The first step is complete."

Arto nodded and stared at the rod as its glow began to fade, turning it from bright red to an ever darkening gray. No one moved until the rod had completely darkened and fell onto the animal skin with a hard muffled crash that resonated through the cavern. A laugh escaped Arto and he looked up at Merlin who chuckled as well. Slapping a hand on the boy's shoulder, Merlin shook his head and smiled warmly. He squeezed Arto's shoulder before releasing it and sitting down on his knees by the bellows.

Picking up the long strange rod, Arto joined Merlin by the fire and watched as the older man raised and lowered the bellow, building up the heat of the fire. Arto slid the long rod into the fire and it vanished beneath the charcoal and wood. Arto then walked over to the strange stone and the packet that Merlin had set next to it. From her position, Morgana couldn't properly see what was inside as Arto unwrapped it, but a moment later her brother raised a set of tongs and a bronze hammer. He placed the hammer on the flat stone and returned to the fire.

Reaching forward, Arto secured the rod with the tongs and drew it slowly from the flames. The tip of it was now glowing red hot. In a smooth movement, Arto carried it to the rock he had set up, picked up the hammer and set the rod on the stone. Morgana gazed on in confusion as her brother lifted the hammer above his head and took a deep breath. The hand holding the hammer began to glow with white magic. In seconds the white light had engulfed the hammer causing the metal to gleam.

Sparks flew as the hammer hit the rod with a metallic crash that echoed in the cavern. The light of the hot metal cast strange shapes over the walls as Arto moved to strike it again. Arto took deep breaths between swings, the glow of magic in his hand shifting into the hammer and then into the metal with each blow. He adjusted his grip with the tongs and struck again as the red hot glow of the metal began to fade. Without a word Arto turned and thrust the metal back into the fire. Merlin raised and lowered the bellows in a smooth practiced rhythm as Arto caught his breath and wiped the sweat off his brow. There was silence as they waited and Morgana heard only the crackling of the fire and the water lapping at the bank as Cyrridven moved closer.

Arto reclaimed the tongs, pulled out the metal and began again. Each crash of the hammer sent another pulse of Arto's soft white magic pouring into the metal which was slowly becoming longer and longer as his blows shaped it. Turning it, he swung, again and again, to force the metal into a narrower and flatter shape. After every few swings, he returned it to the fire as the heated glow vanished, but with each strike of the hammer, the white glow was remaining longer and longer.

Stepping forward, Morgana was entranced by the smooth dance that kept Arto moving between the fire and the stone. Arto's hammer strikes slowed, becoming more and more deliberate as he flattened the metal into a long and narrow shape. It was when he turned it sideways and began to narrow down one end that Morgana realized what she was seeing.

"A sword," she whispered as the tang quickly took shape.

Arto paused only to hold his hand over the length he had
narrowed, checking for the size of the hilt. Satisfied, Arto
drove the metal back into the fire and breathed as it reheated,
now carrying a soft white glow even away from the hammer.
When Arto drew the metal forth once one, Merlin waved his
hand to clear the air of the thickening smoke. Sliding down,
Morgana leaned against the wall, her eyes fixed on Arto as he
resumed hammering at the sword.

Time passed in a blur and the hammering became almost
soothing to Morgana like a heartbeat as Arto switched to a
different, smaller hammer and began to use softer blows to
create the sharp edge of the blade. Merlin cleared the air every
few rotations but never had to place more wood on the fire.
Cyrridven hovered at the edge of the water, watching the
actions of Arto with interest, but never stepping onto the
shore.

The sword was glowing white, shining light across the stone
and illuminating Arto's work. Each blow, however soft, sent
another pulse of magic into the metal. He worked his way up
and down the sword, smoothing out the metal with gentle taps
and bursts of magic. Panting softly, Arto returned the sword to
the fire, set aside the hammer and reached for a waterskin.

"I remember my first sword," Arto said suddenly, breaking the
long silence. "You surprised me: I hadn't thought you'd ever
let me try a sword."

"You were clumsy with bronze," Merlin replied with a
chuckle, his eyes lingering on the glowing white metal.

"True," Arto conceded with a shrug before taking another sip.
"But when we opened that mold, I thought it was the most
beautiful thing I'd ever seen," Arto sighed, rolling his
shoulders.

"And now?" Merlin questioned, looking up at the young man.

"I think this will take that position," Arto murmured as he reached for the tongs.

"You are weary," Cyrridven observed with a frown and a glance at Merlin.

"Yes," Arto agreed with a nod, not stopping his movement towards the metal. "But I need to finish this." His tone was strong and echoed through the cavern. Morgana shivered, there was something in his voice that was startling from such a young man.

Returning to the stone, Arto carefully laid out the blade which was red from tip to tip and pulsing with red and orange. Arto made no move to pick up the hammer and instead set his hands above the metal and breathed out. The white glow of the sword intensified. Slamming her eyes shut, Morgana turned her face away as a blinding light filled the cavern. It faded away in a moment, replaced by a warm pulsing white light from the sword on top of the stone. Arto was on his knees, panting and shaking. Morgana stumbled to her feet at the same time that Merlin rose from his position.

Sweeping forward, Merlin laid a gentle hand on Arto's head before he reached out and gripped the white blade. He turned quickly to Cyrridven and held it out to her. Taking it gingerly, Cyrridven pulled back from the edge and vanished with a swirl of water. Merlin then turned and knelt by Arto, shifting the boy to lean against him. Slowly, they moved away from the stone and Merlin helped him lay down on the now empty animal pelt.

Water erupted up from the surface of the pool with a long arm rising with the sword grasped tightly. The metal was gleaming as droplets of water rolled down the blade. Cyrridven's hand released the sword, leaving it floating just above the water as the droplets slowly solidified around the tang, forming a glistening white hilt, guard, and pommel.

Rising from his place by Arto, Merlin reached out his hands and exhaled slowly. His hands glowed for only a moment before sparks encircled the sword, smoothing the metal and leaving the sharp edges gleaming. Morgana crept forward and was just able to make out the golden sparks moving up the blade, leaving smooth golden lines in the metal. The soft golden glow surrounded the sword, transforming the pommel and guard to a brilliant golden color before fading. Gasping, Merlin fell to his knees against the stone and struggled for breath. Cyrridven's hand rose from the water once again, taking hold of the hilt and sending a burst of water up over the sword.

Groaning, Arto rolled to his side as the droplets flowed down the long blade and hit the water with soft drips. He took a deep breath and rose to his feet, shaking with each step towards the water. Arto rested a hand on Merlin's shoulder as he leaned forward. His fingers tightened around the hilt as Cyrridven's hand turned to water and fell away. With care, Arto raised the sword and released a shaky breath over the blade which glowed white for a moment in response.

"Cathanáil," Arto announced with a wide smile, turning and swiping the sword the air, laughing as it made a loud swish.

"Battle breath," Merlin repeated as he climbed up from his knees. "It will do I suppose."

"Excalibur," a voice whispered from the water with a soft laugh.

"What did Cyrridven say?" Arto asked Merlin with a frown.

"I wouldn't worry about it," Merlin told him, taking a shaky step forward as he struggled to catch his breath.

"Won't she say goodbye?" Arto questioned as he glanced towards the water.

"I suspect that her powers are drained," Merlin replied as he picked up his staff and leaned against it with a soft sigh. "As are ours; we need to leave this place before the Sídhe come wondering what magic we wrought. Neither of us is ready for a fight."

Arto seemed disappointed as he looked down at his new sword, but a sudden yawn made him nod in agreement. They collected the few items scattered around the cave and stumbled towards the passage. Drawing back, Morgana smacked her knee into the limestone wall and barely contained a whimper of pain. She turned back to the dark tunnel as Merlin struggled to form another ball of light before giving up and taking one of the surviving pieces of wood from the dying fire as a torch.

Keeping her arms out in front of her, Morgana carefully followed the small passage, hitting her head twice when she failed to duck. Her right hand followed the slope of the ceiling as her left hand reached into the emptiness ahead of her. Breathing slowly, Morgana tried to stay calm in the darkness as only a few flashes of the torch behind her offered any light. After what seemed like hours, she caught a breath of fresh air and stepped into the dying light of the day.

With a frown, Morgana looked up at the sky, startled by how much time had passed. The gorge was already filling with shadows as the sun began to sink behind the hills. She tightened her cloak around her as her stomach gave a fierce growl and she became aware of how thirsty she was. The forging of the strange sword had blinded her to all else.

Hearing the voices of Arto and Merlin behind her, Morgana stumbled forward to get away from the cave entrance. Her foot caught on the twisted root of a tree and she fell to the ground, sprawling out to keep herself from rolling down the rocky slope. The light of the torch was shining over her before Morgana caught her breath enough to move. Sighing softly, she tilted her head back and looked up at Arto and Merlin, only one of whom looked surprised to see her.

"Morgana?" Arto gasped. "What are you doing here sister?"

Morgana opened her mouth to reply, struggling for a reasonable explanation when she didn't really know why she was there. Arto stepped down the hill carefully, keeping his grip tight on the sword and extended his free hand to Morgana. Taking it gratefully, Morgana climbed to her feet and turned towards Merlin. He was calmly regarding her, waiting for her to say something.

A cold shudder rushed up Morgana's spine making her shiver and Merlin straightened up sharply. His eyes left Morgana and tracked across the gorge. A howl echoed off the high cliffs and Arto gasped, raising the sword in front of him as Morgana spun to study their surroundings.

"We could retreat into the cave," Arto suggested with a quick whisper to Merlin.

"Then we will be trapped," Merlin replied. "There is no other path away from that pool."

"Could Cyrridven help us?" Arto questioned, looking around almost frantically as his hand started to shake.

"Her powers are too drained, I doubt she would even hear our call for aid."

Heart pounding, Morgana reached down and snatched up a small branch from the ground and raised it to the torch. It caught on fire and she stepped away from Merlin, peering out into the low light.

"Their entrance is closer to the village," Morgana reminded them. "They aren't that close."

"The distance is great on foot, but little to a Hound or a Rider," Merlin told her darkly. "And we cannot outrun them."

"But last night you were able to destroy them," Morgana reminded him, looking at Merlin over her shoulder.

"Our task took longer and more magic than I expected," Merlin intoned with a look at Arto before he looked back at Morgana. "They will not harm you, run while you can."

Gaping at Merlin, Morgana took a slow step back before her eyes moved to Arto. The young man was struggling to keep the sword up, his arms and legs shaking. He was panting and half leaning against a short knotted tree on the hillside. Her mouth was suddenly painfully dry and the chill in her limbs was becoming unbearable. Instinctively, Morgana reached up to touch her brooch and moved further away from Merlin and Arto. She couldn't think, she could barely breathe as hunger, exhaustion, fear and doubt all gnawed at her.

Hoofbeats rumbled in the distance, coming closer and closer with each passing moment. Morgana turned and looked out to the mouth of the gorge as the last light of dusk faded from the sky, leaving an inky blackness complete with heavy clouds above that blotted out the moon.

"Arto," Merlin whispered in a low voice. "Run if you can; do not let them get the sword."

"What if they take me into the tunnels?" Arto whispered back, his voice thin, but steady.

"Don't let them," Merlin ordered shortly as he tried to call forth his magic again, only to have his hand begin to shake badly. "Curse the Sídhe!"

Movement at the mouth of the gorge made Morgana tense up, but her feet still did not move. Behind her, she heard Merlin shift and Arto suggest retreat into the cave once more. Two orbs of light appeared, a once welcome sight, but now illuminating two Sídhe Riders and a pack of four Hounds as they burst around the curve of the gorge and into view.

Snarling filled the gorge as the Hounds rushed ahead of the Riders and began dashing up the slope of the hill. Morgana screamed and stumbled back, nearly tripping over the same tree root as a Hound ran past her and lunged at Merlin. With a pained grunt, he swung his staff and hit the Hound in the side. It growled and lunged again, latching on to the edge of Merlin's robe. Next to him, Arto raised the sword and brought it down on the creature's neck.

There was a flash of white light that nearly blinded them all and the Hound was gone. Grinning with victory and panting with exhaustion, Arto swung wildly at the Hound trying to attack him from the side as Merlin caught another Hound in the head.

Looking down the hill, Morgana caught one of the Riders looking at her with a frown and a measuring gaze. She swallowed and glanced back to Merlin and Arto who were losing ground. Merlin grunted in pain, muffling a scream as a Hound sank its teeth into his left arm. Arto turned away from a Hound attacking him to thrust Cathanáil into the chest of the Hound. Behind Arto, the Hound crouched and then leapt off the ground.

"No!" Morgana screamed, throwing her hand out towards Arto.

Light sparked in the night, blinding in the darkness and the Hound gave a terrible cry of pain before falling back to the ground. It struggled to rise but fell and dissolved. Gasping, Morgana dropped the torch she'd been carrying and looked down at her hands in alarm.

"Morgana!" Merlin shouted in warning as the last two Hounds turned their attention to her.

One circled to her left and snarled only to get hit from behind by Arto and vanish in a burst of white light. The second jumped at her, its jaws just missing her leg. Breathing in quickly, Morgana allowed her old training to take over. Magic sparked in her right hand, its warmth flowing over her cold palm and casting a sharp bright glow around her. The Hound growled and moved and Morgana pushed the magic away from herself. They collided right in front of her, the Hound howling as it dissolved.

"Traitor!" a Rider shouted from the gorge.

Jumping to the side, Morgana avoided a magic orb that collided with the rock wall behind her with a hiss. In the corner of her eye, she saw Merlin pulling Arto back towards the cave, but quickly focused her attention back on the Sídhe as she dove sideways to avoid another attack. The air was forced from her lungs as she hit the hard ground and she hissed in pain as a rock dug into her side.

One of the Riders was trying to urge his horse up the hill, while the other dismounted and pulled his sword. Looking up at them, Morgana glared and growled under her breath. She pulled herself up to her knees and started gathering her magic once again. The silver sparks spun around her fingers in both hands, jumping together and growing larger and larger even as she called forth more of them. Just ahead the hooves of a horse clacked against the stone and a Rider's boot broke a branch. Looking up to meet violet eyes, Morgana raised her hands, grit her teeth and threw all of her magic at them.

Silver light blasted forward, striking both Riders in the chest. It swirled around them, enclosing them in a veil of light and magic. There was no sound as the light tightened around them. Morgana closed both hands into fists, never moving her eyes away. Then, with a deep breath, she shoved both hands forward, opening her fists. The light exploded outwards, filling the gorge with light for one brilliant moment and leaving no trace of the Sídhe Riders.

At the base of the gorge, the remaining horse gave a fearful whiny and turned to run. Climbing to her feet, Morgana raised her chin and created an orb of magic in her palm. She threw it with all her remaining might at the horse which vanished in a shower of silver sparks. Collapsing forward, Morgana groaned at the ache all throughout her body. She felt Merlin step up beside her and saw him offer his hand in the corner of her eye. With Merlin's help, Morgana stood up, almost knocking Merlin over before she managed to stabilize herself.

"Well done," Merlin told her in a cheerful voice with a wide smile. "So, are you ready to be a Mage of the Iron Realm now?"

Morgana didn't answer him as her attention turned to her brother. Arto rushed up and wrapped his arm tightly around her, the pommel of the sword digging into her back. She didn't care, leaning forward to return the embrace. Closing her eyes, she brushed strands of her brother's hair for a moment as she caught her breath. When she opened them, Merlin was watching them with a pleased expression that she didn't find as irritating.

"And now we are three," Merlin announced before his expression hardened.

Arto pulled away from Morgana, but remained at her side while he turned to Merlin to ask, "What happens now?"

"Oh my boy," Merlin sighed as he stepped forward and put a hand on his shoulder. "This war has only just begun."

34

Awakened Mage

Alex moved slowly as she began to wake, but struggled to open her eyes. Shifting, she rolled her shoulders and felt the soft mattress beneath her give slightly. She breathed in deeply, stretching out her arms underneath the heavy comforter. Alex sat up slowly as she wiped the sleep away from the corners of her eyes before opening them. The last of her sleepiness vanished as Alex found herself in an unfamiliar bed and looked at a wall with vintage ivory wallpaper. She blinked and glanced towards the large window to her left. Soft white curtains hung closed over it, but the brightness of the sun was still lighting up the room.

"Good morning," a familiar sounding female voice greeted with a hint of relief and amusement.

Turning her head, Alex looked towards the voice and relaxed when she found Morgana standing in the doorway holding a silver tray in her hands. The professor was smiling gently and dressed the most casually that Alex had ever seen her with blue jeans and a green turtleneck sweater on. Her triskele necklace glistened in the light as she walked forward to a nightstand to Alex's right. Morgana set down the tray and picked up a small teacup that she held out to Alex.

"This will help you recover," Morgana informed her.

Nodding, Alex took the teacup and sipped at the liquid slowly. It tasted sweet and she quickly drank it all, realizing how thirsty she felt. Morgana took the empty cup from her and set it back on the tray. Turning to the side, Morgana pulled a small chair out from the corner and to the side of the bed where she sat down.

"What happened?" Alex asked slowly. "And where am I?"

"You are in the guest room of my home," Morgana explained to her. "It is late Sunday afternoon." Morgana frowned slightly and studied Alex's face before asking, "What do you remember?"

Alex paused at the question and tried to think. The haziness in her mind was slow to part, but there were flashes of the tunnels she'd seen in her dreams. Maybe she'd had the dream again, but then the memory of her capture, escape and fighting the Sídhe returned, causing a shudder to go through her entire body. Trembling, Alex clutched at the blankets covering her and struggled to breathe. Morgana leaned forward, grabbing her shoulder and keeping her steady.

"Deep breaths Alex," Morgana commanded sternly and she struggled to obey. "Hold it in." Alex did so and Morgana nodded at her side. "Now breathe out slowly."

Exhaling slowly, Alex looked over at Morgana and then her eyes fell to her hands. She released her grip on the blankets and turned her palms up, looking at them as if she'd never seen them before.

"I… I…" Alex stumbled, her mouth moving silently.

"You used magic," Morgana finished with a smile. "You saved yourself and all the children that the Sídhe Riders captured."

"I remember… Ryan and his sister. I killed the guards. We ran into the Riders coming in on our way out. I was so scared…"

"Easy," Morgana said gently, wrapping a comforting arm around Alex. "You took a blow to the head, things may be hazy. It's alright. What matters is that you got out."

"The children?" Alex asked, looking at Morgana hopefully.

The Professor released her and moved back with a chuckle. "The children are fine. Merlin and I arrived at dawn at the entrance after tracking the Riders back to the tunnels. We found you there along with the children. You collapsed from exhaustion. While I took care of you and made sure that you were stable, Merlin… tweaked the memories of the children."

"Tweaked their memories?" Alex demanded with a touch of horror seeping into her voice.

"The children, their families, and the police believe that a group of kidnappers came through town last night and attacked family homes. Apparently, they found an old basement in the woods to hide the children, but the children escaped when the men left for supplies. Merlin is in Portland right now building a trail for the police to follow there and then into Canada."

"Is that necessary?" she asked, frowning at the idea.

Morgana reached over to the tray and picked up a tall blue glass that she handed to Alex. This one was filled with cool water which Alex forced herself to sip slowly.

"Humanity let go of its belief in magic for many reasons," Morgana reminded Alex gently. "The old stories are not the modern fairy tales that make magic beautiful and wondrous. For most of its history, magic had fearful roots and was connected to creatures in shadows that meant more harm than good." Morgana shook her head and sighed, "Humanity couldn't control that. Humanity likes to be in control so it let go of magic and sought instead mastery over what it could control. First, it was metalworking and irrigation and the next thing you know they are splitting the atom and making gemstones artificially."

"But couldn't they help us?" Alex pressed with a small shiver. "There were so many of them and I almost didn't get the children out."

"In theory, some could help us," Morgana acknowledged with a nod. "But it is a risk Alex; if certain people found out about magic would they want us using it for their benefit or its real purpose? What if they didn't want the threats defeated because magic would decrease once again? There are so many risks and in the age of cell phone cameras, the internet and multinational terrorist groups I hesitate to let the mages become another source of power."

Nodding slowly, Alex took another sip of water and nibbled at her lip. "So Ryan doesn't remember me?"

"If he sees you around town, I suspect that he will feel unexplainable gratitude towards you. He saw so much that it is likely he will dream about it from time to time, but would you really want him to remember?"

The question made Alex shake her head. They were silent for a moment and Alex finished the glass of water before looking down at herself. She was in the t-shirt and shorts she used to sleep in and glanced up at Morgana with a frown.

"The others are helping cover for your absence. I gave Nicki your key after I got you here and she returned with some of your things. The story she gave your roommate is that you joined them for a gaming session at Aiden's house and got sick to your stomach."

"Oh," Alex mumbled before tugging up the sleeve of her t-shirt to check on her arm.

There was a thin red line where she had slashed herself and she carefully touched it. It was tender, but in far better condition that she would have expected. Tossing back the sheets, Alex looked down at the wound in her leg. There was a curve of small medical stitches, closing up the torn skin, but the sight made Alex feel nauseous and she pulled the sheet back over the wound.

"Did you take me to the hospital?" Alex questioned once she could speak again without gagging.

"No," Morgana chuckled. "I'm almost three thousand years old Alex, I've been a doctor a few times."

"You have?"

Morgana raised an eyebrow, but replied, "Merlin and I go in phases. Thirty-six years ago I was a surgeon and he was a photographer. Legally, I'm the daughter of his previous identity and he's the son of my previous identity. It helps us keep the modern legal paperwork straight and under control."

"Okay," Alex agreed slowly. "I hadn't thought about it like that."

"It's not important," Morgana dismissed before she reached up and turned Alex's head to feel the bump. Alex hissed softly and Morgana made a considering noise. "It may be time for some more healing magic. I used some on your arm and leg already. As much as I could manage to help speed things along."

"But what about the Sídhe?" Alex asked, pushing the Professor's hand away. "Will there be more tonight?"

"No," Morgana explained, rising from her chair and stepped further to the side so she could check the bump. "Merlin and I killed a few Riders last night and tracked the rest back to the tunnel entrance so that we could seal it off. It took some doing, but we severed the connection."

"So, it's over?" Alex asked with wide eyes, twisting to look over her shoulder at Morgana.

"No," Morgana told her gently. "They still have most of the tunnel and will reestablish the connection between realms soon enough. I expect we'll see Hounds again by late March and the tunnel to be repaired for Riders by May. It bought us some time."

"To do what?" Alex asked with a huff, her shoulders slumping.

"To train you all to work as a team," Morgana explained with a chuckle. "So that next time you have to fight you don't come out a wreck."

"Hey, I tried!" Alex countered. "I put on some armor, most of it just wouldn't fit." Alex glanced around the room. "Where is it anyway?"

Morgana laughed and stepped away from Alex, patting her shoulder. "It would have vanished when you left the tunnels. Don't you remember the stories of fairy gold? It turns to rubbish or dirt when it comes into the hands of a human."

"But in the tunnels-"

"The tunnels are under the Sídhe's power," Morgana explained. "And outside the tunnels, a Síd's own power will keep their weapons intact, but a human cannot. Whatever you used in the tunnels is gone."

"They took my dagger," Alex grumbled.

"Aiden found it early this morning, along with your car. It's back on campus and he has your dagger. I suspect that you will be forced to tell them of your adventure in exchange for your dagger."

"He found my car... what about the woman who the Sídhe attacked? Ryan and Amy's mother?"

"Ah yes, Theresa Day; she took a blow to the head and suffered blood loss, but made it to a nearby house. She's in the hospital and expected to recover, but it will take a few weeks due to the exposure to the cold she suffered."

"If she was alive then why didn't the Sídhe-"

"Blood loss; the Riders carry their swords to frighten humans, but they avoid human blood. They left her there to die rather than risk coming into contact with her iron blood."

"Yeah," Alex chuckled, a small smile on her face. "I figured out that trick."

"I was wondering," Morgana said as she sat back down and tried not to look curious. "So what happened?"

"I was at a party last night-"

"On Imbolc?!" Morgana tutted with a shake of her head. "Alex really?"

"February 1st hadn't started yet!" Alex defended quickly.

"Alex, the next day starting at midnight has nothing to do with the turn of the seasons. Imbolc started at sundown, not midnight. The Riders had from sundown to sunrise, the same as they did on Samhain."

Alex opened her mouth to reply but shut it with a sigh before flopping back on the bed. She hissed as the bump hit the pillow, but the pain soon passed.

"That wasn't clear," Alex grumbled.

"Apparently not," Morgana intoned. "But it may have worked out for the best. Merlin and I were nearly overwhelmed ourselves twice last night. The Sídhe sent out almost everyone that they had."

"There weren't many guards," Alex admitted with a frown. "The room with Ryan and Amy wasn't even guarded once the prince left."

"The prince?" Morgana repeated, leaning forward. "What did you hear?"

"Uh, the Sídhe with the kids, Eolande or something was arguing with this guy who wanted Ryan." Alex swallowed and Morgana nodded in understanding. "They were talking about the laws and that the Council would have to make the changes once the Riders returned."

"So they're using a Council of the princes," Morgana said to herself. "That's interesting."

"Good interesting or bad interesting?" Alex asked, turning to face Morgana.

"I'm not sure," Morgana admitted. "During the first war, the Sídhe were ruled by a Queen who had seized enough power to do what she wanted without any approval. She was killed at the end of the war, but it seems that no one has gained enough power to replace her."

"That's good right?" Alex suggested. "There isn't one ruler, but arguing nobles."

"Except taking the Iron Realm would be a good way to secure power, so every warring prince and would-be prince will be throwing all their warriors and resources at conquest."

"There's only one tunnel," Alex countered with a frown, struggling to understand.

"Yes, that no one person controls and I doubt they'd be willing to work together to enforce security. With everyone fighting, it would make sense that the tunnels weren't properly guarded. Everyone had their guards with them. Potentially, that makes it possible for random Sídhe seeking slaves to come to the Iron Realm or slaves to use the tunnels to escape." Morgana sighed and shook her head, "If we're lucky it will at least be brownies."

"Wait," Alex snapped looking at Morgana with wide eyes. "Back up, what are you talking about?"

"Many of the small faery creatures like brownies or pixies or phookas are from the realms that the Sídhe conquered. Near the end of the last war, most of the fighting was centered in England so they poured into Ireland and Scotland to escape slavery. During the final battle of the war, hundreds of them escaped all at once. Like the Sídhe, they suffer a weakness to iron so many of the species that escaped into our world have died off." Morgana shrugged, "Although I do know of a tribe of phookas living in Montana, but they don't cause much trouble. If the Sídhe are in fighting then slaves escaping here might be a side effect along with unsanctioned marauding."

Morgana frowned and shook her head. "I'm just not sure if this will be good for us or bad for us."

"What happens now?" Alex asked, her head spinning with the idea of brownies and pixies potentially coming to Oregon and the fact that Irish Phookas lived in Montana. Her stomach grumbled, causing Alex to flinch slightly.

"I'll make you some food and then if you feel up to it, I'll take you back to campus so you can attend classes tomorrow. Although, you may want to stay home ill and rest up some more."

"But I have more questions," Alex insisted, sitting up again. "And we need a plan to stop the Sídhe."

"I'll set up a meeting time with Merlin," Morgana promised as she moved to the door. "You've earned the right to answers." Morgana paused and gave Alex a sad smile. "You did very well Alex, I'm sorry that you had to go through that, but as your teacher, I am very proud of you."

Smiling in return, Alex swallowed and nodded. Morgana took a step out the doorway before she turned back to Alex and asked, "You mentioned Eolande; did you kill her?"

Blinking, Alex tightened her hand and nodded.

Morgana released a deep breath and said, "Good."

Then she vanished out the door and down the hallway, leaving Alex alone with her thoughts. Looking back down at her hands, Alex flexed her fingers carefully. She felt disconnected from the memories of the tunnels. She'd never harmed anything other than the occasional fly and spider but could remember the resistance followed by a smooth slide of stabbing the Sídhe. Her hands trembled and Alex swallowed, trying to shake off the thought.

That she'd done magic, real magic was the next thing that came to her mind and it was a much more pleasant one. Her skin tingled and she could already visualize the dark sparks jumping in her hand. Alex didn't understand what kind of magic it was; it wasn't an element like Aiden or Nicki's or a mental force like Bran's, but she did have it. Exhaling slowly, Alex began to call the sparks forth when a shout from down the hall made her tense up.

"No magic!" Morgana snapped from the kitchen.

Sighing, Alex stopped the attempt and turned slightly so she could adjust the pillows into a better seated position. She leaned back against them with a small huff and watched the hallway, waiting for Morgana and something to eat. Her fingers flexed slowly, curling around the hilt of the remembered dagger despite Alex's attempts not to think about it. Closing her eyes, she breathed in and out slowly and reminded herself to be grateful for how things had turned out.

35

The Iron Soul

Wednesday afternoon was colder with fresh snow covering the ground as Alex climbed out of her car in front of Professor Cornwall's home. She'd rushed out of World Mythology class without telling the others where she was off to in order to make the meeting. A blue SUV sat in the driveway and Alex knew that it wasn't the red sports car that Morgana drove. Taking a deep breath, Alex slung her bag over her shoulder and headed for the front door.

Professor Cornwall's house was across the river from the main town, all the way on the northern side of the lake on a curvy back road that led up into the trees. The Victorians style house had a tall tower and a rounded front pouch with a light gray paint job and white trim. Alex tapped her shoes against the porch stairs to knock off the snow and tugged off her knit cap to smooth down her hair before she rang the doorbell.

Merlin opened the door and smiled widely as he gestured her inside. Pulling off her bag, Alex set it on the wooden bench by the door so she could hang her jacket up on the coat hooks above. Merlin was waiting by the archway leading into the living room for her with a soft smile. Her stay on Sunday hadn't allowed Alex to see much of the house and she stepped into a large parlor with classic looking sofas and chairs that were a rich red color and looked great. Morgana breezed into the room through an archway on the far side of the room, carrying a very familiar looking silver tray which she set down on a large wooden coffee table. Alex sat down awkwardly on the red sofa as Merlin and Morgana both claimed nearby chairs. Reaching forward, Alex claimed one of the glasses of iced tea and took a quick sip before looking back at her professors.

"You have questions," Merlin stated calmly, claiming his own glass of iced tea. "I agree with Morgana that after your… adventure in the tunnels you've earned the right to some straight answers."

"I don't know where to start," Alex admitted with an exhale. Morgana and Merlin were both silent as Alex gathered her thoughts. "The Sídhe enslave all the words they conquer? Haven't other worlds fought back?"

"Almost all of them," Merlin assured her, "But their worlds had no distinct weapon against the Sídhe who were physically and magically stronger than them. Our world has iron, but they had nothing."

"And mythological creatures are from those worlds?"

"Only some of them," Morgana explained with a nod. "The 'fairy' creatures in Irish and Scottish mythology mostly, but some of the species spread across Europe by the end of the Roman Empire leading to fairy stories in places like Germany and France."

"What about the Nordic elves?" Alex questioned. "Were those Sídhe or something else?"

"No, one of the Sídhe princes managed to make a tunnel into Scandinavia in…" Merlin trailed off with a glance at Morgana.

"116 C.E.," Morgana supplied. "But it was a minor attempt and the tunnel's magic collapsed due to the protections we had in place and interference of some others that were in the area."

"Others?"

Merlin held up his hand and quickly said, "We'll go into the mess of Old Ones, dwarves and the negative effects that that tunnel had on the Sídhe that used it some other time." Merlin shook his head and chuckled. "Needless to say there is a reason that Norse Mythology is as colorful as it is with beings from other worlds."

"What you need to know is that other than the war three thousand years ago there has never been another war with the Sídhe. The magic used to seal our realm from theirs at the end of that war did its job. Other than the Nordic attack that ended very badly for them and convinced the Sídhe not to try until the protections failed, we haven't had a war with them."

Alex shifted and took another sip of her iced tea, her mouth suddenly very dry. "Did they always take… children like that?"

"Yes," Merlin answered sadly. "I remember an attack on my village when I was a young man. A Rider took an infant girl and mocked us with the fate in store for her."

"As far as I know I was the only human child ever released," Morgana informed Alex slowly. "And I was originally taken as an infant. There is a great deal of… grooming that takes place to ensure that children don't fight them. It is why the Sídhe prefer to take children."

"And Eolande?"

"My trainer," Morgana confirmed with a sigh. "I was surprised when you mentioned her, I assumed that she was killed when I became a traitor to the Sídhe."

"It's fitting then that one of your students killed her," Merlin remarked with a smile. Morgana shrugged but smiled slightly at the statement.

"So those protections that you mentioned, the ones that stopped them before, how do we make those?" Alex asked, leaning forward. "How do we stop them now?"

"The six of us combined might be able to create a small protective field for the area," Merlin admitted. "But the level of power needed to seal off our realm from their branches of the Tree of Reality… it's immense. There is only one force of Earth capable of it."

"The Iron Soul," Morgana breathed, her voice wistful. "It is a soul, a spark of life that was created by the Earth itself and imbued with the ability to draw on all the power of the Earth. They have a natural affinity to iron and can cast incredible amounts of power into it."

"The original protections are called the Iron Gates," Merlin explained. "The Iron Soul, a young man named Arto three thousand years ago, used a special iron sword to call forth the power of the Iron Realm and created Iron Gates over all of the Sídhe tunnels. The power in those gates echoed outward, blocking not only the tunnels but the whole realm to the Sídhe."

"So we can't do it again," Alex questioned softly, her shoulder slumping. "Without this Iron Soul, it's impossible."

"The Iron Soul is here Alex," Morgana told her softly. "The soul is reborn roughly every seventy-five years into a new human life. They have no memory of their previous existence and almost never manifest their powers unless there is a threat."

"Wait, you said his name was Arto," Alex interrupted. "With a special sword." She glanced between them, her mouth gaping. "Who was watched over by Merlin. You're talking about King Arthur. You said he wasn't real."

"My brother's name was Arto," Morgana corrected. "Not Arthur and he lived long before the age of castles and chivalry."

Merlin chuckled at Morgana's response. "The legend of King Arthur is a story born from the tales and histories of Arto and a few other incarnations of the Iron Soul in the British Isles. It is not a true story... although over the years story tellers have rediscovered fragments of the truth."

"And he's here, in town," Alex pressed, glancing between the two.

"He is," Merlin agreed.

"It's Arthur Pendred isn't it," Alex half asked, half groaned. "I knew there was something different about him, but none of the others felt a Connection with him."

"Indeed, we believe Arthur is the latest incarnation of the Iron Soul. Your vision even had elements of a blacksmith's forge, which had been connected to the Iron Soul since the beginning." Merlin agreed, excitement rising in his voice. "As to why you felt magic from him, we are not certain."

"But you have a theory?" Alex asked, giving Merlin a wary look.

Morgana glared at Merlin and moved to say something, but Merlin spoke faster. "I am afraid that one of the fragments of the story that was rediscovered was the betrayal of King Arthur by his wife and best friend. When Arto led the war against the Sídhe, he created an alliance by marrying a young woman named Gwenyvar. Sometime later he met and befriended an Irish warrior who joined the cause named Luegáed. Years later they are recorded as Guinevere and Lancelot, but the story is the same. Their betrayal led to the death of Arto, the first Iron Soul and nearly lost the war for humanity."

"That's sad, but what does it have to do with the present?" Alex asked with a frown.

"The Iron Soul is reborn naturally, but Gwenyvar and Luegáed are reborn every few lifetimes alongside him. I believe that they are seeking to make things right, but the story always repeats. They may not intend to betray him, but they always do."

"Merlin thinks that you can change it this time," Morgana interrupted, giving Merlin a hard look. "He thinks that was why you were drawn to Arthur Pendred."

"I was drawn to him because he's hot and a great guy," Alex protested. "But he's dating my roommate anyway."

"We know," Merlin replied giving Alex a hard stare. "Jennifer isn't it?"

"Yeah, Jenny Sanchez…" Alex's eyes widen and she gaped at Merlin. "And his best friend Lance Taylor." When Merlin nodded, Alex shook her head and shouted, "Oh come on! You've got to be kidding."

"We were a bit surprised by it too," Morgana agreed with a nod before taking a sip of her iced tea. "It's not usually that easy to identify them."

"Jenny would not do that," Alex protested. "She loves Arthur and isn't the sort hurt someone on purpose."

"Neither was Gwenyvar," Merlin said, ignoring a snort from Morgana. "Ignore her, she never thought Gwenyvar was good enough for Arto."

"And how she proved me right," Morgana growled.

"But-" Alex gasped, shaking her head. "But if it always happens then what can we do?"

Morgana and Merlin glanced at each other: a silent exchange that Alex knew better than to even try to understand took place. Merlin sighed and turned back to Alex, folding his hands in front of him.

"There is very little we can do. Over the centuries, Morgana and I have tried to find ways of averting this fate; sometimes we can make it a little less terrible, but we have never found a way to completely prevent it. Once Gwenyvar even died young and was reborn almost right away resulting in an age gap on top of the dangerous pattern of behavior."

"Merlin thinks you felt Arthur's natural magic because you have a connection to him," Morgana informed her, leaning on her elbow and studying her carefully. "He thinks you can stop it."

"I still say that the right person can change everything," Merlin declared, straightening up.

"And I still say that you've been reading too many of your own stories. Alex just survived her first real encounter with the Sídhe and you're trying to put the responsibility of preventing a cycle that has repeated twelve times on her."

"It is better than your solution," Merlin argued. "The Iron Soul is supposed to be reborn on its own, not be forced by your rituals."

"It was necessary then and it might be necessary now!"

"Okay!" Alex shouted, ending the argument as she tried to catch her breath. As they stopped fighting, Alex took a deep breath. "Okay," she repeated. "I've still got questions, but maybe that's enough for today. I'll already have a hard time looking at my friends as it is without hearing any more of this."

Nodding, Morgana gave her a slightly apologetic look and Merlin blushed.

"I agree with Alex," Merlin said after an awkward moment of silence. "That's enough for today.

"Yes," Morgana agreed with a nod as she rose to her feet. "I did promise you a year," she said quietly to Merlin.

"Thank you," Merlin replied with a nod as he stood up. He gave Alex a rather forced smile and headed past her towards the door.

"I should be going," Alex announced setting her iced tea back on the tray. "But thank you," she added as she stood up.

The room was tense as Alex moved over by Merlin to pull on her coat and Morgana waited in the doorway to the living room, watching them both. Merlin gave them both a nod, swinging his scarf around his neck. He shared a quick look with Morgana and stepped out the door. Alex moved to follow, but Morgana caught her arm gently.

"Do you remember the importance of Imbolc?" Morgana asked Alex as she turned to look at the professor.

"It's the start of spring," Alex replied with a small shrug. "One of the seasonal transition days."

"That's correct," Morgana agreed before she brushed a strand of hair behind Alex's ear. "But to my people and many who followed us it was a day of rebirth and a day when new things began. Life winning over the dark of winter."

Nodding slowly, Alex tried to make sense of why Morgana was telling her this. It was a nice sentiment, especially given that the Sídhe had returned to the Iron Realm.

"I tell you this because it matters that you found your magic on a day like that," Morgana informed her with a smile. "You struggled to find who you were and you did. You found yourself in that dark place and then you came out into the light of the Imbolc sunrise." Morgana chuckled and shook her head. "I know you are scared, Alex. Merlin expects a lot of those around him. He embraced this life a very long time ago and sometimes forgets that it isn't like that for everyone. Do what you can, but don't let him or anyone else put more on you than you can take."

Nodding, Alex bit her lip, trying to keep the whirl of emotions under control. Stepping outside, Alex took in a deep breath of fresh air, noting gratefully that it wasn't dark yet. She came to a stop and turned back to Morgana.

"What caused you to get your magic back?" Alex asked her. "You said it happened when you were my age."

"About your age," Morgana corrected, but she nodded. "The Sídhe tried to harm someone I cared about and my choice was to stand by or save them."

"Arto," Alex guessed and Morgana nodded. "Do… do you miss him?"

"Often, but Arthur Pendred and every life that has come between him and Arto are not my brother. They carry a part of him, but it is not the same as him returning. Sometimes I have to remind myself of that," Morgana admitted softly before she swallowed and shook her head. "I'm sure that you have homework to do and that the others will be eagerly awaiting a chance to find out where you slipped off to."

"May I tell them?" Alex asked, tightening her grip on her bag.

Morgana gave her a searching look and then nodded. "Yes, you should. Let them hear it from the one who has been in the tunnels and seen the Riders. Your insight and experience can help them." Morgana sighed and looked out past Alex and towards the lake. "I'm afraid that this war has only just begun."

CPSIA information can be obtained
at www.ICGtesting.com
Printed in the USA
FFOW03n1407271117
43799512-42706FF